Critical Acclaim for Neal Asher

"British author Asher is rapidly becoming one of the major
figures in 21st-century SF."
—*Publishers Weekly*

"Asher…projects the terror-haunted sensibility of our time into
a future of limitless brutality…Asher displays great virtuosity."
—*The New York Times Book Review*

"Gritty. Now there's a word you don't often hear in connection with
science fiction—and more's the pity…This unique style is all Asher's…
deeply satisfying…. And, he leaves you eager for more…"
—*SF Site*

"Asher's galaxy is full of color and sleaze, and his story rattles along at
high speed. There are surprises, double-crosses, elaborate lies to be seen
through, astonishing escapes from certain death, and last-minute rever-
sals. Fast-moving, edge-of-the-seat entertainment."
—David Langford

"Asher…writes with a low-key, mordant sense of humor, never really
going for over-the-top, laugh-out-loud moments. He creates a sort of
dissonance with his remarkable imagination and clear prose. He'll describe something so patently weird and oversized, something so incredible, so complex, so insanely bloody or vicious with an utter clarity and
aplomb that is seemingly at odds with what we're seeing. He charges
into the absurd with a gusto that is courageous and outrageous."
—Rick Kleffel, *T*

"If anyone still imagines that like ⬛⬛⬛⬛⬛⬛ ion-
thriller-horror genres means that ⬛⬛⬛⬛⬛⬛ n't be
good SF, then they need to pick up….
—*Interzone*

THE OWNER VOL. 1

THE DEPARTURE

THE OWNER VOL. 1

THE DEPARTURE

NEAL ASHER

NIGHT SHADE BOOKS
NEW YORK

Night Shade books may be purchased in bulk at special discounts for sales
promotion, corporate gifts, fund-raising, or educational purposes. Special
editions can also be created to specifications. For details, contact the Special
Sales Department, Night Shade Books, 307 West 36th Street, 11th Floor,
New York, NY 10018 or info@skyhorsepublishing.com.

Night Shade Books® is a registered trademark of Skyhorse Publishing, Inc.®,
a Delaware corporation.

Visit our website at www.nightshadebooks.com.

10 9 8 7 6 5 4 3 2 1

Library of Congress Cataloging-in-Publication Data is available on file.

Print ISBN: 978-1-59780-447-9

Cover illustration by Jon Sullivan
Cover design by Claudia Noble
Interior layout and design by Amy Popovich

Printed in the United States of America

For all the readers out there—

the silent ones, those who say hello on the internet,

and those who demand I write faster!

1

THE PEOPLE RULE

Throughout the early years of the twenty-first century, Internet blogs and news groups displaced the slow, moribund and politically tribal newspapers. As Internet technology became easier to use, TV news incorporated itself into it to survive, thus also sliding out of political control. However, as politicians worked diligently to weld together the main blocks of world nations into a coherent and oppressive whole, and their grip on people's everyday lives grew steadily tighter, governments increasingly monitored, censored and stifled the Internet. Consequently, the stories appearing on the main news services only infrequently strayed out of approved bounds. The news returned to being either a mouthpiece for the main parties or else one hundred per cent tabloid pap. The twenty-fifth Mars mission, in 2124, of course got plenty of airtime, as the then slightly antiquated Mars Traveller VI sped on past Mars to be cannibalized within the asteroid belt, its fusion engine dismounted and attached to an asteroid consisting almost completely of metals, and that was blasted back to near-Earth orbit. In that time, the nations of the two main political blocks were steadily sacrificing individual power to a massive, corrupt and hugely wasteful centralized government, so what didn't make it to the main news was that funding for further Mars missions had meanwhile dried up, as the steadily expanding bureaucracy of what developed into the Committee—a totalitarian world government—leached up increasingly scarce world resources.

The gene bank squatted next to the Leuven monorail: a fat cylinder half a kilometre tall sitting just on the fringes of the government sub-city comprising 90 per cent of the Brussels urban sprawl. Because of its supposedly apolitical purpose, the bank didn't warrant Inspectorate guards—its security system consisting of old-style palm and retinal scanners. However, if there was a problem here the Inspectorate could get a unit of enforcers on site within minutes and, Alan Saul noted while he swept past crowded pavements in his stolen car, other more frightening security patrolled the area.

The three tall shepherds strode into view from behind the gene bank just as he turned into a slipway leading up to the staff car park. These sinister machines were fashioned of gleaming metal and white plastic. They each stood on four spider legs, their knee joints rising a metre above their inverted teardrop, tick-like bodies. Saul spotted that, while two of them had their crowd-control gear neatly folded in below their smooth bodies, one of them had a man bound up in its adhesive tentacles, his arms and legs hanging slackly. Obviously the robots were on their way back from a food riot, and this one had yet to deliver its captured subversive to the Inspectorate. They moved on out of sight, stepping delicately through crowds cramming an urban pedway over that way.

Saul pulled up at the entrance to the car park, fingers tight on the steering wheel. The woman to whom this crappy old Ford Hydrovane had been allotted—for no such thing as ownership existed in the New World Order—was off on sick leave, dying in an All Health hospital after picking up MRSA6 during contraceptive implantation, so Saul did not expect any problems at this stage, but the sight of those shepherds had burnt a hole in his calm. The cam installed at the entrance read the bar code in the lower corner of the stolen car's screen before sending the signal to open the razormesh gates. He drove in, shut down the turbine and, picking up his holdall, paused for a moment just to breathe and dispel the tightness in his stomach.

After restoring a modicum of calm, he exited the vehicle and headed at an easy pace towards the entrance, checking his surroundings as he went. The razormesh fences enclosing this place hardly seemed necessary, since only a few people were gathered outside, and they did not seem inclined to break in, instead having encamped on an abandoned building site. There they seemed intent on growing some kind of crop on a patch of ground where carbocrete had been torn up to expose the underlying soil. This was not an uncommon sight, since many zero-asset citizens were forever in search of some way to fill their bellies.

Within the parking area, squat conifers growing from narrow islands of soil between the rows of cars were evidence of one of the Gene Bank orga-nization's many successes. They were of a species extinct for ten thousand years, then resurrected from DNA extracted from the mummified gut of a ground sloth raised out of the La Brea tar pits. It was a success that would never be repeated under the Committee. Now that one of their numerous focus or assessment groups had ostensibly deemed it a waste of resources, the leaders of Earth had publicly denounced Gene Bank. But that being an announcement primarily for public consumption, Saul felt the real reason had to be something more complicated.

At the entrance to the building he stepped over to the retinal scanner and paused for a moment while its red laser flickered in his right eye. The screen of the palm scanner lit up next, so he placed his right hand up against it and waited for the beep of acceptance. This procedure seemed to take a little too long, and he felt sweat begin to prickle down his spine. Maybe Janus, the comlife he'd remotely loaded into their security system, had not penetrated, or his artificial iris had malfunctioned, or maybe he'd accidentally scraped some of the multi-refractive nanoskin off his palm—the coating that reflected back into the scanner just whatever it sought. Or just maybe an X-ray scanner he did not know about had identified the contents of his holdall. But no, with a click the locks disengaged, the green light came on, and he pushed his way through the revolving doors. Once in the lobby, a waft of air-conditioning cooling the sweat on his face, he realized precisely what must have happened: seldom used layers of security had been reinstated because someone *impor-tant* was coming here, and that had just slowed things a little.

Pausing for a moment to clip on a bar-coded name tag, he studied his surroundings. Numerous potted plants stood along the walls, piped into a water and feed system, while stretching up the side of one of these, an agribot like an iron centipede was busily clipping away dead matter with its forelimbs, to be then fed into its maw and mulched up inside, subsequently fermented, then shitted back into the pots. Having necessarily taken a great interest in the burgeoning population of robots occupying the world, Saul knew that microscopic manipulators extruded from the tips of its second set of limbs would be picking off even the smallest pests, pin-lasers burning off blooms of fungus, microscopic spray heads on its underside targeting whatever remained with very specific fungicides and insecticides. But even technology like this, employed out on usable farmland, had been failing to produce enough food for thirty years.

Doors opened behind him.

Saul turned to watch a woman enter, then pause to wait as her male companion underwent the security procedure and came through to join her. They both looked subdued and, like all but high-end government officials, ragged and worn, thin-faced and with dark shadows under the eyes. They ignored him as they hurried through to the offices located on this floor—reception staff aware they were due a visit likely to shut them down and tip them out onto the streets, which was a fate they just might not survive.

Once they were out of sight, Saul pressed a fingertip to his temple to call up a menu within his iris. It appeared as a small screen apparently floating off to one side ahead of him, and he scrolled down it by sliding his finger lower, selected something with another press of his fingertip and continued searching. Skin nerves at his temple, linked to the processor embedded in the bone lying underneath, acted like a fine-tuned ball control. Finally he found the blueprint of this building, the diagram appearing to him on a large square virtual screen seemingly rising out of the floor just a few paces ahead. After reminding himself of the layout, he shut the thing down and quickly headed for a nearby bank of lifts, which took him down into the basement.

As he stepped out of the lift, an immediate drop in temperature sent a shiver down Saul's spine. Ahead lay a long corridor lined with doors opening into the mapping rooms, which in turn opened into the main store of deep-frozen cylinders containing the DNA samples waiting to be mapped. To his right a short corridor terminated at the door leading to the combined library and control room. Opening his holdall to take out one particular item, Saul strode over, pushed the door open and entered.

Aiden King sat at a line of consoles, a big display screen above him running graphics charting the progress of the mapping computers, one frame open on something he had obviously been working on—clearly some sort of presentation. Behind him lay the door into a staff toilet, beside which stood a vending machine filled with Food Agency-approved drinks, low-sugar chocolates and plastic-wrapped sandwiches.

Saul glanced up at a security camera set high in the wall, but if Janus hadn't dealt with that by now it was simply too late. King was taking a break, eating a grey-looking sandwich, his feet up on the console. He abruptly dropped his feet to the floor, tossed his sandwich back on to his plate and sat upright.

"Citizen Avram Coran?" he said, obviously surprised. The Inspectorate Assessor wasn't due for half an hour, but it was not unknown for government officials to turn up early to start throwing their weight around.

"He's not here yet," Saul said mildly, heading over towards the man.

King began to stand, still looking slightly bewildered, then dumbfounded when he saw his own name on the tag Saul wore. Too late. The space between them hazed and crackled with energy. King jerked upright, stiff as a flagpole, miniature lightnings skittering over his lab coat and earthing from his shoes into the floor. Eyes rolling up into his head, he toppled like a falling tree and slammed down on his back with wisps of smoke rising from his clothing, a smell like burnt wiring permeating the air.

Saul slipped the ionic stunner back into his pocket and sat down in King's chair even as the man shuddered into unconsciousness. Quickly keying in a code gave him access to Janus. The screen blanked for a moment, then opened a display signifying that Janus was ready. He sat back, breathed in through his nostrils, out through his mouth, slow, calming, then coldly studied the graphic of a slowly turning ammonite shell.

"Any problems?" he enquired, picking up King's sandwich and taking a bite. It tasted relatively good, and actually contained thin slivers of bacon far too salty to have been Food Agency approved, so obviously it hadn't come from the vending machine behind him.

"Simple systems," Janus replied flatly. "Easily acquired."

"So no Inspectorate interference?"

"None—they expect no problems here. Only the relocation order has been sent."

"Any idea yet where the stuff here is going?"

"The data is presently going to distributed terabyte storage, to be copied and consolidated at multiple locations. I've yet to ascertain where it is being sent from there."

The data consisted of thousands of terabytes of DNA maps, even though compressed and with interconnecting hyperlinks where code repeated in different samples. Some 20 per cent of all the species of Earth had been mapped—mainly the larger fauna and flora. Experts here and at other banks calculated that samples of another 60 per cent of the total awaited, unmapped, in storage, whilst a further 20 per cent remained to be either collected or discovered.

But knowing the destination of that data was a sideshow. Saul had only discovered that it was being rerouted whilst researching Avram Coran, who was his main reason for being here. Coran ranked high in the mainland European Inspectorate Executive, but had never been to Inspectorate HQ London, so wasn't personally known there. Upon discovering he was coming here, to such a low-security operation, Saul had felt this an opportunity he could not afford to miss. Coran, though disappointingly not the interrogator Saul was *most* anxious to meet, was perfect nevertheless for his purposes. If it had been *him*, the man who haunted Saul's nightmares, that would have made the operation here even more satisfying, but again, a sideshow.

"What about the physical samples?"

"Nothing on Govnet. I've tried searching Subnet in the hope that someone involved in the physical transportation has mentioned the relocation, but nothing yet."

"The likelihood of transvan drivers getting loose at the mouth is remote, don't you think?" said Saul. "Showing too much curiosity about government orders usually results in a little *inducement* in a white-tiled cell."

Saul was very sure that the human mind could not quite process the effect of the pain inducer, which was useful for the Inspectorate because it made sensory reprogramming easier. After some months of such treatment, dissidents were either returned to society as terrified and obedient robots, or became too damaged to function at all. The latter, if they were lucky, ended up paying a visit to a "Safe Departure" clinic, after which they went through the mulchers feeding community composting tanks. The unlucky were sent to trash incinerators and, as Saul was well aware, were often still alive when thrown in.

"The white tiles are a human affectation," Janus noted. "And the inducers will soon no longer be required."

Saul stared at that revolving ammonite. Thousands of dissidents had been euthanized after the failed experiments, but now the technology was nearly ready. Soon the Inspectorate would be able to edit, copy and cut-and-paste a human mind like a computer file. Hannah Neumann was the name connected to all this—another individual he was anxious to meet. After cracking a supposedly secure database to find the most likely candidate responsible for having installed the hardware inside Saul's skull, Janus had found her, and found out how the Inspectorate was using her work. But what got him just now was Janus saying "a human affectation."

What is an artificial intelligence? Janus, a mass of synaptically format-ted software, mimicked a near-copy of a human mind but with sensory inputs adjusted to allow it to exist on Govnet, distributed and hidden. Janus's memories were only those it had acquired since it initiated two years previously, but the AI was constantly growing, its vocabulary and reactions changing. Saul believed he himself must have created Janus, because what expertise he possessed seemed to lie in the realm of computer systems. He also surmised that Janus was a risky option, but nevertheless had a head start. The Inspectorate were almost certainly putting together comlife just like it, which would eventually track it down. Saul had limited time to find out who he was, to hunt down his interrogator, and then to exact his vengeance on the Committee.

"The Inspectorate Assessor has just arrived," Janus informed him, open-ing up a frame on the main screen so as to display this gene bank's roofport.

Coran had arrived in an aircar—only government departments sent their officials around in these aerofan-driven creations of orbitally manufac-tured high-tensile bubblemetals and ceramofacture hydrogen engines. The dwindling supply of such high-tech materials made vehicles like this an expensive option. Janus focused up close as the vehicle settled in a cloud of dust and its passengers disembarked. An Inspectorate enforcer, who was both Coran's driver and bodyguard, accompanied him.

Saul still possessed enough knowledge of world history to know that the Inspectorate had its near equivalents in the past. It had started out as something like the Gestapo combined with the Waffen SS—secret police, interrogators, the enforcers of politically correct thought. In the beginning it had kept to its home territory—the government offices, the prisons and the adjustment complexes—then, like Himmler's black-uniformed force, its territory had expanded. However, unlike Himmler's force, it had been allowed time to take over and absorb the police forces, armies, navies and air forces of the world, so that now its purpose included security, law en-forcement and police actions up to and including the use of tactical atom-ics. But for most civilians the Inspectorate would ever be associated with that sudden hammering on the door in the middle of the night, and the subsequent disappearance of relatives and friends.

Clad in the kind of expensive-looking grey suit those in the Inspectorate Executive favoured, Coran of course sported state-of-the-art comware: fones in each ear engaging via optic to temple plugs, palmtop at his hip and doubtless cameras and retinal projectors actually in his eyes. He was short and stocky, and Saul suspected he ran muscle-tone programmes during the night, complemented by the kinds of steroids banned from public consumption. He looked to be about thirty but, since cosmetic surgery and the new anti-ageing drugs were also available to his kind, he might have been older. Studying the man, Saul felt a clench of disappointment in his stomach. Coran certainly wasn't Saul's interrogator, but nor was his face that of any of those others who had made guest appearances out of Saul's subconscious over the last two years—the total span of his remembered life. No matter, Coran was obviously one of the same kind. Such an official would be precisely the sort Saul needed to help him gain access to the cells of the British Inspectorate headquarters over in London.

Saul hopped out of the seat, stooped to hoist King up by his shoulders, removed and donned the man's lab coat, then dragged him backwards through into the toilet. He lifted King up on the toilet seat, leaning his head against the hygienic-wipe feeder, locked the door from the inside then climbed up out of the booth. He was stepping out, buttoning up the coat, which was fortunately loose enough to give him freedom of movement, just as Janus announced, "Contact from Sharon Thader. I am running an overlay on you of Aiden King's face."

Saul quickly dropped into the seat as a frame opened on the screen before him, to give a vid feed from the upper office of Thader, the manager of this place—a swarthy, tired-looking woman with badly applied make-up.

"Aiden," she began, "Assessor Coran is on his way down to see you, and you are to offer him every assistance." She now glanced warily to one side. Coran obviously having just departed her office, she now spoke in a desperate rush. "Do what he says or we're in trouble. Margot Le Blanc's Assessment Group is reviewing my appeal and we can hope that at worst we'll just lose some of the data and samples before this is stopped."

"Let's hope so," he replied.

All they had here was hope, vain hope. The French Region Delegate, Margot Le Blanc, one of the five hundred and sixty Committee delegates, was a career politician favoured by Chairman Messina. She would do nothing to jeopardize her position.

Thader gazed at him oddly, before closing down the communication. Obviously he had not given the expected response, but she didn't continue the exchange. It was always best not to say too much over vidphone.

Reaching down to his holdall, Saul took out various items and secured them about his person. He left the surgical saw inside, however, and kicked the bag underneath the console just as the door began to open.

Preceded by his bodyguard, Avram Coran entered, and Saul turned, assuming a politely helpful expression.

"Citizen Aiden King," Coran acknowledged, studying him for a short spell before turning to gaze at the big screen. Coran had never met King, as Saul knew, though there was always the danger that the man had studied the staff files before Janus started tampering with them. Coran's present lack of reaction signified that he had not. "You understand why I am here?"

"To ensure that the data relocation and physical relocation of samples is under way, to make an assessment of resource usage here at this gene bank, then report back to the Committee," Saul parroted. But, really, it wasn't entirely clear why a man of Coran's rank had been sent. It seemed the closing down of Gene Bank entire, of which this place was just one branch, and the relocation of its resources, database and stocks of genetic materials, possessed an importance Saul had yet to divine. Coran was here to start in the basement and work his way up, to shut it all down and individually deliver new orders to the staff. All staff had been instructed to remain at their stations; even Thader had probably been instructed to remain at her desk up in the penthouse offices.

Coran shook his head at Saul's apparent naivety. "I rather think the Committee has more important things to do with its time, don't you?"

"Certainly," Saul agreed. "I meant report back to the Assessment Group. My apologies."

"So, if you could explain this to me?" Coran gestured to the screen.

Since here was an important man and he was still sitting in his presence, Saul stood up, but he must have moved a little too quickly, because the bodyguard moved to interpose herself between him and her charge.

Even more visibly augmented than Coran, she towered over him with most of what was female about her buried inside muscle and subdermal armour. Pale cropped hair topped a high forehead over reptilian engraft eyes, and the metal struts of cyber assists ran down the backs of her hands. Saul had to wonder what drove someone to thus visibly augment themselves with so ugly a result. What kind of self-esteem did she possess before she had allowed this to be done to her? In what regard did she hold herself now?

She wore the usual pale-blue uniform, visored cap and bulletproof jacket, and around her belt hung the usual array of tools: the cylinder of a telescopic truncheon, an ion taser stun gun, a short machine pistol and a selection of gas grenades. However, one other item on her belt gave him pause. The fifteen-centimetre-long, square-sectioned device, with just a simple combined slide and press-button control inset below a small screen shaped like a segment of orange, was a disabler—a nicely portable version of the pain inducer they used in those Inspectorate white-tiled cells, or from trucks to quell riots. If he'd possessed reservations about what he now intended, the sight of that item would have dispelled them. Saul rarely entertained reservations.

"That's okay, Sheila. Let the citizen show me what they have here."

As the bodyguard stepped back, Saul turned to the console, incidentally noticing how Coran now moved himself out of his reach. Though, of course, very little about it appeared on the government-controlled news services of Govnet, plenty of gossip had spread on the Subnet during the increasingly few occasions when it managed to function. Attacks on officials like Coran were becoming more frequent, because people were desperate. Since the bloodless annexation of Australia forty years ago there was nowhere left to flee to—or even dream of fleeing to—and, directly after that, things had begun to go downhill rapidly. Especially when Earth's government, the Committee, removed the right to anonymity from the electronic voting system, and democracy took its final asthmatic breath. But that was just politics and would have been ignored with usual civilian complacency, were it not for the fact that those same civilians were now starving in massive numbers, and also that the Committee had turned killer.

Saul called up the presentation that King had been working on, and expanded it to fill the entire screen. Here were scans of some newspaper articles from back in the nineteenth century. Speaking off the cuff, he said, "The first gene bank, as we know it, was set up in the twentieth century in reaction to the steady extinction of species, though of course seed banks had been around for a lot longer, and for entirely different reasons. But only in the last hundred years have we made a concerted effort to sample every surviving species. Our stated goal here is to compile a complete gene bank of all life on Earth."

Coran held up a hand. "You may have noticed that I'm not a tourist and therefore not here on a guided tour. I understand you've been managing to extract samples from museum exhibits of extinct animals, and that further digs were financed to obtain samples from prehistoric species in the La Brea tar pits?"

"Yes," Saul nodded. "We were also running wormbots down into the Antarctic and Arctic ice, and then there's reverse chemical and pattern mapping."

"Reverse mapping—that would be the method used to try and obtain the genetic code of...dinosaurs?"

"Not just dinosaurs, but any and all prehistoric life forms we can find."

Coran nodded slowly. "Which strikes me as stepping somewhat outside your remit?"

Saul suppressed a snake of cynical amusement. Here before him stood a man who worked for an organization that had sent hundreds of thousands off for adjustment, approved the experiments in cerebral reprogramming that resulted in many being lobotomized, and which also presided over numerous not so secret executions of various "dissidents." Yet now he seemed to be seeking a justification for the closure of Gene Bank. But, then, that was how people like Coran operated: justified by his vision of the greater good, anything was permissible, including murder.

It occurred to Saul that maybe he himself wasn't that much different.

"There are many benefits to be obtained from mapping the genomes of extinct species, and we now have the technology even to reverse extinction," he noted, going to the heart of it. "Even now a department of World Health Research is growing a lichen that went extinct some twenty thousand years ago, and some of the chemical compounds it produces are used in the newer anti-ageing drugs."

Coran shrugged. "A visible benefit, perhaps, but what is the benefit of keeping on ice the DNA from creatures like that?" He pointed at the screen.

Saul glanced back, the screen having automatically moved on to some ensuing display.

The last tiger had died in London Zoo forty years ago, but Gene Bank retained DNA samples from every kind of tiger it had managed to jab a needle into over the preceding fifty years, and had then successfully mapped that DNA. Gene Bank possessed digital maps of the essence of tiger and could, using artificial wombs, resurrect the species with all its variations. The tiger had been a great success story for this place, which was doubtless why King had chosen it for his presentation. Saul's cynical amusement increased, since he already knew what was coming.

"How, precisely," Coran began, "can you justify the expenditure of millions of Euros just to save such a species? Where, exactly, will such an alpha predator fit into the society we're building?"

Real nice society, Saul felt. Of course, there were no more wars, just police actions, though sometimes the truncheon used weighed in at about a kilotonne, and the undertakers had to wear hazmat suits. *Despite the world population topping eighteen billion, nobody goes hungry, so there certainly aren't any food riots—just "dissident actions."* There were no more riots, or rather, they ended abruptly when the Inspectorate used its pain inducers in place of water cannons to reduce the crowd to a writhing screaming mess, whilst sending in the shepherds to snatch up the ringleaders in their sticky tentacles. Committee ideology was environmentally sound and rumours about the problems with the North African desalination plants were untrue. There were fish in the Libyan Sea and southern Mediterranean—pictures were available. The Sahara was green now—pictures of that were available too. *And only a month ago didn't Chairman Alessandro Messina himself say that we are more free than ever before?*—after community political officers conducted a survey only last year to prove this point. The Press had greater freedom too, now being government-run and unburdened by financial concerns. *People don't disappear, see; they always come back ready to sing the praises of the Committee.*

"As the Sol system colonization gets under way, perhaps we'll one day have room here for tigers," Saul suggested, though he knew that was about as likely as Singapore rising from the radioactive saltwater swamp it had become fifty years ago.

The Committee's massive and always expanding bureaucracy was a hungry beast, and its hunger seemed to have grown as urgent in recent years as that of the citizens it governed. Though there always seemed to be good news from space, funding for projects beyond Earth's orbit was being hacked down to the bone. This was particularly bad news for Antares Base on Mars. The colonists there would not be coming back and, unless they showed great ingenuity, would gradually run out of essentials and all be dead within five years.

Coran allowed himself a superior sneer. "I would like to see the mapping computers now."

"Sure," Saul said, his stomach tightening up again now they'd reached the point where the talking would come to an end. "Let me show you the way." He smiled at the bodyguard, holding his hands out to either side as he moved round her and led the way towards the door.

Stepping out into the corridor, he again called up a schematic of the building, then made it a realtime overlay updated by Janus. The first room on the left gave access straight through to the main store of sample cylinders. An automated system collected these, one at a time, to take them through to the mapping machines in each separate room. Once the contents of a cylinder had been mapped, it was returned to the store, and once all the samples in the store were mapped, in a process that usually took anything up to a year, a refrigerated transvan would pick them up to take them back to a larger store near Paris, then later replenish them from there. Except the Paris store now lay empty, as places like this were being closed down and genetic sample cylinders rerouted, no one knew to where.

"I am emptying one clean-crate of cylinders," Janus informed him via the bonefone embedded behind his ear, then transmitted another schematic displaying the outline of a human body with augmentations highlighted and labelled. Just as Saul thought, the bodyguard Sheila had some non-standard stuff in there, but it shouldn't present a problem.

He led the way into the first room.

"It's fully automated," Saul explained, gesturing to the packed machinery, then walking over to the glass booth attached to the mapper. Inside, a brushed-aluminium cylinder lay on its side, half a metre long and ten centimetres in diameter. Protruding from one end of this were layers of segments separated by thinner layers of insulating foam, all positioned along a single rod. Whilst they watched, an arm terminating in a miniature grab lowered itself over one of these segments, which slid round to present a sample. The claw closed and extracted a thin glass tube, swung it to one side and deposited it in a box that hinged out from the mapper itself, before releasing it. The box closed up into the mapper, then revolved out of sight.

"It took years to map the human genome back in the twentieth and twenty-first century," Saul explained. "We've advanced some since then and can conduct the same process in a matter of days."

"It's still an expensive process," Coran noted. "I've studied the break-downs. Mapping one sample costs over eight hundred Euros—equivalent to the community credit for one week for a standard family."

"Certainly," Saul agreed, but couldn't help adding, "Or about the cost per head at an Inspectorate staff dinner." Without looking round to see Coran's reaction, he headed towards the door at the end of the room leading into the main store, heaved the handle down and drew it open. Cold air washed out. "This is our main store."

"I am not entirely sure that I like your attitude," remarked Coran snip-pily, as he followed Saul into the icy aisle between the racked crates.

Handlerbots working in here were arrayed along the near wall like steel and plastic herons, either loading or unloading the conveyor belts running to the mapping rooms. One other robot stood at the far end of this store, where it had removed and was steadily unpacking one of the big round-cornered crates taken from the rack along the rear wall, then standing sample cylinders neatly beside it, like skittles. Such rapid unpacking was not normal procedure here, but Saul doubted Coran would notice that. Saul advanced towards this separate crate, and stared at it for a long moment, his hands clenching into fists. Then he turned abruptly. Its familiarity had set his skin crawling, for it looked just like *his* crate.

"Your likes and dislikes are a matter of complete indifference to me," he stated.

The bodyguard had moved in ahead of Coran, and over to his right, her attention having strayed to the line of robots. Saul waited until both she and Coran were within a couple of metres of him, then he pointed back towards the door.

"This interests me," he added.

Just a contrived distraction.

Coran turned to look but, now having eliminated the robots as a source of potential danger, the bodyguard was again completely focused on Saul. The air hazed, crackling, as his stunner fired its full charge. She staggered but didn't go down, as copper wires running down through her uniform discharged through her boots. Just as Coran began swinging back towards him, Saul stepped in, the edge of his right hand coming round to slam hard into the man's throat. Coran crashed into the rack beside him, lost his footing and went down, gagging.

Even as Coran went down, his bodyguard recovered, throwing herself forward, telescopic truncheon already in her hand and extended. Turning, Saul dropped the stunner and thrust-kicked her left knee, whereupon she stooped slightly, and took his first twisting karate punch to her solar plexus. This slammed her to a halt, but her subdermal armour and bulletproof top absorbed most of the shock.

A horrible grin appeared on her face. Saul had attacked an Inspectorate Assessor, and herself, so the gloves were off, and she could justify an extreme response. Her grin winked out, however, as his second punch flattened her nose and drove her back further. She whipped her truncheon across, but he pulled his head back just enough for it to miss. He then drove a punch into her upper ribcage, just below her armpit where there was not so much protection, caught her right wrist and pulled her towards him, drove his knee into her groin, an elbow into her face, followed by stamping down on the arch of her foot. She managed to get in a left-handed blow to his stomach, which he took, before smacking his forehead straight into her already broken and bleeding nose. Then he pushed himself away.

It was over, she assumed, knowing that although slower than him, she could withstand this kind of punishment, and eventually get a grip on one of the other weapons strung on her belt. She dropped her truncheon and groped for the disabler, already relishing the prospect of using it, then her eyes grew wide as the cylinder clamps of one of the handlerbots closed around her neck, its two sets of jaws scissoring shut on hydraulics—one set directly below her jaw and the other a couple of centimetres below that—and hoisted her off the floor. She kicked out for a moment, tried to get a grip on the clamps, but they were already sinking deep into her flesh.

Belatedly she tried for her machine pistol. Too late. A gristly crunch ensued as the upper clamp moved ten centimetres to the side, snapping her neck. She hung shivering for a moment, then sagged, lifeless.

Saul turned his attention to Coran, who was now up on his hands and knees, and still choking. The angle of Saul's blow hadn't been enough to crush his larynx or to sufficiently bruise his neck that the swelling rendered him either unconscious, or dead.

"You should have used your gun," Janus berated him. "You put yourself in unnecessary danger."

Saul pressed a hand against the automatic still concealed under his lab coat. The magazine contained ten caseless, ceramic, armour-piercing rounds that would have punched straight through Sheila's jacket and subdermal armour.

"It would have made a mess," he replied. "I don't like mess."

"The ice-scraping cleanbots would have dealt with it."

"Even so," Saul said, realizing that the sight of that crate had affected him more than he wanted to admit, and the memories it evoked were the reason why he'd chosen to use his hands.

Coran managed to turn to gaze up at him with bloodshot eyes. Saul considered smashing the man's head against the floor, but he didn't want to damage Coran's face. He kicked him back down, pressed his foot against his back, grabbed both his arms and pulled upwards, snapping his spine. Next he flipped Coran over, face up, put a hand across his mouth and pinched his nostrils closed. A short while later it was all over.

Panting only a little, his breath gouting in the still air, Saul paused to gaze at the two whose lives he had so quickly extinguished. He tried to feel something, but found nothing to feel, then stooped to hoist up Coran's corpse and dump it in the now empty crate. Next he took some of his other equipment out of his pocket—a scalpel and the kind of small combined detector and test unit they used in hospitals when dealing with ID implants—and turned to the still suspended woman. After rolling up her sleeve, he soon found the location of the ID implant in her right forearm—a small bullet of hardware about two millimetres thick—and after cutting round a subdermal plate under her skin, levered that up to get to the object underneath.

"Throw her in the crate," he said out loud, whilst pressing the implant into the test unit. It should not have been damaged and to check that wasn't the point of the test unit. ID implants shut down if they remained unsupported outside of a human body for long enough, but the test unit would keep this one active.

Moving on rubber treads, the handlerbot gripping the woman trundled over to the box and dropped her in on top of Coran. Saul spent some moments rearranging their limbs until he could slide the lid on and engage the seal. Yes, it was a crate very like this, or perhaps smaller, unless his mind was playing tricks—a crate like this one that he was born in.

***

Transition to consciousness had been a slow thing. Saul was born in darkness, his mind filled with memories of pain—a chaotic montage of physical damage that had apparently reduced him to little more than bloody and burnt meat on the edge of death—and memories of his interrogator. Saul saw him clearly, clad in a tight pale suit straining at the buttons over a steroid-honed physique, a diamond stud gleaming in his ear, slicked-back black hair, his hatchet face wearing an expression of deep concern that did not reach those glittery blue eyes. Saul expected to hear him speak in his usual convoluted and politically correct manner about "treachery," "the purpose we serve," and the "common people," and he awaited the return of pain, his body's memory of it as hard as iron under his skin.

Yet the pain now stubbornly refused to make itself felt. Eventually he flexed his fingers and they felt fine, opened his mouth and licked his tongue over dry lips, shifted the rest of his body inside the cramped one-metre cube in which he found himself. Still no pain, though he was aware of movement, a steady rumbling underneath him, and objects impacting or brushing against the outside of his confining space.

"Where the hell am I?" he asked abruptly, the words seemingly rising unbidden.

Immediately, as if someone inside there alongside him spoke straight into his ear, a flat, androgynous voice replied, "You are in a plastic shipping crate moving on the conveyor to Loading Hopper One of the Calais commercial incinerator."

He knew exactly what that meant and started struggling, pushing at the slick plastic all around him, driving his fists upwards against the lid.

"Get me out of here!" he shrieked.

"It will be necessary to shut down the conveyor system, then put it into reverse."

"Then fucking shut it down!"

Immediately the rumbling underneath him ceased, things crashing and clanging all about his crate, which was tilting at an angle. Then the conveyor went into reverse, the crate upended and his full weight came down on his shoulders and the back of his neck. After a few minutes of this, something crunched onto the crate, bowing in the sides of it all around him, hauled it up and rapidly shifted it to one side. It dropped suddenly, crashing onto one corner, denting that corner in, then fell down flat.

"Do not be alarmed," the voice urged him.

Something crunched against the crate again, picked it up and dropped it again. Cracks developed, through which he could see light, then the lid began to split away. The next time the crate hit the floor, he heaved himself against the lid, sprawling out, and even the surrounding dimness seemed too much for his eyes.

The whole place stank of rotting matter and smoke. He jerked round as the wide conveyor, mounded with rubbish, once again jerked into motion, then he abruptly scuttled to one side as, above him, a steel grab on a hinged crane arm swung back to position over the conveyor. Studying his surroundings, he saw he was now squatting in the belly of a sorting machine, over to one side of which rested a mound of scrap metal destined for recycling.

"Are you injured?" the voice asked him.

Nightmarish memories told him that all the king's horses and all the king's men would have merely fetched a spade and a bin liner, but, studying himself more closely he saw only a few cuts on his hands from broken glass scattered on the floor. Perhaps other damage lay concealed under the paper overall he wore, though all he could feel was some bruising and a tight cramped stiffness. He stood up carefully, his spine and knees clicking and sudden cramp tightening his feet. He gazed down for a long moment at the things enclosing his feet—items made of the same compressed paper as his overall, but thicker on the underside—and could not for the life of him remember what they were called. Then he looked around again, wondering where the strange voice issued from.

"Who the hell are you?" he asked. "And where are you?"

"My inception name is Janus," the voice replied. "I am speaking to you via a fone implanted in the bone right behind your right ear, but I am myself constantly changing my location over Govnet servers."

Saul understood at once. "You're an artificial intelligence." He paused to consider, before asking a question that only then occurred to him.

"My name is Alan Saul but…" Though now clear in his mind, his name seemed like a label on an empty box.

"You have stated you are Alan Saul," Janus replied.

"That's not enough," Saul declared. "I don't remember…me."

"My circumstances are similar, since my inception was only twenty-six hours ago."

A terrifying panic washed over Saul. He *knew* the world he existed in. He knew how it operated, and knew he possessed large mental resources. But gaping holes lay open in his mind, like naming whatever those things were on his feet, and why he had been interrogated and why his body showed no signs of the torture he had suffered. Or like how he had come to find himself in a crate heading towards an incinerator, or his entire life prior to that point, and, beyond his name, who he *really* was. Two years later, as he applied a surgical saw to Avram Coran's neck, he still did not remember most of his previous life. But by then he had learned enough about the Inspectorate to know how he had ended up in that crate, and he also remembered enough to know that his route there had been different from other victims.

His interrogator had used wiring installed in his head to directly edit his mind. Afterwards, as fragmented memory surfaced, it arose with edited-in physical damage that had not actually occurred. So he distinctly remembered hanging in a frame while being skinned alive, the Inspectorate enforcers slicing up lips of skin and then closing hammerhead tongues on the bloody edges to peel them back; or being lowered into boiling water; or just sitting strapped in a chair with a lorry tyre shoved down tight over him, waiting in terror for the moment they would toss the burning match onto his petrol-soaked body.

And, of course, he also remembered the interrogator forever watching, with arms folded, a judgemental but attentive expression on his face as he asked questions Saul did not remember. There had been no intention of returning him to society, just to torture every scrap of information out of him before his final disposal. He didn't know what that information was, nor did he know how he had acquired the hardware in his head.

But someone did know, he was sure: Hannah Neumann.

2

IGNORING MARS

Just as with the Moon landings, way back in the twentieth century, the missions to Mars of the mid- to late twenty-first century were always reported in the main news and sold as astounding achievements for humankind. The preparatory landings of robots to erect the first buildings of bonded regolith, drill for materials and begin running small autofactories, kept the story in the public eye. That the new fusion drives reduced the flight time to Mars from years to months also helped maintain interest, and it rose to a peak when the first humans arrived there and walked out to plant the Pan Europa and Asian Coalition flags. The Marineris disaster, and the subsequent relocation of the ground base, later brought it all back into the news when interest began to wane. But by the thirtieth mission, the latest news about Mars began getting shunted into second place by the latest scandal about a paedophile footballer or the latest religious fanatic with an overpowering urge to convert unbelievers into corpses with a slab of Hyex laminate, a canister of nerve gas or some nasty biological concocted in a home genetic lab.

ANTARES BASE

A snake of red dust hung in the air, marking Varalia Delex's trail across the plain. In the pink sky Phobos hung over the horizon like a skull, and the distant sun was a bloodshot eye overhead. She paused for a moment to check the tracking arrow on her wrist screen, though needlessly. Since not a breath of wind stirred the dust and visibility remained good, she could see clearly as far as the horizon through the thin air, and there, confirmed by the direction arrow on her wrist screen, sunlight gleamed off metal polished by the jeweller's rouge of the Martian peneplain.

"Are you there yet, Var?" Miska enquired over radio from Antares Base.

"Another ten minutes," she replied.

"Make it quick. Ricard's on the prowl."

Miska sounded nervous, and well he might, for Political Director Ricard had ordered that all excursions out on to the surface must now receive direct approval from him. Through her suit, Var rubbed at the recent surgery on her arm. If Ricard became suspicious and tried to check on her location through the system, he'd locate her as being in Hydroponics, where her ID implant now resided in a test unit. But if he tried to physically locate her instead, he'd soon discover she was no longer on the base.

"He give any explanation of why he's shut us out of Earth-com?"

"No, did you expect one?"

Political directors did not need to give explanations, and those that asked for them usually ended up in an adjustment cell to correct their thinking. But to get people to Mars had cost upwards of fifty million per person, and the only non-essential personnel within the base were precisely those who would not be so treated, meaning the five Inspectorate execs and the twelve armed enforcers, whereas "adjusting" one of the essential personnel would turn that one into a liability they could ill afford. This was why, as technical director of the base, Var had been given the power to request veto over any decision Ricard made that might endanger the base itself. Only now, that power, backed up by orders from Earth, seemed to be fading. Ricard had cut Earth-com and begun to make decisions—enforced by his men—which might end up getting them all killed.

"Still nothing from Gisender?" she asked.

"Nothing at all," Miska replied. "Feeds from the crawler do register major damage and massive air loss, but she would have been suited. There's no reason why she can't drive it in."

Except if she's dead, Var thought.

Over a hundred and seventy people had died here, fifty-four of them when the Marineris Base was crushed by a rockfall, the rest in and around Antares Base. All the dangers of Earth were here, including overzealous enforcement, along with a whole load of new and interesting ways to expire. Though it was next to impossible to inadvertently punch a hole through the mesh fabric of an external activities suit, it still possessed plenty of seals in it that could fail. Over the years, forty-three people had asphyxiated outside the base as the result of such failures. Then there were all the odd chemical compounds generated when Martian materials were introduced into the hot, moist and oxygenated environment of the base. Before Var's time, four people had died trying to produce viable soil from the Martian dust: a spill of water had resulted in an explosion of sulphur dioxide, and they had died inside the laboratory when emergency bulkhead doors had closed—needlessly, Var reckoned, since the gas would have affected few people beyond the laboratory itself. But, then, safety protocols had been strict for years after the first explosive decompression of part of the base complex. Other interesting ways to die included heavy-metals poisoning, some esoteric cancers solely the product of this place—one of which had killed Var's predecessor—and suicide, which was often the ultimate choice of some who had been forced to come here against their will. Just like Var herself had been forced.

Her loping stride eating up the distance slowly brought the crawler into full view. One of its big fat tyres, she noticed, was flat, which was unusual because they would usually self-repair and reinflate. She could now see that the front screen was also broken—another unusual event, since the laminated glass shouldn't yield to anything less than a bullet. Only as she drew closer did she see the line of holes stitched across it, and realize that bullets were precisely what it had yielded to. And when she finally reached the big vehicle, and peered through the broken screen, she saw why Gisender had stopped talking.

"She's dead, Miska. The fucker had her shot."

No reply.

"Miska?"

Var walked round the side of the vehicle to the airlock, scanning for footprints in the surrounding dust but seeing none. She paused for a moment and looked back in the direction of the base. Whoever had shot at this vehicle had done so from a distance, probably from Shankil's Butte, which reared up from the plain five kilometres away from here, and just three kilometres from the base. Doubtless the killer had used a scoped assault rifle, which would work easily enough at that range in the low gravity here. One of Ricard's enforcers, undoubtedly.

The outer airlock door opened easily enough and, requiring no equalizing of pressure, the inner one opened at once. Stepping through the small cargo space, circumventing two big reels of optic cable and the cutting tools Gisender had used to obtain it, Var entered the cockpit and peered in through Gisender's visor, her own stomach tightening with rage and grief.

After Ricard shut down Earth-com and put recent communications off limits, Gisender had ostensibly gone in search of salvage from the old base in Valles Marineris, but had really gone to obtain a copy of those same communications from the secondary signal station up on the lip of Valles Marineris. And here was the result. Though intellectually Var had accepted that her friend might be dead, only now, finally seeing her right up close, could she accept it in her heart. Even in this condition, Gisender still bore some of that Martian look of false health, with the rouge of Martian dust ground into her skin, as it was ground into all of them, but her dried-out features told the truth. Her lips had shrivelled away from her teeth, and her eye sockets were all but empty now that the moisture had been sucked from her eyeballs. That fucker Ricard must have found out, somehow, and had her murdered.

Var really needed to know what was contained in that communication.

EARTH

Behind Saul, as he headed out, Janus made the handlerbot that had first emptied the crate now pick it up and carry it over to the cargo lift. Usually these crates only went up as far as ground level, where they were picked up by a transvan from a loading bay at the back of the building. But this one was going right to the top.

"No problems?" Saul asked.

"If there are any problems I will inform you," Janus replied—somewhat snootily, Saul thought.

Back in the mapping control room he retrieved his holdall with its waterproof lining and shed King's lab coat, though he retained the false ID badge, before heading again to the lifts. There he hit the button for the roofport, and was glad to find the lift empty as the doors opened. His heart went into overdrive when it halted only two floors up and a nervous-looking man clutching a laptop case stepped in. But lift etiquette being what it is, the man merely ignored him and jabbed the button to the floor he required, exiting two floors later. Finally the doors opened on to the roof.

Three aircars were parked there and, oddly, a helicopter. It was probably a casualty of the supposedly smooth transition from fossil-based fuels to fusion energy and hydrogen transport, Saul surmised. That smooth transition seemed to be failing along with everything else, with the result that people were dying every day, in the hundreds of thousands. He now made straight for Coran's vehicle, holding out the implant test unit before him, the car's locking system responding to it by disengaging. Stepping inside, Saul tossed the holdall on to the back seat and set the tester down beside him. The console arrayed before the single joystick had also unlocked, so he pressed the start button and immediately the aerofans began to hum up to speed.

"Now we have a problem," Janus informed him.

"And that is?"

"Coran's boss is trying to contact him via his fone."

"What's the boss's name?"

"Ahkmed Argul—but I suspect the proper form of address in this case is 'Director.'"

"Yes, quite. Route him to my fone, and give me voice overlay."

"Where *have* you been, Coran?" Argul immediately enquired.

"My apologies, Director," Saul replied. "The mapping basement of the gene bank here is a fone deadspot."

"I see. I've also been informed that your bodyguard is out of contact, too. I do hope you aren't having problems there..."

"Aiden King was being a little unhelpful, so I left Sheila down there to have a chat with him. Besides that, everything is proceeding as per schedule."

The car's aerofans up to speed now, he raised the joystick up one notch, to take the machine about a metre off the deck, then eased the car back and round towards the cargo lift, which lay just behind the tail fan of the helicopter.

"Good. Oversight is anxious to get this done, as resources need to be redistributed fast."

Interesting. Saul decided to fish for information. "Such a tight schedule," he observed as he settled the car down again.

Argul made a hacking sound of irritation. "Coran, we don't discuss the schedule over the air, and I think you know why I'm really calling."

"My apologies. I haven't been feeling so good since eating a sandwich from King's vending machine."

"Remiss of you," said Argul, "but I'm not accepting any excuses. Where is that distribution report for the Straven Conference? You've got three days before that's due to be the main topic of discussion, so make damned sure it's in."

"Yes, sir, at once. I've been a bit snowed under…" Saul shut down the car, and climbed out, heading round to the cargo lift.

"And Coran, if you do another of your disappearing acts, that'll be another two points taken off your status. That's not something you can afford right now—you know how difficult it is staying on the shortlist."

"Disappearing acts?" Saul echoed. How very interesting, and what was this shortlist?

There came a long pause. Even though, with the overlay, his voice sounded to Argul like Coran's, just as earlier, along with a visual overlay, it had appeared to be Aiden King's to Director Thader, Saul again wasn't using Coran's normal speech patterns and perhaps Argul sensed this. In a way this might all be quite useful, because Coran's apparently odd behaviour now might go some way towards explaining what was to come. Not that Saul intended any such explanation to be necessary.

"Well, just get things sorted out and go back to that report," demanded Argul, and cut the connection.

Standing beside the cargo lift, Saul jabbed a button and the doors slid open, revealing the crate inside.

"We okay with the cams up here?" he enquired.

"The cams will show Coran walking out, with his bodyguard close behind him. However, there will be an extensive investigation and they will get round to studying images from the Argus Network, which I cannot change."

"Which is why," Saul replied, "I'm not looking up."

With not one centimetre of Earth's surface—unless covered by cloud—being missed by the satellite cameras, the Argus Network should have been a tool of oppression to exceed the shepherds, spiderguns, razorbirds, static readerguns, inducers and the armed might of the Inspectorate military. But, even now, computer processing was still insufficient to handle all the image data. Comlife run in the main Argus Station could perhaps eventually solve that problem for the Committee, then they'd be able to put all the HF lasers online to punch down through the atmosphere with pinpoint precision, and any form of rebellion would be driven literally underground.

Sometimes, when Saul considered what he was planning, his arrogance astounded him, since after he established who he really was and enjoyed a very *personal* meeting with his interrogator, he intended to remove the Committee's biggest and most potent toy.

Operating the cargo-lift control so it would slide out its floor, bringing the crate right up to the hatch back of the car, he then unfastened the lid and tipped the crate over. Sheila spilled most of the way into the back of the car, and he spent some minutes and worked up quite a sweat manoeuvring her forward into the driver's seat. Coran was much lighter, so easier to heave into the back seat of the car. Both tasks were smelly, since both had voided their bowels the moment they died—he just hadn't noticed the stench down in the chill of the storeroom. Returning the crate to the lift he sent it back down, where one of the handlerbots, controlled by Janus, would repack it with sample cylinders and stow it back in the rack.

Shortly after this, he climbed in the back along with Coran, extracting the surgical saw from his waterproof holdall. Coran's head came off easily, though messily, and digging the ID implant out of his arm wasn't much of a problem either. Head and saw then went into the holdall, shortly followed by Coran's palmtop and the contents of his pockets, but Saul retained the ID implant as he stepped out of the rear of the vehicle, depositing the holdall on the ground before closing the back door and climbing into the front alongside Sheila.

With her ID implant operating in near-proximity, the car's console was still running. He programmed a course into the autopilot, out and away from Brussels and over towards London, then took one final item from his pocket—a short black cylinder with a timer nestling in a recess in one end. He placed it on the floor below the console, just over the forward aerofan, and set the timer running. Next he took her ID implant out of the tester and replaced it with Coran's, and dropped the tester into his pocket. Her chip he dropped on the seat beside her. It would shut down in a short while, but that would not affect the autopilot.

Again starting up the aerofans, he jerked up the joystick and applied its lock. He had just enough time to step out of the vehicle, slamming the door behind him, before the fans got up enough speed to develop lift. He stepped back, dust blasting all around him as the car rose into the sky. About twenty metres above him, the autopilot kicked in and guided the vehicle off over the cityscape.

When the Hyex grenade detonated, about midway across the English Channel, its devastating effect would be complemented by the aerofans flying apart. The car and the two bodies inside would be shredded, to rain down in tiny fragments. Most of those fragments, being bubblemetal, would float, but the rest would simply disappear. Since he'd cut off Coran's head inside the car they wouldn't know he now had it, even after studying the satellite images, and they'd never recover enough for proper forensic reconstruction, at least not in sufficient time. Staff files took over two weeks to update, so no one but those directly involved would know that Coran was dead.

He now headed over to the personnel lift, called it and waited, head bowed, then stepped inside as soon as it arrived. The moment the doors had closed, he dropped the holdall, stripped off his jacket and turned it inside-out to present its blue lining, then took a matching baseball cap out of his pocket and jammed it on his head. Next he took up the holdall, stripped off its outer layer of plastic, which he scrunched up and shoved in his pocket, then inverted the handles to turn it into a backpack, and shrugged that on to his shoulders. Shortly afterwards he exited the lift on the ground floor and departed the gene bank, his appearance now somewhat different from the one the satellites would have recorded up on the roof.

"They will almost certainly obtain samples of your DNA," Janus noted.

"Well, that'll be interesting," Saul replied, as he turned left and headed away from the car park towards the personnel gate in the razormesh fence.

"Perhaps your DNA is retained in some hidden file?"

"In that case keep watch and see what you can find."

Only a few months after he'd escaped the Calais incinerator, he'd managed to turn his own DNA into data, then got Janus to penetrate the Inspectorate database to run a search. He wasn't recorded there, which seemed odd considering how the Inspectorate had obviously taken such an interest in him.

Now it was time to further lose any satellite tracking because, despite transforming his appearance, and despite Janus shafting all the cam images and generally trashing all monitoring systems within the gene bank as he left, once investigators finally realized Coran was missing, they would use recognition programs on recorded data to track everyone leaving the building today. He needed now to head somewhere crowded and chaotic, which pretty well defined most places on Earth, but even then, without certain preparations, he would have had problems with the numerous "community safety" cameras and other forms of surveillance. This was why Janus's next destination, and his own, lay about half a mile up the road: the MegaMall SuperPlex.

***

"Who put me in that crate?" Saul had asked Janus, desperately wanting to attach a name to the hatchet-sharp features of his erstwhile interrogator.

His new friend didn't know, but certainly did know who had delivered the crate for disposal.

The incinerator complex wasn't high-security, since big dumper trucks loaded with waste were constantly in and out, and many outsiders were sorting through the mounds of rubbish either for something to sell or something to eat. However, as with everywhere else, cams were sited throughout the area, like black eyeballs impaled on narrow posts.

Stepping out through the inspection door, he squatted to watch a big dozer take a bite out of a massive heap of garbage, the regular trash sorters rushing in dangerously close to be first to get to any finds. The dozer shoved this latest bite up a ramp of compacted trash and on inside to the throat of the conveyor system, which led into the sorting plant Saul had found himself in. Behind this, the incinerator itself loomed like a gas-storage tank, and he *knew* that beyond it lay a decommissioned power station which the heat from the incinerator had once run. This knowledge, like all the rest lurking in his skull, was just there—he had no idea of when or how he had acquired it.

"I have managed to reinstate the cam system and I see you now," said Janus. "Your yellow overall is highly visible."

Saul waited until the dozer rumbled out of sight, then ran over to join the crowd about the rubbish pile. Within a moment he spotted a bin liner spilling clothing and stepped over to snatch it up just as some toothless old woman reached for it too. With silent determination she wrestled to retain her hold and the bag tore open, spilling its contents. He quickly grabbed up a pair of Mars camo combats and a long sleeveless multipocket coat, and retreated. Both items of clothing looked like they might fit, but there was nothing to replace his already ragged foot-coverings—whatever they were called. Ducking out of sight behind a pile of mashed-up kitchen cabinets, he donned this clothing, then stood up and headed towards the exit.

A miasma hung over the place and sometimes throat-locking gases wafted across it. A road ran parallel to the chainlink fence, and beyond this lay huge ash piles like the spill from a coal mine. Once, this incinerator complex had been considered a jewel of the green revolution. Here waste was automatically sorted, sometimes dismantled, and dispatched for recycling. What remained went into the incinerator to be burnt cleanly, all the noxious gases and the CO_2 scrubbed from the smoke. The fires heated up water that ran through pipes to the adjacent power station, then through heat exchangers to extract every last erg of power, then back again. Now the pipes had long since rusted through, the sorting plant worked only intermittently, and the scrubbers had clogged. Everything now went into the incinerator and its smoke cloud sometimes caused a yellow smog over the nearby port, more reminiscent of ancient London than this modern age, while they heaped the resultant poisonous ash on what was once agricultural land, alongside ancient mountains of plastic bottles and edifices composed of decaying cardboard. Gazing out across this landscape, Saul saw a shepherd striding along in the distance like some Wellsian war machine inspecting the transformation of Earth.

The gates stood open and Saul strode out through them, turned right and headed towards the parked transvan. It was the vehicle, Janus informed him, that had reversed up to the conveyor system, its driver then climbing into the back to heave out a single crate. It was parked beside another transvan, whose rear doors stood open, but Saul wasn't close enough to see what was going on.

"How many people there?" he asked.

"Two individuals," Janus replied.

Glancing round, Saul noticed how those indigents outside of the processing plant kept looking over towards the two vans, but not approaching, which was odd. Parked vans were always a draw, since they might contain food or something else of value.

"The second transvan contains cigarettes and alcohol and some sort of transaction is being conducted," Janus added.

Saul snorted in amusement. The external cam system had been out of action here until, for the AI's own use, Janus reinstated it, so until that moment this area had been a deadspot. Cigarettes were illegal and he'd no doubt that the alcohol being sold rated some way above the All Health limit of 5 per cent ABV. The two were conducting business that had been something of a tradition about these parts for over a thousand years. The second transvan clearly belonged to a smuggler, but only as he drew closer did Saul see who the first van belonged to. The Inspectorate logo of hammer and glove encircled by the multicoloured chain representing a united world was clearly visible, and this explained why the indigents were keeping well away. The driver, he noted, wore a grey Inspectorate overall and baseball cap, since even that lofty organization had to employ someone to shovel the shit.

His interrogator, he knew, would not be here, such a task being far beneath him.

As Saul approached, the negotiation had obviously come to a conclusion, for the smuggler—a dreadlocked white woman wearing a sleeveless coat, much like the one he himself had acquired, over tight pseudo-leather trousers—was pocketing a wad of cash Euros and turning away, whilst the Inspectorate guy loaded a large box into the passenger side of his van. Saul picked up his pace and, spotting him, the woman quickly slammed the back doors of her vehicle, her hand dropping to something concealed under her coat.

"*Vous voulez?*" she enquired watching him warily.

"Natch," he said easily. "ZeroEuro."

She nodded and headed round to her driver's door. He supposed that was a response she had been hearing all too often, as Committee delegates and financial experts worked diligently to enforce a much more easily monitored cashless society. Coming back round his own vehicle the man gave Saul the hard eye and dropped his hand to an ionic stunner at his belt.

"One moment," Saul said. "There's something you need to know." He pointed up towards a nearby cam post.

The man glanced up at it and looked abruptly worried. "What is it, citizen?"

English, then. Saul raised a finger to his lips, then turned to watch the woman climb into her van and close the door. The van's turbine quickly wound up to speed and she reversed out onto the road with a horrible grating of the transmission, spun bald tyres on the macadam and headed off. Saul turned back to the man and stepped closer.

"The cam system here," he began, moving closer, dipping his head conspiratorially.

In that moment, as a calm readiness suffused him, Saul felt sure he must have received training somewhere before ending up in that crate. But, oddly, it felt to him that only during the few minutes since his incinerator rebirth had he acquired a sudden capacity for such ruthlessness. His covered foot slammed up into the man's testicles, bending him forward, and Saul moved in, hook fist into the gut, retracted then up, heel of the hand smashing nose. The man went down like a sack of offal. Saul stooped and turned him over onto his face, took his stunner away, jammed his arm up behind his back and drove a knee down behind it.

"You just delivered a crate to the incinerator," he said. "Where did it come from?"

After sneezing blood for a moment, the man managed, "Head...quarters."

"Be specific."

"In...spectorate...London...Adjustment Cell Complex."

"Why all the way across the Channel?"

"It's just always been that way."

Saul integrated that and blinked. He just *knew* that the trash-trains had been running rubbish out of London to the Calais incinerator for nearly a hundred years. Somewhere, he surmised, some bureaucrat had chosen the same destination for what needed to be disposed of from the adjustment cells, probably because procedure declared that all government waste should go for green disposal. It was horribly funny, in its way.

"You know what's in those crates, don't you?" he said.

The van driver went still for a moment, then, "No...fuck no. I'm just a driver!"

Saul wondered how many crates the man had brought over here, and how often those inside them had woken up, if they were still capable. "Just a driver" didn't have much need for an ionic stunner, and he guessed the man used it when his cargo got a little too noisy. Saul released him to step back, and the man rolled over to wipe blood and snot from his face.

"You're a fucking liar," Saul said flatly, pointing the stunner at him. "And I was in that last crate."

"I'm only doing a job!"

"Who gave the disposal order?"

"I don't know!"

Saul fired and lightnings shorted to the ground all around the driver as he jerked and grunted into unconsciousness. Saul stared for a long moment, considering what he now knew. The Inspectorate had obviously had him in their cells and then sent him off for disposal. He had been a marked man but was now supposedly a dead one. He walked over to the driver and searched him, finding cash money, a palmtop and little else. No papers, but the man wouldn't need them, since he'd have an ID implant embedded in his arm. Saul then took off the fellow's foot coverings and held them towards the nearest cam post.

"What are these?"

"They are boots," Janus supplied.

"Boots are the rear compartments in ground cars," he argued.

"Nevertheless, what you are holding are also boots—or perhaps shoes."

The words just weren't there in his head and their absence both frightened him and locked inside him a sudden determination. He pulled on the footwear and stood up, then walked round and climbed into the transvan.

"I need to be free of the Inspectorate," he declared.

"That is not possible. The Inspectorate is everywhere on Earth."

Saul had no reply to that.

He started the van's turbine, then realized something significant. He had told the driver he was in the last crate the man had delivered here. This information would eventually reach the driver's masters, as he tried to explain the loss of his vehicle, and one master, one *interrogator*, would certainly know who Saul was, would know he was alive and start looking for him. As he reversed the van out onto the road, Saul ran it over the driver's chest, then stopped the vehicle and searched under the passenger seat for a while before stepping out with a heavy wheel jack to finish the job. As he drove away he noticed some of the indigents cautiously closing in. They would take the driver's clothing and maybe, just maybe, the body would disappear too—subsequently to turn up in sealed plastic packets on a stall in one of the black markets. It was an all too common occurrence in this new age.

***

The Mall possessed twelve main entrances. The four at the top consisted of two providing access from adjacent multi-storey car parks, one from the monorail and one set higher which connected to the aerocar port. Four more entrances lay underground, connecting to the tube network and the subterranean highway, whilst the remaining four were at ground level and at each point of the compass. Saul headed for the ground-level entrance facing south where, and even as he arrived, the hordes began jostling him and governing his pace. Checking his watch, he saw that ten minutes remained before the grenade detonated to scatter Coran and Sheila across the polluted waters of the Channel. In retrospect he realized he might get unlucky with the debris ending up on one of the giant cargo barges bringing goods in from China, or the supposed breadbasket of North Africa, which meant Inspectorate Forensics would be able to put things together a bit quicker. Finally entering the Mall itself, he began to notice something odd about the crowds, and notice a stink in the air, and then realized he faced more immediate problems.

The stink was desperation.

"We have another problem," Janus informed him, on cue.

"Yeah, don't I know it," he replied.

Nobody looked at him oddly for openly talking to himself; such behaviour wasn't unusual when most people wore fones and conducted most of their conversations with people several kilometres away from them. He studied those around him, the hollow cheeks and cheap clothing already turning thready at the seams, the collapsible flight bags and the scarred forearms resulting either from fucked-up All Health ID implantation, or the illegal removal of the same. Everything about them announced minimum-welfare and zero-asset status. No cash here, none at all. And, glancing at the store fronts, he saw little they could buy with their triple Cs—their community credit cards—though, inevitably, the doors to a Safe Departure clinic stood open to offer a free service for all. An angry murmur permeated the air, and even as he moved deeper in, a fight broke out at the entrance to a store that obviously did offer a little something on its shelves.

"The Inspectorate is closing the upper levels," observed Janus.

Damn, that meant he'd have to move fast to get to the multi-storey before things turned ugly here. However, the imminent chaos was to his benefit, since it would very much confuse matters when the whole area went under a communications blackout. He just needed to be out of the middle of it before Inspectorate riot police turned up with their disablers, weighted batons and gas—a scene that he'd witnessed all too often. Of course, they wouldn't use shepherds inside the mall, because of the lack of space—they'd be waiting outside.

After selling the blackmarket cigarettes and booze, then selling the Inspectorate transvan to be immediately broken up into spares, Saul had acquired enough cash to buy a cut ID implant and have it inserted in his arm. The people that did this were very professional, and their hygiene standards much higher than those of All Health. They didn't ask him why his own implant was blank, and he didn't ask where the new one came from, even though he knew that an ID implant died once its temperature dropped 10 per cent below human body temperature. Maybe they murdered people for their implants? Maybe they lurked like vultures about the dying rooms in hospitals whenever the "Safe Departure" nurses called by.

However, before Saul left the place the surgeon who had injected the implant acquainted him with the facts. During euthanasia, he explained, implants were deactivated, so the surgeon's source were those who sold their implants for cash to buy things unobtainable with a triple C. This was not part of the knowledge Saul had possessed at the time, so it had been either lost along with his shoes and boots or he had been one of those people the Committee defined as a Societal Asset—therefore maintained in living conditions some way above subsistence level because of some expertise, though also kept under constant political supervision.

***

"It is estimated that over eight million people have died in the food riots across Asia," Janus informed him. "The Inspectorate used inducers to begin with but, under direct instruction from Chairman Messina, cut power and water to the most uncontrollable areas for ten days, then followed that with air strikes before sending in the armour, including spiderguns and shepherds."

On the road winding through the Provence countryside, Saul paused by a steel "gate"—an object whose name he had only just acquired during the last week—and leant on it shakily, gazing out at a robotic harvester that sat weeping rust in a field overgrown with weeds. Also in the field were people, scraping at the ground with handtools in search of tubers and wild garlic, or collecting edible seeds, while beyond them the sun was setting, an eye red with fatigue, on the horizon. No real crops here either, but at least this soil was better than the dustbowl he'd trudged through on the other side of the Luberon sprawl. The conditions here were the reason for the protest assembled around the government compound in the century-old town that formed the core of the sprawl—a peaceful but desperate affair to begin with. The nexus of the protest had seemed well organized and the participants' demands clear. They needed fuel for the robotic harvesters, like the one sitting inactive out here, but more important, they required more than the subsistence trickle of water they were receiving from the Rhône-Durance dam. They needed enough for irrigation.

However, most of the crowd were zero-asset-status citizens who were hungry, thirsty, pissed off about a power shutdown that showed no sign of ending, and doubly pissed off because lights shone inside the compound at night, when the rest of the town was dark. And to heap on a further unacceptable indignity, only that morning two articulated lorries full of provisions, with armed enforcer escorts, had driven into the compound. Committee bureaucrats never went hungry or thirsty.

When the Inspectorate then turned up and started making arrests, things soon turned nasty.

"You got that from the Subnet?" Saul asked, rubbing his hand up and down his arm as he turned to watch scattered groups of citizens trudging up the same road. These people weren't fleeing what had happened back in the Luberon sprawl, merely carrying their meagre belongings and getting away in search of something better. It had soon become apparent to him that there wasn't anything better, unless you were a government employee.

"Yes, just before the Inspectorate hackers crashed it again."

He snatched his hand away from his arm. The limb was undamaged though, when they turned the truck-mounted pain inducer on the crowd, it had seemed to work like an invisible flame thrower. He'd only caught part of it before managing to throw himself into an alleyway, yet it felt like his arm had been burnt down to the bone. He meanwhile caught a glimpse of a shepherd snatching up one of those who had been addressing the crowd, from among those screaming in agony, writhing on the ground, shitting and puking. It didn't carry him away either, just brought him up to its underside and shredded him, dropping the bits. The sight dragged unbearable memories of Saul's interrogation to the forefront of his mind and he ran away, as much to escape from them as from the inducer and that murderous robot. He managed to get past the enforcers erecting barricades, but a machine gun chattered, bullets thumping into the carbocrete right behind him, so he was forced to use the cover of a line of rusting cars to get safely away.

"Nothing about what happened back there?"

"The Subnet is still down."

"What have you been able to get from Govnet? Usual shit about them scraping out the last of the shale, and the Arctic oil wells being down to the dregs?"

He moved on, sipping from his water bottle and ignoring the shrivelled apple still in his bag. He wasn't hungry any more—seemed to have moved beyond that state.

"I have further penetrated secure communications and am building a general picture of the situation. There is too little energy from the fusion-power stations, not enough hydrogen being cracked to take up the slack, and the power-station building project has stalled."

"Why?"

"Insufficient funding."

"Yet there's enough funding for maintaining the Inspectorate and projects like the Argus Network?" He paused for just a second. "Don't bother answering that—just tell me more about this general picture you're building."

Janus sketched out more of that picture and filled in the colours, mostly shit-brown and battleship-grey. As well as energy stocks, water supplies across the world were low—it sometimes happened, just like here, that officials had to make a choice between supplying a thirsty population or crop irrigation, and, managing to make no choice at all, ended up with dying crops *and* a thirsty population. Janus was able to report one instance of great quantities of food rotting inside warehouses because of the lack of power to supply either the refrigeration systems or the vehicles for transporting it. Meanwhile, just a few kilometres away, a scramjet airport was being extended at great cost, just so that Committee delegates and their numerous personal secretaries and bodyguards could more rapidly zip from location to location while going about their important government business.

The overall picture was that, yes, resources were in short supply for the general population, but only because Earth's massive government apparatus sucked up nearly 80 per cent of them. And, though Saul instinctively attributed that to the Committee's huge parasitic bureaucracy, something still didn't quite add up. At the same time, government organizations seemed busier than ever, killing off industries, rerouting supply lines, while huge amounts of materials and equipment were being shifted to unknown locations.

"I'd like to believe that this crisis is going to result in Committee rule collapsing," Saul remarked.

"No," Janus replied, "the Committee controls far too large a proportion of world resources."

Saul nodded to himself, seeing hints of another picture that perhaps Janus had not spotted.

"A resources crash was inevitable, wasn't it?"

"With the world population at its present levels, yes."

"So Messina and the rest of those shits take an even tighter grasp on the reins of power, and hoard resources for their own use. After it's over, they'll still be holding those reins very tightly indeed."

"Yes, that seems to be their intention."

"How many people will die before the situation stabilizes?"

"Stability will not be achieved until the population level returns to that of the early twenty-first century."

"So that means about twelve billion people dead. And the remaining six billion ruled by a government that would even like to control their thoughts."

"Yes."

Moving higher up the hill, Saul gazed back to see columns of smoke now rising, big aeros hovering about them like steel vultures, lit up by the fires below, through which shepherds were striding. The stars were starting to come out, as they always would, no matter what happened down here.

Twelve billion people were going to die, and even if the five hundred and sixty delegates comprising the Committee disappeared in a puff of smoke then and there, those billions were still inevitably destined for the lime pits. He wasn't sure which he hated most, the oppressive government of this world or the mindless, ever-breeding swarm it governed.

He looked higher into the sky, focusing on the numerous satellites shooting across it, many of them doubtless part of the Argus Network. Then he spotted Argus Station itself, a three-quarters wheel five kilometres across, built from the nickel-iron asteroid they'd shoved back out of the asteroid belt using the fusion engine cannibalized from Mars Traveller VI, and which now formed its hub. The mirrors that supplied concentrated sunlight to its two cable-extended smelting plants gleamed bright on either side of it, like eyes. At that same moment, all the frustration and anger he'd been feeling for some time, hardened into a cold kernel inside him.

He decided then he would take it away from them.

3

ARGUS IS WATCHING

As larger and larger proportions of Earth's surface came under Committee control, so did larger and larger sections of the Internet, till it simply gained the title of Govnet. Very little featuring upon it could appear without government approval, whilst Committee political officers even edited and censored what had appeared on it previously, in an effort to rewrite history. Only a small portion of the original Internet survived, often crashed by hackers working directly for the Inspectorate, and it was only there, on the Subnet, that people learned about the final Mars mission and the funding cuts that made further missions an impossibility. There they learned also how the one hundred and sixty colonists would not be coming back home, and how the remaining Mars Travellers were destined for the Argus smelting plants. Of the whole programme only the big fusion drive from VI remained, still attached to the Argus asteroid up there. Yet to be enclosed within the station ring, it remained fuelled and ready, the intention once being to use it to position the station itself at the Lagrange point between Earth and its moon. That was before the Committee decided to position it closer in, as a base from which to establish the Argus satellite network—its ultimate tool of oppression.

Saul was halfway up an escalator when it all kicked off. One moment angry people crowded the Mall, trying to spend their community credit on the few goods available, the next moment these same crowds became a rabid mob intent on tearing the place apart. The escalator jerked to a halt and he found himself being jostled and shoved as all those about him began trying to climb the rest of the way. Grabbing the shoulder of a man next to him, he hoisted himself up on to the sloping aisle between two escalators and ran up it, grateful for stainless steel filthy enough for his boot soles to grip. Ahead of him a woman had got the

38

same idea but, either drunk or ill, was taking too long about it. He shouldered her aside and continued on up, jumping back down amidst the thinner crowd at the top, just as others began following him. Then, from somewhere down on the ground floor, towards the south entrance, an appalling concerted screaming arose.

The enforcers had arrived.

Their intention should have been to try and disperse this mob, but with typical idiocy they'd started using either disablers or larger pain inducers on the way in. Excellent move: now they were driving the panicking crowd into a crush deeper within the Mall. Or perhaps they were under deliberate orders from the Inspectorate Executive? Just hit any protest hard and don't worry about casualties, since more body bags mean less mouths to feed?

More people jammed around the doors leading to the multi-storey car park and, as they slowly edged in, he heard the thumping and hissing of teargas canisters going off. Even better: now people wouldn't be able to see where they were going so that they could quickly disperse. As some of the acrid chemical wafted between himself and the cam suspended above, he took the opportunity to lose his hat, just to further frustrate any future computer tracking of him.

When Saul finally pushed through the doors into the car park it became immediately evident that most of those coming through this way weren't heading for their cars. Yes, there were plenty of vehicles, some of them already starting up and pulling away, but many others rested, thick with long-settled dust, on flat tyres, whilst others had obviously been systematically raided for spare parts. Some local people, it seemed, were managing to obtain blackmarket hydrogen for their vehicles and thus keep them running, however rarely, so spares were needed. And in a cam deadspot like this, thieving was bound to be rife—not that the Inspectorate really responded unless it was theft of government property.

As most of those around him fled towards the exit ramps, Saul headed towards the stairs, while unshouldering his backpack and converting it back into a holdall, then discarding his jacket. Three floors up, he stepped out into a much cleaner level of car park, with strip lights functioning and security cameras hanging from the ceiling. The Hydron SUV, with its mirrored windows, was parked over to his left—still gleaming and, as far as he could tell, untouched. As he approached, it unlocked itself, responding to the implant embedded in his forearm. He climbed into the driver's seat, dumping the holdall beside him.

"Secure," he said, and locks clonked shut all around him.

A traffic jam slowed his departure from the car park, until he tried the executive exit, where two Inspectorate enforcers waved him out under the loom of a shepherd. Obviously the theft of this government vehicle had not yet been reported, but then its usual driver, a bureaucrat working for the Water Authority, wasn't in any condition to report it, since he currently lay at the bottom of a reservoir with a slab of carbocrete roped to his chest.

Saul drove slowly and carefully out on to the highway, and only when the last shepherd was out of sight did Janus direct him to a cam deadspot where he could pull over, climb into the spacious rear of the vehicle, and set to work.

After placing Coran's head down on a plastic sheet, Saul removed the man's fones and put them to one side. Then, opening the vehicle's tool compartment beside him, he folded up a flat screen above a plasfactor specially designed for the theatrical profession, and set it running. He first cleaned Coran's face of blood, then sprayed a quick-setting sealant around his neck to prevent further leakage. Next he ran a scanner from the dead man's forehead down to his chin, then down each side of Coran's face, then over his hair; the head's three-dimensional image appeared on the screen. Next he clicked the screen stylus against the image of Coran's hair to get the required dye mix, which the plasfactor provided for him as a spray. After that, he instructed it to run the template, as he converted his own white hair to Coran's dark brown.

On the screen, Coran's image shifted over to the left, and on the right appeared a three-dimensional image of Saul's own head. The two slid together and overlaid to provide a visual representation of the computer making the required depth measurements. Removing a small medical kit from the toolbox, Saul next focused his attention on his arm. Calling up the menus in his eye again, he searched through and found the one accessing the implant presently under his skin, and shut it down. Next he took out the tester containing Coran's implant, sterilized it, and his arm, then inserted the chip into a small injector to drive it under the skin of his forearm beside the others he hadn't yet got round to having removed. Plenty of scar tissue was evident in that location, as this was the eighth identity he had stolen—or rather remembered stealing, for there had been scar tissue there before. Perhaps having no real identity of his own made this easier for him.

By the time this was all done, the plasfactor had finished its work and extruded a mask which, when glued into position, would fool most recognition systems. Once he arrived in London, all he would need to get into the

Inspectorate cell block was another layer of the multi-refractive nanoskin on his palm, his artificial iris—oh, and the expensive suit neatly boxed beside him. He hadn't bothered with trying to use Coran's—too messy.

***

The first time he did it he thought he'd activated a holographic advertising projector, but then he knew that couldn't be right. Who would bother advertising in an industrial complex overgrown with weeds and now only occupied, for as long as it was safe, by car breakers and those going about other nefarious deeds—like those selling cut implants? He studied the menu hovering to the right of his vision, and realized it must originate from within him.

"Janus," he asked, "do I have a computer implant in my skull?"

"Yes. My signal is relayed to your bonefones through it," his unseen companion replied.

"I can see a computer menu hovering before me," Saul explained, "presumably relayed to my optic nerve from that computer implant. But how do I operate it?"

"The control is in the skin of your right temple," Janus replied, "though the menu is projected up in the artificial retina inserted in your right eye." Artificial retina?

He came to a halt and just stood gazing across cracked concrete, noting how a straggle of GM broad beans had punched up through it. Those were another reason people would come here, since they were a ready source of food, though some of the strange proteins they contained could cause stomach cramps. When he reached up and probed his right temple, a sequence of submenus flickered across his vision. He needed to get himself somewhere he could spend time working all this out, so decided on a nearby warehouse.

On the floor, just inside the busted door, lay four skeletons, one of them obviously a child's, and all of them with bullet holes punched through their skulls. He just glanced at them, then went and sat down with his back to the wall, only then wondering why the sight did not shock him. He knew, just knew, that though these victims might have run foul of the underworld, a more likely explanation for their deaths lay with the government. It was now the biggest killer on the planet, and they'd probably been too much trouble for Inspectorate enforcers to bother processing. He turned the thought away and concentrated instead on the menus.

It soon became evident, once he got back to the first of them, that something was highlighted: IMPLANT ID. Managing, with practice, to select this, he checked through and discovered the menu provided the code of the new implant in his arm, along with options to reprogram it with new personal details. After a little investigation he found he could only edit the identity in the implant to a limited extent. Profession and personal history could be changed, but physical details were firmly set. The surgeon who had injected the implant into his arm had warned him that it would only get him through public scanning, which merely registered that a certain person was in a certain place at a certain time. Now it seemed more options were available to him, though he would not be able to slip through any recognition security.

Gazing down at his arm, he wondered about the reason for all the scarring. In the past, before he ended up in that box heading for the incinerator, had he taken other people's implants in order to assume their identities? And if he had done so, he doubted that their owners would have willingly given them up. So what was he previously? What the hell was he? It now seemed quite likely that he had once worked for the organization he'd run foul of. Maybe he had served as an Inspectorate agent of some kind, perhaps working undercover to expose dissidents? Had he then decided he agreed more with the dissidents than with his masters? He needed to find out the truth.

Leaving the industrial estate, he headed south, always keeping under cover whenever the Inspectorate cruisers came by, avoiding large population centres where possible—though, of course, with the urban sprawls covering much of France, that wasn't always easy—and surviving as best he could. He ate from trash, consumed GM beans, once shared a stew with other indigents, and only wondered after his stomach was full where they'd obtained the pork. He had used his cash frugally but had spent it all by the time he reached Provence. Only on his return journey up the west coast did he really begin to use Janus as he suspected was intended. Creating a community credit account did not cause the AI any difficulties, nor did obtaining a triple C, but Saul's real problem was finding anything to buy with it. However, that situation started to change once Janus upgraded him to Societal Asset, and he could now gain access to those shops that weren't rated at or below subsistence level.

But he needed more, so his first new identity was that of a low-ranking bureaucrat in the Department of Agriculture. He left the man's body in an empty grain silo—certain it would never be found, because the silo would never be used.

***

The London sprawl occupied a vast portion of southeast England, extending right to the Essex coast and including the massive floating airport in the Thames estuary, where once stood Maunsell forts. Saul didn't come in by scramjet since even Committee Transport Oversight had decided it wasn't cost-effective to run a scramjet route from Brussels to Maunsell Airport. Aboard an executive rotobus—a giant bubblemetal transport driven by twelve aerofans and hydrogen Wankl engines—he gazed into the well-lit smog over the urban sprawl and contemplated how satellite cameras would simply be unable to penetrate it.

"Are you here for the Straven Conference?" asked the woman in the seat beside him.

She was a grey suit with cropped ginger hair and a disapproving mouth as tight as a cat's arse. He reckoned she must be a delegate's staffer, since some big Inspectorate bodyguards occupied the seats near the door leading into the forward luxury compartment, where doubtless one of the five hundred and sixty was having his or her every whim catered to. He'd so far managed to avoid talking to her by the usual method of focusing on his much modified and barely functional laptop and pretending to be extremely busy and important, occasionally taking imaginary calls over Coran's fones whenever she ventured a conversational gambit. He simply did not want her, or anyone, inspecting his face too closely. The silicon mask was indistinguishable from real skin, and its join, running under his chin to up behind his ear then following his hairline, was invisible. Air pockets and electro-muscle also enabled the mask to move along with his face, and capillary pores even transferred some sweat from underlying skin. However, he felt it lent him a certain unnatural deadness of expression that someone might be able to detect—might have been trained to detect.

"No," he replied. "I'm here on Inspectorate business."

She nodded her head wisely and ventured no further enquiries, since probing into Inspectorate business was a good way of becoming Inspectorate business. With his laptop turned away so she couldn't see the screen, he typed in: "What the fuck is this Straven Conference?" remembering that Coran's boss had mentioned it too. His question was directed to the large proportion of

Janus presently residing inside the machine, and the AI replied via embedded bonefone.

"They will be discussing the societal consequences of raising the price of staple food items in Britain, i.e. how they're going to deal with the ensuing increase in riots when ZA citizens here start sliding below the subsistence level like they are in France, and also whether the plan for sprawl sectoring will work."

"Sprawl sectoring?" he typed.

"Movement restrictions are already in place for ZA citizens. Meanwhile, certain sectors with high ZA populations are being fenced off, and any societal assets moved out. The intention is to further isolate those sectored areas with automatic pain inducers and readerguns, when available, or by bringing online parts of the satellite HF laser network to keep those areas contained."

"Concentration camps, you mean?"

"Doubtless the Committee will eventually come up with a *final solution*."

Janus had obviously moved on to another stage—this was the first time Saul had noticed such morbid irony coming from the AI. Of course, if large proportions of the useless zero-asset population were contained and starved, they would be less likely to be able to cause trouble. The Committee Population Logistics Support Group would much prefer those destined to die to do so quietly and without too much fuss.

With a roar, the rotobus drew in over Maunsell Airport, which bore some resemblance to an old-time aircraft carrier, though it extended ten kilometres long and three wide, stabilized all around by massive bollards punched down into the seabed. He'd chosen to use this method of travel here because no Committee bureaucrat came by tunnel any more—that was reserved for cargo or trash trains, and for dissidents in sealed crates. As the aircraft settled, the great hinged arm of a docking corridor opened out towards it like a giant grasshopper's leg, whilst the fuel and luggage collection posts rose from the deck below to engage and automatically carry out their tasks. Off to the right, a scramjet running on conventional turbines now, with its speed down below Mach 10, lowered its wheels and came in to land like a black swan envisioned in some cubist's nightmare. Perhaps it carried other Committee bureaucrats from further afield, heading for the Straven Conference.

No staff out there on the runways, he noticed, and on a raised aisle between the rotobus section of the airport and the scramjet strips squatted Dalek readerguns ready to ensure that only essential personnel could venture out. The guns, which constantly checked ID implants against an internal database of approved codes, were deadly accurate up to a thousand metres. The three bullets, which each would fire at one go, were low-penetration wadcutters less likely to end up in any one else near the intended target—though anyone nearby would probably end up covered in bits of the intended target. During the clear-up after another riot, in another place, he'd witnessed what had happened after some Inspectorate exec in charge decided to offline the identification routine. On that occasion they didn't bother to sort the bits into bags, but used dozers to push the heaps of remains up ramps into tipper trucks, then hosed the smaller gobbets down the drains.

"I wish you luck with your conference," he told the prim bitch beside him, as he slid his laptop into its slim compartment inside his briefcase.

"It's not about luck," she told him. "It's about the correct application of resources and knowledge-based societal planning."

What did she have on the way over? Oh, yeah, the champagne dinner, of which she'd eaten only about half before peremptorily summoning the stewardess to take the remains away. He remembered, over by another scramjet port, once eating flight-meal leftovers some enterprising official was selling for a hundred Euros, cash, per half-kilo.

"Of course," he said, smiling. "You are absolutely right."

He actually wanted to snap her neck, but comforted himself with the thought of the scumbags he'd already rubbed out, and the mayhem he intended to cause, starting in a few hours from now. Maybe she would become a victim of that. He certainly hoped so.

The softly carpeted exit corridors led to security procedures not much different to those of Gene Bank, since the major security hurdle he'd penetrated had been to get on to the rotobus in the first place. He avoided baggage collection and headed straight out to the large arrivals lounge. This place swarmed with people, and he realized he was probably the only one here who did not actually work for the Committee. Of course, the restriction imposed on public travel—it quickly becoming the privilege of the government bureaucrats only—had started way back with numerous bogus crises used to divert the public eye from what was really fucking over the planet: too many people. That was a problem no democratic government could attain office by offering to solve, and one that would only be cured either by Mother Nature applying her tender mercies, or by some totalitarian regime applying Nazi-like final solutions. It seemed that, here and now, Earth had both.

He strode right across the lounge to the exit doors, beyond which taxis were drawing up, loading up with passengers and pulling away. Escalators also led up to aerocar and aerocab platforms but though, as Avram Coran, he rated that kind of transport, he chose ground taxi instead. Even with his status rated high, he wanted his profile to remain low, and those arriving at the Inspectorate headquarters here by aerocar would become the subject of much scrutiny. Stepping through the doors, he headed over to the nearest vehicle—an old hybrid Mercedes with a combined one-litre multi-fuel and electric engine, which by its smell had been running on synthetic diesel.

As he climbed into the back, the driver didn't bother looking round. "Conference?" he asked in a bored voice.

"No, Inspectorate headquarters. Cell Complex A."

At this the driver did turn to peer at him through the security screen. He guessed that, in another age in Germany, this would have been like finding one of the Gestapo had just got into your cab. Inspectorate officials enjoyed their power and weren't averse to using it.

"Certainly, sir," the driver replied, very politely, and eased out into the traffic, the Mercedes running on electric until out in the open, then switching over, with only a slight change of tone, to diesel.

The exit road ran down the side of the airport, then up on to a bridge crossing half a kilometre of oily-looking estuary, then over mudflats traversed by numerous pipes from a nearby desalination plant, which stood silent and unlit. Where dirty-looking salt from the defunct plant had been mounded had since become a dumping ground for excess sprawl waste, and upon this roosted hordes of filthy seagulls, pigeons and raggedy starlings. Shacks were visible down below, and half-seen figures moving about in the glow of campfires. Pickings were probably extremely lean now, since even the rankest of food rarely made it as far as a waste tip.

At a roundabout the cab took the second exit, though Saul noted other cabs heading in the opposite direction, and within minutes the road passed through a gap in a long fence still in the process of being erected, and into a GUL section of the sprawl where an attempt had been made at Green Urban Living.

Compressed-fibre tenement blocks rose on either side, interspersed with independent waste incinerators or digesters running tenement-block generators and hot-water systems. It was easy enough to spot the ones still functioning by noting which blocks still had lights shining from their windows. Here and there long garden allotments speared off like side streets, every scrap of exposed soil crammed with vegetables, chicken coops and occasional pigsties. Around these strips rose fences, sometimes repaired with whatever had become available—fibre building board, old doors, parts of the bodywork of cars—though the more well-to-do tenements, perhaps with government employees still in residence, used ceramic-link fencing topped with razorwire. Every allotment was occupied—the participants from each tenement rotating the responsibility of guarding such a valuable food source.

Though certainly not self-sufficient, Saul knew that the system here had worked well enough when the tenements were first built, but as the population continued to rise and what were once single-family apartments absorbed a load of two or three families each, the cracks soon developed. Many of these areas were now considered no-go for the Inspectorate, and even the block political officers were powerless in districts where someone could be killed just for a bag of onions.

After passing the last tenement, the cab drove out again through a gated fence, similar to the one they'd driven in by, though this time it was complete. Readerguns were positioned on either side, and probably unnecessary Inspectorate guards sat in a lit-up guard booth. The gun barrels immediately tracked the vehicle's progress, a laser doubtless scanning the bar code on the car's screen, whilst a radio pulse also elicited responses from both his own and the driver's ID implants. Saul noted how buildings had been demolished to make way for the fence, and to clear a space about twenty metres wide on either side of it. To the left, as the cab entered a more salubrious neighbourhood, he noted a minibus tipped over on its side, its bodywork peppered with holes and blackened by fire. It looked to him like those who had been trying to escape from the sectored area behind might still be inside. Just beyond this point, the driver breathed a sigh of relief.

"Not your usual route?" Saul suggested.

"I normally take the M25C, through the Chelmsford arcoplex, sir," he explained. "But this is the quickest route to IHQ—though I won't be coming back this way."

"Why not?"

"Readerguns ain't reliable."

"Why did you choose this route this time, then?" he asked.

The driver remained silent for a moment, perhaps remembering who his passenger worked for and frightened lest his comments might be taken as some sort of criticism of the authorities Saul represented.

"No readerguns here last time." He hunched his shoulders, clearly not wanting to say any more, but finally impelled to continue, "Weren't no fence neither."

So sectoring was well and truly under way, and no one wanted to be on the wrong side of the fence when all the gaps were finally sealed.

***

Saul had studied Argus Station for a year before information about the place became increasingly difficult to obtain. With Janus's help, during that year, he managed to gain access to hidden files and secret information. He learnt that the station's population then stood at just over a thousand, and it was a damned sight closer to self-sufficiency than any GUL developments or the green villages of the early twenty-first century. However, right from the start that self-sufficiency had been difficult to assess, what with the frequent changes in staff, space planes running up supplies or bringing down to Earth the loads of bubblemetal rendered out of the station's asteroid, along with numerous other products that could only be manufactured in zero gravity. It wasn't a closed system, therefore, and this applied particularly to its nascent ecology.

The station's rotational arboretum helped keep the air supply oxygenated, and its trees supplied a multiplicity of other products: wood, fibre, resin, fruits and, from just two of the trees, also natural rubber. Both rotational and low-grav hydroponics provided cereal crops, vegetables, soya beans, cooking oils and sugars, whilst the farm provided oddly shaped eggs, the flesh of chickens, farmed salmon and tank-grown artificial proteins that could be flavoured and textured to resemble the meat of just about any animal.

But to maintain this the horticulturalists of Argus were frequently supplied with seeds, eggs, stasis-preserved life and genetic material from Earth—Gene Bank providing that material, which on the station they implanted in gel-eggs to grow in artificial wombs, or multiplied into seed germs. These produced extinct strains of chickens, rare mushrooms, cereal crops untouched by genetic modification, worms to work the soil, and odd parasites to kill off some pest inadvertently brought aboard the station. Only by constantly monitoring and constantly tweaking things had they managed to keep this makeshift ecology running. Separated from a regular supply of the stuff of life, it would fall apart and everything there would die. But perhaps they had solved that problem now, for in the last year traffic to and from the station had ramped up, and every day vast loads of materials and equipment were disappearing into it.

Only later did Saul learn that Gene Bank itself was about to be closed down, its information and resources relocated. The hatchet man for this task, an Exec called Coran, was unknown at IHQ London outside of the Inspectorate database, and therefore working outside the heavy security that usually surrounded such people. Much easier to get to.

"Anything on Coran yet?"

"Nothing at all," Janus replied. "All they know is that an aerocar went down over the Channel, but they haven't even started to look for it. They have no ID on the car either, since apparently there was some problem with Air Traffic Control registering it."

"Your work?"

"No, just inefficiencies in the system—the same kind of inefficiencies that allow me to exist."

Saul nodded to himself and then studied his surroundings. On the side of the street behind him were numerous well-lit suburban houses dating back to the twentieth century. They all looked in good repair, with neatly trimmed front lawns, cars parked in some of the drives, and a surprising lack of security cams or lights, but, to the cabby's obvious disgust, to get to this street it had been necessary to pass through another guard post watched over by readerguns and enforcers. This place was not one of those being sectored, however, but a gated community reserved for government employees, and the place lying behind the combined ceramic-link and razormesh double fence in front of him was where most of them were employed.

Cell Complex A consisted of numerous long, low, flat-roofed buildings regimentally positioned one after another, hundreds of them, with the ten-storey blocks of the main Inspectorate HQ lying in the distance beyond. Perhaps it was his recent brief conversation with that bitch aboard the rotobus that inclined him to decide this place resembled Auschwitz-Birkenau. Clutching his briefcase he headed over to the gate.

This particular entrance provided a pedestrian access for those staff living in the houses behind him. On one side of a mesh entrance tunnel sat a guard booth with readerguns perched on its roof. Readerguns were also positioned on poles along the inner fence, spaced a few hundred metres apart. The only security at the gate into the tunnel was a reader signal directed to the implant embedded in his arm, which resulted in the gate automatically swinging open. The real security lay at the far end of the tunnel, the set-up here being that if anyone tried entering here who shouldn't, they wouldn't be getting out again. As he paced along the tunnel, he glanced over to one side, noting guard dogs patrolling between the two fences. They were big bastard mastiffs with honed-steel spur implants running up the back of their forelegs, cropped tails and ears, and—so Janus informed him—a genetic tweak enabling them to carry as much lethal bacteria inside their mouths as Komodo dragons.

The guards in the booth, clad in the light blue uniforms of Inspectorate enforcers, observed him walking through, and one of them, after checking a screen before him, abruptly stood up and headed for the booth exit. Either Saul had been rumbled or they were reacting to the fact that an Inspectorate Assessor of his standing was now entering through what was effectively the servants' entrance. Without a doubt they would assume his visit indicated a surprise inspection instituted in Brussels, which usually resulted in someone getting the shitty end of the stick.

Just before the gate at the far end of the tunnel stood a scanner post, and he noted, on approaching it, a sliding gate above and preceding it and gates on either side. If the scanner picked up any anomalies, the gate behind would slam down and trap him, whereupon those in charge would have a number of choices. They could arrest him, or let a readergun shoot him, or open those two side gates and provide a tasty treat for the mastiffs. It definitely said something about the mindset of those running this place that they should provide themselves with such an option. Seeing those side gates dispelled any last qualms he felt about what he intended to do. Now he had none, none at all.

He halted at the scanner post and waited until the retinal scan laser flickered in his eye, before stepping forward to place his hand on the palm scanner. Recognition programs also read data from his implant, scanned his face and cross-referenced and double-checked, before the gate ahead of him sprang open and hinged itself aside. As he strode forward, he glanced over to see one of the mastiffs turning away and heading off, perhaps disappointed that only doggy snacks and dry mix would be on the menu today.

Saul then stepped out into the area beyond, on to slate-grey carbocrete slabs once the product of CO_2-trapping plants across the European Union, later Pan Europa.

The guard he'd seen leaving the booth earlier appeared round the end of a compound surrounded by iron palings, within which stood a scattering of fat-tyred electric cars with trailers attached. He guessed that one of these had been used to transport, to some larger gate, the crate he'd found himself inside two years earlier, there to be collected by transvan.

"Citizen Avram Coran," the man greeted him.

He was a standard Inspectorate enforcer, without the kind of augmentations the bodyguards employed, yet who wore a bullet- and stab-proof jacket as part of his uniform, and carried a machine pistol, ionic stunner and telescopic truncheon. His shaven head and heavily muscled, thickset physique could have fitted easily into a black uniform adorned with silver thunderbolts at the lapels, Saul reckoned.

"Citizen," Saul replied, with a nod of his head.

"We were not informed of your visit," the guard tried.

"That would rather defeat the purpose of my visit."

The guard's face fell; an inspection, then. "May I assist you, sir?"

"You may." Saul pointed towards the compound. "My first port of call must be the Complex Security monitoring room."

The guard turned away and headed over to the gate leading into the compound, which immediately slid aside as a smaller scanner beside it read his implant. Walking inside, he climbed into the driving seat of an electric car towing a small trailer fitted with a perspex roof and four seats. The vehicle's engine was utterly silent as it pulled out, the only sound those fat tyres on the flaking carbocrete. Saul climbed into the back as it paused, his briefcase perched on his knees—the very image of an officious inspector.

"We've been very busy here lately," the guard told him, glancing over his shoulder as he pulled away. Saul deliberately showed a flash of annoyance, but the guard missed it. "We're even having to double up on some of the cells, and that's never a great idea. Sharing a cell with another prisoner can give each of them psychological support, isn't that right?"

Damn, despite him being considered the perpetrator of a feared surprise inspection, he'd now got Mr Friendly Guy guard with a case of verbal diarrhoea, or perhaps this man was just the sort who babbled whenever nervous. Then, again, he might be letting "Inspector Coran" know about the doubling up as quickly as possible, since it was probably against the regulations.

"I'm sure that doesn't mean sufficient psychological support to make any of the inmates too difficult?" he suggested.

"We're trying to use it to our advantage." The guard nodded enthusiastically as he steered the vehicle into an aisle between two cell blocks. "After a few days, we move one of the inmates and tell the one remaining that their cellmate died under inducement…weak heart or something. Anyway, most of 'em aren't in here long enough for it to become a problem."

"Really," Saul said, noncommittal.

"Nah, we only run the full course on SA citizens. The ZAs get the short and dirty course, and if that don't work we ship 'em over to E Block."

E Block stood over by one of the larger entrances, where the transvans came in. They kept the plastic disposal crates there. The euthanasia block was a place where sometimes they didn't bother killing those intended for disposal in the crates, because a bullet in the back of the head or an injection or electrocution sucked up funds that were better spent on a ministerial lunch, and the living victim would not manage to fight his way out of the sealed crate anyway. That savings had probably been suggested by a government auditor, perhaps the same one who had failed to notice how wasteful of funds it was to still ship the crates across to the Calais incinerator. Saul had also learnt that sometimes relatives on the outside managed to put together a large enough cash payment to the staff of E Block, and to the transvan driver, so that the crate with its living occupant never actually reached the incinerator.

"Things are gonna change, though," his driver added.

"Really." Saul still affected a lack of interest, whilst he surveyed his surroundings. All about him he'd been seeing various staff of the cell complex hurrying importantly here and there, and he had studied every individual in hope of seeing the face of his interrogator, but now, for the first time, he saw one of the inmates. He was clad in bright yellow paperware overalls, hands cuffed behind his back, a plastic rod connecting his ankles so he could just about walk, though with a painful, waddling gait. Two guards walked behind him, occasionally prodding him with telescopic truncheons which, judging by the blood spattered over his shoulders and sticking his hair close to his head, they had obviously felt cause to use earlier.

"No more ZAs for adjustment—that's the word," Mr Chatty added.

Saul rolled that one over in his mind and couldn't avoid what it implied. Why bother wasting resources in adjusting to correct political thought those never destined to be part of the wonderful world society? They'd end up like the skeletons he'd seen in that broken-down industrial complex, like the corpses washing up on so many shores—those being only a visible proportion of the whole, he suspected, most of whom ended up in community composters and incinerators.

"Here we are." The guard gestured ahead.

The Complex Security monitoring room bore some resemblance to a squat version of an old-style air-traffic control tower. The guard pulled his vehicle up outside the doors and turned to Saul again. "Will you be needing me to drive you anywhere else?"

"Yes," Saul said. "But first I would like you to accompany me inside."

The guard acceded with a shrug to this unusual request, stepping from the driver's seat as Saul stepped out of the trailer. His next actions, unlike much else he had organized here, had not been meticulously planned and left him at a bit of a disadvantage. Janus had been unable to penetrate the firewalls established here, hence Saul was carrying a large proportion of the AI around with him in the laptop inside his briefcase. To get Janus into the system required a hard-link—an optic cable plugged into one of the computers here, and the portion of the AI loading, then disabling the firewall to let in the rest of itself—after which things should go smoothly, if bloodily, enough. However, the staff of the monitoring room certainly wouldn't want him plugging his hardware directly into their computers, no matter what his rank, no matter who he might seem to be. He therefore needed to deal with them.

Entering the monitoring room required passing through just as much security as at the gate into the cell complex. He went through first, the guard following, but once inside he gestured the man towards the stairs ahead, while scanning the foyer as he did so. No one in evidence down here but still plenty of complex staff busily hurrying to their next appointments outside, so at any time one or more of those might enter behind him. His driver climbed the stairs ahead of him, glancing over his shoulder.

"They'll know you're here," he said conspiratorially, as if he himself had nothing to do with informing them.

"That won't be a problem." Saul awarded him a brief smile.

Double doors opened into the monitoring room. Sitting at consoles lining three of the walls were seven staff, all wearing enforcer uniforms. A suited woman likely to be Inspectorate Executive began walking towards him, her expression slightly puzzled. Slanting outwards from above the consoles, windows overlooked the mazelike network of cell blocks, and from here he could see readerguns positioned on every roof at each corner. Just for a second he hesitated, some stab of conscience slowing his hand. But it swiftly evaporated.

"You are citizen Avram Coran," began the Inspectorate woman, her mouth tightening as prissily as that of the woman who'd sat next to him on the rotobus.

He stepped forward, past his erstwhile driver, reaching out as if to shake her hand, then locked his stance and chopped backwards, hard. Cartilage gave under the edge of his hand, and his driver staggered back making wet choking sounds. Dropping his briefcase Saul turned and stepped in close to the man, tearing both the machine pistol and the ionic stunner from his belt. He then turned and fired one short burst from the machine pistol. The Inspectorate woman flew backwards, that burst of fire also stitching holes across the backs of two of those at the consoles immediately behind her. Even as she crashed to the floor, he fired to the right with the machine pistol and to the left with the stunner. Two staff managed to get to their feet and grope for weapons at their belts. Shattered glass rained down outside from the monitoring room, shortly followed by one of them. The second danced an electric quickstep until Saul shot him through his forehead.

Saul's driver lay on the floor, still making gurgling sounds. Clicking the machine pistol down to three-shot bursts, he fired once into the man's chest and shut him up. One of the console operators, a fat greying man, was trying to crawl for cover, his back bloody and his legs dead behind him. Three more shots spread his brains across the marble-effect tiles. Somewhere out of sight, someone was emitting short panting gasps. Stepping round one of those government-approved vending machines, he found her huddled up against the wall, in a spreading pool of blood.

"No…why? No…"

"Doubtless a question you ask yourself every day," he suggested, before he shot her in the face.

Nice to be able to so clearly identify the bad guys, and as far as he was concerned, anyone found within the confines of this place, and not a prisoner, did not deserve to live. That was a privilege of which he now intended to deprive a very large number of them.

4

ALL HEALTH

Even after national health services across the world turned into a lethal joke for the recipients of treatment, the Committee insisted upon amalgamating them to establish a worldwide service, free to every user. However, with status classification being established in parallel, what free treatment you received from All Health depended on how useful you were to society. Of course, since bureaucrats and politicians ran society and were, in their own opinion, the most useful members of it, they planned their own health care to be some leagues above that of the average citizen. But with the Committee world bureaucracy consisting of over 20 per cent of the population, even before taking into account the useful workers of state-run industries and services like All Health itself, there just weren't the resources to go around, and therefore their plan lay far from reality. Only the top percentile received twenty-second-century medicine: the cancer-hunting microbots and anti-ageing drugs, the bespoke magic bullets and grafts or even organs grown from their own body tissue, the internal monitors and offline heart pumps ready to spring into action should the actual organ fail. At the other end of the scale, zero-asset citizens received healthcare on a par with that of the decrepit national health systems of the twentieth century, but with the not inconsiderable drawback that the superbugs now enjoyed a lead of a century and a half. Treatment in long-established hospitals presented a major risk, and people fought not to be taken in unless very sure that their ailment would otherwise kill them. Mobile hospitals were a slightly better option, and mobile black hospitals better still, but if you were zero-asset you were unlikely to be able to afford them unless you too were making cash money illegally.

NEAL ASHER

ANTARES BASE

Var backed off and scanned the interior of the crawler. Gisender's knapsack lay beside her seat, so Var hoisted it up on to the console and opened it. Inside she found a flask, empty, and a lunchbox, empty too, both so prosaic and pathetic, but also a data disc. She powered up the crawler's com screen, glad to see it still working despite the bullet holes torn through the console, popped the disc out of its case and inserted it into the slot below the screen. It whirred up to speed and immediately a menu appeared. For the moment she ignored it, reaching down next to pick up Gisender who, now dried out like a mummy, was as light as if made of balsa, and carried her into the rear of the crawler. She placed her gently down on the floor, her body reclined on its side since it had frozen in the sitting position, and found a tarpaulin to cover her.

"I'm sorry," she said and, as tears started to well in her eyes, she turned away angrily and re-entered the cockpit to occupy Gisender's seat, and there began scanning the menu.

Var assumed there must be some problem with the crawler's computer or the disc itself, for the file containing personal messages directed to base personnel was empty, as were the other files containing software updates, Govnet search results and even the latest shipment manifest. However, some files were full: eyes-only stuff for Ricard, which she could not access, and the one containing the latest announcement from Delegate Margot Le Blanc—the usual weekly lecture that all base personnel had to sit through in the community room. Var opened it and let it play.

Le Blanc blinked into existence on the screen. As usual she was seated at her wide, polished and empty desk in her office in Brussels, above her head the space-exploration logo affixed to the wood-panelled wall behind her: a space plane penetrating the ring chain of the united world, all its links differently coloured to represent the various regions of Earth. The woman looked grave, but then that was nothing unusual, and Var felt a sneer appearing on her own face—such as she could never allow herself while watching such a broadcast within view of Ricard or any of his staff. Above desk level, Le Blanc wore a tight grey jacket straining at the buttons over her matronly running-to-fat body and a short-collar blouse, whilst out of sight she doubtless wore a neatly matching skirt and sensible shoes.

An Inspectorate brooch cinched her blouse at the throat, but she wore no other jewellery, no make-up, had her hair in a page-boy cut, and a white and utterly utile fone in her ear. Her hands were neat, but meaty, the nails unvarnished. It seemed to Var that cloning technology must be more advanced than she had supposed, for many women in the upper echelons of the world bureaucracy looked just like Le Blanc.

"Citizens of Antares Base," she began, as she always did, but this time how she continued was very different. "It is with a heavy heart that I address you today. Most of you, having been away from Earth for five years, and some for even longer, will be unaware of how circumstances have changed here. When you departed upon your great venture on behalf of the people, you left an Earth blossoming under the auspices of Committee rule."

"Yeah, right," said Var who, like many on the newest complement of technical staff for the base, had been secretively accessing the Subnet before her enforced departure. That was just about the time that the Inspectorate nuked Chicago and, as Var's fellows were waiting at Minsk to board their space plane up to Traveller VIII where she awaited them in a holding cell, when the Committee had announced the restructuring of the East Saharan irrigation project. "Restructuring" always meant something had gone drastically wrong, so that probably meant starvation in the North African sprawls, along with rioting and the deployment of Inspectorate military.

"However," Le Blanc continued, "the forces of chaos and disorder are never completely vanquished and are always ready to take advantage should the opportunity present. Dissidents and revolutionaries are ever ready to try and destroy the socialist dream; ever ready to sacrifice the lives of the people on the altar of some ridiculous, selfish ideology. These people have been working against the Committee for some time and, though they have on the whole been defeated, some of their plans have come to fruition and have caused…problems." Here Le Blanc paused to shift about in her seat, as if she were suffering from haemorrhoids. "Of course, they can never win, and the damage they can cause to a society as strong as ours will always be minimal, but because of their actions, some restructuring is required."

There it was, that word: *restructuring*.

"Because of the activities of these mentally subnormal people, we, the Committee, have decided, for the good of the people, to reallocate world resources. This is merely a momentary impediment, and I can guarantee you that we shall once again progress beyond it. Once this is behind us, further Traveller spacecraft can be constructed and supply lines can be re-established. Meanwhile—"

Var hit the pause button and just stared at the little screen. *Further Traveller spacecraft can be constructed?* What the hell happened to VII, VIII, IX and Messina's ego-trip project the *Alexander*? She felt a horrible frustrated anger at this, for she had overseen the construction of the Traveller VIII and had been overseeing the construction of IX and the *Alexander* when they pulled her. She set the communication running again.

"—it is certain that you will face some hardship whilst you are maintaining humanity's foothold on another world, but I am sure you will do so with the fortitude of true citizens of Earth. Some of you will find your final resting place in the red soil you labour upon, but be assured that your sacrifice will never be forgotten." Le Blanc held up her fist. "Solidarity, citizens. With great regret I must now close down all communications while I and my fellow delegates focus our energies on the problems we face here. I leave you with the blessings and felicitations of the Committee." The image blinked out to be replaced with the United Earth logo. Stirring music ensued; it was Holst, *The Planets Suite,* "Mars."

"You fucking bitch!" Var exclaimed, but wondered why she should be surprised.

Right from when she had arrived here, five Earth years ago, things had been going wrong. Those who had been due to return on Traveller VIII had discovered that their space plane, the plane that had deposited Var and her fellows on the surface, did not have enough fuel to lift off again. Traveller VIII meanwhile had swung round Mars and, without delay, headed back to Earth. The delivery of new supplies had also been a fuck-up. Yes, the tonnage had been shipped, but half of the things they most needed here had not. Instead of the required soil biota, furnaces and replacement injectors for the fusion reactor, they'd received two shrink-wrapped shepherds and a tonne of aerofan spindles. This had been ascribed to the usual bureaucratic fudge which could be corrected with the next delivery, but, no, it seemed things were already winding down even then. This was how projects got abandoned: increasing screw-ups as each government department involved withdrew, until the inevitable announcement of restructuring, reallocation or, in this case, "We're going to leave you to die now, sorry and all that."

"Bitch!" Var repeated, then her attention strayed to a com light blinking on the console. "Miska?" she queried. Still no response via the coded channel they had been using, so perhaps something had gone wrong with that and he was now trying to talk to her through the crawler's com. She hit the respond pad, but it wasn't Miska's face that appeared on the screen.

"Ah, at last," said Ricard. "Miska shut down your com channel, and has been reluctant to provide me with the code." Ricard turned to look down to his right. "Haven't you, Miska?"

Var heard Miska's voice followed by a fleshy thump—probably an enforcer's boot going in. Ricard swung his gaze back to Var.

"You killed Gisender," was all she could say.

"It was necessary to neutralize Gisender until certain protocols were in place." He paused, shrugged. "Hard decisions have to be made, Var. With your expertise, this is something you must understand."

Var let that go for the moment and instead asked, "So you didn't think we needed to know Le Blanc's last message?"

"As I suspected, you've seen it. That's unfortunate."

"How long, exactly, did you think you could keep it from us?" Var asked.

"As long as necessary. Such an announcement might have led to incorrect behaviour, and even disorder."

"Incorrect behaviour," Var repeated woodenly. "We could all die here and you're still fretting about *that*. Are you fucking mad?"

"And disorder, Var," he said gravely. "Disorder could lead to the destruction of government property—property it has cost billions to transport here. It is my remit to ensure this base remains functional and staffed, ready for when the supply route is re-established."

"You *are* fucking mad."

Ricard continued obliviously, "Certainly, some downsizing will be required and the assigned status of present personnel will have to be re-evaluated."

"There are no Travellers coming, Ricard. We've been left here to die!"

He nodded mildly. "The old Travellers are presently being recycled through the Argus bubblemetal plants, but new vessels should be available in between fifteen and twenty years."

Var sat back hard, as if he'd punched her. Only now, as she really thought about it, did she realize what Ricard was implying. They all knew that, with present resources, the 163 people here—now 162—could survive unsupplied for only about five years. But it seemed Ricard had received private orders, and had made his own calculations. *Downsizing?* The only downsizing she could think he might be referring to was a reduction in the number of people using those resources. So, when he talked about *re-evaluating* status he meant deciding who he could afford to kill.

But if he thought their time here could be extended to ten or fifteen years, using such methods, he was still seriously mistaken, or had been seriously misled. Doubtless some Committee apparatchik had told him that a small complement of personnel could survive here, and when that small complement started to die, as they inevitably would, they would use up fewer resources and be less likely to damage any of that government property he had mentioned. The Committee clearly wanted to keep the Mars foothold open, the Mars base available. Staff weren't so important, since replacements could be selected from a pool of billions.

"Surely you know you're being lied to," she said. "If we have any chance of survival here it's with *all* personnel working on the problems we face."

"Don't you see?" he said. "Incorrect thought already, and yet you are an intelligent person who has only just viewed Le Blanc's communication."

Var stared at him for a long moment before saying, "So I'm guessing my status has just been downgraded."

Ricard smiled cheerfully. "Certainly not! You are a valued member of the Antares Base staff, whose knowledge will be essential over the coming years."

"But Gisender wasn't," she spat.

He shook his head, his expression mournful. "Merely a computer and power-systems technician—the kind of person who was useful while resources were abundant, but who would soon have become surplus to requirements."

That really brought home to Var his cluelessness. He simply had no real idea about the necessities of survival here. Gisender had been exactly the sort of person they needed, someone who could actually repair things rather than merely head down to Stores for another plug-in replacement. Var also had no doubt that Ricard considered himself and his executives and enforcers to be utterly essential, even though they were people with skills generally limited to micromanaging and bullying.

"So," he continued, "I want you to return here to Hex Three, without informing anyone of your…discovery. To that end I've sent someone to bring you in."

Even then she saw it, striding out from behind Shankil's Butte and heading towards her, kicking up little puffs of dust each time its two-toed feet thumped down on the peneplain. It seemed Ricard or his men possessed more technical skill than she gave them credit for, because one or more of them had assembled a shepherd and, in some ultimate expression of reality imitating art, a machine like something out of H. G. Wells's *War of the Worlds* was coming to seize her—out here on the surface of the world that gave it birth in that writer's imagination.

EARTH

In the terms of the society in which Saul found himself, he was a sociopath, though perhaps that might be considered a normal condition in a society that so easily eliminated its innocent citizens. But then who was innocent? Just by following the dictates of selfish genes in an overpopulated world, people were effectively killing each other. Yes, the Committee had turned killer as it expedited the coming resource crash, but that crash in and of itself wasn't the product of either this political doctrine or that; it was the product of people—manswarm—endlessly breeding. Saul often felt great self-doubt, considering himself a killer without conscience, somehow damaged and not sane, but assured himself that this must have been how he was before, probably made that way by training, indoctrination, something external.

It was a comforting illusion of his that, as the product of civilization, he had once been civilized, and that to become a killer had required some traumatic twisting of his psyche. But, whatever way he looked at things, he knew that to succeed in his aims he must be even more ruthless than those now preparing to cling to power while billions died. It seemed a rather extreme demand on oneself.

It took Saul only a few moments to find an undamaged console, and then a chair not soaked with blood. A couple of those working in here had been wearing machine pistols like the one he had just used, and having deprived them of these weapons, he laid them down on the console and gazed outside.

Some people were standing about in stunned groups, the odd individual pointing towards the monitoring room, but he noted enforcers clad in body armour and grey camo-fatigues beginning to respond—running towards him. To give himself just a little more time, he picked up one of the weapons and fired at one approaching group, not particularly aiming. Carbocrete and earth erupted beside them and they ducked for cover behind a cell block. He fired again, here and there, sending others scurrying for cover, then sat down and opened his briefcase.

After unfolding his laptop on top of the console, the screen instantly bringing up Janus's ammonite icon, he used a coil of optic cable to plug it into a nearby port, then waited a second until the icon started blinking.

"Are you good to go?" he enquired.

"I am," Janus replied.

Immediately a loading bar opened up at the bottom of the screen, as the portion of Janus contained within the laptop began to load itself into the system here. Saul rattled his fingers on the console for a moment, then spotting some further movement down below, picked up a machine pistol and emptied its entire clip in that general direction. However, further out within the complex he saw another troop of Inspectorate enforcers cross the gap between two buildings. They were carrying armourglass shields and heavy assault rifles, and perhaps all that now slowed down their further response was not yet knowing if any hostages were being held here. Doubtless the cams above his head would soon apprise them of the facts, then, given the chance, they would attempt to turn this monitoring room into a pepperpot.

"I am in," Janus informed him, its icon now appearing on every unbroken screen.

"Cam system first," he suggested.

"Already done," Janus replied.

"Is there a central locking system?"

"Yes, to all cells. However, three cells in maximum-security block A7 also need to be manually unlocked."

"Well, open up everything you can," Saul instructed, more just for something to say than anything else, for he knew that Janus would already be doing so. Even now, cell doors would be popping open all across the complex, with prisoners looking up in fear of another visit from their tormentors, but finding no one there. Some such prisoners, he knew, would just crouch inside their cells, too terrified to avail themselves of the open doors. Others would take the chance though, knowing that trying to escape would not make things any worse for them.

"ID implant codes located," Janus informed him. "I am deleting prisoner IDs from the readergun system now, and simultaneously uploading staff IDs."

"Have you found the one I described?" he asked.

"There are four who come close to your description."

Four faces appeared on the screen, all dark-haired men clad in enforcer uniforms, but none of them possessed those hated features.

"He's not there," he said, at once feeling both disappointed and relieved, for what he was about to do was just too impersonal. He wanted to meet his interrogator face to face, and then kill the man with his bare hands. "Just don't forget that Coran's ID must be excluded," he added. "And make sure Hannah Neumann's ID isn't considered a staff one, as we don't really know for sure what her position is here."

"I have located her. She is classified as a prisoner and is located in A7."

From where he sat, Saul watched one of the readerguns swivel and fire off a three-shot burst, the flare from it just one bright flash and the report only one sound—the shots so close together it was impossible for the human eye or ear to distinguish between them. The guts and much of the chest of an Inspectorate enforcer splashed a grey concrete wall, just before the rest of him slammed into it. Other readerguns began to open up intermittently, then built to a steady thunder as Saul used the fingertips of his right hand to tap out a little ditty on the surface of the console before him. Finally, as the thunder started to die, he stood up and headed for the stairs.

Exiting the lower doors of the monitoring station, he ducked low and quickly slipped behind the vehicle that had brought him here, but a quick glance around revealed that no one was paying attention to him any more. The devastating and gory effectiveness of the readerguns had become immediately apparent. Corpses slumped at the termini of great red splashes of blood and body parts, or lying in spreading pools of blood, were now scattered all across the carbocrete. Whilst he watched, a woman tried to find a better hiding place by moving along a nearby wall. The gun positioned on the building opposite turned and fired, the three shots tracking down her body from the top, first taking off her head, then blowing her spine out of her back.

He stood up a little nervously, but the readerguns did not respond to him as he climbed into the electric buggy and engaged its motor. The short drive over to Cell Block A7 seemed part of a journey through some lower circle of hell: just canyons of concrete and the partially dismembered dead, blood splashes and body parts. There were no wounded here because the guns were almost incapable of inaccuracy at such close quarters. Only the particular position or angle of each detected target dictated the placing of the shots, but they were always at once lethal, wadcutter bullets slamming nearly head-sized chunks out of the most vital parts of the human body. Saul's mouth was dry and he felt slightly sickened at the carnage he had achieved, but those feelings were dominated by the other colder and more ruthlessly cruel side of him.

Cell Block A7 looked little different from all the other blocks in the vicinity. He noted where an enforcer had tried to get inside but a gun had brought him down on the threshold. Saul dragged the soggy corpse aside before opening the door and stepping through. To his right was a small monitoring station, and two people whirling towards him.

"Have they stopped?" asked the woman, clearly scared and horrified.

The man started reaching out for her arm, as if to draw her back, perhaps realizing that anyone entering at that moment probably had something to do with what was happening outside. One burst from the machine pistol flung them both backwards into a vending machine, where they collapsed to the floor under a shower of hot coffee and milk powder.

Moving into the corridor beyond, Saul shoved open a door. A cell, but unoccupied: a single toilet in the corner and nothing else, that sole comfort provided only because Inspectorate enforcers did not want to handle shit-smeared prisoners.

What lay behind the door opposite came as a surprise, for the cell doors on this side of the corridor all opened into one single long room, the intervening walls having been torn out at some time in the past, and replaced here and there with glass partitions. Directly ahead of him lay a very high-tech operating theatre. He entered and turned right, passing two hospital beds on opposite sides of the aisle. A man occupied one of the beds, with numerous monitoring machines hooked up, optics and fluid feeds running into glued-together incisions in his skull, screens to one side running images that might even have been his dreams. Ahead lay further computer hardware, also squat tanks he recognized as artificial wombs, all containing small organic conglomerations rendered almost invisible by the masses of wires, tubes and optic threads plugged into them. He stepped back into the corridor through the next door along, and opened the one opposite. In the corner of this cell squatted a man who just stared at him blankly, his stubble-covered skull webbed with stitched-up wounds.

"If you run now," Saul said, "you have a chance to escape."

The man stood up. "Readerguns?"

"Targeting the staff only," Saul explained.

The man stepped past him into the corridor and strolled off slowly down towards the exit. This wasn't exactly the reaction Saul had expected, and the man's speed of comprehension was somewhat unnerving.

Saul moved along to open the remaining cell.

Hannah Neumann had been provided with more comforts than the other prisoners, but then she wasn't here for adjustment, since what resided inside her head was too valuable to risk being damaged by such crude measures. Her double-length cell contained a bed, toilet and shower and even a small kitchen area. She had also been provided with computer access, beside her terminal stretched a work surface strewn with computer components, paper read-outs, extra screens and processing units, and above this the entire wall was shelved with books. She turned her swivel chair away from the terminal and gazed at him with a kind of beaten acceptance.

Though sixty-five years of age, Hannah looked no older than twenty-five, so obviously they'd considered the new anti-ageing drugs sufficiently stable to use on her. She was slim, clad in a short jacket, like those often worn by dentists, over red jeans and trainers. Her hair was brown and up behind her head in a plastic clip, face pale and thin with dark shadows under her eyes. She scanned him from head to foot and, glancing down at himself, he noted too the splashes of blood staining his expensive suit. Her gaze finally came to rest on the machine pistol.

"I heard the readerguns firing out there," she said. "I take it there's been a breakout."

"Certainly," he replied. "Prisoners are escaping but the readerguns aren't shooting at them."

Her expression was at first puzzled then started to show fear. He turned towards the door. "I don't have time for explanations. You must come with me, now."

She stood up, and meekly followed him out through the carnage.

***

At first Hannah had assumed the readerguns were test firing, but when she heard the screaming, and the firing just continued, she reckoned on a breakout. A tightness in her chest and throat prewarned of familiar panic, and she was fighting to quell that as he stepped through the door. With blood spattered on his Inspectorate exec's suit and a machine pistol clutched in his hand, she recognized him at once.

Killer.

Oddly, when here stood a real and deadly reason why she should panic, the panic attack subsided like the liar it was, to be replaced by the genuine article: *fear.*

Even when he told her that the guns were killing the staff, her assessment of him didn't change, for he must be an Inspectorate killer sent to ensure she never escaped. Her legs shaking and only a sudden effort of will stopping her peeing her knickers, she went with him meekly, hoping desperately for something, some way out, just some way of delaying the inevitable. He led her out into the room where Ruth and Joseph kept constant close watch on her, saw the pair of them lying dead and frosted with milk powder, coffee still pouring from the machine beside them and mingling with their blood. Outside, the readerguns were firing only intermittently and, stepping through the door, she could see why. Everyone caught in the open appeared to be dead.

Hannah felt she should be sick, but only numb blankness filled her.

"This way," he said, leading her to an electric truck.

She glanced at him, only then realizing that the readerguns could not have been responsible for killing her guards. He had done it. Who was he? And why did his face look so odd?

Corpses everywhere, and here and there orange-overalled prisoners were unsteadily making their escape. As she and her captor reached the main gate, she saw the windows of the guard booth smashed, and even a couple of the mastiffs lying bullet-riddled in their extended enclosure girdling the compound.

"Transvan." He was pointing her towards the nearest vehicle.

"Who *are* you?" she asked, finally.

He gazed at her with those cold eyes that seemed somehow wrong in that face—and yet somehow familiar.

"A question I, too, am curious to know the answer to," he replied, staring at her with peculiar intensity. "And to which I hope you can supply an answer."

She climbed in through the passenger door of the transvan. What else could she do? Or what else did she want to do? Underneath the shock, she felt something like excitement stir. Her life had been one of perpetual confinement and political supervision, the imminent threat of an adjustment cell just around the corner. She had never expected anything else. And now he was taking her out into a world she had never expected to see again.

Malden, she thought. He had to be one of Malden's people.

But why had he grabbed her and not the revolutionary leader himself? The man must still be back there, still in his cell...unless he too had escaped, perhaps leaving the complex via a different route? Perhaps she had been taken out separately so as to cut down on the risk of both of them being caught?

The killer beside her drew the transvan to a halt at the gates, where the post-mounted recognition system just bleeped acceptance and opened them. While driving through, he took his machine pistol out of his lap and dumped it on the third seat, between them.

"I thought you were Inspectorate...here to kill me," she said, since it now seemed clear that was not his intention.

"I think you underrate your value to the Committee," he said. "If you were that dispensable, they would not have allowed you the anti-ageing drugs, or supplied you with everything you need to conduct your experiments." He paused to glance at her expressionlessly. "Including the human subjects."

"Not my choice," she replied, feeling a surge of guilt.

He continued, "I've little doubt your escape will warrant the outlay of massive resources and any number of lives, just to put you back under lock and key."

"You think so?" Perhaps he was right, though it just didn't feel like that. The threat of adjustment or execution had been hanging over her just too long.

"Oh, yes," he continued, a note of bitter sarcasm in his voice. "They want you regularly turning out all those astounding inventions and innovations that fall within your area of interest. They want further brain augmentation and more ways to connect it up to computer hardware. Your work is leading to developing the first post-humans, which is what many in the upper echelons of government want to become."

It was a nightmare scenario: old and vicious ideologues made immortal by anti-ageing treatments, and super-intelligent through the hardware and software Hannah could create. An awareness of this had always been there, at the back of her mind. She studied him further, then tentatively reached up to the scalp just behind his ear. He glanced at her, but did not deny her investigation, so she probed with sensitive fingertips before snatching her hand away.

"You've got hardware in your skull," she declared. "Advanced hardware."

That was it then: he himself must be one of her experimental subjects, who had somehow escaped and now come back to exact his vengeance.

"And an artificial intelligence living on Govnet," he added.

"An artificial intelligence," she repeated woodenly. *An artificial intelligence on Govnet? None of her experimental subjects could have managed that...* Then something heavy and terrifying came and sat on her chest. Someone possessing that kind of resource, who quite evidently also hated the Committee? *Far far too much of a coincidence...but he was dead.* She'd watched him die, so how could this have anything to do with him? Hannah just sat there in silence turning it all over in her head, lost in a haze of speculation which she only came out of as he pulled into a layby.

"Vehicle change," he said, nodding towards an old hydrocar parked ahead. Then he explained, "This place is a cam deadspot."

Now Hannah felt a weird species of bewilderment, as if she'd just stepped through a hole in reality. She could not remember any time in her life when there wasn't an active camera watching her every move. In her early years, behavioural programs had judged her and passed on snippets of her life to political officers for assessment. In later years, such officers had kept her under constant watch. Not having them watch her now felt really strange.

It meant she could *do* something now. *Say* something now.

"Fuck the Committee," she said abruptly, then felt her face redden, her chest and her throat tightening up. She flicked her gaze towards the various ragged-looking people wandering aimlessly about the area, almost afraid that someone might have heard her. But no real immediate danger seemed to threaten here, which was why her "liar" panic attack returned.

He glanced at her as he took a fuel can out from behind the seat.

"Quite." He leaned across to open her door. "Out, now."

She stepped out of the van, still feeling in a haze and reluctant to move away from the vehicle's protective presence—out into the unwatched open. He rounded the front of the vehicle to stand before her, an electrical device of some kind clutched in one hand. "Step away from the van."

Catching a whiff of diesel from the cab, she obeyed, fully expecting him to now torch the vehicle, but it turned out that the device he held wasn't an igniter but some kind of scanner that he ran up and down her body, pausing for a moment each time it beeped.

"Five trackers on you," he said, bringing the scanner back to the last detected point, where it beeped at her collar. He clicked another button, whilst holding the device in place, and she spotted a bar display rising on its little screen. When that reached the top, a green light blinked on. He pressed another button and a point of warmth expanded at her neck.

"Focused microwave burst," she surmised, that sense of tight panic inside her fading with the warmth.

"Burns them out," he supplied.

He found another two in her clothing: two dermal stick-ons which, after he dealt with them, left her skin reddened. He then paused the scanner device over her thigh.

"I'm afraid this is going to hurt," he said flatly.

"What…what do you mean?"

"You've got a tracker embedded in the bone of your thigh."

She saw the bar display rising and didn't know how to protest. He triggered the device and at first the expected pain failed to register. But then it started to grow, a bone-deep ache that just kept climbing in intensity. She found herself gritting her teeth, her eyes watering, then her leg just gave way under her. He caught her around the waist, holding the device in place for a moment longer, till he finally retracted it.

"Okay," he said. "Come on."

He helped her hobble over to the hydrocar, and she was more than glad to climb inside. Sudden light caught her eye and she looked round to see fire blooming inside the transvan cab. She then looked round at the scattering of indigents up above on the concrete bank, watching the show.

"What about *them*?" she asked.

"They'll disappear quick enough once the Inspectorate appear."

He passed her a blister pack of painkillers and an analgesic patch, then concentrated on pulling the hydrocar out into a gap between passing autotrucks. Feeling no embarrassment, she pulled down her trousers and pressed the patch into place. She was so used to being watched. From behind came a whoomph and, glancing back again, she saw flames belch out of the gap where the transvan's screen had been. Seeing this destruction too, the indigents began moving off.

"You expected deeply implanted trackers?" she said.

"I expected more than just one."

Another vehicle change ensued in an underpass, presumably another deadspot, and again it was a place inhabited by ragged, aimless people. But then where wasn't, these days? Everywhere Hannah looked, she could see hopeless souls trudging about with the demeanour of seniles in late-stage dementia, even though many of them weren't noticeably old. Her head felt light as she sat staring out of the windscreen at these sad beings, but, even so, something seemed to begin unwinding inside her—years and years of it. Her leg aching after having to walk from car to car, she swallowed some of the painkillers, then realized her abductor genuinely had expected more than just one deeply implanted tracker, for the pills were strong. She didn't remember sleeping, but after an odd hiatus she found they were driving along a carbocrete rural road, then parking on a patch of old concrete, amidst fields. Here, at last, no people in sight—which seemed very strange.

He hid the vehicle under a filthy canvas sheet whose colour matched the concrete, then guided her round by a trampled path, to a hatch that he pulled up. He then led her down below, and lights came on as they entered some sort of underground bunker. Next he tore off his mask—the layer of silicone rubber she had somehow known was there—to reveal features that she recognized at once.

She gazed at him for a long moment, not quite sure how to handle this.

Then she nodded slowly. "I thought Smith had killed you, Alan. I thought he'd finally got what he wanted."

Thinner-featured, of course. Hair dyed a different colour from its usual acid white. Something almost unhuman wearing a human face and finding it didn't quite fit. That was him; that had always been Alan Saul. Of course she was glad to see him alive, but it meant that a whole bunch of complicated emotions, once securely cached in her mind, were no longer quite so secure.

"Smith," he echoed, momentary rage transforming his expression, shortly displaced by puzzlement. He shook his head. "I know my own name, but that's about all I know."

"You don't remember Salem Smith?"

"No."

She should not feel disappointed with his amnesia. Considering what Smith had done to him, it was miraculous he possessed a mind at all—or that he was even alive.

"Alan Saul," she confirmed tightly. "But don't even bother looking on Govnet or the Subnets for anything regarding yourself. You erased everything, and your work was so highly classified they put nothing back. Even I'm only allowed access to parts of it—after it's been vetted by a committee of fourteen science-policy advisers."

"My work?"

She told him.

5

PROHIBITION WORKS!

The greater the power and extent of the state, the more room there is for corruption. The more inept state services and industries become, the more pies it takes its huge cut from and the more regulation it imposes, the greater the call for black markets. This last fact is one governments consistently failed to learn, even after the stark lesson of American Prohibition. Deadspots are where you'll find them. Inspectorate officers grow rich in cash by selling the locations of such deadspots to the underworld, which in turn makes its cut from those it opens up such spots to. The breakers come there—those who burn out the tracers in stolen vehicles and disassemble them for their components, those who take apart computer hardware to sell to others maintaining the Subnet, and those who chop up human bodies for usable organs—usually to be sold to low-echelon officials not yet enjoying twenty-second-century medical care. Retailers come to sell other blackmarket goods: food disapproved of by All Health, like high-fat dairy products, sugary drinks and sweets; cigarettes, drugs, illegal ABV booze, coffee and tea without the cumulative emetics to discourage abuse. And then there are the black surgeries dealing in illegal implants, ID implant excision and exchange, gunshot wounds, and all those injuries and illnesses not catered for under All Health—but only for those who can afford them.

In a totalitarian state, some people are just too dangerous to be allowed to live. Saul now considered his second-hand knowledge of the person he had been. He was a brilliant, brilliant man, indeed a genius, but with a huge drawback in that he was also only a marginally functional human being. It could be called autism, or maybe Asperger's syndrome, but Saul liked to think that so focused on his work had he been, he simply had not found the time, space or energy to deal with the trivialities of normal human relationships. Able to speak and read even before he could coordinate his limbs, his previous self had been sent immediately into special schools, but even they could not quite handle him and he ended up being home-tutored by educational experts. By the age of ten, he also outpaced these experts, and thereafter had taken charge of his own education. Had Saul been a child of zero-asset-status parents, all this might have caused great problems, and sufficient funding and resources might have been hard to find, but his parents were high-level Committee executives and able to lavish attention on him.

For Saul, every test, both mental or physical, was of overriding interest and in nothing he tried did he fail to excel. He practised martial arts, taking his second black belt in shotokan karate whilst studying for eight doctorates in the physical sciences and three in the arts. Very soon he began to produce: making vast improvements to the software of agricultural robots, then designing a new kind of materially inert microbot that could hunt through the human body for cancer cells without causing rejection problems. Next he applied the same inert materials to someone else's invention of a chip interface to the human mind, so it too would not activate the immune system. That was Hannah's invention.

Saul thus became a "societal asset" even as the Committee was just inventing the term. When Committee political officers realized how valuable he could be, he was seconded to a gated science community secure in the Dinaric Alps of Albania and there, for the first time, and like all the other scientists thus seconded, he came under intense political scrutiny. This was where he had first met Hannah.

"That was forty years ago, Alan," Hannah told him.

"How old am I?" he asked.

"Somewhere in your sixties," she replied. "Just like us all, you received anti-ageing treatments."

"I see." He nodded. "So how, then, did I end up in a crate heading for the Calais Incinerator?"

"You didn't do what you were told. You kept antagonizing them." She gazed at him steadily. "Most of the community thought you a brat. They'd been working under the eyes of political officers since their school days, yet you'd experienced none of that."

"How...how did I antagonize them?"

"Probably the first example was what you did thirty years ago when you were into splicing nanotech and viruses." Hannah shrugged. "They still haven't been able to work out what you actually did, and neither have I. You created something: a splicing of the cancer-hunting nanite you'd developed and a retrovirus used to fix the genetic faults that lead to some cancers—one of the so-called magic bullets. You injected it into yourself and actually edited your own DNA. You wouldn't tell them what you'd done, and that's when they really started to get pissed off with you."

"Why wouldn't I tell them?"

"I think you had developed an extreme dislike of Political Director Smith."

That name again. The mention of it caused some sort of deep reaction and, as on previously hearing it, he again chose not to analyse the feeling.

"He wouldn't allow you unsupervised contact with your sister," Hannah added.

"I have a sister?" Saul felt a surge of something inside—something difficult to identify.

"You do. As brilliant as you, apparently, and seconded like you to work on government projects."

"Her name?"

"I don't know. You never talked about her much."

That tight emotion wound itself even tighter inside him, and he glanced up, visualizing the Argus Station somewhere above them, seeing void beyond it, and some sort of resolution.

"Janus," he said, "find her."

"I have already begun searching," the AI replied. "Unfortunately, with your own files deleted, I don't have much to work on. Females with the surname Saul number two point six million, and if all reference to you has been deleted then there'll be no record that they had a brother called Alan. It is also possible that she is now listed under a married name."

"She'll be listed in a protected-asset file."

"Which makes the search even more dangerous and difficult."

After a moment, he shrugged the problem away. "Keep looking whenever you have the processing space available." He was aware he felt strong emotion about his sister, but pursuing his present course now seemed more important. In fact he had the odd feeling that by sticking to this course, the matter of his sister would be resolved, and that it was inclusive—yet that made no sense at all.

"They could easily have forced me to tell them what I did," he said to Hannah.

"They searched your files but couldn't find very much, because you kept most of what you achieved inside your head. They'd already tried the viral nanite on a political prisoner, and it killed him quicker than cyanide." She added, "You got away with a lot simply because your mother was high up in the Committee Executive."

"What about my father?"

"Dead by then."

"What happened next? What finally made them put me in that crate?"

Hannah explained the history.

One of the scientists working in the Dinaric community, a woman who always came under the most intense scrutiny because the political officers knew she disagreed with the whole concept of world government, had created a very powerful form of Hyex laminate which she supplied to the Albanian Separatists. They then blew the periphery fence and got her and five other scientists out, but that effectively spelled the end of the community. The Applied Sciences branch of the Inspectorate Executive now decided it would be better to separate the scientists into small groups, each focusing on one discrete area of the various projects the Committee wanted quickly advanced. One group worked on fusion-drive technology, one on satellite imaging and recognition programs, another on gerontology and yet another on GM bacteria used to clear up pollution, and so forth. Hannah's particular group had the goal of connecting up the human mind to a computer, whereupon Alan Saul, his focus now straying from nanotech and retrovirals to artificial intelligence, was seconded to her group under the supervision of Political Director Smith.

They did some superb work, finally managing to install a terabyte processor inside a human skull, though never able to connect it up completely to the human brain, only managing to wire it in through the sensory nerves. Saul decided he wanted one of these processors inside his own skull and so, with his usual blinkered focus, he hacked into research-team security when Smith was absent, and falsified the orders...

"I inserted that processor in your head, Alan," Hannah now told him. "I thought it a stupid risk to take, but I never disobeyed orders. I assumed you had suggested it to Smith and he'd agreed, perhaps after you claimed that by using the technology you might be able to crack the mind-silicon interface."

Saul had then been concentrating on trying to copy the function of the human mind into software, on silicon, to make it easier to crack that same interface. Smith and his advisers were getting both very worried and very excited about this work, and when Alan used some of his comlife, as he called it, to punch through security so easily, it seemed that their worries were justified.

"Smith hated you, though I don't think he could have done anything about that if your mother had still been alive, but she'd died a month before." Hannah shook her head. "I tried to excuse your behaviour by telling Smith you'd gone a bit strange after your mother's death, but the truth was that you showed no reaction to that at all. It just didn't seem to interest you."

Smith finally cleared permission to take Alan off the project and send him for adjustment. But that came a little too late, because Saul crashed computer security systems and all the research computers before escaping. While in the outside world, he created false community credit, a false identity, and even managed to penetrate secure Committee files to erase all details that might be used to track him down. Alan Saul thus disappeared from most computer systems and most live computer files, except for the discs retained at the Dinaric community. It was the information on a single disc like this that enabled newly developed recognition software to track him down. Enforcers arrested him while he was living in a ministerial apartment in the Caribbean, and handed him directly to Smith for adjustment.

"He used the hardware inside your head and pain inducers to torture you," explained Hannah. "He even brought me and the rest of the team in to watch, · just so we understood where any disobedience would lead. When he'd finished, you didn't have a mind left; in fact large parts of your brain suffered lethal bleeds, and tissue had died inside your skull, too. They then dragged you off for disposal, so I don't know how you can be here now."

So Smith was his interrogator. Even as Hannah finished speaking, Saul also knew why he hadn't died. A memory lurked just at the periphery of his mental perception, a ghostly hint of the person he had once been. He realized that to lose his mind was his greatest terror, and Smith, knowing this with the instinct of all sadists, had therefore chosen that way to destroy him. He also realized that he had done something to ensure that both his brain and his mind would prove difficult to totally destroy, perhaps something involving that retroviral and anti-ageing fix. Nevertheless, Smith had come very close to his objective:

Saul still possessed a mind, but not the mind of the original Alan Saul.

"Was I violent?" he asked.

"Never," she replied. "In fact, if you had been capable of real violence, I don't think they would ever have caught you."

So that was it. The first Alan Saul had not been sufficiently ruthless, but had ensured that his creation would be.

***

The British government had established the World War Two bunker in preparation for a Nazi invasion, perhaps to provide just one more safehouse amidst many for dissident forces or a government in hiding, but what remained of its history was unclear. It was Janus who found it for Saul, then carefully erased all reference to it from official computer records, but he needed to ensure that no local knowledge of it existed either. It lay amidst agricultural land, just fifty metres to one side of a road composed of carbocrete blocks along which only robotic harvesters ran. It was a location frequented by very few humans now.

To gain access to the croplands he had to assume yet another identity but, wanting to use the bolt-hole long-term, he did not lift that identity from a corpse. Janus created a new persona for him, and to acquire it he needed to visit an All Health clinic to have the necessary ID implant injected into his arm, which struck him as even more risky than killing off another bureaucrat. All agricultural land now being private government property, only approved workers were allowed anywhere near it. Any intruder was at risk of being spattered by readerguns mounted on the harvesters or independently mobile and stalking through the crops like iron spiders—in fact, the precursors to modern spiderguns—or in danger of being attacked by razorbirds, with a similarly messy result. He'd already seen the decaying corpses of those who had tried to supplement their rations: their remains got ploughed into the soil after harvest, old bones shattered by the disking that broke up the clods of earth.

Driving his recently requisitioned mini-digger up from the roadway, Saul came to a concrete area enclosed on three sides by block walls, now overgrown with weeds and occupied by rusted-together piles of swarf and machine parts and an ancient truck probably belonging to a scrap dealer from some previous age. He recognized this area as a bay intended for mounding beets before they were transported away—from the time before such vegetables were wrenched from the ground by robotic harvesters, washed and then mashed up, before the mulch was injected straight into one of the many processing plants scattered across the local landscape.

"You are heading in the right direction," Janus informed him. "Another twenty metres and you should be right over the entrance."

It lay behind the beet bay, where brambles and nettles fought for predominance with GM beans, so there was no visible sign of it on the surface. Scraping downwards a metre through this tangle, he unearthed a layer of cracked concrete and managed to pull away a lot of this before revealing a rusted cast-iron lid. This he tore up to expose steps heading down underneath the beet bay. He picked up his torch, climbed out of the digger and descended.

Because it was concealed inside a hill, only the lower floor of the bunker had flooded. The large upper chamber and four side rooms were packed with all sorts of interesting rubbish: sacks of solidified fertilizer, a table and chairs made of plastic now as brittle as eggshell, a kitchen counter with an old gas stove, the gas bottle underneath it; a generator that had obviously broken down, then been taken apart and abandoned; some cups, plates and cutlery in decaying kitchen units which, judging by the date of a newspaper stuck to the table, must have been only a hundred years old. He had much work to do.

It took him a full month to get the required equipment in place. He first ran a buried power line from a harvester recharging station, then a pipe from the surrounding irrigation grid. Pumping out the lower floor revealed rotten crates filled with the rusted shells of food tins, and also an escape tunnel filled with rubble. After running a dehumidifier inside—one stolen from one of the grain-processing plants—he sprayed every surface with a layer of sealant. All the while he resided there, he kept the dehumidifier running and never required any of the irrigation water, instead using water leeched from air that was constantly moistened by the damp surrounding concrete.

Whilst Saul made the place comfortable, Janus worked its magic in the local agricultural security, until such time as Saul would no longer require his new identity—the recognition systems just ignoring him. When finally ready to act, he was fully linked via the agricultural network in Govnet and the intermittent Subnet, and possessed a weapons cache, an excess of computer hardware, and his own cams installed in the surrounding area as an additional layer of security sitting below Janus's access to the government cams and read-erguns. Also a plentiful food supply, and all the other comforts of a home.

THE DEPARTURE

***

"This place is mine," he told her, which was a statement you just did not hear these days. The Committee owned everything and allotted to its citizens those things they might require on the basis of their status—their usefulness. And, with what Hannah had seen, she knew that people did not even own their own bodies, while the property of their minds now lay under constant siege.

"No cams in here," he added. "No monitoring of any kind."

"Nice place," said Hannah, looking round, tears welling in her eyes.

This was incredible, like a dream they'd once shared: no government watchers, none of those constant flushes of embarrassment in case she might have behaved in a manner some political officer might find questionable. Being here seemed like stepping back, over a century or more, to the time when people actually owned their own homes and government intrusion stopped at the front door. Yet, perhaps understandably, she now felt clumsy and somehow foolish. So long had she lived within set parameters defining both her behaviour and what she was allowed to say that suddenly without them she felt almost lost.

"A temporary accommodation," he explained. "Nowhere on Earth is safe."

"So where next?" She swallowed drily, tried to get herself back under control. *Grow up. For Christ sake, grow up!*

"I have attained my first goal," he said emotionlessly. "I now know who I am, so it is time for me to attain my next goal." His face showed extreme emotion, raw hate. "Now I must show these fuckers they've really made an enemy."

"How?"

When he told her how, she wondered where the hell that idea had come from. He studied her with fevered intensity, perhaps waiting for her to declare him insane, but usual definitions of sanity did not apply to the person he had once been and probably did not apply to the person he was now. She considered what he had told her about this artificial intelligence on Govnet. He'd mentioned a name, Janus, which was revealing in itself. In light of her own research, and what she knew of his previous work, she could see where this inevitably had to go.

"You are incomplete," she said, her voice catching. "And once complete you'll be much more able to do what you want."

"I *know* that, but it's still not going to stop me."

He didn't know. He just had no idea of what was possible…Then, again, he had come looking for her first even though, from his point of view, she was merely a footnote to his main goal, just a way to learn about his past. Belatedly she wondered if his older self had prepared his present mind for this, impelled him to go after the one person who could give him the tools to bring his plan—his vengeance—to fruition. Yet she had once known that other self so intimately, and this seemed too cold and cruel a calculation, even for him.

"I'm not talking about what memories or what portions of your mind you've lost." She took a firmer grip on her emotions, wiped her face shakily. "I'm talking about what it's possible for you to become."

"Become?"

Hannah paused, suddenly horrified with herself, then after a moment continued, "I was currently working on a full organic interface of the human mind with an internal computer, and thence with computer networks. Unfortunately that interface, the new cerebral computer and software, are still back at the cell complex."

She explained further, and it seemed like her words just plugged themselves into his brain like programming patches, yet did nothing to slow down the impetus of something unstoppable. He frightened her at an almost visceral level because of his capabilities, even with his mind fractured, damaged. However, the thought of once again falling into the hands of the Inspectorate frightened her even more, for even here in this damp underground bunker she was experiencing a freedom of thought and expression not previously allowed her, never allowed since the moment the first community political officer had told her to carefully watch her parents and report any incorrect behaviour.

"I have to go back, then," he concluded.

"Yes, perhaps," she agreed, wondering what price she was prepared to pay for her own continuing freedom and survival.

"The Inspectorate won't be expecting that," he noted, whilst carrying out the prosaic task of pouring hot water from a kettle. "But still it's a risky venture. My plan will require substantial revision."

She felt a scream of laughter rising in her chest. *Risky venture?* He'd just broken her out of Inspectorate HQ London, slaughtering most of the staff in the process. Yet, even so, he obviously wanted what she had to offer. Was it because of that ghostly memory of who he had once been, of the powerful intelligence that lay wrecked inside his skull? Was it the promise of turning his mind into something post-human, superhuman, that tightened his expression into something dangerously predatory? Maybe it was more complicated than that. Maybe his old self wanted to live again, and this was the nearest it could get to him, out of the land of the dead.

"The artificial intelligence is the key," Hannah told him. "They would only allow me just small portions of the comlife presently being developed, and it works every time—for a little while at least. And if this Janus is capable of penetrating government security like you've just demonstrated, then it's far in advance of anything I knew about." She used some of the tea he'd just made her to wash down another painkiller. The ache in her leg was not so bad now—it just felt like she'd bashed it against the edge of a desk.

"You've had people connect up?" he asked. "Fully?"

Her tea was just as she liked it: strong with two sugars. It bothered her that somehow he had remembered this small fact, yet nothing else about her.

"Yeah but, with the comlife they allowed me, it was like trying to direct-link laptops using different computer languages. Janus is almost certainly like all the other comlife you created: an almost direct synaptic copy of your own mind."

"Alan Saul lives again?"

"No, there should be no memories there…unless you did something no one knows about while you were a free agent. But you claimed Janus activated at about the same time you woke up in that crate?"

"Yes."

"That's…odd."

"Perhaps Janus just initiated before but wasn't conscious, and then started searching for the coded signal from the hardware you installed inside my head?"

She nodded. It could be that his earlier self had prepared the AI just before his capture, and that it found him only after the guards removed him from the interrogation cell, perhaps when his brain re-engaged with the processor lodged in his skull. However, she felt a horrible intimation: perhaps Saul had connived at his own capture, knowing that he needed to become something else, and that only by destroying what he already was could he…no, no, that way lay madness.

"You'll go alone?" she asked.

"Far too risky to take you back there," he replied.

She didn't quite manage to hide her relief.

***

It now being night-time, diode lamps bathed the cell complex in an unforgiving glare. Between the security fences where the mastiffs had once patrolled, leggy, bunched-up steel shapes squatted—spiderguns at rest. The inner areas now swarmed with Inspectorate investigators, and from the surrounding mess, Saul assumed they'd only just managed to get the readerguns offline. With thin plastic-film overalls covering their clothes, workers were identifying corpses, scooping them into body bags, then loading them on to electric carts to be conveyed to nearby ambulances. The crowd here was good cover, because one more investigator on the scene would be of no particular note. Also, since they'd yet to unscramble the mess Janus had made of their system, they wouldn't have figured out who had entered or left during this incident, so no one would be particularly wanting to interrogate Avram Coran. Abandoning his car in the internal car park, he acquired a transvan, drove it over to Cell Block A7 and reversed up to the doors, beside an enforcer's armoured car.

"What's the situation now?" he asked.

"All security is offline and all the computers down," Janus replied. "They had to shut everything down just to stop the readerguns."

Good. Confusion was just what he needed. He climbed out of the transvan.

"You two," he pointed to two of the Inspectorate enforcers outside the doors, "come with me."

The things Hannah really needed could be fitted into his briefcase: namely the secondary processor and implant hardware enclosed in a cylinder lit with LEDs to show they were powered up and running interface software; also the organic interface, which resided in a container the size of a cigarette packet—again under power but this time to keep the scrap of semi-organic tissue frozen. However, she had drawn up a secondary list of surgical items, and they would fill up a crate like the one Smith had dispatched him in to the incinerator. It took about half an hour to get this stuff loaded, and just as he headed for Transvan Gate Two, an Inspectorate forensics van, trailed by an Inspectorate limousine, passed him heading in the other direction. He guessed there would be some delay whilst they sorted out how they were going to conduct their investigation, so hopefully it would be a little while before someone got round to mentioning that an Inspectorate officer had already removed certain items from the scene.

On through the gate and out, then into the nearest tunnel. He parked in the underpass where previously he had made the second vehicle change, fifty kilometres from the burnt-out van he'd used in order to get Hannah out. Even though not precisely following the previous route, he was now using the same vehicles a second time, and this worried him. Before moving the crate over to the car, he ran his scanner over it, and found it loaded with trackers, so he just took off the lid and spilled it and its contents out the back of the van, knowing that the whole lot would be spread out among the indigents of the sprawl by the time the Inspectorate even started looking. However, the only trackers he found on the essential items were fixed on their containers and therefore easy to dispose of. Fortunately the items themselves were aseptically sealed, ready for surgical implantation.

By early morning he reached the bunker where Hannah, having only just roused from his bed, greeted him wearily.

"You did it," she observed.

He dropped the briefcase on the worktop and pulled out the objects she had requested.

"Is that all?"

"Too many trackers on the other stuff," he said. "We'll have to acquire it from elsewhere."

She looked disappointed, but seemed to shrug it off and move on. "That means we'll need equipment from a high-tech surgery." She scanned her surroundings and frowned. "Preferably the use of a high-tech surgical theatre."

"Mobile black hospital."

She nodded in agreement, which surprised him. How could she have learned about such illegal concerns from her prison?

"Problem," Janus abruptly warned him.

"What sort of problem?"

Hannah looked at him oddly, but he pointed a finger at his bonefone, and she nodded in understanding. Janus did not reply; all he got was a fizzing noise from the fone.

Of course, it had all been too damned easy. He grabbed up a scanner from the work top and ran it over himself. Nothing, so what had he missed? They must have worked out what happened to Avram Coran and been tracking him by satellite the moment he departed the cell complex—he could see no other possibility. He abruptly stepped over to the two screens allowing him a view outside. The agricultural security net was offline and most of his own cams were now down, the screen becoming a patchwork of fizzing squares with only a few clear views. He realized the clear views came from cams with direct fibre-optic links, but they were enough. One big aero had landed in a nearby field and another was still descending. Inspectorate enforcers were pouring from the first and heading across directly to the old beet storage bay.

"We've got trouble," he said, gazing at the screen disbelievingly, the evidence before his eyes not yet really impacting.

"Oh, Christ." Hannah's voice was full of weary pain.

"They're using EM blocking, and have knocked out the agricultural network here," he observed. "I can't talk to Janus." He abruptly felt a strange sense of loss, not remembering ever having gone without the voice of Janus in his ear...never in all his two-year lifespan.

"We're dead," said Hannah.

He turned to study her. "I might be, but they'll sacrifice anything at all in order to take *you* alive." Simple fact of life: while she was close to him they'd use ionic stunners which didn't have a great range, maybe disablers or gas, but they certainly wouldn't be firing live rounds. His mind abruptly kicked into gear again and he jerked round to gaze down at the open briefcase, then after a moment he walked over to a cupboard standing against one wall, took out a package and returned to drop it into the case.

"An optigate?" Hannah enquired, eyeing the box as he slammed the case shut.

"More specifically: a teragate optic socket with skin port and inert fibre-grid exterior."

"For installing in a human body."

He nodded. They used such ports for access to cerebral computers employed to replace function and control stem-cell regrowth in the severely brain-damaged. It was twenty-second-century medicine.

"But where?" she asked.

He tapped his temple where the control for his internal computer resided. "We haven't enough time for me to explain now." He turned and headed towards his weapons cache. She followed him over, and watched while he donned a bulletproof jacket, belted on an automatic still in its holster, shouldered the strap of an assault rifle, then loaded ammo and grenades into a backpack, though reserving some of the latter for his pockets. He slipped the briefcase and its precious components in too.

"Do you know how to use any of this?" He waved a hand towards the weapons.

"I know, but I've never done so."

"You came with me," he said, "but how long are you prepared to stay with me?"

"For as long as it takes. I'm not going back."

She pulled on a bulletproof jacket, then selected a light, short assault rifle and plenty of ammunition. She also took up a couple of press-button grenades and put them in her pocket.

"Where now?" she asked.

"We go down."

After he'd managed to get things set up in the bunker just as he wanted, and begun formulating the detail of his plan, he had found physical activity a welcome distraction, so had often spent time clearing rubble out of the escape tunnel. At the end of the tunnel he found only bare earth, checked the position of that point on GPS, then dug towards a particular location, sealing the earth walls all along the way behind him with a spray of fibre bonding. His tunnel exited about a hundred metres away from the bunker, through the side of a drainage dyke, and just another few metres from a wide underground pipe.

As Hannah went ahead of him, down the stairs to the lower floor, he felt really reluctant to leave. So much work, so much equipment—and a home of his own. He would have had to abandon it at some point, but hadn't expected it so early in the game. Saul stepped over to one of the computer consoles to input the code detaching the whole system from the surrounding agricultural network, then input another code, whereupon a number of things happened simultaneously. A proximity explosive activated under the entrance hatch, the computer began scrubbing data and overwriting with nonsense, time and time again, and a three-minute countdown began to trigger detonators within the Hyex laminate buried in the bunker walls, and along the walls of the tunnel below. He took one last regretful look around, then followed Hannah downstairs.

A steel door closed off the entrance to the tunnel. He now unlocked and opened it, pointing his assault rifle inside, just in case the cam images he had seen from down here had in some way been subverted. Nobody home, thankfully, but then they wouldn't have had time to do seismic scanning here, so hopefully only knew that he'd descended into a hole in the ground. He moved ahead, rifle braced against his shoulder constantly and his nerves on edge. Fragmented memories surfaced of what happened to him the last time the Inspectorate had got him in its tender care, so the weight of the grenades in his pockets was a comforting one. Whether they took Hannah alive, he left up to her, but they certainly would not be capturing him.

The tunnel curved round, lined with concrete until they entered the freshly dug section, where the walls now looked to be made of fibreglass. He then caught a whiff of something: a perfume-like smell that was characteristic of some insecticides.

"Gas! Run!"

As they hurtled ahead, he could feel the knockout gas starting to haze everything. Soon they reached the exit hatch, where he fought a growing lethargy whilst undogging it. He thrust it open and hauled himself out on to a muddy slope, then had to reach back inside and drag out Hannah, who seemed unable to control her limbs. He slammed the hatch shut.

They lay gasping on the bank, clearing the gas from their lungs, but their limbs still heavy as if they had just woken from a deep sleep.

"Come on, movement'll clear it quicker."

Sliding down the bank, they ended up to their knees in water choked with sickly yellow silkweed, then waded along the V-shaped dyke towards the pipe and ducked inside it. The massive *crump* of an explosion resounded, and a shockwave sent them staggering. Glancing back, Saul saw an enforcer, his clothing afire, slam into one bank of the dyke and roll down it, sizzling in the water and thrashing about, seemingly unable to put out the flames. His screams pursued them into the darkness.

***

Hannah knew something about the illegal hospitals Saul had mentioned—she had learned about them from the kind of people supplied for her experimental work. He had originally planned on heading for such a hospital, but as they stepped out of the end of the pipe, and a mobile readergun stepped down into the dyke ahead of them, it seemed they weren't going to get much further.

The incredible unfairness of it suddenly raged up inside her. "Fuck you!" she shouted, and opened fire, but the kick of her gun put her aim well off, the bullets cutting clods out of the dyke's lip, some distance above the advancing robot. She then threw herself in one direction, while Saul took the other.

Like a harvestman spider, two metres across and fashioned of wrought iron, it crab-walked and slid down the bank, the sharp tips of its extended legs slicing through the mud. As Hannah lay there expecting to die, she noticed how fast Saul moved. Already he was up in a squat on the bank, swinging his weapon round to target the thing, but then he hesitated.

"Shoot it!" she yelled, trying to pull her own weapon out from underneath her.

"Those attacking us would have taken all the readerguns offline, to prevent them shooting their own soldiers or, worse still," he glanced her way, "killing you." He pointed to the robot. "If this thing was back to running its usual program, we'd have been dead less than a second after it spotted us."

Hannah now managed to get her weapon aimed at the thing, but didn't open fire. She just stared, taking in its details and wondering how Saul managed to show so little fear. The robot's main body was a squat upright bullet of metal painted in earthy camouflage patterns, a sensory band under clear glass encircled its circumference. The barrel of its gun protruded like a proboscis, while depending underneath its body, like a prolapsed bowel, hung its magazine and power supply.

"It might have been reprogrammed just to capture us alive," he said speculatively.

She still expected him to open fire, but he abruptly lowered his weapon. The robot was now behaving very strangely, as with one sharp foot it wrote something on the mud bank. After a pause, he scrambled down the bank and waded forward to take a look. Hannah heaved herself to her feet, leg aching again, and waded after him. They both peered down at the mathematically precise letters.

"PWRFL GOVT COMLF TRCKD U THRU ME. J."

"Janus?" she gasped.

"Are you?" Saul asked the robot.

The spider dipped briefly in acknowledgement.

"Powerful government comlife?" she queried.

He glanced at her. "That would be something you should know more about than I do."

"NET UNSAFE MST EXIT," the thing now wrote.

"How?" he asked.

"DWNLD."

"Download?"

Again that dip of acknowledgement.

"We needed it to do so anyway, and we've got the right place for it," said Hannah shakily. That was the next stage, after the installation of further hardware in Saul's head.

"The secondary processor," he observed. Then he addressed the spider, "You're fully loaded to this readergun?"

"NO."

"How do I download you?"

"THRU U BUT COMLF WIL KNO LOCA."

"I have to tell you when..."

"BECON," Janus scribed in the mud, then something crackled inside the spider and, smoking, it sank down into the dyke water, jerked once and lay still.

"Beacon?" He looked round at Hannah.

"Janus must have found you by following the beacon in your processor," she said. "I can only think it's shut down now, probably by Janus, and that you'll be able to find some way to start it running again."

He nodded. "Yeah, but before then we need to find a mobile surgery." He stepped over the now burnt-out robot and led the way along the dyke. As she followed, Hannah's foot kicked against something in the water, and for a moment she gazed down in horror at the skull she had brought to the surface—the thing wearing a wig of yellow silkweed. She then saw bones embedded in the dyke bank, all the way along the bank for as far as she could see.

6

THE STARS ARE OURS

In the late twenty-first century, as the first fusion plants came online and advanced robotics transformed global industries during the "Golden Decade," it truly looked as if the world was set to make the transition away from fossil fuels with elegant ease. Russia, fooled like so many others by this idiot optimism, negotiated an alliance with the European Union and, along with North Africa, a conglomeration was formed that ultimately became Pan Europa. However, Russia, by controlling gas reserves and oilfields, still wielded a big stick, and thus came away from the negotiating table with huge concessions. In this way the massive industrial complexes and spaceports of the Pan Europan Space Agency were established at Minsk even before the Asian Coalition climbed aboard. Space missions were launched from there, thousands of satellites sent up, and it was there, too, that the dream of the colonization of Mars began to look like a reality. Meanwhile NASA, already moribund under its stifling level of bureaucracy, continued a steady decline, and the Russians, essentially, won a race that began with Sputnik's first beep. Thirty years later people were actually living and working on the red planet, and Mars camouflage combats had become a must-have fashion item. Ten years after that, Minsk Spaceport began dying, however; sucked dry by a bureaucracy of an order of magnitude even bigger and greedier than NASA's.

ANTARES BASE

Var shut off communication with Ricard and focused instead on the advancing shepherd. As she saw it, she could not allow herself to fall into the Political Director's power because, even though he had labelled her as essential, giving in to him would still lead to her certain death. They had been abandoned by

Earth, and left here to die, but even so they still had energy from the fusion reactor, they had hydroponics and protein production, materials to utilize, and a hundred and sixty-two people, most of them very intelligent as well as highly skilled and motivated. Yes, they had problems over food, air and water production and usage and, yes, by killing off many personnel these could be eked out, but they would still eventually run out and those few remaining here would die. Better by far to apply all those useful minds to their present problems, since brainpower was all that could save them. Ricard had to be stopped.

Var tried to remember everything she knew about shepherds. Their purpose was utterly specific: they were devised to go into large crowds—riots in fact—and grab up ringleaders already targeted by the Inspectorate, whom the robots generally identified by their ID implants. Ricard had to know by now that Var had removed her implant and, since she wore an EA suit, the shepherd would not be using a facial recognition program to identify her. But then she guessed it wouldn't be difficult for it to track her down, as it wasn't as if she was taking part in a riot. The shepherd had probably been instructed to grab the only human around out here, so the moment she stepped out of the crawler it would have her.

She ran a diagnostic check on the crawler, and was soon examining a list of the damage on the computer screen. The deflated tyre could not reinflate since the pump was offline. Four-wheel drive was out, battery power low, and it seemed that the gearbox contained no lubricant. However, she could engage rear-wheel drive, circumvent the safety cut-out that prevented the gearbox from running, and there just might be enough power to get her all the way back. She performed these things, set the engine running, and the crawler started rolling forward just as the shepherd arrived.

The thing stopped directly ahead of the vehicle, and its adhesive gecko tentacles, hanging underneath its tick-like body, began writhing as if in anticipation. Var shivered, realizing she'd been frightened of these things from the very first time she'd seen one as a child. Certainly, other robots deployed by the Inspectorate were more effective and dangerous, like spiderguns or razorbirds, but the shepherds had established themselves in the public consciousness as the archetypal Inspectorate bogeymen. She floored the accelerator, a horrible grinding issuing from the gearbox as it spun up the rear wheels and sent the vehicle hurtling directly towards the shepherd. The steering wheel was nearly wrenched out of her hands, and she had to strain to keep it half a turn over to compensate for the flat tyre, for it now seemed the power steering was out too. The shepherd scuttled to one side, and allowing the wheel to slip from her grasp let the crawler skid towards it. With a reverberating clang she clipped one of its legs, but it danced to one side, then turned to keep pace with her as she continued towards the base. Of course, she hadn't expected to bring it down, as the damned things were too agile and, anyway, part of their programming covered an ability to avoid ground vehicles directed against them.

After only two kilometres, her arms were aching and an overheat warning kept flashing up on the screen. She resented that. This vehicle was precisely the kind of machine they would desperately need over the coming years, and here she was wrecking its gear box. A further kilometre got her round Shankil's Butte, and now she could see occasional glints of sunlight off polished metal or laminated glass windows. Only glimpses though, because a wind was now starting to pick up the dust again. Good, that should give the cover she needed.

If she entered the base's garage, Ricard's enforcers would certainly be waiting for her there, and if she parked outside the base and tried to leave the safety of the crawler in order to gain access some other way, the shepherd would grab her. She would have to be thoroughly ruthless to stop Ricard, and even as she drove with the shepherd loping along just to one side, she glanced back at the contents of the cargo section. Entering the base, she would become just one against Ricard, his five executives and twelve enforcers, and would be given no time to explain the situation to the others and recruit them to her cause. Miska, Lopomac and Carol would immediately be with her, and so would Kaskan once she told him how Ricard had ordered his wife shot: but Miska was certainly being held prisoner and quite likely Ricard had grabbed the other three also. She needed to even the odds, she needed weapons, but first she needed to get out of this crawler without being captured by the shepherd. And it seemed that Gisender and her range of tools provided the means for all of these objectives.

Antares Base rested in a natural dip in the landscape. After the failure of Valles Marineris base—the unfortunates who occupied it having found that rockfalls, even in the low gravity of Mars, became lethal when erosion dropped boulders the size of this crawler onto your home—this new location had been selected. The robots sent here had first cleared a runway to accommodate planes like the one she could now see over to her right. It was a great manta-winged thing of bubblemetal, perfect for flying in the thin atmosphere of Mars, but which would melt if it ever tried re-entry on Earth. Anyway, it was going nowhere, had been sitting there for five years.

Beyond this landing strip the robots had cleared another area of rocks, and then stolidly erected the first hexagonal building of the base, then the six wings extending from this, then Hexes Two and Three at the ends of two of these wings. Initially the entire structure had been just bonded regolith a third of a metre thick, with gaps left for windows and airlocks. These were then added, fabricated from bubblemetal and laminated glass, which were themselves refined from ores and silica sand mined from the surface, before the smaller robots moved inside to work on the rest. By the time the first personnel arrived here, the fusion reactor had been assembled and fired up. Hex Two, with its geodesic one-way glass roof to admit meagre sunlight and with internal sun-lamps to complement that, was already up and running, with the hydroponics troughs inside already crammed with GM beans, cassava, sugar cane and other high-yield crops. Air and water were provided by a bore drilled down into an underground permafrost pocket—the water was cracked into oxygen and hydrogen, the latter fed straight into the fusion reactor. Hex One contained the laboratories, the artificial wombs and protein tanks, the community room and much else besides. Hex Three contained the garage, the reactor, spacious quarters for the political staff and Ricard himself, whilst everyone else occupied the dorms located along the six wings.

Soon Var was motoring past the partially constructed Hex Four, where an arboretum was to be established, though the new seed stock had never arrived. Here a block-making machine and a couple of construction robots stood idle, like big steel birds peeking out of their coop. Behind this, stretching in towards Hex One, lay Wing Six, but she did not turn in there, instead driving on past it towards Hex Three. As always, on viewing the base from outside, she got the impression of seeing something long-established and old. The bonded rego-lith was not sharp-edged and its colour varied from pale yellow to red-umber streaked with black. It had been bonded in blocks using a special epoxy resin, so the entire base looked like it had been built from stone hewn from the planet itself, perhaps by green giants with more than the usual complement of upper limbs, before they went off to do battle with some neighbouring tribe.

Ricard would probably assume she was heading for the garage, but would want to know what she was up to after she halted, therefore she must park the crawler well out of sight of any of those windows glinting like slabs of mica in the stonework. She chose a wall of the hex that faced in towards the centre of the base, where no windows had been made, and where a couple of large insulated water tanks had been erected. By now the overheat warning continued perpetually and the gearbox was making a sound like ball-bearings being rattled about in a tin can. Upon drawing the crawler to a halt, she noticed a haze of vapour in the cockpit, and bleeding out through the holes in the screen– smoke from that gearbox. The shepherd, obviously recognizing her only possible exit from the vehicle, strode round and squatted just beyond the airlock. Next the com light came on—Ricard wanting to talk to her.

Var stood up, rubbing at her arms. The left forearm, from which Miska had removed her ID implant, was particularly painful. Stepping into the rear of the crawler, she eyed the tools available. Gisender had taken out a saw with a circular, diamond-tipped blade, probably so as to quickly cut open the ducting that the fibre-optics had run through, also some hydraulic shears for severing the optics themselves. These would do nicely; but first there was the shepherd to deal with.

She opened the inner door to the airlock, which extended across the rear of the cargo compartment, unlocked the outer door and pushed it open just a little, and peered out. The shepherd immediately rose out of a crouch and drew closer, only a couple of metres away, and looming above. Even in the thin air she could hear the hissing sound its gecko tentacles made. She returned to the cargo compartment, bent over Gisender and hauled off the tarpaulin.

"I'm sorry about this," she said, lifting up the corpse.

She shouldn't feel so concerned about human bodies, for many had already gone through recycling here, along with the other waste, whilst more recent ones resided in a silo stored for when they would help make up the soil necessary for the arboretum. Manoeuvring Gisender's body through the airlock itself was easy, though she did wonder if its lack of weight would be noticed. She then pushed the outer airlock door open, just enough to shove the dead woman outside. And the shepherd instantly pounced, its shiny legs clattering against the crawler, tentacles spearing down like the tongues of chameleons. Var held back for a moment as the arachnid machine retreated, then she moved forward to peer outside again. The shepherd was striding away, with Gisender tightly clasped against its underside, clearly with no idea that it had retrieved the wrong EA-suited human.

Var returned to the cargo compartment to pick up the diamond saw and its battery box. She took the shears too, though the saw ought to be enough. She needed to act quickly now, before Ricard discovered that his shepherd had only retrieved a corpse.

EARTH

His other preparations, made after he completed the escape tunnel, were good, though Saul had been hoping not to need them. The dyke curved round for nearly a kilometre, the water in it growing fetid and the silkweed becoming a toxic orange. Glancing back, he could see a pillar of smoke rising from the abandoned bunker's location and, worryingly, two shepherds patrolling around it. But only as he and Hannah moved into the shadow of a processing plant did he witness more aeros arriving.

The dyke carried the outflow from apparatus used for cleaning and preserving vegetables. He imagined that the orange tint of the water derived from the antiviral and antibacterial sprays used to extend shelf-life. That was not quite the organic dream of previous ages, but then, over the last century, and faced with the cold realities of trying to feed an out-of-control population, a great many of Earth's dreams had been abandoned.

The outflow pipe ran out underneath a security fence, and many months ago he had cut through the bars of the grating at the near end of it and secured them again simply with ducting tape. It came away easily, and they proceeded through darkness, ankle-deep in toxic water, to an inspection hatch he'd previously altered so that it could now be opened from the inside.

"This way." They crossed a carbocrete yard and skirted the looming silos and juice tanks, also the big storage barns beside which robotic harvesters were parked.

From here, when the season arrived, the great combines, diggers and sievers would depart to harvest the crops, before returning to pump, blow or otherwise convey their loads into the processing plant. Keeping in the lee of a wall made from blocks of bonded ash, the pair of fugitives moved round to the forecourt where lorries and tankers awaited. Some of these were robotic, but others of an older make required human drivers. All these took rapeseed oil and bamboo pulp to fuel plants and power stations respectively, vegetables to MegaMalls or other processing plants where they were further preserved, and cereal crops to be turned into all sorts of commodities. Saul knew, for instance, that the big bread factory in Suffolk used a great deal of bamboo pulp in its flour mix to bulk its products out.

"Over there." He was heading for a nearby grain lorry when he noticed Hannah staring at something over by the fence. He glanced over that way too, but couldn't figure out what had caught her attention until a swarm of flies rose up. Someone had obviously made it this far through the surrounding fields, and then been brought down at the fence.

"Why?" she asked, her voice choking.

It seemed an odd question to be asking him then and there, but then he himself had grown used to seeing the dead scattered across the agricultural landscape, and smelling the occasional stench arising some days after another desperate human being had fallen foul of readerguns or razorbirds.

"Because human life has been cheapened by its sheer number?" he suggested.

Hannah had no reply for that, so they now climbed up into the truck's cab. He paused to watch as a robotic tanker pulled out of the forecourt, probably loaded with sugar syrup that had been processed here during last season.

"You can drive this?" Hannah asked him, her gaze still fixed on the fly-blown corpse clinging to the razormesh. "It won't be picked up?"

"It's always wise to be prepared," he replied, reaching under the dashboard and pulling out the black box he'd stashed there previously, which was linked in to the truck's computer. The click of a switch overrode the recognition system that allowed only approved drivers to operate the vehicle. He pressed the start button and, after the hydrogen turbine had wound up to speed, reversed the lorry round, before heading towards the compound gate. It opened automatically, and soon they were out on the all-but-empty motorway.

"So what other preparations have you made?" Hannah asked leadenly.

"I've got caches of useful items spread across Europe, as well as new identities I can assume. More in North Africa, too, in case things get really desperate." He glanced at her. "But we definitely don't want to go that route, as it would take us further away from where we ultimately want to go."

"Minsk Spaceport," she replied flatly.

***

The apartment Saul decided to use measured eight metres square. It possessed a small kitchen area, a combined toilet and shower, a motorized sofa bed and a home computer. One window overlooked the central megaplex of the residential block, and a screen window could run any view he selected, including ones from the numerous cams positioned on the block itself. Or at least it would if the screen was working. A single lighting array, also containing a community safety camera, was suspended from the ceiling. Generally, only complex computer programs kept watch on the inhabitant of this apartment, but if his behaviour strayed outside acceptable parameters, the visual and audio feed would instantly be diverted to a community political officer, for further assessment. Not everybody endured cameras like this one perpetually watching them, but then not everyone was considered a "societal asset" who needed constant supervision.

"Not *your* place, then?" Hannah remarked.

"Assigned to one of my reserve identities," he replied. "Ownership is merely an anachronistic concept fostered by the anti-society dissident," he quoted.

"So what's your name now, citizen?" Hannah asked, as she paused by the door—holding it open, as he had instructed, with his altered keycard still in the slot.

"Kostas Andreas," he replied, looking round.

"Very…Mediterranean," she observed.

He nodded, pulled over a chair and stood on it to get at the safety camera, smearing the lens with a gobbet of rotten margarine he'd scraped from a pot in the fridge—which, in turn, had been automatically shut down by Block Control after its door hadn't been opened for a specific time. Next he jammed a pen into the little microphone incorporated in the side of the camera and scrunched it around a few times. He then stepped down.

"Okay, you can close the door now."

After doing so, she headed across to dump her holdall on the sofa and hand him back the keycard. "Are you sure that vandalism is not going to be a problem?"

"Cam service personnel are overstretched almost everywhere, but especially here." He looked up at the device as the microphone spat out a spark—the cam now activating in an apartment that had registered vacant until Hannah removed the keycard. "They'll detect the fault instantly, but then it'll join a maintenance backlog over a month long." He gazed at her steadily. "You have to understand that our masters are starting to give up on the whole idea of constant surveillance and ideological correction. They'll only be reinstated when our numbers are sufficiently reduced for them to again be effective."

She nodded, looking slightly sickened by the thought, then threw herself down on the sofa. He'd already told her about this Straven Conference, and the sectoring of ZA sink estates and other population areas. She'd wanted to disbelieve him, but he guessed the corpses she'd recently seen in the fields went some way towards convincing her. He suspected her doubts had lasted only until he abandoned the lorry in what he hoped was still a cam deadspot adjacent to a sector fence. He felt that the two corpses, one lying on the ground and one still clinging to the fence, must have finally persuaded her.

"I think," she said, "that since you took me from the Inspectorate, this is the longest time in my life I've been without someone constantly watching me." She reached up, pressing a fist against her chest, her shoulders hunched and a bewildered expression on her face.

"*I'm* watching you," he said. "Are you in pain?"

"Panic attack." She gave him a tight, forced grin. "They're a constant with me but, as I've recently discovered, I don't get them when there's any real reason for panic." She waved a dismissive hand and lay back, closing her eyes, deliberately pulling her hand away from her chest and resting it flat on the sofa beside her.

"You're watching me," she said, "but I don't think you're about to lecture me about squandering government resources, or deliver any completely inappropriate homilies."

"Misuse of government property is theft from the people?" he suggested.

"Yeah, because all property belongs to the people, but is controlled by the Committee for the good of the people." She opened her eyes and gazed at him. "Better then to say that all property and all people belong to the Committee, for *its* own good." She looked up. "You know they gave me political prisoners who were scheduled for disposal to experiment with?"

Yes, he already knew that, but it seemed she wanted to repeat herself. She wanted to be certain he knew about the crimes she believed herself to have committed. Perhaps she wanted to revel in her own guilt.

"I saw one in your surgery," he said neutrally. "And I released one from his cell. He seemed very self-possessed, so I wonder if he managed to escape."

"Malden," she said. "I hope so too, because, if so, he's going to be a big thorn in the state's side. He's a revolutionary leader, maybe even *the* revolutionary leader. I put as much hardware in his head as I could, and used the organic interface and comlife they allowed me. He is a lesser version of what you yourself can become."

He dropped onto the sofa beside her, saying nothing.

She eyed him sideways. "I had no choice, you know."

"I know."

"After Smith made us watch what happened to you, he kept us grouped together for a while longer. Once they brought in the first human subjects for experimentation, Aira objected." She was staring at the floor again. "He didn't even try to persuade her otherwise, just took her down to a cell and made us all watch while five enforcers raped her repeatedly. When they were done, he just shot her through the head—no attempt at adjustment."

"I can pass judgement on you if you like," he said. "If you consider a serial murderer's judgement of any relevance. You, at least, have done the bad things you've done to survive. I don't have that excuse."

"I don't want excuses."

"What happened after Aira? Where's the rest of the research team?"

"Smith had us separated—the only communication via comlink—and I got to stay in the cell complex. Smith himself got reassigned after that." She gazed at him steadily. "He was made Political Director on Argus."

Motives within motives, and now he had another motive to get himself up to that space station. "So I guess I shouldn't be surprised at how willing you are to help me?"

She frowned. "I just want to be there when you see him again."

"You will be. That's a promise."

"There must be...justice," she said firmly.

It seemed likely to Saul that she would not enjoy his idea of justice.

"Yes, quite."

She nodded, then turned away. "Does that shower work?" she asked, pointing.

He shrugged. "I think the water's turned on, but whether it's hot is another matter."

"Do you have any fresh clothing here?"

"Yes, enough."

Standing up, she stripped off her lab coat, kicked off her trainers, then began unbuttoning her blouse. He rose too, and began heading for the door.

"Where are you going?" she asked.

"To give you some privacy."

She pointed up at the cam. "You've given me more privacy than I've ever enjoyed before in my entire life. Please stay."

She stripped off with determined deliberation, and with equal deliberation he didn't look away. She had a tightly muscular body, small breasts and a slim waist, her hip bones quite prominent. Her pubis was bald, probably electro-depilated, while a moon-shaped scar lay above her right knee. When she turned round he observed a fade-form tattoo at the base of her spine, its pattern regularly changed by any alterations in her skin temperature. He'd had sex with just two different women over the length of his two-year life, and neither of them had looked so familiar to him. His chest felt abruptly tight and he understood that here was the real reason she so willingly stayed with him.

"How long were we lovers?" he asked.

"You remember?" she asked, suddenly hopeful.

"I remember your body." He felt ashamed. "I'm sorry, but that's all."

She headed over to the shower. "From about ten years after we first met, then up until Smith burnt up your mind. I like to think that, besides your sister, I was the only other human being you actually cared about." Stepping into the shower, she gazed coyly over one shoulder. "Maybe we can shake loose some more memories?"

"I'll take a shower right after you," he replied, smiling at her as she closed the glass doors.

He retained the smile for a while longer, then suddenly he switched it off. He'd been operating alone with perfect if ugly efficiency for two years, yet now he carried a passenger and, if he allowed to grow further what he so far only felt a hint of, his ruthlessness might become impaired.

He couldn't allow that.

***

Having placed an apartment door sideways across the communal stairs to act as a toll gate, they searched the woman ahead, removing from her bag a sorry collection of potatoes before letting her through. They'd created their own deadspot by spray-painting over the cams fixed up on the ceiling, which, Hannah supposed, might just mean the cams were now queued in a month-long maintenance backlog. However, the man's corpse lying up against the wall in a pool of old brown blood, with flies crawling in and out of its nostrils, didn't look that fresh. It should certainly have been reported by some responsible citizen, but the fact that his killers showed no particular hurry to be elsewhere seemed to confirm that no enforcers were likely to be coming here. Perhaps it was now policy to give free rein to those thinning out the excess population. Hannah did not like to think so, but after Saul had pointed out the corpses rotting on the fence surrounding a "sectored" area, she was starting to believe some of the things he had been telling her.

"What you got in there?" asked one of the thugs, now turning to Saul and herself.

The four of them—three young men and one woman—were all dressed in Mars and terran combats, rib-effect body warmers with a slick waterproof look, and Velcro-strap training boots. Their dress looked decidedly military, but the only gun visible was an ionic stunner one of them had tucked into his belt. The other three sported home-made weapons consisting of long-handled maces fashioned from lengths of pipe with foam-tape handles, the club end comprising a collection of heavy nuts and bolts welded together into a mass. Judging by the ragged dent in the side of the corpse's head, one of these implements had been used on him. Hannah glanced at Saul, wondering how he would handle this situation, yet not so sure she really wanted to know. But, no doubt, handle it he *would*.

It had taken three days before the Subnet became available through Saul's home computer—accessed via perpetually changing radio frequencies using a receiver it was considered an "adjustment" offence to own. It lasted only four hours before Inspectorate hackers took it down again, but long enough for him to confirm a local deadspot was still in use, and then to learn some other news. Hannah then took a seat beside him to have her first look at what he described as the real world.

With the new food pricing beginning to bite, there'd been sector riots in Manchester, Cardiff and in some of the suburbs of the Outer London sprawl. In the first of these conurbations a Subnet reporter had detailed how a vast crowd surged towards the exit to the Salford sector of Manchester, using short-range missile-launchers to take out the readerguns. As they stormed into the surrounding community, they had grabbed the Inspectorate guards and hanged them with razorwire from the sector's fence posts. But then enforcers had arrived, flying aero gunships and dropping gas grenades. They didn't use knockout gas either, because afterwards they had quickly and efficiently loaded dropside tipper trucks with the corpses, using small vehicles equipped with loading buckets to the rear, and digger arms terminating in tri-claw grabs to the fore. Saul pointed out how both vehicles seemed to have been specifically designed for the sole purpose of removing corpses. Similar mobs in other sectors didn't even get as far as the fences—the readerguns had been reformatted to fire beyond the no-man's-land adjoining the fences, while enforcers were coming in with the gas even as the mobs were gathering. No clear-up within the sectors, though—which perhaps accounted for the smell of carrion in the air here in the London sprawl as he and Hannah set out from his apartment towards the local deadspot.

"It's exponential," Hannah observed, trying to apply a scientific frame of mind to the growing horror she felt. "Start running out of the basics, and it's all going to break down fast."

He nodded in agreement as they strolled down one of the community-block streets towards the communal stairs, since the elevators were out of action again. Hannah noticed that here, even in this block reserved for those considered societal assets only, the people seen out and about all carried backpacks or large flight bags ready to be filled with whatever food they could acquire with their triple Cs or any cash they might possess. Saul explained that the produce grown in the greenhouses on the roof, which about a year ago might only be bought with large wodges of rapidly devaluing currency, could no longer be bought at all, because readerguns and Inspectorate guards were stationed up there now. The few shops in the neighbourhood with goods actually available were easily identifiable by the queues outside. While she nervously waited for him in the apartment, he himself had stood in a few of these during the last few days, using three different identities simply to obtain enough food for the two of them. And still Hannah was hungry, just like those waiting on the stairs.

"Nothing of interest to you," Saul replied to the thug's question.

The man tilted his head, acknowledging the fact that perhaps Saul was going to cause him a problem. "I'll be the judge of that," he replied. His hand dropped to the ionic stunner at his belt, and one of the other men stepped forward, shouldering his mace. Hannah saw then that it seemed the visible corpse was not their only victim. Further spills of blood stained the floor, one still sticky and red with a couple of teeth lying amidst it.

Were the others who had been assaulted still alive, or had they merely been dragged out of sight, just the one corpse left on display?

"Let me show you." Saul unshouldered his backpack and dropped it to the ground, glancing at Hannah as he did so. She slid her gaze away from the corpse, to the fresh bloodstain, then back to Saul. What was he going to do? What *could* he do in this situation? What if they stole the hardware he'd risked his life a second time to retrieve? And what if they stole the payment he had brought to finance the installation of that hardware?

As he glanced down at his backpack, then focused back on the man before him, Saul asked, "Did *you* kill him?"

"He died for a bag of sugar." Grinning at that, the man stared at Saul challengingly. "Thought he was a tough guy."

Suddenly Hannah realized that even if they paid whatever toll was demanded, they would still be in trouble. She felt she needed to communicate this to Saul, but how?

"Inspectorate enforcers could be here at any moment," Saul suggested calmly.

Hannah then noticed that two of the four, including the man standing before Saul, wore badges on the shoulders of their body warmers: an emblem of laurel leaves enclosing an Egyptian eye. They were community political officers.

"They're not interested," the man said flatly. "Now open your pack."

Saul nodded thoughtfully, reached round under the back of his jacket, as if tucking in his shirt, pulled his automatic from its holster and simply shot the man through the throat. He flew backwards till the door caught the rear of his legs and his head slammed down hard on the carbocrete steps behind him. Saul's second shot punched straight through the chest of the next man, spraying gobbets of flesh over the wall behind him before he thumped into it and slid down, leaving a wide and bloody trail. The woman threw her mace at him, before turning to run after her remaining colleague, who had already taken off. Saul stepped aside and the weapon clattered past him, then his next shot lifted the top of her head and sent her tumbling down the stairs. Steadying his gun hand, he next put a group of three shots into the back of the fleeing man just as he reached the next landing. That dropped him as well.

"Christ!" said Hannah, staring at the carnage, then turning to face him. "Christ!" She'd thought he had left all his weapons in the truck, along with hers.

"Not the Alan Saul you remember," he remarked.

She shook her head numbly and moved away to steady herself against the wall. Her legs felt suddenly weak, her breathing an effort. She felt she was going to be sick, but managed to hold on to it, perhaps because there wasn't enough in her stomach for her to bring up.

Saul returned his gun to its holster, shouldered his backpack again, stepped over the door serving as a toll gate, kicked it over then squatted to inspect the haul the four had assembled. It consisted of a couple of bags of potatoes, a few tomatoes and cucumbers, a loaf of bread and some pre-served sausage. He shoved these into a large shoulder bag before searching the clothing of the two lying nearest. Some chocolate and a little cash, but not much else of value, though he did pocket the stunner.

"You carry the bag," he instructed, pointing to the haul of food. Feeling utterly out of her depth, Hannah pulled herself away from the wall and tried to be calm as she went to pick up the shoulder bag. Her foot slipped and she nearly went over, then seemingly out of nowhere came the tears.

"I'm sorry," she said, shaking her head, and angry with herself. "I'm sorry."

He stepped over and she put her arms round him, burying her head in his shoulder, let some of it go, but all too soon he was pushing her away.

"We can't stay here." He nodded towards the stairway behind.

People were gathering on the landing above, staring down. She nodded but, when he started to pull away again, she clasped him even tighter. A moment's pause, then she released him. The flow of tears ceased abruptly, and they headed down.

"I'm sorry, too," he said, once the corpses were well out of sight. "But if we're weak, we die."

"Are you really sorry?" she asked. "You didn't have to kill them all."

"No, I didn't," he said. "I could have taken us safely through and just left them to carry on doing whatever they wanted, to rob and murder."

"That bothers you?"

"It does."

He seemed to say that with such sincerity that Hannah tried to suppress her doubts, for he still appeared utterly unaffected by what he had done—almost like he was used to it.

7

AND THE DREAMS FADE

It has long been a dream of humanity to go out into space, but as dreams become reality they lose their mythological quality, sliding into the humdrum day-to-day, and the dreams fade. The first Moon landings marked the dawning of a new age, yet dropped into second place in the headlines when pitched against the latest "Politician Buggers Rent Boy" scandal. So died the public wonder at the space stations in near-Earth orbit, and at the mission to Mars. It's only human nature, in the end. However, throughout all these ages technology continued its steady advance. The entire computing power of the control room of NASA during those first Moon missions could not match that of an ordinary home PC thirty years later, and then the computing power of a home PC could be fitted into something no bigger than an ear stud a further fifty years down the line. But beyond a certain point, the size of the technology within a computer becomes irrelevant, because there's a minimum size to which you can reduce the button a finger presses. Humans, unfortunately, are the weak component in the circuit, as also in all their logical creations.

Sited on the second-highest floor of a multi-storey car park, the All Health mobile surgery had obviously remained stationary for quite some time, seeing that the power cables extending up from it through holes in the ceiling probably connected to photovoltaic panels above. Gazing at the vehicle and assessing all the people in the vicinity, as he and Hannah headed over, Saul replayed his justification for the four corpses he left behind him, and he wondered how Hannah would have reacted to hearing the truth.

They would eventually be heading back that way, back through that makeshift toll gate on the stairs, and he wouldn't be in such great shape then, so he had removed a potential threat. And, though he needed to be utterly ruthless to achieve his aims, to be honest he enjoyed being able to blow away any scum found in his path. Did that mean he was a sociopath? Just as the four corpses behind him had demonstrated, the quicker civilization disintegrated, the sooner its veneer was peeled away from those prepared to discard their social conditioning to survive. Of course, it was Smith who had peeled away Saul's social conditioning in an adjustment cell. In this case the blame was his.

"Dr Bronstein?" he enquired.

Bronstein had once been a fat man, so now the skin of his face hung in loose folds, just as his newly outsize clothing hung around his body. He sat in a deckchair, smoking a cigar, his feet up in front of him on a crate marked with All Health's logo of a caduceus set against a world map. A bottle of clear moonshine and a glass rested on a couple of crates stacked beside him.

"Yup, that'd be me."

"Business slow today?" Saul asked, looking around.

On the market stalls behind, a pathetic amount of food was on display, while the best business was being conducted out of the back of a transvan. It contained bags of homegrown tobacco, in strong demand because everyone knew that when you're smoking you don't feel so hungry. Here and there lolled guards armed with very up-to-date assault rifles—underworld enforcers. Over to the right, behind an area almost fenced off by car bodies, lay piles of engine parts and burnt-out computer-locking mechanisms. Pillars of tyres formed the entrance to this zone, but no one was currently doing any business there. Saul guessed that the car-breaking business must be on the wane. Over to the left the open side of the car park overlooked the urban sprawl, now lost in the hazy polluted distance. There were plenty of people about, he noticed, but none by the mobile hospital except Bronstein himself.

The doctor inspected the end of his cigar. "It's a matter of priorities."

"Really?"

"You got enough cash for lung wash and a relining you now spend it on bread."

Hannah stepped forward. "I didn't realize that All Health was charging for its services now."

"All Health?" He eyed her wonderingly. "I stopped working for them once they told me to carry on reusing syringes after the sterilizers broke down." He waved his cigar at the vehicle behind. "I'm private now, and this set-up is my pension plan."

"Won't they miss it?" Saul gestured at the vehicle.

"Amazing what records can disappear when you M-bullet a bowel cancer for the right official." Bronstein drew on his cigar again and let out a long stream of smoke. "So what can I do for you?"

"You've got the full auto-surgery with telefactored instruments, clean box and full life-support?" Hannah asked.

"Yup."

"Nerve-sheath scouring and microtools?"

"Yup." He looked slightly puzzled and wary now.

"Sigurd biotic tools?"

"Fuck me, lady, this is an AH unit not a Committee hospital."

"But you must do implants here, so what do you have available?"

"Some Sigurd," he admitted, stubbing out his cigar and taking his feet off the crate, "and old Clavier biotics."

"That should do it."

"So what's the deal?"

"Cerebral implants," she said.

He grimaced. "I do some, but nothing after the Net Chips."

"Not a problem. I'll operate and you can assist."

"Lady, no one uses my stuff."

Saul unshouldered his backpack, opened it and took out a heavy parcel wrapped in newspaper, tore the end open and showed Bronstein the contents. At first he'd considered bringing the considerable sums of cash he'd accumulated, but since a bag of tomatoes now cost upwards of four hundred Euros, he would have needed a transvan to carry the necessary payment. However, there's something people always fall back on in times of hardship: gold. He'd got five bars in the pack, all he'd been able to lay his hands on over the last two years, and hoped he wouldn't need to hand over them all. The doctor let out a low whistle and slowly stood up.

"Best we go inside," he said.

The driver's cab and living quarters took up the entire forward compartment of the All Health trailer bus, the rear section accommodating the surgery itself. The rear door led first into a small office-cum-waiting room, with a desk and computer, but with all the chairs intended for customers and most of the surrounding space taken up by stacks of supplies. Most of the crates bore the All Health logo, but some boasted the blood-red stamp indicating reserved government property. Once they were all inside, Bronstein closed and locked the door, then moved over to perch on the edge of his desk.

"Cerebral implants," he said.

Saul took the briefcase out of his pack, rested it on the desk and snapped it open. Bronstein peered inside for a moment, then reached in to pick up the cigarette-packet-sized container for the organic interface, studying the blue LEDs along one edge, then the miniscreen that ran a convoluted screen saver.

"Organics," he said, as he turned to regard Hannah. "You'd better know what you're doing, lady, because I don't pay compensation here." Next he picked up the box containing the teragate optic socket and examined it in puzzlement.

Hannah gazed through the glass window beside them at the operating theatre. Saul had also inspected this room and been glad to find it spotlessly clean. No used syringes, pus-soaked dressings or bloodstains on the floor, like you'd usually find in an AH hospital.

"I know what I'm doing," she replied firmly.

Bronstein turned to Saul. "I take it you're the recipient?"

"Yes," Saul confirmed.

Bronstein pointed to a door adjoining the window. "Clean port through there. You strip, depilate your head and take a shower, making sure you use the small cleaning head on your mouth, nose, ears and anus, then dry yourself with the fibresept towel and put on some disposeralls. You okay with that?"

"I think I can manage," Saul replied, "but we've yet to agree a price." He felt more than a little edgy. Though he'd undergone implant removals previously in places like this—having done most implantations himself—those had all been under local anaesthetic. He didn't like the degree of trust involved in going under full anaesthetic and letting someone take a scalpel to his head. Yes, Hannah would be doing the procedure, but if Bronstein found the bag of gold attractive enough, Saul had no doubt that he might choose his moment to take her down. Disposing of two corpses would be no problem for him and, as they had witnessed on the way here, no one would be investigating their disappearance.

"Two of those gold bars will cover it," Bronstein replied. "One more, maybe, if there's any complications." He gazed at Saul steadily. "But that ain't your main problem right now, is it?"

"I don't follow you," Saul said.

"You armed?" Bronstein asked.

"Why do you want to know that?"

"Because, if you are, you can take whatever weapon you've got through the shower with you."

That would not be a problem for the automatic Saul was carrying, since it had been over a hundred years since damp could affect the firing of a modern weapon.

"A lot of good that'll…" Saul paused and looked at Hannah. "You mean I'll be conscious during the operation?"

She nodded. "You don't ever attach up such hardware to an unconscious brain, or you get activation problems."

"I see." He took out the three bars of gold and set them down on Bronstein's desk, then headed straight for the door. As Saul went through, Bronstein was already picking up one of the bars to feed through the narrow throat of the kind of scanner a jeweller would normally use. Doubtless many of the doctor's clients now paid him with precious metals or with gems.

The short passageway beyond the door terminated at the shower booth, with a plastic box on a low shelf beside it for the client's belongings, and coathangers arranged above. Saul stripped and placed all his clothing in the box, along with his boots and backpack, but he retained the automatic as he stepped into the shower to inspect its complex controls. He first dealt with his head, the dyed hair dropping as powder into the shower tray from the high-speed tungsten-carbide heads of the shaver pad. Next he spread depilating cream over his scalp from a spigot beside the shaver recess, and following the instructions on a screen just above the spigot, he waited until the timer hit zero before turning on the shower itself.

As he punched the shower button, needles of water jetted towards him from one wall, also from the ceiling and from the floor. At the same time, bactericide UV lights came on. The greenish water had to be loaded with powerful antivirals and antibacterials, for an astringent stink filled the steamy air. Brown water disappeared down the drain as his dissolved hair went with it, followed by the stripped-off outer dermis and reactive soap bonded to particles freed from his body. He detached the dildo-shaped secondary cleaner head from its recess and used it to wash everything the needle jets weren't reaching, starting with his nose and mouth, where it tasted and felt like he was spraying turpentine inside them. After a few minutes of this, the water changed colour again, and began to eliminate the slimy feeling from his skin, till finally it shut down altogether and a small hatch popped open beside him to reveal a rolled-up pad. It smelt strongly of bleach, and he recognized it as a fibresept towel. After drying himself thoroughly, he tried to exit via the door he'd entered by, but it was now securely locked. Feeling slightly stupid, he opened the alternative door, and took up the disposeralls hanging just outside it as he finally entered the operating theatre.

Bronstein came through next, clad in disposeralls too. He glanced at Saul, then went to pick up a remote control. He pointed this at the surgical table which, with a low hum, transformed itself into a surgical chair. "Okay, take a seat."

Saul did as instructed, resting the gun in his lap. He wondered what good the weapon would do him after the doctor folded up clamps from behind the chair so as to immobilize his head, but then the man also utilized a non-standard addition in the form of a mirror mounted on a jointed arm. Still, if Bronstein decided to skull-fuck him with a liposuction tube, Saul didn't suppose he'd be able to react very quickly. Hannah now entered, clad in disposeralls, and carried the secondary processor and organic interface over to a nearby work surface where she could safely open their containers.

Bronstein attached monitoring pads through strategically placed vents in Saul's disposeralls, then hooked up a saline pressure feed. The same feed would also be injecting into him all sorts of antivirals, antibiotics, antishocks, and other drugs beside. Again he felt really vulnerable because Bronstein could easily start feeding cyanide into him for all he knew. In a situation like this, he just could not guarantee safety. While the doctor made all these preparations, Hannah carefully placed the items destined for installation in a stainless-steel tray filled with a clear fluid. This she laid on a trolley loaded with surgical cutlery, which she guided over to Saul's right side. Peering down at the tray, he quickly identified the processor as a white object about the size of a hundred-Euro coin, but with smoothly rounded edges from which radiated hair-thin wires attached to tiny objects like beads of polished ruby. The teragate, by contrast, was an object that could be mistaken for a blackened cigar butt. The organic interface resembled a scale taken from a mirror carp, but with vaguely identifiable capillaries running through it and a spongy-looking collection of tubes at its base where, he guessed, it would be connected into his blood supply and lymphatic system.

As he peered down at these items, something cold and wet was pressed against his scalp, right over his right ear and the jaw below, as Bronstein affixed an anaesthetic cap and half-mask. The doctor then swung in a kidney dish to rest just a short distance from Saul's jaw, and began to adjust the clamps that would hold his head steady. Saul tightened his grip on the gun and watched the doctor carefully in the mirror, but Bronstein soon had everything arranged to his satisfaction, and stepped back round beside the trolley to gaze with curious expectancy at Hannah. By now Saul's head and the right side of his face felt as numb as granite. Hannah studied the half-mask closely and he supposed there must be some sort of display on it, for after a moment she stripped it off decisively, and he felt nothing.

"We'll start with the teragate," she said, taking up a ceramic scalpel. "That's just a swap-and-plug job."

He watched her making quick and neat incisions into his temple, but he couldn't get a clear view of them. Next a slim set of tongues, and a sound as of cornflakes being crushed. She extracted something from his head and dropped it into a wad of tissues that Bronstein held ready, then reached for the teragate socket. By then Bronstein was back, using a suction tube to drain the wound of fluids, as Hannah inserted the socket into Saul's temple with a simple push and twist. Last to go in was a small cap of synthetic skin and, but for the blood all down Saul's neck, it appeared as if no surgery had been performed at all.

"Now for the real work," said Hannah, taking up another scalpel, this one crescent-shaped. As Saul watched her draw it across the top of his head to his temple, then down behind his right ear, in one long neat and decisive slice, he tried to remain analytical and ignore the fact that, despite being numb to pain, he could still feel the tugging of the blade. Next she used a small curved spatula to unzip his head like a bag for a bowling ball, while Bronstein started up the bone saw. At that point, Saul raised his right finger and pushed the mirror aside. That was enough thanks.

After a few minutes of vibration, some manipulation and tugging accompanied by a butcher's shop stench, there was a sucking sound as if someone was opening up an oyster, then a dull clunk, and it didn't take much expertise for Saul to realize that a chunk of his skull now rested in the kidney dish.

Hannah took up the other dish, the one that held the processor and interface, and placed it somewhere near the kidney dish. More cutting ensued, whilst Bronstein wheeled over a pedestal-mounted microsurgery, then retreated as Hannah positioned the machine directly over Saul's opened skull. She locked its nose into the framework that held his head steady, stepped round behind to insert her hands into the telefactor gloves, and studied the screen before her. Then the machine whined into motion, moving tiny implements over distances measured in fractions of a millimetre—at which point things started to turn a little strange.

Saul's internal computer came online of its own accord, its menu flicking up just to the right of his vision and the cursor scrolling through it, selecting options too quickly for him to follow, while finding submenus he didn't even know existed. Code ran down through his artificial retina, breaking and fizzing like a faulty screen, then, weirdly, the operating theatre abruptly expanded to seem a couple of kilometres wide, while Bronstein loomed beside him like a giant studying something on his enormous palmtop.

"Never seen this set-up before," the doctor remarked.

"Not many people have," Hannah replied.

Next the operating theatre appeared claustrophobically small, but did Saul mind? No, he didn't, because he was now gazing across three different sections of the London sprawl simultaneously: a massive visual input, but one that he could encompass and process. However, he managed to enjoy this only for a short time before a sense of imminent threat began to impinge on him. He was now out in the computer networks and fully exposed, feeling certain that something dark and dangerous was looking for him.

"Getting some weird visuals," he slurred.

Hannah did something at that point and the three views shut down, whereupon the operating theatre returned to its normal dimensions.

"You were still open to the Internet," she explained. "It seems Janus restored your link even when it severed its own."

"Janus?" Bronstein enquired.

Did they really need the doctor? Saul felt sure Hannah could complete the operation by herself now that she had the necessary equipment. Perhaps it would be safer if he just raised the automatic and put a bullet through the side of Bronstein's head.

"Not your concern," Hannah replied.

"I'm just curious, obviously."

"Put it this way," she said, "you already know enough now to get yourself permanently adjusted through a recycling plant. Do you really want to know more?"

"Well, things can't get much worse than you describe. Yes, I do want to know."

After a pause in which yellowish three-dimensional space sectioned by cubic gridlines began to expand inside Saul's skull, where surely there could not be room for it, she replied, "If you think things can't get any worse than that, you obviously don't know enough."

"Hey, the Inspectorate catches up with me and I'm in for adjustment anyway—or more likely a bullet through the back of the head. Yeah, I know they can stick you under an inducer until your mind's turned to jelly, but that'll never happen to me."

"Why not?" Hannah asked.

"A lot of us have them now: a Hyex implant at the base of the skull." He paused thoughtfully. "I can kill myself simply with a thought."

"A *lot* of you?" Hannah echoed.

The space inside Saul's skull had meanwhile grown vast. In fact it seemed infinite now; something underlying his mind and his perception of…everything, but still he managed to interject, before Bronstein answered, "He's a revolutionary…Hannah." By then he had the automatic raised and pointing straight at Bronstein's face. The doctor seemed strangely unsurprised by this. "Over there." Saul gestured with the weapon towards the far side of the theatre and, after a shrug, the doctor moved to where instructed, leant back against a work surface, and folded his arms.

"How much longer?" Saul asked Hannah.

"Just a minute or so and I'll be able to glue this bit of skull back in," she replied.

He had just wanted the time frame, not the physical detail.

"What are you two?" Bronstein asked.

"None of your business," Saul replied, calculating the best move to make next. As his capacity for thought expanded, it seemed to be sapping his capacity to act. Other considerations impinged, like, if he shot the doctor now, this place would be filled with a mist of blood that might be infected with something, or he might damage computer hardware linked to the microsurgery.

"Only Committee executives get given the kind of stuff in your head, and they certainly don't come here to have it fitted," Bronstein said.

The doctor had to have some emergency way of dealing with Hannah and himself, Saul realized. Allowing them to walk in here armed had just been to reassure them, but Bronstein would never otherwise put himself at such a disadvantage, since armed customers might decide to retrieve any payment they had made. Saul needed to work out his options before Hannah finished up, because it would be then that the doctor made his move.

"It's still none of your business," Saul replied.

"Maybe we can help each other," Bronstein suggested, one finger going up to his own temple.

He clearly had hardware in his own skull, and was doing something with it. After a moment he exclaimed, "Jesus!" and suddenly looked very frightened. "We have to go!" He pushed himself away from the worktop.

Saul heard sizzling and smelt burnt meat as Hannah sealed blood vessels.

"Stay the fuck where you are!"

Next a smell he recognized as bone glue.

"The Inspectorate!"

Just then something slammed against the trailer van, throwing it sideways until it crashed to a halt. Bronstein's feet slid out from under him, but he saved himself from falling by grabbing the work surface behind him. The microsurgery tore loose from the framework steadying Saul's head, falling to the floor with a sound like a dropped cutlery drawer, and Hannah ended up sprawled across his lap. A great booming roar filled the multi-storey and Saul heard loose objects smashing against the side of the vehicle. Almost simultaneous with this, the paralytic, which Bronstein's clean lock must have administered to her as they entered the surgery, had now activated and dropped Hannah straight to the floor the moment she pulled herself off Saul's lap. At the same moment, Saul found himself incapable of pulling the trigger. His arm dropped, heavy as lead. Consciousness faded.

***

As consciousness slowly returned, Saul felt totally disconnected from his body, his mind cowering alone like a cockroach in some huge tiled bathroom. But then the cockroach began to break apart, each piece of it assigned to a separate tile, as the chaotic structure of thoughts normally organized on an evolutionary organic basis found itself being stored much more logically, and given *room*. The table of elements sat there perfectly clear in his memory, and he found he could view those elements in any order he chose: whether by valency, atomic weight or even chromatic spectra. Spreading out from this mutable table reached a forest of chemical formulae, all just as mutable, whereupon he found disconnected parts of himself idly modelling and filling in the gaps in his knowledge. From all this he could link to subatomic formulae, but by then was positioned on another tile within his mental space, in another cube of the grid…No, such images were too much of a simplification for the benefit of his animal consciousness, for his mental space was multidimensional, the blocks of information reordering and linking up dependent on requirements. He understood this all to be real, as he woke up; his only problem was that he himself did not feel real. If he had believed in the human soul, he would have now felt certain that his own had taken a sabbatical. It seemed that those parts of his brain dealing with self-image and ego had somehow been swamped.

"More advanced than the shit in *my* head, then," said a voice.

He opened his eyes to find he lay sideways in a ratty armchair, surrounded by a haze of cigarette smoke. His head, which felt as if it'd been kicked by a horse, rested on a stained pillow. Focusing his gaze, he saw two armed guards standing by the door. With great care he turned his head to take in the rest of the room.

"Slightly more advanced, yes," Hannah replied, "but still lacking the comlife component." She raised a cup from the table she sat beside, took a sip, then put it down again.

"Why?" asked the man, scratching at a crusty, sewn-up split in his skull as he paced round behind her, coming to a halt beside the same table.

"I've yet to be able to either obtain or build anything useful, and anyway it's too early for installation," she lied to him. Saul could sense her fear, no matter how hard she tried to conceal it. The man standing over her had, after all, been one of her experimental subjects, with hardware implanted in his skull to test it, and doubtless through which he could be interrogated. It hadn't mattered to the government if this procedure killed him; he had been due to die anyway.

"Malden," Saul observed, recognizing the man he had released from IHQ London.

He wore the fatigues of an Inspectorate enforcer, over a heavy-boned physique winnowed of spare flesh. Now sprouting bristles on the scalp and chin, his skull-like head had regained some humanity, but dark circles still underscored his eyes, and stitched-up slices were mapped across his crown and behind his ears. When he snapped a glance towards Saul with bloodshot eyes, it felt almost like a blow. Malden assessed him, making calculations based on this new input of him being awake and cognizant, then dismissed him as he returned his attention to Hannah. After a moment he picked up a hand-rolled cigarette from the ashtray on the table and took a drag.

"How did he manage to penetrate Inspectorate security?" Malden asked.

Saul abruptly felt the imminence of a bullet through his brain. He had used Janus to penetrate Inspectorate security, an AI hiding on Govnet which he could summon at any moment, in turn alerting the Inspectorate to his location, and he would be dead if Malden found that out. Saul sat up, feeling sick and slightly dizzy, and with a thought called up a menu to some inner visual field.

"I used a virus," he said. "I could give you the schematics, but I doubt it will work again now the Inspectorate is aware of it." He paused, in his mental space somehow summoning up a virtual screen and beginning to lay down the coding for just such a virus, in case Malden requested it. Even as he did so it felt as if he had started up some sort of pump in his head, his pulse thundering inside it and a pain growing between his eyes. "Then, again, the Inspectorate has a bit of a problem at the moment, so might be slow to respond." Saul gazed at the man intently. "How is it we are here now and what was that blast?"

Malden gave him a humourless smile. "My people were watching out for the good Dr Neumann here, so consider my surprise when she walked straight into one of our surgical units." He paused. "The blast was a tactical nuke, and Inspectorate headquarters London is now a radioactive crater."

In Bronstein's mobile surgery they had been quite some distance from the HQ, yet were still at the periphery of the blast. That meant more than just the HQ was gone. As Saul absorbed the implications of this information, the part of his mind trying to build a virus just hung, nothing happening. The pain then peaked and the virtual screen dissolved in a jagged mass of migraine lights. He'd just discovered his limitations.

"How?" he asked.

Again that glance: still Malden was comparing the danger Saul represented to how useful he might be, and deciding whether or not to kill him. Saul tried to run a search through his extended mind, and again that pump started up and the pain increased. Nothing happened for a moment, then something seemed to connect inside his head, with an almost physical clunk, and he was in. It was like no search he had ever run before, more like trying hard to remember something. Menus appeared, overlaid and linked, no longer two-dimensional but spreading out in a multidimensional array, and in that instant he *remembered* how to turn on the beacon that would summon both Janus and the Inspectorate to him.

"It was a simple matter," Malden spat. "Inspectorate headquarters had a weapons cache which included tactical atomics. While the staff were hiding from the readerguns, I entered that cache and left them a parting gift. So the moment they offlined their system to shut down the guns, a timer started running."

Such understatement. To be able to open the cache and then access the computer of an atomic, he must have penetrated Inspectorate security on a level similar to that of Janus. Saul wondered if any of the staff had got in his way, and knew that any who had would have died, quickly and quietly. In the sheer ruthlessness stakes, Malden was some way ahead of Saul.

"And what are your plans now?" he asked.

Malden just blinked, then turned back to face Hannah. "Can you copy the comlife I'm running, and load it to him?"

"I could," she nodded. "but the interface in his head isn't ready. It'll take time for it to establish all its connections." Now she gazed at Saul with some sort of warning in her expression.

"How long?" Malden asked.

"A few days."

Malden turned back to Saul. "I plan to tear their world government apart. What I need to know is what *your* plans are. Are you prepared to join me?"

"Yes," Saul replied, realizing that "no" was not a healthy option.

Malden stood up. "We need to move. You'll stay with Bronstein until you're ready. I've meanwhile got to move other assets into place and notify the Council that it begins now."

"What begins now?" asked Hannah.

"The revolution," Malden replied succinctly. "Merrick and Davidson here will accompany you and, if you need anything, Bronstein can contact me in an instant." He stared at Hannah for a moment longer, and she seemed to be trying to shrink in her chair. "I'm still undecided about you, *Doctor*, so don't disappoint me." He departed, saying to the guards, "Take them to Bronstein."

As the door closed, Saul gazed at Hannah. He wanted to know more before acting, but they needed some time to talk. He bitterly reflected upon the similarity between the Committee and "the Council," and wondered just how extensive this revolution might become. No matter if it was big enough to take down the government, he understood enough history to know that revolutions never ever led directly to a less autocratic regime.

"Come on," said one of the guards.

Saul tried to stand up, and nearly crashed out of the chair. Hannah came over to steady him, and he managed to struggle to his feet. He still wore the disposeralls from Bronstein's mobile surgery, and his feet were bare. As, with one guard ahead and one behind, they entered a short corridor outside, he considered what it would be safe to ask her.

"What do you know about this revolution?" he enquired.

"Malden was a prime catch for the Inspectorate," she said, averting her eyes. "That's why they wanted the hardware put inside his skull—so they could get at all the information it contained." She glanced at him briefly. "I was present during his first interrogation, when they learnt enough to know that the Council is worldwide and keeps in contact via unbroken code on the Subnet. They were just learning that the revolutionaries possess arms caches and have agents high up in government, when the interrogation had to be stopped before Malden died."

At the end of a corridor stinking of piss and scrawled with graffiti, they descended a stairway where dirty windows overlooked the sprawl. Above this a distant black cloud trailed across the horizon, strobing with the emergency lights of numerous aeros buzzing about it like flies round a turd. At the base of this he spotted the glare of orange-red fires.

He gestured towards the grim scene. "How much damage?"

"I don't know."

"Inspectorate HQ and about four square kilometres of surrounding 'burbs," interrupted the guard ahead of them.

"A lot of innocent people," Saul suggested.

The guard glanced over his shoulder. "Lot of IHQ staff and other Committee shits who lived in those 'burbs. Might even have been some delegates there, too." He shrugged. "Anyway, the General had to grab his chance."

"You're Merrick?" Saul asked, whilst easily making some complex calculations in his head.

"Yup."

"So the General just killed about four million people."

"Total war," said Davidson, from behind. "Better a quick death than starvation."

Saul controlled his urge to enter a vitriolic debate about this, since he was now supposed to be a new recruit to their cause. He felt in two minds about it all anyway, since billions were going to die over the next few years. Whoever ended up in charge would not be able to change that. Maybe a massive loss of life in order to displace a totalitarian government was a cheap price to pay, when those lives were due to end anyway—that is, if the revolutionaries were likely to be less totalitarian. It just seemed morally wrong, though he then suppressed a self-mocking laugh. Who was he to be sitting in moral judgement over anyone?

Raggedy people, silenced by hunger and lack of hope, just sat numbly on the stairs and in the corridors branching off from each landing. This tenement was ZA, and he started wondering if it lay within a zero-asset sector, until they stepped out into a street thronged with both ZA and SA citizens. A mixed area, then, and clearly one the government had yet to decide what to do with. He was about to step out into the street, when Merrick halted him with a hand held against his chest.

"Wait."

The reason soon became apparent as a shadow fell across the street and people started running for cover. A shepherd paced into sight, its twin-toed feet crunching down on chunks of broken concrete. It paused for a moment, as if thinking to itself, its gecko tentacles writhing under the smooth tick-like body, then abruptly it moved on.

"Fucking things," muttered Davidson.

Merrick ducked out to look up and down the street, then, calling back, "Clear," he moved out.

Parked at the kerb, Bronstein's All Health vehicle showed damage from the blast, with a great dent in the trailer's side and the windscreen of its cab crazed with cracks. Despite the two armed guards escorting Saul and Hannah, no one seemed to take much notice of them. The residents stood about in groups on a street littered with broken glass and chunks of rubble, gazing up at the smoke cloud from the distant firestorm, while posing questions that none of them could answer. He noted a lack of the usual collection of flight bags and rucksacks carried in readiness for the next shopping opportunity. For once these people were not thinking about the source of their next meal.

Their guards hustled the pair of them up to the door accessing the living quarters located just behind the cab. Merrick stayed with them in the space lined with bunks down either side, whilst Davidson moved forward into the cab itself. Their clothing lay ready on one of the bunks, but their weapons now stood out by their absence—as did Saul's gold.

Bronstein headed back to check on them just as the vehicle's engine whined into life. "Do you need anything?" he asked Hannah, with a nod towards Saul.

"The drugs you gave us should be sufficient, but food and drink would be good too," she said.

"You'll find it in the fridge." He was staring at Saul, who could see how pale and sad the doctor looked. Perhaps Bronstein secretly had some reservations about the nuclear incineration of four million people, being a surgeon after all. "I'll be up front," he finished, then abruptly returned to the cab.

Hannah got changed first, ignoring Merrick's faint smile as he inspected her naked body. Then she helped Saul to dress. He kept deliberately emphasizing his debility, though already starting to feel much better. He began to feel even stronger after eating the tomatoes and sausage Hannah had taken from the fridge, washed down with a pint of water and accompanied by the painkillers and antibiotics she supplied him. Merrick seemed pretty relaxed around the pair, abandoning his rifle on the seat beside him, sprawling out his feet and closing his eyes. He probably reckoned that Saul was in no condition to jump him, or maybe he believed that Saul was genuinely now a paid-up revolutionary. However, as Merrick took the opportunity to use the toilet, he took his assault rifle along with him.

"I need the toilet too," said Saul, standing up shakily and clutching his stomach, as Merrick returned. The sudden lurching of the vehicle negotiating through the crowds or around fallen debris was timely indeed. Saul stumbled forward just as Merrick turned his head to point back towards the empty toilet, and a side-fist caught the man precisely on his temple. Saul clutched the front of Merrick's jacket as he went down, guiding his descent on to one of the bunks, and then quickly took hold of his rifle.

Saul turned to Hannah. "I'm not joining any revolution," he announced.

She stared at Merrick, perhaps wondering if he had killed the man. Then she looked up at Saul. "I didn't for a moment think you would."

You have to grab your opportunities when you can, and he now saw one, just as the vehicle slowed down on approaching some sort of encampment sheltering in a highway tunnel. Saul activated the beacon, and an instant later a voice spoke in his head.

"You took your time," said Janus.

"Download to me," he instructed. "Download now."

"You have been found," replied Janus. "The Inspectorate comlife has located in an All Health mobile hospital presently on the A12c."

"Not a problem," he said. "Just download."

"My home is in your head," Janus observed.

"I know, and I repeat: download to me now."

As the vehicle entered the tunnel, they simply opened the side door and stepped out. Saul stumbled and went down, splitting the knee of his trousers just as chunks of data began landing inside his skull, like bricks tumbling into a goldfish bowl.

"I'm drowning," said Janus. And those were the last words the AI ever spoke.

8

MEGADEATH REQUIRED

In the twentieth and early twenty-first centuries, the governments that wielded the biggest sticks were those with easiest access to fossil fuels, primarily oil and gas. Russia, steadily tightening a fuel stranglehold on Europe, wielded a very big stick indeed, in fact one so large that, in a shameful replay of history, everyone looked away when it annexed the Czech Republic, and Red Army troops marched again through the streets of Prague. But then, perhaps, everyone was busy watching the Middle East, and shrieking hysterically about the protectorate America had begun forming there after being dragged into a worsening situation when Israel nuked Tehran and proceeded to roll its tanks into Syria. Or perhaps they were more intent on China's sabre-rattling in Tibet, or India's response of a hydrogen bomb test conducted in the Bay of Bengal—a test, incidentally, aimed at focusing the attention of the new Caliphate of Pakistan, which responded in turn with its own test in the Arabian Sea. Yet, even after all this mayhem, sanity prevailed and the expected World War Three failed to materialize. However, there are those who seriously still think such a war would have been a good thing. For the resultant megadeath would have taken the strain off world resources, while inevitable technological advances could have made us more able to use them effectively. It would have at least given the human race a breathing space, whereas now, without one, the human race suffocates.

ANTARES BASE

Var waited until the shepherd headed out of sight around the other side of Hex Three, where it would doubtless enter through the big airtight garage doors—a process likely to take at least fifteen minutes. With the diamond saw resting on her shoulder and the battery box clutched in her right hand, she started walking and then, once accustomed to the weight and balance of her burden, broke into a steady lope. She skirted the water tank and continued on down between it and the hex wall, to where that connected with the outer wall of Wing Five. Then, after a few paces along the wing wall, she came to the first of the metre-square windows. Luckily, Wing Five was not being used as a dormitory, since Ricard did not like having ordinary station personnel bunking too close to him. Instead, that wing now contained workshops and storage. At this end lay a workshop for the crawlers, with direct access for the vehicles running underneath the hex towards the garage on the further side, while a light-engineering workshop lay further along, towards Hex One, beyond which the wing was divided into a regular series of storage rooms.

Nobody at home, it seemed. Var peered in at a crawler stripped of its wheels and raised on a lift, then transferred her gaze to the bulkhead doors separating this particular wing from Hex Three. These were the same sort of doors as could be found scattered throughout the complex, the sort that had killed those workers processing soil in one of the laboratories. And the doors still operated according to the same safety protocols.

Var placed the battery box on the ground, plugged in the diamond saw's power cable, then set the thing running. It jerked and twisted under the force of its spin, the blade turning to a blur and gyroscopic action making it awkward to manoeuvre. For a second she hesitated—strangely reluctant to harm her own base—then she brought the saw blade down against the window. A thin shriek assaulted her ears as the blade juddered against the glass, raising a spray of fine white powder. As it hit one of the resin laminations, this bubbled between the layers of glass, then the saw pierced all the way through, and internal air pressure booted it out again. A great plume of vapour shot out from the gash, but maybe that would not be enough. Var cut again, then again, the blade slicing open slots that extended to just under its full ten-centimetre diameter. Beyond the blur of vapour and glass dust she saw three of Ricard's armed enforcers charging through the bulkhead doors, with a couple of execs trailing behind them. She gazed at them a little disbelievingly, seeing they'd demonstrated just how stupid they were to come running unsuited into a section already shrieking with decompression klaxons.

Var shoved the blade still harder against the glass, then, with a thump, found herself flung back, in a cloud of glittery fragments, on to her backside. The entire window had blown out, the vapour plume reached thirty metres behind her, but diffused as the thin Martian air sucked it in like a dry sponge on milk. After carefully shutting off the saw and laying it on the ground, Var stood up and walked back to the gaping window to peer inside. As expected, the bulkhead doors had closed, and the five who had foolishly entered were pressed up against them, two of them desperately trying to operate the frozen controls, before sliding to the floor. All of them had trails of vapour issuing from their mouths, as their lungs expelled both air and moisture with a thin shriek. She grabbed the top of the frame and hauled herself up, then carefully over any remaining fragments of glass to drop inside. There she waited as the three enforcers writhed about, fearing they might grab for their weapons if they saw her. It was only then she realized they could not see her, for their eyes had started bulging, the fluid inside them expanding, and vapour wisping away as their surfaces dried out. Even as she watched, she noticed a fresh gust of vapour, as first one eyeball burst, then another.

Var strode across and picked up the discarded weapons: two side arms and a scoped assault rifle—probably the same one used to kill Gisender. The three enforcers were also carrying universal ammunition clips, but a check revealed that only one of the spares contained ceramic ammunition. The rest held plastic ammo, sufficient to kill, but too light to punch a hole through a window, a door or any other vital infrastructure. These went into her hip bag, before she returned to the broken window and stepped outside.

Perhaps she should be feeling some guilt about what she had just done, but found no such emotion inside her. People just like these had made her life a misery from her first conscious moments, then later forced her to make the journey out to this godforsaken world. They deserved everything they got. Like so many others who concealed their rebellion deep inside, she had just been waiting for a chance to strike back—and it felt good.

Pausing, she remembered what her personal political officer had said to her back at the Traveller construction project: *"You're too dangerous to live, Var, but too valuable to kill."* That was just before he informed her that she had been appointed Technical Director of Antares base, replacing the previous incumbent who had recently died of cancer. But as enforcers had taken her off to a holding cell, "the only accommodation presently available," she had known the real reason they were moving her out. They knew she had just discovered the truth about her husband, Latham Delex; how he had not died in an aero accident, back down on Earth, but in an adjustment cell. They wanted her to continue being useful to them, but in a situation where she wouldn't have access to the massive orbital tools of her main profession—tools she might use against them.

Ricard and his staff were now sealed in Hex Three, until such time as they could suit up and find another route out. Var did not intend to allow them the time, however, and quickly strode round the hex to bring the next two windows into view. Here lay the private community room for Ricard's staff. After much fumbling she managed to swap the assault rifle's existing clip for the one with ceramic ammo. Then adjusting the weapon to a three-shot setting, she fired once at each window. One pane blew out but the other held, so she hit it again and it blew out too. Var did not bother checking inside. She'd already seen movement in there, and knew she'd just killed someone else—quite likely more than one. She jogged round the hex to the next windows, and opened fire again.

After that, again approaching the hex, she peered in through the broken windows of Ricard's office and apartment, and was disappointed to see it empty. She moved along, then climbed through the next shattered window and into the control room. Here she found one exec slumped over a console, while another lay writhing and clawing at the diamond-pattern metal of the floor. She headed over to the console and hauled the first one out of his chair, aiming to dump him on the floor. He grabbed her wrist and held on tight, his lungs pumping wildly as he tried to stay alive. She waited patiently until his grip slackened, before shrugging him off, then paused briefly to gaze down at the two of them. Five years she'd known these people, but right now, she couldn't even remember their names.

Sitting down, she reached into her hip bag and took out the data disc she had retrieved from the crawler. She fed it into a slot, from the disc menu selected Le Blanc's speech, then from the control menu selected *broadcast* and *repeat*. A subscreen blinked on, down in the bottom righthand corner, confirming that Le Blanc's speech was now being broadcast throughout the base.

Back outside the Hex again, Var realized that by now Ricard and his remaining staff must be aware of what was going on. They would already be suiting up, grabbing weapons, reacting purposefully. She quickly strode round to the personnel airlock, and fired one burst into its outer door. One bullet ricocheted off, but the other two punched through the bubblemetal, disabling the airlock and killing anyone inside.

Var paused to check the display on the side of her weapon, seeing that only seventeen shots now remained of the fifty-round clip. Just then a shadow speared across the arid ground over to her left, removing her attention from the weapon. A shepherd had arrived.

The machine paused, surveying its surroundings with its blind blunt dome, then abruptly jerked into motion again to come striding towards her. She felt a sudden dry terror, but managed to take careful aim, this time using the scope and setting the rifle to full automatic. As she opened fire, emptying all seventeen shots into the thing, it shuddered and staggered, with chunks of metal and ricocheting bullets flying away from it. Var turned and ran, aware that it was still loping after her, even with one of its legs no longer working properly. Just a few metres from the personnel airlock leading into Hex One, its shadow finally fell across her and its sticky tentacles dropped on her like writhing lianas. They wound themselves around her torso and hauled her off the ground.

EARTH

The pain was intense as Saul's pulse thundered in his head again, but he now seemed to be positioned over to one side of it. In his two-year life he had encountered the number pi only once, and memorized it to fifty decimal places, but it had never been of much use to him, so he'd done no more beyond that. Janus's calculation of pi was delimited only in terms of processing space. The installation software had made a compromise during integration, however, so now Saul could instantly remember the number to five hundred decimal places, then calculate it thereafter. Such compromises and complete displacements were working all through his artificially extended mind, and blocks of information shifted rapidly about as if being moved by some ancient computer-defrag utility. He remembered some parts of the processing plant in which he'd been destined for incineration. Janus had known it wholly and completely: the schematics, computer systems, security, power inputs and outputs, the materials used in its construction, the manufacturers of its components, its overall history and its maintenance log, so Saul now knew all that too, as Janus and he gradually became one.

Govnet remained open to him, so he managed to download data from it for inspection, thus learning that the encampment had been established in a cam deadspot inside the tunnel, probably around the location of a former black market. But, with tentacular code, something started groping its way after him in that virtual world, trying to latch on. There seemed something familiar about this shadowy presence and he wondered whether he was detecting Malden. But somehow that wasn't right; somehow he knew he would identify Malden instantly if the man put in an appearance. As this thing, this comlife, oriented towards him, shifting the information of its substance in some sinister manner, he immediately tried to shut down the radio modem in his head. The result was overload: a spike driven in between his eyes, his vision filled with lightnings. But the modem closed.

"Alan," urged Hannah. "Alan."

He was down on his knees and she was trying to pull him back to his feet with one hand, whilst she clutched Merrick's assault rifle in the other. He raised his head to study their surroundings through watery eyes. To his right stood a row of double-skin inflatable tents, and directly ahead lay a campfire around which a crowd of ZAs was gathered. Many of them were staring at him and Hannah, and some of them were beginning to walk towards them. They needed to get out of here, now.

There was no reason to suppose these people were hostile, but they would certainly want to know about the AH trailer van, and why he and Hannah had deserted it. The state of his skull would raise questions too. Or maybe they thought he and Hannah might be able to provide answers regarding that distant atomic blast.

"Alan!" she repeated.

He was still weak and his head ached abominably, but his awareness of his body, provided by the martial training in his previous existence, had grown to something almost mathematical in its precision. He stood upright, automatically assimilating a mental model of the movements of every muscle and bone in his body, whose names, strength, position and size he now knew, calculating the stresses caused, calculating potential, as he also filled in a rather more sketchy model of his surroundings. This other model he expanded, briefly switching on his modem again to download a city map, seemingly snatching it from beneath the multiple limbs of some shadowy behemoth, mapping the sprawl around him and working out precisely where he wanted to be next in order to further his plans, for they had not changed.

"Who are you?" called the woman leading a group of four zero-assets towards them.

"Rifle," he said, reaching out to close his hand about the assault rifle Hannah held, delighting in the complexity of the structure of both hand and arm, and already seeing much room for improvement.

"No." She did not release the gun.

He turned to gaze at her, targeting the points on her body he could strike to get her to release the weapon, finally deciding that one jab in her solar plexus would be quickest. She met his gaze and straight away let go, looking terrified. Weapon held one-handed, its butt tucked under his arm, he turned back to face those still approaching. The woman halted then and, as if Saul had struck her, abruptly lurched backwards into the man directly behind her. The other ZAs halted as well, and Saul measured subtle alterations in their pose. They went from a belligerent curiosity to something cowed and frightened. What were they seeing? He turned and began heading back out of the tunnel, already downgrading their importance within his mental model.

"Your eyes," said Hannah.

"Bloodshot like Malden's," he stated. "Blood-pressure differential through the organic interface to his cerebellum, caused by increased demand. It will kill him eventually."

"And you?"

"No."

"Why?"

He halted and turned to her. "Because of the viral nanite fix my previous self made." He paused, briefly studying the map in his head of the surrounding sprawl. "Telomeres reconfigured, T-cell boost and an increase in stem-cell division, but with strong immune response to stem-cell mutation. I heal about four times faster than a normal human being, and this body physically adapts to internal and external pressures at the same rate. Also, those little biomechs are still in my bloodstream, constantly running repairs. This is why I survived Smith's torture."

No terror in her expression now, but a look of shock remained, and something like awe. "How can you know that?"

"I worked it out, and that's what my present self would have done."

A motorway flyover now above. A big truck with strobing green lights shot over it, followed by four Inspectorate ground cruisers. He began walking towards a pedway over to his far left. It cut through under the flyover and on the other side of it lay access for maintenance workers to reach the road itself.

"Where are we going?" Hannah asked.

"Closer to the blast."

"Please, speak to me, Alan."

He was already speaking to her, so what was her problem? The answer to that didn't really require much thinking about, but its implications did. The human component of his self had been all but subsumed by Janus, and he now thought with the ordered logic of a machine intelligence. Emotions: what were they but an evolved evolutionary imperative, a chemical anachronism residing in the new him? Love, hate, friendship, fear and happiness, what did he need them for? In the mouth of the pedway tunnel, he dumped the assault rifle in a litter bin—as a precaution, since carrying it might draw the attention of enforcers in the cruisers passing above—then, two paces beyond the bin, a great black gulf opened up in his extended mind, and he sank to his knees again.

What use were emotions? He could analyse them right down to their smallest components and know the reason for them all, then he could discount them from his thought processes and become a totally logical being. What use then for that other anachronism called the survival instinct? He'd run full-tilt into the dilemma of those who saw themselves merely as machines for the transmission of genes, and nothing more. If that was to be his only purpose, what use was existence at all? Why live, why struggle, why seek pleasure and try to avoid pain, in the sure knowledge they were both just a couple more screwdrivers inside the genetic toolbox? Surely oblivion was a better choice?

He didn't need a lump of Hyex embedded in the base of his skull to end it all. Through the organic interface, he could just shut himself down, turn off his conscious mind, erase all data. His autonomous nervous system would continue functioning, but he would then be mindless. He lay a breath away from oblivion at that moment, but even patterns of thought are a product of evolution and the old survival imperative itself had survived the integration process, having as its source both himself and Janus who, after all, was a near-copy of a human mind. Saul realized that to survive he must make divisions, he must retain a human mind to interface with the world, just as the organic interface in his skull marked a physical line of division between the organic and the silicon him. In that instant he began rebuilding the cowering cockroach inside his skull, re-establishing its predominance, turning a human face back towards the world. Finally he stood up again, and the human face he turned towards the world boiled with anger and hate.

"What happened?" Hannah asked.

"Call it existential angst," he said tightly.

She nodded. "Something like that happened with Malden, but he thought it was a fault in the comlife he used."

"You knew?" He looked up.

"I got no chance to tell you." She gazed at him accusingly. "I thought you would warn me before you loaded the AI."

"How did Malden survive?"

"He hung on to his hate."

The much larger and more complex part of himself delivered into Saul's human mind the dry verdict that, though Hannah indeed had some idea of how things had run within Malden's head, she had no idea of what was going on in his own. Saul realized that she had taken a gamble with him; she could not have known what combining Janus with the hardware in his head would result in.

"I, too, hang on to my hatred," he declared.

But was it just the Committee he hated, or the entire human race?

***

As the Inspectorate cruisers, the big trucks of DRS or "disaster response service," the AH ambulances and ATVs sped past, their occupants all ignored Hannah and Saul. Why, Hannah wondered, would they take note of just two more civilians milling around the periphery of the blast zone? If she and Saul had been the only two actually walking towards the great boiling cloud still rising from the firestorm, the only two making their way through the increasing amounts of debris, perhaps they would have been more noticeable.

"Why are there people heading towards it?" she asked Saul.

"Desperation," he replied succinctly. "It's an opportunity for looting not to be missed."

Soon impassable, the highway became a traffic jam of emergency vehicles, though some surprisingly organized individual had kept one lane clear for the bulldozers that approached shortly after she and Saul arrived on the scene. With such a concentration of Inspectorate enforcers, the citizens who flocked along this route, with apparently nefarious intentions, abandoned the main highway long before, heading off into devastated sprawl and dodging between smoking mounds of rubble, while avoiding those buildings that still belched flames. She wondered if they hadn't noticed the shepherds pacing about over there, or hadn't heard the clattering hum of razorbirds. However, one small group of citizens, who she and Saul joined, seemed to be here merely as spectators. She felt that Saul's cynicism might be catching, as she found herself surmising that they had come here to see something appalling enough to lessen the impact of the constant disaster of their own lives.

Survivors came staggering out of the surrounding wreckage, and some others barely crawling. Many of them seemed to be naked, some bearing burn blisters big as fruit, and after their clothing they were now shedding their skins. But there and then, in that moment when screaming might be justified, there was only silence from them.

"They're not receiving any help," Hannah observed.

Though a crowd of these injured had gathered in a clear space beside that section of the highway where most of the All Health ambulances were parked, no one showed any signs of tending to them, and instead they were being driven away from the ambulances by baton-wielding enforcers.

"They cannot all be saved," he remarked flatly.

She glanced at him, feeling something leaden in her stomach. "You're not just talking about those we see here, are you?"

He gestured to the traffic jam of emergency vehicles. "This is probably the result of some automatic disaster-response plan that Committee execs just hadn't yet got round to shelving," he said. "I doubt they would have bothered sending any ambulances, since what's the point of saving a few thousand people when you expect billions of others to die?"

"Can it really be so cynical?" she asked, but with no real question in her tone. By now she was beginning to know the score.

Four of the large bulldozers made their way off the highway, beginning to cut a path through the wreckage. A couple of AH ambulances turned round on to the lane the dozers had just vacated, providing a gap through which further bulldozers could pull out on to the other side of the highway. The big machines weren't making a path towards where Inspectorate HQ had recently stood, but almost certainly scribing a circle with that place as the centre point.

Hannah nodded to herself as the two ambulances now returned along the highway, and other ambulances began breaking away from the main cluster to follow them.

"They're sectoring it," she said.

"I imagine they'll bring in readerguns, in a few hours," he said, then pointed to where a number of large aeros had settled in one of the few clearings amidst the rubble. "We go there."

A double crash barrier lay bent down a slope strewn with burnt rubbish and seared grass, a Dascan Hydrobus lying on its side down at the bottom. The windows were all blackened, yet as far as Hannah could see the vehicle had taken very little damage from its impact with the barrier. Then she saw why: the posts securing the barrier had rusted through and it had possessed almost no stopping power at all. In passing, she saw the red palm of a single hand welded against one window of the bus, but only noted it with a kind of numbness. Enough horror surrounded them anyway, like that woman crouching in a doorway, the only part standing of an apartment block, with her face a dripping mess and her plastic sunglasses melted into her eyes.

"You should have brought the rifle," Hannah said, her voice hoarse to breaking point.

Inspectorate enforcers patrolled within the area where the four aeros had landed, while a cylinderbot circled it, crawling round on rubber treads to deposit coils of razorwire behind it like spider silk. If they had waited any longer, they would not have been able to just walk straight in here the way they did. As they crossed in front of the bot, Saul paused for a moment, then turned and gazed over to the Inspectorate officer who appeared to be in charge.

"Walk just ahead of me," he told her. "You're my prisoner."

"Yeah, I figured that." A panic attack nibbled at her, then dissipated because everything here was just too real for its falsity.

"Citizen Avram Coran, Inspectorate Executive, command designation HQ707," he explained to the exec. "I'm commandeering one of your aeros."

How the hell could he get away with this? But even as she asked herself the question, Hannah knew the answer. Now the AI had fully loaded to and begun integrating with his mind, he possessed all its abilities within his skull. He was Saul *and* Janus all in one, and with every passing moment the synergy between those two components would keep expanding his abilities. But that wasn't all. She hadn't yet told him about the organic interface she had used, just how different it was from the one inside Malden's skull. Whilst Malden's had been made of organic tissue, it remained inert, merely integrating with his brain like a plug-in electrical component. The interface in Saul's skull, however, was an active organism: even now it would be growing neurons throughout his skull and making yet further connections. Quite possibly it would kill him, quite possibly it would turn him into something never witnessed before, but whether that would result in a demigod or a monster, she didn't know.

The two enforcers accompanying the officer already had their machine pistols trained on Saul. All three were staring at him with wary vigilance, and not a little degree of fear. Was it just his red eyes and the stitching in his skull that caused this reaction? Or did something of what was gestating inside him show through to them? Hannah could certainly see it, but then perhaps she was reading more than was actually visible.

The officer meanwhile dropped his hand to the portable scanner at his belt.

"So it seems you haven't studied your atomic-incident protocols lately," Saul said, inserting what seemed just the right amount of contempt into his voice.

"Sir?" the officer enquired.

"Electromagnetic pulse from the blast." Saul pointed at his forearm, where his varied collection of ID implants resided. "Do you really think my ID implant is working right now? It'll take at least an hour for its recovery program to reinstate it."

"You'll understand that I cannot just hand over an aero without checking first, citizen," the man replied.

"You've received no orders about me, Commander Taiken?"

Hannah stared at Saul, whose mind must now be in Govnet, absorbing data, perhaps changing data. Taiken straightened up, now he had been offered some small proof that Saul was of the Inspectorate. For how else would Saul know his name?

Saul continued, "I managed to make contact from my car, after the blast tipped it over." He gestured towards Hannah. "It's important I get her away from here fast, but you don't need to know any more than that."

Taiken raised a hand to the fone in his ear, as doubtless his new orders came through. Then, as was only to be expected, he unhooked a palmtop from his belt and did some checking. He directed its integral cam at Saul for a moment, then pointed it at Hannah. After a moment, he snapped the palmtop closed, nodded to himself, then pointed across to the nearest aero.

"You can take this one." He turned to the two enforcers. "Go check the gas loading, and tell Latham to speed it up with that fence."

Hannah was dumbfounded. That was fast—faster than she could have believed possible. Saul's penetration of the local computer network had to be all but total. He must have been providing data direct to the man's palmtop even as its recognition programs tried to read their faces. He must have drafted orders, and built a whole fiction to back up their presence here.

"Gas?" Saul enquired as the officer turned back to him.

"They're writing it all off," he replied.

Hannah understood. There would be no survivors.

"I'll get you a pilot and put together a squad for you," Taiken added.

"That won't be necessary," Saul replied, and Taiken glanced at him in surprise. "I can fly the machine myself and I need to lock down on security."

"Security?"

"The fewer people who know about her," he gestured at Hannah, "the better."

Officer Taiken didn't like that, since it suggested that not all of his men were to be trusted. As they reached the craft, its recognition system picked up on him, opened its doors and lowered some steps. Taiken stepped up inside first, and even as Saul waved Hannah up ahead of him, she realized something was wrong. Saul seemed to be in pain, pressing the heel of his hand between his eyes before climbing in behind her. Door motors hummed into life, closing the door behind them, and Taiken turned, with a brief look of confusion on his face, just before the edge of Saul's hand slammed into the base of his skull. He went down like a sack of potatoes.

"Ack! Jesus!" Saul stumbled away from the fallen man, and went down into a squat. He retched, bringing up nothing but bile, then just crouched there, gasping.

"Saul…" Hannah took a step towards him, but just then Taiken groaned and began to make an effort to rise. Saul's head snapped up, and she saw his eyes were weeping bloody tears. He lurched to his feet and stumbled over towards Taiken, descending to drive a knee into the man's spine, then, grabbing Taiken's head, he pulled it back and twisted hard.

The horrible gristly sound seemed to punch Hannah in the stomach, and she turned away, pressing herself against the wall of the aero. "Is it necessary always to kill them?" she protested, but that seemed about as effectual as appealing to a guillotine, and she hated the whine in her voice.

"I've shut down all their links to Govnet here," Saul rasped, "but it won't take them long to open up some other channel, once they find they're offline. Then he could identify us."

Already he had the aero's engines starting up, its fans whirling up to speed. It had to be him, since the cockpit stood empty.

"So can others out there," she remarked.

"Yes, I know."

Just that? Did he mean he had already set something in motion to deal with the problem?

He moved past her towards the cockpit, and she followed him inside. As he strapped himself in, he gestured to the seat beside him. She plumped herself down and began to fumble with the straps.

"You have reservations," he suggested, his voice tight and angry.

"You might be just like Malden: possibly worse than what you're fighting."

Saul winced, wiped his eyes and studied the watery blood smeared on his hand. "You heard what they're intending here?"

"They're going to gas the survivors."

"Whether I'm worse than them or not is irrelevant," he snapped. "This is about survival now, not morality."

He took the override off the controls before him, and grabbed hold of them, then lifted the aero up into the sky.

***

Lights still jagged across his vision, but the pain in his skull was beginning to disperse. Apparently, each time he pushed himself too far mentally, as he had back in the aero camp, either the software or the hardware crashed in his mind.

Things had been fine while he was approaching the camp, reinstating his internal radio modem at last and cautiously exploring his near surroundings in cyberspace. Govnet had lain around him like an infinite city constructed of edifices of information, webbed with highways and lanes, paths, rivers and canals of information all in transit. With a thought he had highlighted the networks relevant to the Inspectorate, picked out the aero section, and absorbed as much data as possible related to the imminent gassing of survivors and the squadron of aeros being used.

Therefore, once in the camp he had jumped inside the nearest aero's computer in an instant, made a coded link direct to the modem in his head and simultaneously disconnected the craft from Govnet. He had then disconnected all local hardware from Govnet too, by scrambling connection software, isolating the aero camp, and incidentally cutting himself off from that distant dark thing he had first sensed in Bronstein's surgery. But by that time his pulse was thudding inside his head and the pain growing constantly.

He had managed to hold on just long enough to get himself inside the aero, and to eliminate Taiken, but then had come the crash. Yet, each time he recovered from one of these painful episodes, like now, it seemed his abilities were expanded. Saul now considered dumping the aero and going into hiding until whatever was going on inside his head was completed and he had found his new limits. But he soon dismissed that idea, for the longer he waited, the greater the likelihood that the Inspectorate would move to tighten up computer security because, certainly, someone or something out there had got to know about him. He needed to now move fast and with utter ruthlessness to achieve his goal.

By confining his mental compass to the aero and its systems, he could see everything in them with a clarity that had been missing before. This vehicle was a fast transport with jet assist, internal and external readerguns, external missile-launchers and inducers, state-of-the-art armour and autodefences. And, having seized control through the command override, it had become his absolutely.

Now airborne, he considered the evidence he'd left behind. Time to remove it. All the aeros possessed similar command overrides, so could be flown and their weapons controlled remotely—this to prevent them being hijacked.

Useful that, and precisely the route he now followed to hijack them.

The identities of the two enforcers who had actually seen Hannah and himself, he transmitted to the recognition systems of the aeros still on the ground, and fixed a delay of about two minutes. After that brief time, the other crafts' readerguns would identify the two of them as dissidents, and that would be the end of them. He doubted the Inspectorate would be able to—or even be bothered to—work out what had happened, or at least not until his and Hannah's journey was over. He neglected to mention this to her, however. Next he finally severed his connection to the aero camp.

That was it. Done.

9

BLAME THE ROBOTS

In the twentieth and twenty-first centuries, massive processing power and memory outpaced other technologies. It took many years before the software was invented to utilize it efficiently, and before sufficiently intelligent systems could be designed. When those were finally invented, this advance created its own mini-revolutions in personal entertainment and access to information; unfortunately it also created a mini-revolution in the ability of governments, already increasingly totalitarian as political elites gathered more and more power to themselves, to monitor their citizens and become even more totalitarian. Following the socialist dream into the territory of nightmare, those elites now took increasing control of society. Next to catch up was robotics, displacing the weak human components utilized in so many walks of life, and in the end those not included in the massive bureaucracies that controlled Earth became just client citizens—mostly on the dole, mostly zero-asset. Was the technology itself to blame: should people have Luddite-fashion smashed it? No, technology is merely a tool and any blame always rests squarely on the one wielding that tool.

Saul chose a less-travelled route: up over the North Sea, to land for refuelling at Trondheim, then crossing the Scandia province of old Norway and Sweden, down across the Baltic to cross erstwhile Lithuania, finally to Minsk. Refuelling was no problem. It merely required a minor penetration of the airport computers, since unscheduled Inspectorate aero flights weren't uncommon. Just a minor headache there, and a few warning flashes across his vision. This time, as with his previous minor penetrations of Govnet, no sign of that other presence on the net. He calculated the degree of noise he could create before attracting its attention, now knowing that the moment he did anything related to Coran or Hannah, that would be the equivalent of a shout.

After he landed, a tanker of liquid hydrogen waiting on the carbocrete hooked up its bayonet hoses and completed the job within twenty minutes. Then they were off again, and all the way as far as the Baltic he saw only two other aeros and just a few vapour trails from the high-atmosphere scramjets of space planes. But as soon as they entered Lithuania troposphere traffic became much heavier, with definite aero-lanes visibly punctuating the sky. The activity here was very much more than he had expected.

Information garnered from the Subnet showed that the fortunes of Minsk Spaceport had been on the wane until the Committee started building the Argus satellite network, and that now it was even busier than before. He knew that many of the aeros he saw flying the route from Lithuania to East Germany would be loaded with drugs, data-crystals, 3D silicon chips and the like, whilst the big trucks on the twelve-lane autobahns below him were loaded with bubblemetals or products of the same from the surrounding industrial complexes. The traffic using the same route into the port was mostly of empty vehicles and staff buses, though some commodities were still shipped up to the station. However, the Argus Network was all but complete, and supplying Argus Station itself and ferrying down vital materials and technologies that could only be made in zero gravity would not account for this furious activity. Some other operation was under way.

It was difficult to say where the actual Minsk sprawl began, because in Lithuania the Vilnius sprawl had absorbed Kaunas and also blended across a forgotten border with the district of Minsk. As with the rest of the world, none of the old national borders now divided this area, just various regions of Committee political authority. However, Minsk Spaceport remained under its own authority, the lines of division from its tertiary industries clearly marked by security fences, readergun towers and a no-man's-land seeded with mines. Ahead, just inside this massive fence, aeros were spiralling down towards a twenty-storey vehicle park that squatted amidst the glassy administration towers located beside the square kilometres of primary direct-support industrial estates attached to the spaceport. It resembled the grey edifices of the ancient communist regime—the kind of buildings demolished during Russia's emergence from communism, but now being built again under Committee rule.

Air Traffic took control as they approached this spiralling descent, and the orders he'd falsified on the way here gave them primacy, so Traffic inserted their craft lower down in the queue. As the big machine descended, sometimes only tens of metres away from other aeros, so that the roar of surrounding engines penetrated even the high-tech insulation of their craft, he unstrapped himself and headed to the rear. Hannah came to watch as he dragged Taiken's body to a large integral chest half-full of squat gas canisters, and then shoved it inside.

"Getting here was the easy part," he said.

"Masterly understatement."

Her irony had returned, so her sleep during the ten-hour journey must have restored some of her equilibrium.

He shrugged. "But though the next part will be difficult, failure is not an option."

"Was part of your installation software an arrogance program?"

Again linking into Govnet and the subsidiary spaceport network, cyberspace became as real all around him as the physical world. It seemed in fact part of the real world—just an extra perception of it somewhere between sight and thought, but with the added factor that he could manipulate it. His mind perpetually groped for suitable analogies for describing to himself what he was doing. To a certain extent it seemed like being inside a control space in virtual reality where information came in apparently physical units, to be moved about by hand and ordered by voice, but even this close relationship between man and machine amounted to no more than a more complex keyboard-and-mouse combination. It seemed he had completely closed the gap between man and machine; being actually *in* the machine, and part of it.

"When someone knows his own capabilities and states how he intends to use them, is that arrogance?" he asked.

"It's how it was said," Hannah replied.

He nodded, realizing that he really had been arrogant, because already he began detecting increased activity on Govnet, and a sampling of the communications soon explained why. Security had upped a level shortly after the destruction of Inspectorate HQ in the London sprawl, but was now ramping up to condition red. Massive troop movements were in progress, critical facilities being locked down, Committee delegates disappearing into their private fortresses. Chairman Messina was off the radar, and execs from the next echelon down were taking refuge in bunkers. Someone had just poked the Inspectorate wasp nest with a big stick, and it wasn't Saul. Perhaps this explained why that other presence out there seemed unable to find him.

"Malden," he said, as their craft slid into the side of the aero-park and turned to head for its designated slot.

"What?"

"Seems the revolution has started."

Fourteen separate Inspectorate HQs had been hit, all across the world. Tactical nukes were used against two of them, four had been stormed by well-armed insurgents, most of the staff slaughtered and only a few captives taken. One was destroyed with thermal Hyex missiles whilst the remainder had received a taste of what they dealt, for the revolutionaries had used nerve gas. Eight scramjets had been hit by ground-to-air heatseekers before they got up enough speed to outrun the missiles. Three actual Committee delegates had been assassinated, hundreds of lower-echelon execs knifed, shot or blown up. These incidents were just part of a much larger widespread whole that included less lethal sabotage with, for example, a garage of Inspectorate cruisers being disabled, com towers blown up, and viral attacks affecting Govnet. He now related much of this news to Hannah.

"I'd say they don't stand a chance, but there's Malden..."

"Much of what I'm seeing seems likely to have been organized beforehand," Saul interrupted, as the aero settled into its slot. "I don't think Malden would be satisfied with just taking out another Inspectorate HQ. He'll go for something bigger."

He checked the inventory of equipment aboard their craft, and then, opening a tool chest, took out a couple of large rolls of duct tape before turning and instructing the aero door to open ahead of them. After stepping down to the carbocrete floor, he turned to help Hannah down, but she ignored his hand and moved away to put some space between them. He didn't react to that rebuff, since he was busy penetrating the cam system in order to cause a temporary fault. Once this sufficiently developed, he decided it was time she ceased to be just a passenger and tossed her one of the rolls.

"Cover the serial number on the far side," he instructed.

She nodded and moved round to the other side of the craft, whilst he covered the number on this side. As Hannah returned, his next mental instruction closed up the machine and locked it, and in considering how to make things even more difficult for anyone who found this machine, he *remembered* numerous viral programs from that part of his mind that had been Janus. He used just one virus, but including elements of yet another one and a little bespoke tailoring, and it left the machine pondering, so that, about the time they stepped into the park lift, the craft shifted over to auto-defence. He had not set the readerguns to just kill any who got too close to it, but the moment someone started tampering, by either trying to force open the doors or peel that tape off, they would be in for a nasty surprise.

The lift took them down eighteen storeys, to where it opened into a security area with a row of gates operated by combined palm and retinal scanners. Just beyond the lift, Hannah came to a halt, uncertain and obviously frightened, as she turned to look at him for reassurance.

"No problem," he said, beckoning her after him, while trying to ignore the stabbing pain growing between his eyes.

Penetrating the security all around them, he simply shut down the scanners and then opened the gate ahead. Beyond it lay an open area with readerguns mounted on the walls—a kill zone. He instructed the readerguns to ignore them both, but knew that would not be enough. Another push and he was into the Minsk security mainframe, inserting sketchy identities for the spaceport's recognition programs, which now either opened any barriers ahead or simply overlooked the intruders.

"You're terrifying," remarked Hannah—but abruptly moved up beside him and looped her arm through his.

"Yeah, maybe," he replied, turning his head away from her to flick a bloody tear from his eye. "But there's something out there looking for us that might be just as capable. It keeps zeroing in on me every time I create enough noise on Govnet."

"Malden?" she asked.

He shook his head. "No, it's the 'powerful comlife' Janus mentioned."

"But they don't have anything." She looked confused.

"Seems they do."

She was very thoughtful for a moment. "Are you making too much noise now?"

"I don't think so. Just local penetration."

Local penetration wasn't enough, however. At some point a diagnostic program would detect the alterations he had made, so he just hoped he had given himself and Hannah enough time.

Sliding glass doors drew open ahead of them, and they stepped out on to a pavement beside which were parked automatic ground taxis resembling stretched-out flying saucers. In the distance, between two glassy octagonal-section office blocks, the orange flames of a cluster of rocket motors blasted into the sky a long black shape with triangular rear wings and stubby nose wings. The space plane passed behind the tower block to his left, steadily accelerating upwards at an angle of forty-five degrees. Somewhere high above the Baltic, when it hit Mach 5, its scramjet would kick in, taking it up to Mach 15, and its wings would fold into its body. By then its trajectory would be vertical, the scramjet finally shutting down through lack of air, and Earth's gravity bringing the plane's speed down to below a thousand miles an hour. Then would begin the long slow deceleration and manoeuvring towards Argus, if that happened to be its destination.

"You realize," he said, "that without what I can do and have done we'll end up in custody within minutes—and with that comlife out there there's still a chance that'll happen anyway." He glanced at her. "I can't turn back now, but if you want I'll get one of these"—he nodded to one of the autotaxis—"to take you to a ground-level gate. The security system here will simply let you out, but beyond that gate you'll be on your own."

"Is that what you want?" she asked, pulling away from him a little. "I'm sure I'm a liability you can ill afford."

That wasn't actually what he wanted, but some nasty part of him was wondering if he only kept her with him because he needed an audience. In an eyeblink he distanced himself both from the machine and from his human anger. No, he wanted her with him because he knew that, even though great dangers lay ahead, she was safer with him than on her own. All those protective instincts of a man with his mate were operating, and the idea of her falling back into the clutches of the Inspectorate horrified him. Did this mean he loved her? He didn't know. *What is love?*

"As far as I'm concerned, you're with me all the way, Hannah," he said. "But I won't stop you now if you want to leave."

She pulled herself closer again, reached up behind his head and drew him down into a kiss. It was long and passionate, her body pressing against his, and he felt himself responding. Drily analytical, another part of himself noted that he was wasting time. With a flash of irritation, he sent that part off to roam cyberspace—to make preparations and keep watch for that other thing out there. The kiss finished, they now approached one of the taxis, which opened its doors for them, and they climbed in the back.

"Staff Embarkation," he instructed, and the vehicle pulled out on to the road.

He sat in the back with Hannah pressed up against him, her head on his shoulder and the smell of her hair in his nostrils. He connected up again, becoming more of himself once more, feeling a brief bitter ache as he recognized that to be more human he needed to be actually less complete, the human him just being a part of the whole. His inner vision of himself seemed to be one of interfaces: some central entity sitting neither in cyberspace nor in that grey fatty tissue inside his skull, its senses operating through the fleshy gene transporter within this taxi, within cyberspace and the silicon, wires, optics and electromagnetic signals that were its medium, touching the physical world through those surrounding cams and sensors he chose. Did he know what love was before Smith sent him to the incinerator? Was human love possible for him now that it seemed he was no longer really human?

Humming contentedly to itself, the taxi pulled out on to a two-lane highway, away from the park, then joined a six-lane highway where massive trucks loomed about them like mobile buildings. Saul studied these, wondering just what the hell they were carrying; again aware that such massive movement could not be accounted for by standard operations, as of a year ago. Then, with a feeling of unease, he observed that some of these vehicles were troop transporters, and when the taxi swerved into another lane to let two Inspectorate cruisers race by, he sat upright. Surely this could be a reaction to Malden's revolution, because Minsk would be considered a prime target?

"What is it?" Hannah asked, noticing his reaction.

"Lot of security activity."

Just a brief modem connection revealed how local network security had escalated. Something had got them really bothered here, some major penetration, yet it wasn't him. However, this made it increasingly likely that his own interference in the mainframe would be quickly detected. His head started to throb as he tracked diagnostic traffic and tracer programs.

"We've got trouble," he added.

The taxi turned off on to another two-laner utterly devoid of traffic. They sat apart, now gazing out of the windows at their surroundings, taking in sprawling factories with steam towers belching white clouds, cranes etched against the sky, stationary since all construction here had ceased, then the bloated hemisphere of a fusion-reactor building, kilometres of above-ground pipes, with those glassy tower blocks nailing it all to the ground. Notable by its absence was any sign of life that wasn't human. Neither trees nor grass were visible, and the only green on view glinted in traffic lights or showed on faded signs in Cyrillic declaring the environmental credentials of this place. Saul gritted his teeth, now aware that a search engine had begun riffling through identity files. Almost certainly it would find the two sketchy ones he had put there and immediately delete them.

Then would come a location trace…

"Get ready to run," he warned, lights again beginning to jag across his vision. He should be able to deal with nearby cams and readerguns, and hopefully that would be enough.

Soon the taxi turned off again into a single lane that curved round to one side and across a bridge over one of the big highways, then down again. Thunder from above and a dark shadow drawing across, as another space plane hurtled into the sky. Even so high up, the thing seemed massive, and he remembered that standard transporter planes like that one overhead spanned six hundred metres from nose to rocket engines, and were capable of hauling two hundred tonnes of passengers and cargo up into orbit. Amazing that humans could build such a massive, complex and wonderful piece of technology, yet could not apply the same degree of logic and intelligence to building their societies or preventing their eventual decline. He watched the thing continue to rise, as the taxi drew up right beside the doors leading into the long, low Embarkation building. There was now a hollow feeling inside him, a blend of both awe and regret.

Then, suddenly, a massive disruption in the Minsk network, whilst simultaneously something exploded within the back end of the space plane, extinguishing that punctuated glare of its motors and throwing out chunks of dark metal trailing spears of smoke. It dropped out of the sky with all the aerodynamics of a falling chimney pot.

"Mother of God!" Hannah exclaimed.

He groped for information throughout cyberspace, hit disruption wherever he looked, then oddly found easy access to cameras positioned on high buildings, giving him multiple views of the disaster. He watched the plane trying to stay level but, with one of its rear wings tearing away, its nose came up as it descended. Another view gave him four seconds of its underside hurtling in, silhouetted against fire, until its rear end struck the building on which the cam was positioned. Back to another view of that same edifice, the plane carving through it, its position in the sky and angle of descent hardly changed by the impact, the wreckage of the top half of the building now strewn across factory complexes below. Then the plane went in like a wounded black swan descending on to a lake, churning up and spraying the lower buildings like water. As the nose slammed down, it disintegrated, becoming a train-shaped firestorm within which could be seen the burning black bones of its structure. It cut a swathe of devastation ten kilometres long.

Only when the final debris rained down did Saul consider why it had been so easy for him to access these views of this disaster. Someone had got there before him, to position the cams.

"Let's move," he said, shoving his elbow against the door of the taxi.

It wasn't opening, which meant that from somewhere an instruction had been sent to lock it down. He turned and looked behind him, spotted an armoured troop carrier motoring into sight.

Then something out there. Some pattern forming in surrounding and seriously disrupted cyberspace. Something tentacular expanded, a shadow cast by someone's manipulation of the network, yet Saul immediately recognized that this wasn't the comlife that had been hunting him. Hannah became like a distant creature trapped in the taxi, alongside that set of mobile fleshy sensors that seemed to be a minor part of himself—yet within which resided the essential him. It *had* to survive because, even in this new state, he knew himself unready to depart physical existence; knew that without that human connection he would lose any real reason to stay alive.

This new comlife, he realized, was taking control of Inspectorate aeros that were even now ascending into the sky to head for the crash site. They began firing upon each other.

Missile streaks cut above the devastation caused by the space plane, and cartridge cases rained down from machine guns firing continuously. Two of the aeros just dropped like bricks, trailing smoke, and slammed into the ground, one exploding and the other just turning into a flattened mess of wreckage. Another aero blew a fan and began spinning around about its other main fan, until that too blew and tore its guts out. It also went down.

Saul saw it then: a single craft departing the battle, between its fellows, neither firing nor being fired upon. It flew past the face of a tall building built in the shape of a cowl—one he recognized as he withdrew from cam systems and used only his eyes. The building lay just half a kilometre away from them, and he watched the aero fly into view, settle into a hover and revolve towards them. He knew in an instant that they weren't the target—those troops back there were—but, trapped inside this taxi so close to them, he and Hannah would die.

***

Hannah had told him that in his previous incarnation, as well as being a semi-autistic genius with enough going on in his head to frighten members of the Inspectorate, he had excelled in the martial arts. And, as he had since discovered, he still did. His body still possessed the muscle and coordination developed through all that previous training. However, that alone would not have been enough—it was knowledge acquired from Janus that tipped the balance. His AI, which was now part of him, knew the design of autotaxis like this one down to the smallest detail. The lockdown was a security protocol usually employed by the Inspectorate to secure suspects remotely, before they themselves could arrive on the scene.

A lockdown would seal the doors, then shut down the vehicle's computer so those trapped inside could not access it to open them. No mental access for him there, but he knew precisely how the vehicle was constructed. Two steel locking bars had engaged to the rear of the door, and these could only be physically disengaged from outside by arresting officers. The window glass wasn't glass at all but a laminated perspex which here, in the spaceport where many *important* people might use the taxis, was capable of stopping a bullet. The weakness lay at the hinges, being angled steel plates riveted to the body and the door, connected by five-millimetre steel hinge pins. He spun in the seat, grabbed a hand support provided for less able passengers, drew back both his legs and kicked out hard at the front of the door, over those hinges, the force of the blow running from his rigid arms right down through his body. The top hinge broke, the door tilting out. He kicked it again, and the second hinge broke away, but the door still hung suspended from its two locking bars. Leaning over, he shoved the door forward off its bars, and it clattered to the ground.

Saul got out, turning to drag Hannah after him, but she was already close on his heels. Behind them, troops were still piling out of the armoured car and, noticing someone trapped in a taxi just ahead, he realized the lockdown hadn't been directed at only his taxi. Somebody began shouting, and he saw a crowd of people, outside Embarkation, pointing over towards the aero. A glance in that direction, fire flaring under the craft, a stream of missiles spewing out, smoke trails heading directly towards them. Less than ten seconds, he calculated, as he grabbed Hannah's hand and they ran.

One man stood at the scanner beside the entrance to Embarkation, the glass doors drawing apart for him. Saul shouldered him aside, just hoping the readerguns in the foyer beyond would still ignore them. Just for a fraction of a second, the sight of numerous potted plants—the first green he had seen in a while—fazed him, but then he dragged Hannah towards a guard booth stretching all along the left side of the foyer. The doors to this stood open, an enforcer halfway across the blue-carpeted floor, on her way to the main doors. The woman turned towards him, to say something, he didn't know what. He pushed Hannah ahead of him to reach the door into the booth, where she threw herself on the floor with her hands over her head. An enforcer within the booth turned on his revolving chair, hand dropping to the ionic stunner at his belt. Saul dropped down on top of Hannah, shoving his fingers in his ears just as a sound impacted like that of an avalanche in a scrapyard.

Then came the light and the fire.

***

The blasts blended into one hollow roar, and Hannah felt something grab and drag Saul backwards off her. Heat washed over her legs and then the roar receded, as if some angry fire god had just paid a brief visit, then departed. She raised her head and saw that the vacuum created by the blast had dragged Saul halfway out of the booth. Glancing up she realized the armoured glass had been blown in, sheets of it now resting against the back wall to form a low ceiling. The enforcer seated in the revolving chair had not ducked fast enough and lay on the floor, his head weeping blood.

Saul stood up and mouthed something at her. She gazed at him, puzzled and stunned. Her ears were ringing and his words an indistinct mutter. He studied her for a moment, then, crouching below the armourglass, reached out a hand to haul her up, and they ducked out of the booth.

The autotaxis outside were gone or, rather, all she could now see of them was the remains of a hydrovane embedded in the rear wall of the foyer. Outside, she could see other burning wreckage, and smoking fragments she did not want to identify. The glass doors lay strewn in mostly hexagonal chunks, each the size of a spectacles lens, across the floor. The plants were blackened, some of them burning, but the carpet below, though scorched and hot underfoot, yielded neither smoke nor flame, from its fire-resistant ceramoplastic. An arm lay on it before them; a torso, one leg still attached, reclined beside a steaming money tree positioned against the far wall. The enforcer they had seen on the way in lay flat on her back, utterly still, her uniform seared but surprisingly little damage to her body; merely a little blood in her ears and nostrils, despite the fragments of glass all around her.

"Why?" Hannah managed to utter, her voice oddly off-key.

He replied, but again she heard only that indistinct mutter. She pinched her nose and blew, popping her eardrums, shook her head. Hearing returned slightly: the sounds of metal and rubble falling on hard surfaces, the oily crackle of fire and a couple of whumphs, of things exploding, maybe gas canisters, fuel tanks or overheated batteries.

"Seems the revolution just arrived," he said, the words now clear but a perpetual buzzing behind them. He beckoned her after him and headed towards the rear of the foyer, where long corridors, ceilinged with smoke, speared towards the trains used to transport passengers to the space planes.

More people were starting to appear, and the first to reach them, running down that corridor, were two Inspectorate enforcers. She noticed that both possessed the kind of mods more usually seen in bodyguards: subdermal armour, black artificial wide-spec eyes, and the exterior control units at elbow, shoulder and wrist that showed they possessed implant motors and bone reinforcing. But she knew in an instant that if they got in Saul's way they were dead.

"What the hell happened?" one of them asked.

That he even asked demonstrated that communications must be down—if only temporarily.

"Hey, I'm damned if I know," Saul replied.

The enforcer stared, hand dropping to the butt of his machine pistol, doubtless taking in Saul's reddened eyes and the marks of surgery on his shaven skull. Hannah knew that, in this situation, Saul was sufficiently abnormal for the enforcers to want to detain him, and when Saul moved to step past, the man reached out and grabbed his upper arm in a cyber-assisted grip. The killing would resume very shortly.

"You know a space plane went down?" Hannah interjected, before she even knew where she was going with this.

"We saw." The enforcer was still gazing at Saul suspiciously.

"It was probably wreckage that hit here. Officer Coran needs to get to Damage Control now before this situation gets any worse," she declared imperiously. "Don't you two have things to do?" She stabbed a thumb behind her. "There are people back there who need your help."

The bluff was good, but needed reinforcing. Saul did not disappoint her. He looked down in annoyance at the hand closed on his arm, then up at the enforcer, just the right amount of arrogance in his expression. "Govnet," he said, "is severely disrupted, so I am unable to obtain full access." His gaze strayed to the bar code on the top pocket of the man's uniform. "What's your name, officer?"

The enforcer let go of his arm as if it had suddenly heated up, seemed about to say something further, then abruptly stepped past and headed towards the foyer, his companion pausing only for a moment before trailing after.

"I just saved their lives, didn't I?" Hannah said.

"Yes," Saul acknowledged. "Yes, you did."

More staff appeared in the corridor further along, some heading towards the foyer and others moving away. Two teams clad in fluorescent hazmat suits were pushing wheeled stretchers towards the incident. Moving beyond these, Hannah and Saul got far enough away to just be part of the crowd, and entered a lift to take them down a floor to one of the train stations. Once inside the lift, Saul pressed his hands against his head.

"No, not now." He looked up. "Did Malden suffer this pain?"

She nodded. "Yes, he did." The lie tasted sour on her lips.

The sliding doors drew aside and he forced himself into motion again. They crossed a short platform to board a waiting train. Five other people were already inside, deep in nervous conversation.

"Our flight has to be cancelled," said a woman wearing the same grey flight suit as the rest of them. "For Christ's sake, that plane just dropped out of the sky!"

"Don't bet on it," replied her nearest male companion.

"No, don't," said one of the other men. "We'd have been notified of a blanket grounding, and been recalled by now."

The woman looked at her watch. "There's still time. I'll bet the orders'll catch up just when we're strapping in."

"Ever the optimist, Eva," said another woman.

"They'll need to know why it happened," Eva insisted. She then noticed Saul and gazed at him disbelievingly for a moment, before abruptly looking away. She glanced queryingly towards one of her companions, who shrugged. Always better not to ask.

After a moment, the train moved out of the Embarkation complex, following its rails out towards the hectares of carbocrete comprising the spaceport runways.

***

The front end of the space plane reared up out of the surrounding support vehicles, fuel silos and tangles of umbilicals like some monstrous Gulliver trying to escape its Lilliputian captors. It rested on the specially formulated carbocrete like a prehistoric beast reformatted for a new cybernetic age: all hard angles and black solidity.

The train drew to a halt at the end of its line, directly opposite a large mobile building poised on enormous caterpillar tracks, from which an entrance tunnel rose towards the belly of the plane itself. The five on board with them exited the train first, carrying an assortment of laptops and short cylindrical flight bags containing their personal effects. Saul and Hannah were certainly the odd ones out, and because of that would come under scrutiny. Time for him to once again penetrate local computers to ensure that they got safely aboard. He did not relish the prospect and wondered if he had been foolish to push so far so quickly. A mental crash now and it would all be over for them both.

Saul linked into Govnet, found it still disrupted, then into the subnets of the spaceport and brought his focus down on to everything concerning this plane, and it didn't take him long to find problems. The woman called Eva was right: a general order had been issued to cancel all further missions, and the concert of groaning and swearing from the five ahead confirmed that they had now received this instruction through their fones. Orders specific to space-plane crew and passengers were that they must return to quarters whilst an investigation was put in place. All space planes were to undergo a thorough inspection.

These were the orders on the surface, but there seemed a great deal more activity going on below this. The spaceport authority was aware that the plane had been brought down by computer penetration, the same sort of penetration that resulted in the aeros turning on each other and wreaking destruction elsewhere about the port. Saul discovered that the missile firing, having wiped out an Inspectorate security squad sent to apprehend suspects at Embarkation, was under heavy suspicion, and further squads had been dispatched. It seemed likely to him that he and Hannah had been detected, but so far the Inspectorate just had a general location.

Deeper penetration now, the thumping in his head growing, and some invisible tormentor trying to drill him another eye socket.

He sent orders to whatever crew was aboard the plane, and in its surrounding infrastructure, to expect an investigator plus his assistant. By way of a cam within the train he made visual files of both their faces and sent them through, with no more than the name Agent Green, and which gave him complete authority here. After the five crew had climbed back aboard the train, ready to return to their quarters, Hannah and he disembarked.

"We are now investigators," he told Hannah as they stepped from the vehicle.

"Very good," she replied. "But how does that help us get the plane off the ground?"

"We'll see when we get there."

She stared at him. "Nothing planned here? Nothing prepared?"

"No, but I know how to fly this thing now and, once I have it isolated up in the air, there's nothing they can do. I don't see them quickly making a decision to shoot twenty billion Euros worth of their own hardware out of the sky, and once the scramjets fire up they won't be able to."

She flinched and shook her head. "I wish I could trust your superior intelligence, but obviously I can't. Even a space plane travelling at Mach 15 can't outrun a laser."

"You're talking about the Argus Network?"

"Of course."

"Then you *can* trust my intelligence. The lasers were designed for accurate antipersonnel use against people on Earth's surface, and even when they're at close range they haven't got the power to penetrate a carbon nanofibre, heat-dispersing hull."

"I'll trust to your judgement," she decided, doubtfully.

"Yes, you must."

Outside the train, the chilly air was redolent with the odours of oil and some other acrid chemical smell. He shrugged his jacket more closely about himself, then reached up to touch his scalp as the cold added to his misery by causing sharp stabbing pains all over it. He was also hungry and thirsty, not having eaten since they delved into the supplies aboard the aero they had used to travel here. He realized that the computer hardware in his skull, and the constant pain from the surgery employed to install it, had distanced him from his body to the point that he was neglecting it. He glanced at Hannah, who had made no complaints even though she must be as worn down as himself, but he could do nothing for either of them now.

"Just play along," he said, as he pulled open the door into the mobile building before them and stepped up inside it.

Within lay a suiting room: spacesuits on hangers along one wall, test equipment against another, and various hoses trailing along the floor. He wanted them wearing suits but wasn't sure how he could achieve that if he was supposedly here as an inspector only. No one around but, lightly linked into nearby cams, he observed a technician now approaching down the entrance tunnel. Time now, he felt, to begin isolating this plane, to begin cutting it off from surrounding Govnet. Yet penetrating the plane was proving difficult, as if it was already partially isolated. Perhaps the spaceport authority had done this to prevent penetrations similar to the one that brought down the other craft. Now the technician stepped into view and Saul concentrated on him, trying to read his features through the constantly flashing lights.

"Agent Green," he announced to the technician.

The man was shaven-headed, a scar running down from his forehead and over his right eye, which was a double-pupil engraft. He looked like he should be clad in an enforcer uniform rather than the orange tech overall he was wearing. He showed little reaction to Saul's odd appearance. Perhaps seeing his own face in the mirror over many years had inured him to such sights.

"You're the inspector," he said.

"I certainly am," Saul rasped. "And I want to start here with these." He gestured towards the suits, meanwhile searching local software for explanations of the suiting-up protocols, and how the suits worked. "Myself and my assistant are going to suit up."

The man merely shrugged—*you're the boss*—and said nothing, which annoyed Saul because now he had just found a justification for why he, as an inspector, wanted to don a suit. The suits possessed sophisticated comware that linked into the plane's computer. He therefore intended to check this facet of the system for possible sabotage.

"If you don't mind," he suggested, gesturing to the entry tunnel. The man shrugged again, looking slightly bored, then returned up the tunnel and out of sight.

"Copy me," he said to Hannah as he stepped towards the rail of suits.

First they stripped off, then donned padded undersuits. Skin-stick sanitary devices went on next, and Hannah discovered it was fortunate that her pubis was hairless. Next the integral trousers and boots, with the urine pack on one hip and a power pack at the other. Nothing provided for storing shit—the suits were made for only short-term use. The trousers possessed expansion and contraction points that automatically adjusted. The tops next, sealing at the waist, numerous electrical and plumbing connections made there; gloves with wrist seals hung at the belt. The helmets were tight against the skull, with bowl visors that slid round from the side. He twisted his visor round for a moment, clicked a control at his wrist, and when a series of computer menus lit up on display he pushed the visor aside. They both next took up packs containing belly airpacks and other peripherals. The suits were not bulky at all, rather like motorbike leathers, so moving around in them was easy. They were ready.

"Okay." He led the way up the entrance tunnel, where the technician waited for them, leaning against the wall.

Saul was still having trouble worming his way inside the computers of the space plane, then abruptly everything collapsed and he could see clearly inside. No one at home, which made things a damned sight easier. Checking systems he saw that, but for the disconnection of a few umbilicals, the plane stood ready for launch. The technician waved them ahead of him to a ladder leading up to the airlock situated in the belly of the plane, and they proceeded through the airlock and up into the rear of the passenger compartment. Saul then experienced a moment of complete confusion when the images in his mind did not match up properly to what he now saw.

Too late.

A cold barrel was pressed against the back of his neck, and two men clad in white spacesuits grabbed his arms and dragged him forward. Two more grabbed Hannah, and just too many guns were aimed at them for him to do anything to resist. All of those occupying the plane were armed with assault rifles or other military hardware.

"Welcome aboard," said Malden.

10

WILLINGLY DON YOUR CHAINS

If you forcibly deprive someone of that airy concept called freedom, he will resent you and, given the chance, he will fight to regain it. Better, as governments all across the world discovered long ago, to have people willingly give up their freedoms, to actually collude in the process; then, before they realize their mistake, their chains are adamantine. Make the process slow enough to sit below immediate perception and they will grow accustomed to their enslavement; they even might not realize they are wearing any chains at all. By so slowly depriving people of what were only really considered inalienable rights during a brief period in human history, and in only a few countries, did the Committee come to power. But how did it get the people to willingly forgo all control over their own destinies? Simple, really: it used the formula proven by the governments that were its original components. First make the people afraid…

ANTARES BASE

As it strode away from the airlock, Var struggled against the shepherd's grip, which wasn't as secure as it should have been. The burst of ceramic ammunition she had fired into it had damaged the robot, some of its tentacles left merely as stubs waving in the thin air, whilst others just hung slack. With her free left hand, she reached into her hip pouch and took out one side arm, aimed and pulled the trigger, firing up inside the tick-shaped body, towards the gaps in its armour. The robot shuddered, things shorting out inside it, and molten metal and fragments of plastic ammo rained down on her. Then the stub end of a tentacle smacked hard against her forearm, right where she'd had her ID implant removed, and the gun spun away. The shepherd adjusted its grip, tossing her about like a fish in a net. She felt a rib crack, but now her right arm was free. Again into the hip pouch, this time her hand closing on the hydraulic shears. She brought them out, closed them over one snake of ribbed metal and set their little hydraulic pump running. The shears sliced with ease through the tentacle and it dropped away, dead. Another tentacle, the shears closing on it, then she fell free.

She bounced once, twice, in a cloud of dust, the shepherd already moving two or three lengthy strides away from her before it came to an unsteady halt and began to turn round. Up on her feet in an instant, and running, she saw a figure step out through the airlock.

This could be one of Ricard's men—there was no guarantee all of them were in Hex Three, and in fact it seemed likely the bulk of them were standing guard over the technical staff attached to the base. The figure held up a hand, something clutched in it, and waved her down with the other hand. Instantly recognizing what he held, she dropped. He threw, and the cylindrical package arced over her head.

Light flared and something whoomphed. A blast picked her up and tumbled her forward. One gleaming shepherd leg cartwheeled past her in Martian air suddenly thick with dust. Then the figure was helping her up and she recognized Lopomac's pudgy face, his skin webbed with ruptured capillaries, yet to heal since the decompression he had survived three months ago. Pausing only to snatch up the rifle she had dropped, he pulled her towards the airlock and inside.

"You saw Le Blanc's little speech?" Var asked, after she removed her EA suit helmet in the suiting antechamber.

"No," Lopomac replied, resting the assault rifle across his shoulder. "We were too busy watching you fucking over Hex Three."

Carol was waiting here, Kaskan too, his eyes reddened. All three were watching Var with something approaching hunger. Carol and Kaskan wore EA suits too, as if all three had been readying themselves to come out to her, before Lopomac destroyed the shepherd and got her back inside. Should they go out again? She didn't know. She needed to assess the situation here first.

"We've been abandoned," she said, probing her cracked rib. "The Committee has left us out here to die, though apparently someone back there convinced Ricard that a reduced base staff can survive the fifteen or twenty years, until they build another Traveller to send out here." She decided not to mention Messina's *Alexander*—it didn't seem relevant.

"Another Traveller?" Lopomac echoed, puzzled.

"All the others have gone through the Argus bubblemetal plants." She then focused on Kaskan. "Kaskan, I'm sorry…"

"No need." He waved a hand in irritation, almost dismissively. "I saw what that shepherd grabbed from the crawler before Ricard turned it round."

Her throat tight, Var turned to the other two. "What's the situation here? Ricard captured Miska, and I'd have thought he would have got you two as well."

"Kaskan saw Ricard and two of his enforcers dragging Miska off towards Hex Three, and told us," said Lopomac, something odd in his expression.

"Ricard seemed to have forgotten about the cams up on the roof, too," said Carol. "We were watching when you rounded Shankil's Butte with that shepherd almost on top of you just about when he sent us a summons. We decided we'd best not respond, and broke into the geology storeroom instead."

"Hence the seismic survey charge?" suggested Var.

"Lopomac's idea," Carol explained. "He decided we needed to first lose our ID implants, then cut the cam-system feed, and then arm ourselves."

Good, that meant Ricard would not be able to keep track of them, though he would know which airlock she had used, so they had to get out of here fast. Lucky for them it had been decided that Antares Base should not carry readerguns. "How many charges?" she asked, now heading towards the door, the others falling in behind her.

Carol grimaced and held up a single cylindrical charge, its detonator and detachable remote control already in place. Really, it surprised Var that any of these things had been available, since they'd stopped doing seismic mapping on Mars over five years ago.

"Speaking of which"—Lopomac nodded towards the assault rifle—"you got any ammo for this?"

Var reached into her hip pouch, took out the remaining clip and examined it. "Plastic only, I'm afraid."

She tossed it to him. He caught it negligently, held it up and frowned at it. Then, showing none of Var's hesitation, he removed the empty clip and replaced it with the new one, setting the rifle over to single shots. Var meanwhile opened the door from the suiting antechamber and stepped out into the corridor.

"The situation is this," Lopomac said, as he followed her out. "Ricard has two enforcers guarding Hydroponics. He's got four in the community room, along with that shit Silberman—where all staff were summoned just ten minutes ago."

"They'll have seen Le Blanc's speech," said Var.

"Not much help while they're under guard."

"Miska?" She halted at the end of the corridor, wondering where it would be best to head now.

They seemed reluctant to say anything for a moment, then it was Lopomac who spoke. "We didn't break out those charges just because Ricard summoned us, nor because he'd got a shepherd up and running." He paused, not looking at her, but frowning down at the assault rifle he held. "On the way to Hex Three, Ricard stopped off at an airlock—the outer door is still open because someone is lying across the threshold." He looked up. "We guessed that someone isn't Ricard or one of his men."

Var felt the tight ball of doubt in her gut expand and dissipate through her limbs, to leave her with a colder and more pragmatic clarity. If there had been any doubt that Ricard intended to carry through his orders, it had just been dispelled. Her own ruthlessness had now been utterly justified.

"Very well," she said succinctly. "Silberman is the only exec Ricard has left. I killed the other four. I also killed four or possibly more of his enforcers over at Hex Three." She awaited some response to that, but only Kaskan reacted.

"Good," he said, "but maybe not good enough."

She nodded. "Ricard still has Silberman and the six you mentioned in the community room and Hydroponics, plus himself and two others still over in Hex Three. We have to deal with them or we die—if not very soon then later, when he truly fucks things up here."

"They're all armed. Ricard controls the reactor and we can't afford to use that seismic charge or get into a fire fight in Hydroponics," Lopomac pointed out, adding, "Even with plastic ammo. Then there's that." He pointed to one of the nearby metre-square windows, providing a view across to where she had entered, and then out towards Hex Three. The dust was settling and, coated with it, the remains of the shepherd looked like some strange Martian cactus. However, just beyond it, the second shepherd was striding into view.

Var reached into her hip pouch to take out the remaining side arm, then just stared at it. Ruthless she might be, but simply not ruthless enough.

Kaskan was right: even with potentially a hundred and fifty people against them, Ricard's men still held the upper hand. Four or five assault rifles—and she guaranteed that Ricard still had some ceramic ammo available—could easily turn that number of people into mincemeat. But even if the enforcers presently in the Community Room were somehow driven out, they could simply withdraw to an airlock antechamber like the one she and her friends had just departed—easily defended—then head out of the main base. No one would follow, not with assault rifles trained on the exit, and certainly not at risk of being snatched by a shepherd.

Thereafter, Ricard controlled the reactor, which meant, essentially, that he could shut down all systems. Eventually the air would turn foul and he could dictate whatever terms he chose. She suspected he would just wait until there was no need to turn those systems back on again. He was stupid enough.

"We need to take off the head. We need to get Ricard," she decided.

"We can't get to him through Wing Five," said Lopomac. "We'd need to repair the window and repressurize before we could open either of the bulkhead doors, and that would mean going outside just to get to that section."

"Maybe we can make it to Hex Three without that shepherd getting to us first," she suggested weakly.

"Maybe," said Lopomac, "though the closest we can get to it without actually going outside is the Hydroponics hex, where Ricard has two enforcers. If I didn't know him to be so stupid, I'd reckon he was covering that approach, too."

"I can kill the two in Hydroponics," said Kaskan.

"But how do we do that without risking the glass being smashed, and wiping out any chance we have of surviving here?" Var asked.

"I'll give the plants too much of a good thing."

EARTH

Rows of seats ran down the middle of the passenger compartment, while either side was walled with aluminium cupboards. A large video screen to the fore provided a display from the cockpit, almost as if a hole had been cut through the craft's exterior to show a carbocrete runway curving away to the right. Flexi-displays were hooked on to the back of each seat, facing the passengers behind. They were of the kind that could be removed, bent into a curve, and lodged inside space helmets to give a 3D effect. Inset into the arms of each seat, ahead of the sockets for oxygen hoses, were VR half-gloves for calling up any chosen view or entertainment.

The two soldiers dragged Saul to one of the front-row seats and manhandled him down into it, then shoved Hannah into the seat just beside him. She glanced to one side, noting the technician now stripping off his overalls and donning a spacesuit like his fellows. Two guards remained standing over her and Saul, with squat, ugly machine pistols trained on them.

"Can you think of any reason why I should not kill you immediately?" Malden demanded, stepping into the space before them and leaning back against the bulkhead.

"You want to know who and what I am, and why I am here," Saul instantly replied.

"That's true, but you nearly fucked up this entire mission."

Saul pressed the heel of one hand between his eyes. Before he could reply, Hannah said, "How? We didn't even know about this mission."

Malden's gaze strayed towards her. "You led the Inspectorate straight to Embarkation, and now we've got more on the way. Luckily I've given them other distractions."

"The space plane?" said Saul.

Malden's gaze swung back to him. "A distraction to facilitate our boarding this space plane, but I used the aeros to remove what I thought was a threat to us."

"You thought I worked for the Inspectorate."

"What was I to think? Inspectorate enforcers were heading here; you were ahead of them. It was only after I hit them that I realized they were after *you*, upon discovering your sloppy penetration of their security here. Did you deliberately follow me?"

"No. Pure coincidence—or more likely our aims are the same."

Malden then just stared at Saul, almost statue-like, his eyes a deep, dark red and with fractured blood vessels webbing his face, and Hannah realized that Saul's prediction was on the button. Malden was dying, and it seemed likely he knew it. Perhaps this was the real reason he had not killed them. Maybe he hoped she could do something to help him to change that verdict or, if not, maybe he hoped Saul might somehow replace him.

"So why are you here?" Saul asked.

"I intend to take Argus and the Argus Network out of Committee hands."

Saul tilted his head, with a flash of amusement. "Really?"

"Really."

"That's…interesting."

"Why are *you* here?" Malden countered.

"I'm here to take Argus and the Argus Network out of Committee hands."

Malden gazed at him blankly for a moment, then stepped closer, studying Saul more intently.

"It's true," Hannah interjected. "You're not the only one who doesn't care for our rulers."

"Yet, despite your dislike, you worked for them willingly enough," Malden commented.

"That's not fair."

"Little is fair, in this world." He returned his attention to Saul and continued, "Do you know they never decommissioned the Traveller VI engine on the Argus asteroid? They kept it at first because they were going to reposition out at the Lagrange point between Earth and the Moon, then as a safety protocol. They've kept that engine fuelled and workable for decades just in case the asteroid needed to be used against anything bigger coming in out of the Oort cloud."

"Yes, I do know," Saul replied. "But why does it interest you so?"

"I'll use it to drop the asteroid on Brussels," said Malden. "The impact should depopulate much of Europe and take out most of the Committee and nearly forty per cent of the Executive." He paused. "Centralized world government is never ever a good idea."

Hannah sat quietly chewing that over. Saul had previously stated his intention of seizing control of Argus and the satellite network, and now that she looked at it in the light of Malden's statement, it didn't seem enough. Had Saul intended to do something similar? Because, once he had taken control up there, the question remained: what next?

"That seems…drastic," said Saul.

"You disagree?"

"Let's say I have moral doubts," Saul hedged.

"Why?" Malden asked.

"Perhaps I'm not so careless of human life as you," Saul suggested. "Anyway, I'd have thought the power of the Argus Network would've appealed to you."

It was like seeing two big cats facing off in a world full of herbivores, but Hannah felt one of them was severely underestimating the potential of the other. Malden had been an intelligent and resourceful man, who was now running some serious hardware and software in his head. Saul had been a genius with an intelligence difficult to describe, let alone measure, and the additions inside his skull were of an order of magnitude more powerful than Malden's, or at least they would be when the organic interface had made sufficient connections.

"Of course, it does," Malden replied. "But Argus Station is not essential to that network. In fact, once I've seized control of the network and taken the Argus computers out of the equation, I can operate it from down on Earth."

Hannah seriously doubted that would improve the situation on Earth for anyone.

From outside came a series of clattering booms as umbilicals detached. Hannah glanced round to see two of the soldiers closing the airlock hatch, while others were returning to their seats to strap in. The erstwhile technician came across to them and pulled their straps into position, and from where they inserted in sockets down beside their hips, there came the click of locks closing. After he stepped over to Saul, Hannah reached down and tentatively tried to disengage her own strap. No joy. It seemed the locking mechanisms of the straps could be controlled via the plane's computers, so they wouldn't be going anywhere until Malden gave instructions to unlock.

The man then unwound hoses and multi-core electric leads from their suits to plug into sockets in the chair arms. She knew enough about space flight to know these were to control the pressure function in suit capillaries, so the G forces wouldn't knock them out.

"A lot of innocent people are going to die anyway," said Malden, as he stepped to one side, then took the seat alongside Hannah. "But the sacrifice is worth making just to cut off the government's head."

Hannah thought maybe it was time for her to make the comment that it was all very well for him to make such sacrifices, since he wouldn't be one of those dying, but she reconsidered. Very likely he would be one of those soonest dead.

With a lurch, the space plane set itself into motion and from outside came the sucking roar of turbines winding up to speed. The movement was undetectable on the screen for a moment, but then Hannah noticed a cam post sliding past them as the plane followed the curving route ahead. The curve then straightened out, and the plane climbed over a massive bridge with barriers running down either side. For half a minute they got a view across the spaceport to where columns of black smoke belched into the sky, then off the other side of the bridge, the plane turned to face a long runway spearing into the distance. It paused there, shuddering, as the racket from its turbines grew to a scream, then with an abrupt roar the seat punched her in the back as the craft shot forward. The acceleration just kept on climbing and climbing, and even at that point she could feel the G-function of the suit tightening it around her legs and the lower half of her body. Then the nose was up, and the same forces trying to shove both her and her seat through the floor.

She turned to see how Saul was taking this punishment, and saw blood trickling down the side of his face. He reached up with an arm seemingly made of lead to touch it, and observed blood on his fingers. How well could his new surgery stand up to this kind of treatment? He glanced at her questioningly, but she just shook her head. She didn't know.

Then the pressure was off and the plane banking. In front of them the screen divided, one view showing an anvil of cloud ahead and the other revealing the Minsk spaceport sliding by underneath. No sign now of the crash site below, which brought home to her the sheer scale both of the port itself and, by inference, of everything the two big cats here were up against. But soon that view was lost in cloud for a few minutes before the plane punched through into bright sunshine above an endless plain of white. Now the screen lost its division, as a display appeared along the bottom—Mach 3.2 & 20 min to SCRAM—and it began counting down.

"I don't quite know what to do with you," said Malden, and Hannah assumed he was addressing her until he leaned forward to look across her at Saul. "It seems you *do* have similar aims to my own."

That was a concession at least.

"What about me?" Hannah asked.

"You will help me." It was not a request. Under Malden's control, she saw herself in exactly the same position she had experienced under the Committee. "What software is he running?"

She met his gaze. "His own."

Malden returned his attention to Saul. "Hannah told me you were once

Alan Saul—one of their most brilliant researchers—until Smith used pain amplifiers and cerebral reprogramming to destroy your mind."

Saul shrugged. "Alan Saul is gone. I'm a two-year-old."

"Smith runs security aboard the Argus Station."

"I know."

Malden just stared for a long moment, obviously making his calculations. "Argus Station is heavily firewalled with numerous cut-offs between it and Govnet. Most importantly it has a plain old-fashioned off switch to completely disconnect it from Govnet."

"The EM field they turn on to block solar radiation whenever there's a storm," Saul agreed.

"You know, it's been very difficult to obtain information from up there for some time...I tried accessing by satellite uplink but failed. Security is far too heavy and when I started trying to steal access codes, the EM field came on and cut the station system out of the circuit. Its own internal network is maintained by coded shortwave radio when the EM field is off, and line-of-sight laser and hardwire when it's on."

"Hence you going there with soldiers?"

"I need to get inside the station, to be effective. I need to disconnect the transformers supplying the EM field to be sure I won't be cut out."

"I myself intended just to sneak aboard," said Saul.

Malden shook his head as if listening to the plans of a child. "Then, the moment you started taking over, all Smith would have needed to do was switch on the EM field, cutting you out of the circuit, then hunt you down."

"I'm sure I would have found a way round that," Saul replied huffily.

Despite Saul's obvious capabilities, Malden gave a superior smile now. Hannah realized he was thinking like a revolutionary, locked in that groove where it seemed the only solution to anything must involve guns. Perhaps some part of him assumed that taking over a space station must require drama. Obviously Saul wasn't averse to guns himself, but Hannah realized that, by having an optic plug installed in his head, he'd negated the need for troops. His huffy response to Malden was just a pose, and he was way ahead of the man.

"I can either leave you aboard this plane," Malden said, "in which case it's certain station security will come looking for you—or you can come in with us."

"That a good idea?" asked Scarface.

Malden glanced at him. "He knows the situation." He turned back to Saul, weighing him up. "You *do* understand the situation?"

"If you leave me aboard the plane, Smith gets me and I'm dead. And even if I try to betray you to Smith, I'm still not going to be his best buddy. I'll still end up chewing a bullet."

"Our objectives are essentially the same, too," Malden said. "And by working together now—and in the future—we can be a lot more effective."

"Agreed."

As Malden returned his attention to Hannah, she felt the locks on her straps disengage.

"You will be accompanying us, too," he told her. "I'm going to be needing you later."

He wanted to live. Did he also visualize building an army of cyborgs like himself and Saul to rout the remains of the totalitarian state down below, after the asteroid had done its work? Until he replaced that state with one of his own, nearly indistinguishable?

The countdown on the screen slowly clicked its way down towards zero. At two minutes, the space plane shuddered, and shortly afterwards a great hollow roar grew in volume and Hannah knew it must now be opening its scramjet intakes. Next came a mutter, like some steel giant grumping to itself, then a crash followed by massive acceleration. That same steel giant next came and put his foot on her chest, then pressed his weight on that foot. Her vision seemed to tunnel, and she could only just see the frame newly opened on the screen, showing the rear view of a great ribbed flame like a scorpion's tail whipping out behind; below it the maps of Earth were rapidly shrinking.

"They'll know you're coming," Saul said tightly, his voice hoarse.

Hannah looked across at him, saw more blood running from his scalp, and watched as his eyes folded up into his head, exposing their whites. Despite wearing the same sort of suit as she did, he was blacking out, but she could do nothing for him just then…or perhaps ever.

***

At first the whole structure seemed like a toy, and only by seeing another space plane, like the one they were aboard, clinging to one of the massive docking pillars stabbing out into space, like an iron redwood growing from the station rim, could he recalculate the scale. An object moving across the outer surface of the station wheel, which he had at first taken to be someone in a spacesuit, he now realized must be some sort of vehicle or robot the size of a bulldozer.

A big technical control centre had been built on what might be described as the top of the asteroid, which sat at the centre of a three-quarter ring five kilometres in diameter and over a kilometre wide and deep. Three cylinder worlds held this ring in position, each of them a kilometre wide and nearly two kilometres in length, spaced at three quarters like spokes, their near ends connected to the asteroid itself, whilst at the fourth quarter, projecting from the rocky surface directly towards the break in the ring, sat the massive Mars Traveller engine.

Two further spokes were positioned evenly in the two gaps between the three cylinders. These were the two ore transit tubes that ran from the asteroid's surface to connect with the smelting-plant docks located in the rim. Extending out from the plant docks, on massive cables, were the smelting plants themselves, positioned about a kilometre out from the station—these looked something like giant combustion engines surrounded by a spider-web of cables and further scaffolding to support the foil parasols of folded or un-folded sun mirrors, all again surrounded by vapour spilling from the processes conducted within.

Up close, Argus certainly did not look so neat as it did from the surface of Earth, and it now seemed much larger than the last government-approved images of it that he had viewed. The sections between the spokes, from the asteroid to the station rim, were infilled with lattice walls with numerous accommodation units and other features sandwiched between, all connected by tubeways through which ran wormish trains. The levels expanding outwards from the original wheel were not being built one at a time, so in some areas three or four "floors" of the station extended out into space, webbed throughout by structural members, with random chequer-square sheets of bubblemetal scattered across them. In fact there seemed no clear dividing line between where the station ended and space began.

"Keep your head still," Hannah instructed.

Scarface, whose real name was Braddock, had found him another helmet to replace the one he'd managed to fill with his blood, and then given Hannah a battlefield medical kit. Apparently each of these soldiers was carrying one.

Having stopped the bleeding, she was now using a stapling tool to put his scalp back together. Wound glue would only last if he didn't exert himself for a week or so, which seemed unlikely.

"How bad is it?" he asked.

"Very minor," she replied. "You know what head wounds are like."

Now she was spraying artificial skin over his scalp, and finally she turned his head round and concentrated the spray over his right temple. He just met her gaze and said nothing. That she was further concealing the nub of synthetic skin covering the teragate socket in his skull told him she had picked up some idea of his intentions.

He looked round as Malden towed himself in from the space plane's cockpit, gazed over to where one of the soldiers was throwing up in a sick bag, then focused his attention on Saul.

Saul had to admit that Malden seemed to know a great deal about how Argus Station operated. In the beginning, it had been Saul's intention to take control there in the same way he had taken control of that gene bank and then Inspectorate Headquarters London, by feeding Janus into the system and letting the AI do all the work. Now Janus resided inside his head, was actually part of him and, had he not used a bit of forethought, he would have possessed no way of physically linking into a computer system. But he had considered this, which was why that teragate optic plug resided under that nub of synthetic skin at his right temple. He could only assume that when Dr Bronstein had made his report to Malden, he had neglected to mention the details of the operation Saul had undergone. And Saul preferred not to enlighten him.

"You okay?" Malden asked.

Saul had managed not to throw up as they went zero gravity, and now nausea pills were dispelling the rest of the sickness. Obviously they weren't working so well for others aboard, including Hannah, who looked decidedly ill.

"I'm good," he lied, for really his head felt as if someone had been sandpapering the inside of his skull, and though extended processing within lay available to him, he felt almost frightened to use it. "So what's the plan? They have to realize this is no regular flight by now."

Malden nodded. "They've denied us docking and demanded to know who we are, and what we want. I insisted we're just the expected flight, but they've checked with Minsk and know the assigned crew isn't aboard, and that this plane took off without permission." He shrugged. "They've also just put the

EM shield up, but that could be because of the solar wind."

"And?"

"We don't use the dock." Malden moved over to his seat and strapped him-self in. Immediately after that, text appeared along the bottom of the cabin screen: PREPARE FOR DECELERATION.

"Get strapped in, guys. This could be tricky," warned a voice over the inter-com—obviously the pilot.

Hannah pulled away from Saul and strapped herself in. He picked up the new helmet from his lap and clicked it down on its neck ring, before doing the same. A frisson of fear tightened his gut. If Malden wasn't going to dock this plane, that probably meant they were going for a space walk.

Spikes of flame stabbed in on either side of the screen view, jerking Saul forward against his straps. Then one constant flame erupted from the left, swinging the nose of the plane round, the momentum trying to throw him into Hannah. The station slid aside, then the plane came under massive de-celeration, this time thrusting him back down into his seat. Manoeuvring next, the nose swinging back rapidly and the station grown huge, filling the screen, one of its surface-mounted steering thrusters—an engine the size of a train carriage—became clearly visible, projecting at forty-five degrees from the station rim, then abruptly dropped away. A glimpse of Earth, and then starlit space. Main engine now; a double blast again slamming him backwards. Lines cut down through the forward view, cables and the belly of a big smelting plant slid above like an iron Zeppelin. Then the main engine came on yet again.

"Helmets!" Braddock shouted. "Suit-integrity check!" Why the hell did he want them to do that, whilst still inside the plane? Then Saul realized the docking was going to be violent. He closed across his visor and, using the small control panel on his left forearm, called up the integrity check in the liquid-crystal laminate in his visor. He then turned to Hannah to instruct her on what she must do, but she was already busy working her own panel. Good for him to be reminded that the technology of her spacesuit was child's play to someone like her.

Then they hit.

11

PLAIN PLANES

In the early years, rocket scientists took elements of the NASA space shuttle, and the privately developed craft then being used by the optimistically named Virgin Galactic, and amalgamated them to create their early two-stage shuttle. This consisted of the hydrogen booster or carrier section which, after throwing the shuttle up into space, was then capable of coming down to land by itself. Even then, with engines becoming steadily more powerful, the engineers realized how overcomplicated and prone to problems was this system. They needed to thoroughly rework the technology, discarding much of what had gone before, and this they did after Airbus successfully tested its first passenger scramjet. Perhaps, under a different regime, the enforced amalgamation of the two projects would never have happened or the huge funding required would not have been available. It could also be argued that without the bureaucratic screw-ups and political oversight of the science, it would have happened faster. However, despite many difficulties and many disastrous crashes, the first Earth-to-orbit space plane made its inaugural flight during the second half of the twenty-first century.

A crackling sound first, as of something heavy falling through a forest of sticks. The screen abruptly filled with a swirl of fire and debris, then their space plane began to shudder. Only when the flame cleared a little could they see a framework ceiling sliding over above, its spaces only partially filled with bubblemetal panels, and a similarly constructed floor appearing below. They were punching their way through into the side of one of the partially constructed rim floors of the space station. The shudders continued, interspersed with an occasional gut-wrenching crash. The roar of the engine cut out, and flame wisped away on the screen ahead to reveal the tangled ruin of bubblemetal beams rimming the tunnel they had cut through. Then a further few crashes as the plane thumped at last to a halt, and they were in zero gravity again.

"Straps and belly-packs," Braddock called, using the PA system of his suit as he unfastened and propelled himself from his seat.

Saul pressed down the buttons detaching his own straps, glad to see that Malden had left the locks off, then reached down and pulled out the pack containing his oxygen supply and CO_2 scrubber from under the seat.

"Hannah," he said over com, but just got a fizzing and no response from her. The EM shield of the station was obviously screwing radio communication, even over such a short distance.

A flat aluminium box twenty centimetres thick and about a quarter of a metre square, the belly-pack clicked straight into the suit, with bayonet fittings on its back. At once the suit's software began running diagnostics, displayed in the visor. Next all he had to do was unplug his suit's air-hose from the chair arm and insert it into its socket in the side of the box, and after a moment the display indicated its readiness—confirming he had ten hours of air. Then he turned to where two of Malden's troops were opening the inner hatch of the airlock.

Those two went through first, dragging a couple of large cylindrical objects with them. Immediately after them, another four went through, then another four—each set of four attaching their belts to a combined safety- and optic-link line, then cramming themselves into the airlock. Malden beckoned Saul and Hannah to follow himself and Braddock, and they comprised the next four through, the line connecting them all and providing a communications link, but only between the four of them.

As the pressure in the airlock dropped to zero, their suits expanded slightly, stiffened and carried out further auto-diagnostics. Braddock exited first, the line between him and Hannah drawing taut until she followed. Saul pushed out next, with Malden behind—a cautious positioning on the line that reminded Saul that he was not fully trusted. Once outside, he could see how the massive length of the space plane was jammed into a network of distorted or snapped bubblemetal beams. Towards its rear, about the rocket-motor output, something like heat haze shimmered, but everything else stood out in sharp-edged clarity—with no atmosphere to distort the view.

Ahead, the two other groups of four were already moving off, widely spaced, and beyond them he saw how the first pair of soldiers had joined together those two cylindrical objects to create a single cylinder about the size of a coffin. He had assumed they would all be attached to the same line, for safety's sake, but then understood why not. If they were fired upon out here, it wouldn't be a good idea for them all to be bunched together.

"Let's go," said Malden, his voice now sounding clear through the optic connection.

Braddock used a reaction jet, fired from his forearm, snapping the line taut and towing them after the others. Glancing back, Saul saw the next four on their way out, but then returned his focus to their immediate surroundings.

They followed the path the space plane had already bashed through the surrounding structure, Braddock occasionally altering their course with his reaction jet or by thumping a foot or hand against some piece of twisted wreckage. Open space lay ahead, strewn with stars, then became visible above, too, through gaps in the bubblemetal plating. Reaching the point where the plane had punched into the structure, the first soldiers propelled themselves downwards and out of sight. Once Saul's group reached the same edge, where supporting beams were sparse, they floated out over a long drop to the original outer hull of the station, which extended into the distance like a massive highway. Just visible over the rim, to the left, jutted the top of the technical-control centre.

Braddock slowed them with the jet, then guided them down after the others.

"Malden," Saul enquired, "are we all using the same airlock?"

"We're not using a station airlock."

"What do you mean?"

"You'll see."

Those who had already reached the main hull of the space station below began to walk out across it. Only upon seeing this did Saul check stored data on his spacesuit to find one item called "gecko boots."

"Boots," Braddock informed them as they reached the hull.

"Hannah, you'll find—" Saul began, but she broke in.

"I know." She stepped down onto the hull, and followed Braddock as if walking through tar.

Some distance ahead, cables extended out to one of the two smelting plants. They now headed towards these, circumventing the huge convex glass of a sun-catcher—for directing the sun's rays inside—with the tilted monolith of a steering thruster lying to their right. Soon they reached the edge of the smelting-plant dock, and Saul peered down to where massive cables terminated, then up towards one of the big smelting plants perched like a steel rose atop a tall steel stem, around which craft buzzed like feeding bees. They descended, pausing only momentarily on a huge docking clamp to peer down into the seemingly bottomless well of an ore-transit tube leading down to the surface of the asteroid itself. Finally reaching the shadowy bottom of the dock, they moved out across it just as a big skeletal ore-carrier rose out of the transit tube only a hundred metres away from them, its hundred-tonne body sliding upwards in utter silence, massive guide wheels running on the cable. Now, directly ahead of Saul, the first two soldiers turned the cylinder upright and began fixing it to the hull.

"What is that thing?" he asked.

"Vacuum warfare penetration lock," Malden replied. "Built by the Chinese about eighty years ago. The Committee doesn't bother with such stuff now, as they have no opponents up here whose space stations or satellites they might want to penetrate."

The forward eight held back, squatting down on the hull, heads bowed, whilst the two who had positioned the cylinder retreated as quickly as they could.

"Shield your eyes," Hannah warned, before he could warn her.

Arc light flared bright around the base of the cylinder. He caught only one glimpse of it but enough to leave hard afterimages in his eyes, which reminded him of those migraine lights he had been experiencing too much lately. After a while the glare faded, and when he looked again the cylinder had sunk half of its length into the hull. Molten metal spat out all around it and snowed away into space, radiating white and red at first, then turning into gleaming confetti. On the cylinder's surface, rows of spiked treads, traversing its length, propelled it downwards. When only half a metre of it still stood above the surface, it jerked up again a few centimetres as gas erupted about it, steaming away into vacuum. Then it sank again, with green foam bubbling around its circumference, lumps drifting away like spindrift until enough had hardened in place to block escaping air. After a moment one of the soldiers walked over and opened the hatch located on the outer end.

"Braddock." Malden beckoned.

Braddock nodded, detached himself from the line and strode ahead. Saul watched as the man went head-first down into the lock, the hatch closing behind him. After some delay, the soldier on the surface opened the hatch again and the next one went down. The procedure was surprisingly quick, and it seemed no time at all before Saul was cramming himself down inside that uncomfortable thing, to drag himself through into the side of a wide pipe lit by chemical lights that the soldiers had stuck against the walls.

Five of them were now gathered to one side of the airlock, facing along the pipe in the same direction, whilst another three stood on the other side facing the opposite way, towards where the pipe terminated against a glass wall through which could be seen a vast chamber filled with the massive engine and cable drum used for winding in the smelting plant. It struck Saul as a very dangerous position to be in, there being no cover at all, which was perhaps why the air soon filled with a constant shriek as Braddock and two others hurriedly cut their way through the far wall using a diamond saw, a glittering cloud of metal swarf etching strange even patterns in the air about them, formed into swirls by the electrical activity of both the saw and the hardware of their suits. While he watched, the saw abruptly shut down and Braddock inserted a short, polished pry bar to lever out a wall plate. This he nudged away, and it began floating up slowly to settle against the curve of the pipe directly above him.

Hannah came through next, shortly followed by Malden.

"No firing unless they're armed," Malden said, using the PA speaker of his suit.

That seemed very generous of him, but in reality he wanted to delay alerting station security to their presence for as long as possible. People might see them and still not know they were intruders.

Soon all the troops were safely in the pipe, and again Braddock led the way, hauling himself through the new hole in the wall. When Saul's turn came he paused on the other side to study an enormous cavity that stretched in every direction, and recognized it as a floor of the station yet to be walled out. Whilst one of the soldiers started up the saw again, cutting through another plate, Malden pointed back at the wall they'd just passed through.

"Do you see?" he asked.

Braddock had carefully positioned the hole he had cut, for it emerged through a section of plain wall. Elsewhere numerous ducts cut across, shielded wires branching off to form large squared-off spirals, with some sort of laminate enclosed in clear plastic running round the gaps between.

"For the EM field," Saul suggested.

One of the biggest problems with living in space had always been cosmic rays and the dangerous bursts of radiation from the sun, which the Earth's magnetic field protected people from down on the surface. With the advent of cheap and plentiful energy from fusion combined with the nearly hundred-year-old invention of room-temperature superconductors, it had become possible to build and run magnetic shielding for this station. It was, however, a very heavy energy user and interfered with local electronics, which needed to be hardened to withstand it, so was only initiated at moments of greatest threat. But even now, the results still weren't in on its effectiveness. Certainly people working up here would be much safer than those who had first ventured into space two centuries ago, but how much safer was a moot point.

"A feed from the fusion reactor runs through the transformers and waveform modulators to reach these," Malden explained. "We just need to cut that link."

Saul didn't know why the other man felt the need to explain.

"Do you feel it?" Malden asked.

"Yes," he replied.

Of course he felt it. It was as if someone had turned on an AC transformer in his head to create a vibration he could only describe as hot tinnitus. He was grateful when the next hole had been cut through and they dropped gently into an internal corridor, though the shielding in its walls merely muffled the effect to a bearable drone.

He had seen numerous pictures of the interior of the Argus Station during Govnet broadcasts, and these had always shown an aseptic high-tech environment populated by technicians clad in clean grey and white, with reassuring Inspectorate execs clad in futuristic-looking suits overseeing them, and just a few enforcers patrolling the gleaming facilities. However, the reality was nothing like advertised. Scraped, dented and dirty walls enclosed the corridor, and scattered along it were piles of equipment, crates and large plastic water barrels. Oval doors were ranged along one wall, most of them closed but some opening onto rooms packed with similar rubbish.

"Go to station air," said Braddock, pushing aside his visor.

Saul undid his visor, then wished he hadn't. The place stank like boiled cabbage and some astringent chemical, all underlain by something like body odour. As they set out in a slow loping walk, he noted an open crate filled with small cardboard boxes, to which clung a wash of rust-coloured water, and from this arose the smell of putrid meat.

"Nice," Hannah noted, then stopped to peer at a cockroach moving in slow bounds across the corridor floor like some huge somnolent flea.

"Looks like a dumping ground," observed Malden. "Let's hope there's not too many people here."

No sooner had he said it than one of the oval doors ahead opened and a woman clad in filthy overalls and towing an arc welder pushed her way through, welding smoke billowing out all around her. She glanced towards them and paused, then briefly bowed her head and hurried further up the corridor, to disappear into the next room along. The advantage for them, right then, given the society they lived in, was that such people kept their heads down, averse to asking questions.

"It's about a hundred metres further down to get to the transformers," announced Braddock, checking the display on a palmtop. "They're no longer near the surface."

So even Malden had not possessed up-to-date knowledge of the station, Saul realized. It must have grown massively. He tried linking into the station network, but as before, the modem in his head just received static. Having glanced into the room the female welder had just exited, and having continued checking all around him since entering the place, he'd observed no facilities for computer access, so must stick with Malden until he came across something he could use.

"How do you shut down the transformers?" he asked. "Explosives?"

"We just disconnect them from their power supply—no need to blow anything up."

Malden surprised him with that, but then he guessed that, once the man assumed control here, he wanted to be sure not to get fried, should solar activity ramp up. Saul wondered how long after assuming control it would take Malden to achieve his goal, then depart. Certainly he would need to make it impossible for anyone to shut down the Traveller engine, or in any other way divert the asteroid's course down to the surface. Maybe it would be necessary for him to access readerguns here and depopulate the whole place first.

The droning inside Saul's head grew yet more irritating and crackly as they finally reached the end of the incredibly long corridor. Next they entered a cageway penetrating down through numerous floors, before they traversed a short tubeway to a door that gave access on to a platform overlooking one side of a massive chamber, with steel steps leading down to the floor below. He could not help wondering what idiot had decided to install ordinary Earth-scale steps here.

At the centre of the great chamber, packed into a framework extending twenty metres on each side and rising from floor to ceiling, were what he presumed must be the transformers themselves, since these vaguely cuboid objects closely resembled antique wire and laminated-steel transformers. Supported by the quadrate scaffolding that filled the rest of the chamber, pan-pipes clusters of heavy ducts wove away from these transformers like some nightmare road junction, before finally disappearing through the walls. The entire area was strewn with cables connected to control boxes and access panels that seemed to be scattered at random. Fluorescent tubes attached to the scaffolding illuminated all of this, and the whole place stank of hot electronics. In Saul's head, the droning became merely a mumble underneath a nerve-shredding mosquito whine. He couldn't tell precisely how much of the sound lay inside his head or actually in the air around him, though Braddock nearly had to shout to issue his next order.

"You know the drill!" he said.

The soldiers separated into groups of four, taking different routes through the surrounding scaffolding towards the transformers. Malden, Braddock, Hannah and Saul himself descended the steps, or rather they launched themselves straight down to the floor and approached the transformers directly. As Malden led the way, Saul noticed a trickle of blood issuing from one of the man's ears. Obviously the hardware sitting in his skull rested there about as uncomfortably as that in Saul's own skull.

"This is it!" Malden yelled as they arrived below the massed transformers. He stepped over to a large console peppered with switches, plunger circuit-breakers, dials and buttons seemingly dating from the last millennium, but probably needed because the usual computer-control hardware and software would not be robust enough here. He began by clicking over a long line of twenty switches and the steady drone in the air stuttered, the mosquito whine in Saul's head wavering. Next Malden turned to the row of twenty plunger circuit-breakers, and as he shoved each one down, the dial above it dropped to zero, and the noise decreased in level each time. When the noise finally ceased, Saul felt hollowed out and slightly bewildered.

"It'll take about a minute for the charge to dissipate," Malden explained.

The fizzing from Saul's modem waned to nothingness, and he already began to *feel* the computer network establishing itself around him; radio and microwave channels beginning to open up. Malden was now checking the positioning of all his soldiers throughout the chamber, so Saul launched his own penetration of the network, began putting all of himself online. It opened up around him a multidimensional reality into which he could slot himself. He began tracking and interpreting the information, starting to feel the shape of the codes and their purpose, and quickly managed to seize an updated schematic of the entire space station. Then Malden was in there with him doing precisely the same: becoming a node within that network and extruding informational tentacles. Saul glanced towards him, but Malden still wasn't even looking at him; in fact seemed unaware of any other presence in the network.

With more of the network opening to him, other links began to open, too, and one piece of traffic in particular called for Saul's attention. He remained wary of it until he recognized it as something instituted by Janus before their integration: the results of the search for his sister. Something tightened inside him and he wanted to inspect this data at once, but time ran out. Suddenly, looming on a horizon of pure information, there appeared a great black shape like a clenched fist, or a thundercloud expanding. It was the comlife that had been hounding him from the first moment he had opened his mind to the net.

"Malden," he conveyed a warning, in some manner beyond normal speech.

Malden sensed him at once, at last focusing on him within that virtual world. In the real world he turned and raised his machine pistol, aiming it straight at Saul's face.

"Withdraw," he instructed brusquely, "or die."

Saul hesitated for just a moment, and Malden shifted his aim slightly, firing a burst just past him, ricochets zinging around behind. Saul began pulling himself out, shutting down his connection, but he kept his mind working at its optimum—all of his mind.

"There's something else here," he declared. "Comlife."

"Withdraw," Malden repeated,

Saul pulled out completely, and Malden lowered his weapon.

"Reality wins every time," he said, and smiled.

Yes, it did, and in his enhanced state Saul saw the reality here with a painful clarity. The station schematic in his head revealed massive reconstruction inside, huge additions outside, but specifically it showed all points of access to this particular place. They would use low-velocity, soft-plastic slugs capable of penetrating spacesuits and human flesh, but less likely to damage the equipment located in here. A maintenance tunnel lay below those ridiculous steps, and that was one access point they wouldn't be using. For why use such a narrow approach when those above it enabled a much wider field of fire? Already every soldier present here would have been located precisely by the monitoring system.

He stepped back beside Hannah and tightened a hand around her upper arm, leaning in close. "Get ready to run," he urged her.

Braddock was gazing at them suspiciously, swinging his machine pistol back towards them. But soon enough he would find other distractions.

"Too easy," Saul remarked to the soldier. "They were ready for us."

Malden turned. "They were lax. They were—"

All at once he seemed to lose the ability to speak, just mouthing words but nothing coming out. He slapped one hand to his face, digging in his fingers before letting it drop, then screamed loudly and began to slump. Keeping his machine pistol trained on them, Braddock moved towards Malden, as the man finally collapsed to his knees, his head bowed.

"Your revolution served the purpose of the people down below." Malden said in a voice not his own. "But it serves no purpose up here." His head snapped upright and he turned it towards Hannah and Saul. "But I'm so glad you brought me these two traitors to the State."

Weapons fire erupted, a stuttering mechanical sound like faulty diesel engines starting up. Numerous sources began laying down a withering fire. Up above, a figure flew backwards to slam into a scaffold pole, shattered bullets and fragments of his suit spraying out all around, and a mist of blood behind him. He grabbed the pole, trying to reorient himself, but the harsh slapping impact of bullets just continued, till eventually his grip slackened and he tumbled slowly away. The firing continued amid shouting transmitted over com. As Saul turned away, dragging Hannah after him, something exploded over to their right, where he glimpsed a splash of blood up one wall.

Braddock hurled himself aside as impacts tracked across the floor, throwing fragments of blue plastic in every direction. Their path terminated at Malden, who began to shudder convulsively as shots tracked up his back, the rounds shattering inside him but failing to penetrate all the way through. He vomited blood as the force of the shots threw him forward. Elsewhere someone began shrieking as he gyrated downwards, a bullet hole in his airpack acting like a jet motor. He slammed against the side of a transformer, next into the floor, then spun round and started to rise again. A short burst of fire tore his airpack apart, and most of his chest.

They were now under the steps, where Saul pulled open a circular hatch only half a metre in diameter and pushed Hannah down towards it. Bullets rattled against the stairway above, peppering more blue plastic through the air. Braddock, over to his left now, stepped out briefly and fired upwards, but the intensity of return fire forced him back under cover. He was shouting, the words resonating in Saul's ears, asking for a response but receiving none. Saul felt that if whoever had spoken through Malden's mouth really wanted them all dead, dead they would be by now. But the speaker wanted Hannah, and also wanted Saul.

They crawled through the maintenance tunnel as fast as they could. Firing echoed behind them, and he turned back to see Braddock entering the tunnel, shooting behind him from the cover of its mouth. No firing in return this time; none at all. Then out into a long low room lined with gas cylinders, illuminated by their helmet lights only.

"What happened to Malden?" Hannah asked breathlessly, but he could sense she had already guessed.

"The comlife got him."

"Got him?"

"Went straight into his skull and spoke through him, which it could do easily enough since it is comlife with a human component."

"The way he spoke…" she began, but didn't want to say out loud what she was thinking.

"You mean with Interrogator Smith's voice?"

She bowed her head. "We're dead, aren't we?"

"Either that or we may want to be," he replied.

Just then the EM came back on, whining in his head.

***

"Who is this Smith, then?" Braddock gazed at them intently.

Hannah sat herself upright in the confined space, and looked across at the man. Braddock was resting against one wall, with his machine pistol in his lap; he could turn it on them in an instant.

"He's the political director up here on Argus," said Hannah, a slight catch in her voice.

"I know that," Braddock snapped, now focusing his gaze on Saul. "But there's something else. How the hell did he do that to Malden?"

"Hannah?" Saul enquired, looking across at her for an answer.

She dipped her head and stared at the floor, trying to dispel her doom-laden thoughts so that she could restore her mind to its analytical best. She now looked up at Saul. "He was our political director, so he must have taken whatever he wanted of my research and applied it to himself—whether with government permission or not, I don't know." To Braddock she now continued, "He's the same type as Malden, but managed to outmanoeuvre Malden because he was well prepared, and because he's been running the hardware in his skull longer and knows better how to use it."

"What about him?" Braddock indicated Saul with a tilt of his chin.

What about him? Hannah wondered. Saul had obviously expected to come up here and snatch control of the station as easily as he had taken control of the cell complex, and if there had only been normal humans and computers for him to overcome, he would have had every chance of succeeding. But, first, Malden had stood in his way, and now a comlife poisonous spider lurked at the heart of things. And, just to add to their woes, station security officers were now searching for them, so this little hideaway would not remain safe for much longer. Could Saul triumph over such odds? Was he strong enough yet? Gazing at him, she had to wonder just what was going on behind those unreadable red eyes. She now spoke to try and boost her own confidence:

"The hardware and software inside his skull is far in advance of that used by both Malden and Smith—his intelligence, too," she explained. "He just hasn't had a chance to use it yet."

"What, my intelligence?" Saul joked.

Hannah did not respond to this attempt at humour. It was dry and disconnected anyway, since Saul was somewhere else, his gaze directed overhead and his face expressionless. It almost seemed as if an empty mannikin sat in his place.

"What do we do now?" she asked.

"I am considering our options," he replied.

"Perhaps if you could let us in?" she suggested.

His gaze dropped to focus briefly on her, then on Braddock.

"I am simply bringing more of myself online," he explained icily. "Even though I cannot connect to the local network, I can that way more accurately analyse the circumstances that brought us to our current position, and from there divine a solution."

His gaze drifted away from them as he continued speaking, till it almost seemed as if it wasn't actually him speaking—as if the real Saul was elsewhere and had delegated the tiresome task of turning thoughts into words to some subprogram of his mind.

"Obviously, Smith took an interest in the attack upon his old stomping ground of Inspectorate HQ London, so located Janus on Govnet, and through Janus located my bunker. His abilities are such that he could not have failed to locate Malden, once Malden had started operating as comlife. He did not *fail* to locate him. From his own words, Smith clearly allowed Malden to conduct his little revolution, possibly with Committee approval or possibly not…"

The ensuing pause was lengthy, his lips still moving according to some subroutine, then finally the voicebox re-engaging. "Smith was sensitive to anything involving the name Avram Coran, therefore must have tracked that identity back to reveal how I obtained it at Gene Bank…He's been on top of me and Malden right from the start, I think." Saul refocused on Hannah, his voice becoming marginally more human. "But I still wonder why he allowed Malden to get away with what he did down at Minsk. I suspect Smith's agenda might differ from the Committee's."

"Good to know how we got here," Braddock interjected, "but I'd rather now know how the hell we're going to get out."

"Smith has tight control of the station network, and will be watching out for me. If I try to penetrate it, he might be able to do to me what he did to Malden. I need to create a diversion and find another route in, if I am to kill him."

There it was, stated with cold precision: *kill him.*

"How, though?" Hannah asked.

"Robots," Saul replied succinctly, a statement of fact, his gaze again elsewhere.

"If you could explain?" Hannah suggested.

"Once the EM shield is on, all electromagnetic communications go down. The computer networks throughout Argus Station are maintained by physical wiring and line-of-sight laser. However, for the robots both those forms of connection will only be intermittent, since they are constantly on the move. They will be running on their own programs for the duration of shielding, and only updated every time they physically connect up, or connect by laser, or when the shields go down."

"Smith can't be in the robots," declared Hannah. "At least not fully. Maybe they possess stripped-down copies of his AI component within them, but there's not enough processing space for much more."

"I doubt he even bothers," Saul said.

"We need to find robots?" Braddock asked.

"We do."

"Readerguns are going to be a problem."

"Quite true, but not until we depart the rim and head inwards, to where they are concentrated. And I have no intention of going there just yet," he said decisively. "Come on, we've been here long enough."

They'd reached their current narrow place of concealment via an even narrower crawlway designed for some of the very robots Saul was talking about. He now headed for the exit leading to this, then paused.

"Solar activity must be high," he observed.

"What?" Hannah asked.

Saul continued, "I can see no other reason for Smith to keep the EM shield up and running, when it severely hampers his search for us." He glanced round. "Only hardwired cams and detection systems can be used, since most portable detection equipment won't work, and those searching will only be able to communicate with each other by using hardened consoles. As we have noticed, both consoles and the access points for them are few in this section of the station." He nodded as if confirming this to himself, and entered the crawlway.

Hannah followed him in, Braddock close behind her.

"Where are we going?" Hannah demanded as Saul abruptly halted in the crawlway.

"To find larger and more effective versions of this chap who is directly ahead of me," he replied.

"What's ahead of you?" asked Braddock.

Hannah wormed her way further, till she was pressing against Saul. She felt him go tense for a moment, then relax as if such physical proximity had first irritated him, then been discarded as irrelevant. Up beside him, she could get a close look at what he was talking about.

"Maintenance bot," she informed Braddock.

The robot was about the size of a badger, and indeed had the same body shape, but was fashioned of metal and provided with numerous pneumatic starfish feet rather than four legs. It had halted on detecting a blockage ahead of it—namely Saul. He reached out and grabbed the machine, turning it on to its side so he could inspect it. Directly underneath its front end was a connecting plug enabling it to socket into a data port and upload new instructions, should the normal radio option be closed. On the side facing up lay a single panel which Saul flipped open. Inside were various chip sockets, but obviously not what he wanted. As he turned the thing over, Hannah noted the glassy hemisphere of a laser com unit on its back, but that wasn't what he wanted either. Opening the panel on the other side, he revealed two coiled-up cables, one for recharging and the other an optic with a gigagate plug. Hannah well knew that all optic gate sockets were manufactured to take the smaller plugs.

"Plugging in?" she suggested.

He silently answered by peeling artificial skin from his temple, then slid his nail into the plug of synthetic skin underneath and levered it out, before uncoiling the optic and inserting it into the teragate socket in his own head. After a moment, he set the robot upright and sent it scuttling ahead, but not so fast it would risk pulling the cable from his head. Soon they were heading out into a wider area which seemed to be used as an oxygen store, judging by the cylinders clustered all around them. Saul stood, then picked up the robot and cradled it in his arms like a pet.

"What now?" Hannah asked, eyeing the machine.

"We need construction robots. Heavy robots."

"Why?"

"Because readerguns and machine pistols won't bring them down straight away and because, with the right programming, they can kill." He turned to look at Braddock. "Are you prepared to help us?" he asked.

Braddock gazed at him bitterly. "I'm out of alternatives."

"Good. Well, stay alert. You know what'll happen if they capture you."

Utterly logical, guaranteed to appeal to Braddock's sense of self-preservation, Hannah thought. Almost like following a formula.

Braddock nodded and, like a good soldier, checked the workings of his weapon before loading it with a fresh clip. Saul led them to the far end of the store where another robot had been bolted to the floor, its single function being to load the gas bottles stockpiled here onto a conveyor.

"This leads out to the edge of the station," explained Saul, pointing up the conveyor.

Abruptly, the loading robot opened out its single arm and clasped a four-fingered claw around one of the gas bottles. The conveyor started running for a second, then shut down.

"The fuck!" said Braddock, stepping back.

"It's under my control now," Saul told him. "Let's go."

He climbed onto the conveyor and, after some hesitation, Hannah climbed up behind him. The belt then advanced a short distance to let Braddock get on and, with the soldier in place, it started running again. Hannah understood that she and Braddock were only witnessing the surface activity, and that Saul must be running some complex programs in his head as he used the line-of-sight laser from the "badger" robot to similarly seize control of other machines in their immediate vicinity. Though this might well save them from capture and then inevitably torture and execution, she had to wonder what might come next. How important would Saul consider human life as he sank ever deeper into the *machine*?

12

WHO ARE THE SLAVES?

Since before the start of the twenty-first century we have had robots, but they were then generally unsophisticated: automated machine tools, independent lawnmowers incapable of overcoming molehills, and other clunky under-powered devices. Following Moore's law, the memory and processing power of computers had been growing exponentially for years before the software started to catch up, and thus—seemingly following an inversion of the evolutionary process in which brains developed before bodies—we come to the sophisticated independent robot, and that, like so many other developments in the twenty-first century, took power. Already robotics experts were running sophisticated robot minds in computers, but had yet to fully develop the hardware. There was no point in doing so—the mechanisms were rapidly becoming available but, generally, the reach of the robots made from these would be only as long as their power cables. The new nanotube batteries and super-capacitors changed all that, so within just a few years, robots became capable of doing things only humans could do before, and a few years later they went beyond the capacity of their masters, but still, slaves they remain.

ANTARES BASE

The two enforcers were actually inside the Hydroponics hex, and why not, for the air was always pleasant and the lights much brighter and more cheerful than anywhere else within the base. The bulkhead doors were closed, of course, to prevent the moisture-laden special mix of air spreading out through the rest of the base, and also to keep the human-oriented air out of Hydroponics.

"Here," whispered Kaskan, pointing up at the computer screen as, crouching low, he pushed the chair aside and moved up to the console.

They were now in Wing One, in the small control room attached to Hydroponics. Here resided the computer that monitored the plant life, controlled the lights, the fluid mix in the troughs, and the gas mix of the air. Here also were packed tanks of various chemical fertilizers, as well as cylinders full of fungicides, for though they had managed to establish a small ecosystem here without introducing harmful insects, fungal infections were common.

Lopomac remained outside to guard the corridor, and Carol paused by the door, while Var crouched behind Kaskan. All of them were suited in readiness for entering the airlock leading out of the adjacent hex. They had to keep low because of the windows ranged along one wall, just a metre away from the computer screen, which overlooked the interior of the Hydroponics hex.

"A higher level of CO_2 helps the plants grow," Kaskan whispered. "We keep it at just the right level to prevent anyone working there from getting asphyxiated—but that can be changed." He reached up, operating a ball control to call up a menu, then touched the screen, shifting upwards a marker on a bar control, but Var reached over and caught hold of his hand.

"If they start suffocating they might fire their weapons," she said.

Kaskan shook his head. "No, it'll be gradual anoxia." He nodded towards the windows. "I'll raise the nitrogen content too, so they'll start to feel tired, maybe a little ill and certainly a bit confused. If they realize something's wrong, they'll head for the bulkhead door to try and escape, and that exertion will probably be enough to knock them out. The door, of course, will have automatically sealed by then, and even if they do fire their weapons it'll be at that door, which won't cause us a problem."

"How can you be so sure?"

Kaskan just gazed at her steadily, but it was Carol who answered from behind, "Because he's seen it happen often enough."

Of course, Kaskan was one of those who had been due to depart at the time Var and others arrived. He'd been here during the first blowouts, during the period when it was discovered that not all the regolith blocks were completely solid and impermeable. Var remembered Gisender telling her about the time after one blowout, when even oxygen had been rationed and they had been forced to live right on the brink of asphyxiation for nearly a month. Many had not made it. Many had simply died in their cabins. Some, like Kaskan and Gisender, had been very suspicious of Ricard's activities during that period, because the political director had seized control of the atmosphere regulators.

They waited long minutes as the bar on the graph Kaskan had altered rose up to the marker he had set. Kaskan meanwhile kept utterly still. Var was tempted to peek through the window to see what was happening with the two enforcers, but she knew that just the slightest miscalculation now would leave them all dead. Then, as they waited, the intercom crackled into life.

"It would seem that the usual suspects have gone missing," Ricard announced. "Lopomac Pearse, Kaskan Lane, Carol Eisen and, of course, our Technical Director, Var Delex."

For one spine-crawling moment Var feared Ricard had located them, but now she could hear that Ricard's words were issued from the public-address system throughout the base.

"Director Var has murdered Gisender Lane and caused a number of atmosphere breaches, murdering nine Inspectorate staff along with Miska Giannis. She has also destroyed valuable government property, so it is inevitable that she must be seized and duly tried. However, her guilt does not attach to the other three, who, if they return to the Community Room straight away, will be treated fairly. Surely all four of you must be aware that you have nowhere to run, and surely you understand that, unless you hand yourselves over, I will have to order my men to use deadly force against you."

"Bastard," Kaskan muttered.

"He's just playing to the crowd," Var observed.

"Like anyone will believe him?"

"They'll pretend to believe him. What else can they do?"

"Having now seen that broadcast from Delegate Margot Le Blanc, you must all understand that we face hard times, in which hard decisions will have to be made," Ricard continued, "but be assured that the Committee has provided me with a restructuring plan for our survival. Delegate Le Blanc mentioned those dissident elements back on Earth that have brought us to these straits and, as we are seeing, those same elements are here. We cannot allow them to threaten our survival. We must remain strong and firm in our purpose. There…there is much work still to do."

As Ricard seemed to run out of steam, Kaskan checked his watch, nodded and carefully rose from his crouch to peer over the screen. At that very same moment, a series of shots slammed into the windows, a terrible racket of plastic bullets smashing against the glass. Kaskan ducked again as the glass finally broke, large laminated chunks of it falling inside the computer room.

"What the fuck?" Lopomac hissed from the door.

"A whole fifty-round clip," said Kaskan. He glanced around. "Plastic ammo." He looked up at the atmosphere sensors in the ceiling, and just then a reverberating clang sounded from the corridor outside, as the nearest bulkhead door closed in Wing One.

"I never thought of that," admitted Kaskan. "But it doesn't do them any good—the pressure is higher in there."

Var shook her head. One of the enforcers had shot out the internal window in an attempt to let in breathable air, but with the pressure differential all he had done was let some of the unbreathable stuff escape from Hydroponics. Further shots erupted, this time smacking against metal, followed by a clattering noise and gasping, someone falling and then something breaking, the sound of liquid spilling. Kaskan stood up, and Var stood too.

"Best to close up our helmets," she advised.

They all complied, then Kaskan dialled down the CO_2 and nitrogen on the screen graph. Var realized it would take some minutes before the air in there became breathable again, which would be too late for the two enforcers. Kaskan led the way over to the broken windows.

Greenery so crowded the hex troughs that they were difficult to discern. One trough had been holed, so that nutrient-laden fluid was spilling on to the floor. One enforcer lay curled up against the wall, while the other sprawled a few paces away, his machine pistol lying just outside of his reach. By now both men were utterly motionless.

"The bulkhead door into the hex should open now," Kaskan reported over com, turning to gesture to the corridor behind where Lopomac stood. "The safety protocol cuts out once the mix is the same on each side of a door."

Lopomac led the way out, followed closely by Carol and then Var. The short corridor, which terminated at the bulkhead door leading into the hex, was blocked by a similar square door at the other end. Lopomac approached the hex door, pulled down on the lever to disengage the seal, and a pendulum mechanism swung the door on its top pivot back up into the wall cavity. As she stepped into the hex behind him, Var peered up at the geodesic dome, considerably relieved to see it unharmed.

"That was close, Kaskan," she remarked. "Too close."

"You're right," he agreed. "I'm sorry."

Now she felt a stab of guilt at berating someone who had so recently lost his wife—the kind of grief she herself understood so well—and who, despite the unacceptable risk, had now provided them with further weapons and dealt with a further two enforcers. But, when the public address system crackled into life again, it seemed that they had still not done enough, quickly enough.

EARTH

Braddock swung his weapon hard—hard enough to crush the man's skull—then caught hold of his shoulder and shoved him down to the floor, pinning him there. Saul stepped out from where he and Hannah had been hiding and headed over, his mind working at high speed as he assessed his current position here on Argus Station and calculated what he must do next.

It all seemed to make perfect sense to him now he had closely studied the results of Janus's search for his sister. She had come up here, into space, because her speciality was in massive construction projects like those conducted up here, as well as synthesis, and other scientific disciplines besides. Yes, he himself had come here to exact his vengeance on the Committee, to take Argus away from the rulers of Earth, a belated motivation being the knowledge of Smith's presence here, but underneath all that obviously lay something of the person he had been previously. On some level he had known that his sister was up here, and just as that same inner self had driven him to search for Hannah, it had similarly been driving him to find the only other person he cared about. But now it seemed his sister was not here after all. She had been forcibly transferred to Mars, so now, perhaps, a new course to pursue…

But first he needed to stay alive.

Saul again reviewed some of the data recorded within the processors in his brain. Most of the massive ongoing construction and reconstruction was being carried out by robots, ranging from machines the size of monorail carriages which were used to transport materials about the rim, to others only the size of a cockroach, designed to install or repair small electronic devices. A huge number of robots laboured in the three cylinder worlds—the arcoplexes—which were parts of this station he'd known very little about until downloading the schematic. Meteor-repair welding bots constantly searched for holes made by the large amounts of debris drifting out here. Mining robots cut like woodworm into the underside of the central asteroid, while others laboured out in the smelters. Cleaning robots and maintenance robots were constantly at work throughout the station. And his experience with the pair of robots they had recently encountered did nothing to dispel the certainty that these were the answer.

From the little cleaning robot, data flow had been immediate, and within a second, and without ill effects, he had encompassed it as part of himself. He reprogrammed it and tightened its computer security, shutting down its response to station signals and making it accessible only by a ten-digit code constantly changing according to a formula that only he—and it—knew. Controlling the robot's laser com, he had opened a communication channel with the loader robot and at once included it in his personal network. He had input the same changing ten-digit code to the larger robot, then reverted to straightforward laser com, without the code, to check its security by giving it new instructions. No response to this. He tried running every code-cracker he had available, but still no response. Even then, he realized that, given a few hours, he might have managed to get through and therefore, given the same time, Smith would be able to get through too, and break his control of the robots. He must not allow his former interrogator sufficient time to do so.

Saul glanced at the maintenance technician, who still seemed to be breathing despite the force of Braddock's blow. Saul calculated that the low gravity here, and Braddock's purchase on the floor being only through his gecko boots, had diminished the blow's force by about 40 per cent. Turning to study the contents of the technician's toolbox, Saul began undoing the clips holding the upper section of his spacesuit. Once he had stripped it off, he selected the necessary tools, then quickly removed the little robot's cowling, its processor, power supply and communications laser. Next obtaining sufficient optics and carbon power cable from the bot's control systems, he linked the power supply and processor into his suit's hardware and main processors, which were located behind the oxygen pack, then stowed them in an arm pocket of the jacket. He epoxied the laser to one shoulder of it, before once again donning it, then ran the optic from his skull into a port situated in the rear of his helmet, before putting that on.

"Seems a bit of an unstable rig," commented Hannah doubtfully.

"You should know better," he replied. "It's all about programming."

"You can do this?"

He didn't reply as he concentrated on optimizing those disparate items of hardware. In the end, if you avoided shoving a power cable into an optic plug, or an optic into a power socket, it really *was* all about programming and therefore possible to get most modern computer modules to work happily together. He could now operate the com laser, as before, but most importantly it enabled him to avoid running an optic from his head *outside* his suit, which would have made it impossible to close his visor, as he would need to do the moment they passed through the first airlock.

"He'd better be able to do this," muttered Braddock.

"Just ahead of us there's an area of the station that's still under construction," Saul said. "That's where we'll find construction robots."

"Him?" Braddock gestured to the prostrate technician.

Saul knew precisely what Braddock meant. If the technician came to before they were ready, he would certainly alert Smith. And once Smith saw the remains of the little robot, he would guess Saul's intentions. He was about to instruct Braddock to kill the technician, when he caught Hannah's eye. It would be nice to say that some degree of compassion influenced his next instruction, but it just wasn't there.

"Tie him up," he said, "securely."

Braddock took a roll of duct tape from the toolbox and set to work, while Saul stepped across to the scattered remains of the robot, scooped them up and took them over to one of the EVA units affixed against the wall—a one-man vehicle with large manipulator arms used for exterior repairs—opened its hatch and tossed the pieces of robot inside. Even if the technician was found, it would hopefully take Smith some time to work out what Saul had been doing here.

"It'd be better to kill him," Braddock remarked, having bound the man securely to the side railing.

Saul agreed, but realized that such a drastic step would push Hannah further away from him—the emotional considerations weren't too difficult to slot into his calculations. The risk of this man regaining consciousness, and somehow getting free to report to Smith, was worth taking. Though, admittedly, only if Saul had not overestimated the value he was ascribing to Hannah within the formulae in his head.

The conveyor had brought them to the outer edge of the station, almost a kilometre and a half from where they had penetrated it, which almost certainly put them outside the main search area for a while. In that odd, seemingly unhurried gait which was the best anyone could manage here, Saul led them along the corridor to the point where it transformed into a walkway cutting left into open and incomplete station structure—just a vast gridwork of girders and distant walls. Soon they came up alongside what looked like a large room suspended in the open structure, with a single door and windows running round the outside. Closer inspection revealed metal arms extending from its corners, terminating in double clamping wheels. These could be clamped to structural beams, so as to propel this "room" to wherever its occupants next wanted it to be. It was a mobile overseer's office; a base of operations in the immensity of this unfinished section.

"Looks like no one home," observed Braddock, since no light shone from within. In fact, the only light hereabouts issued from fluorescent work lamps scattered sparsely throughout the surrounding area, presently powered by the station's EM field.

"Looks that way," Saul agreed, halting to peer at a cluster of shapes suspended underneath the mobile office. "Except for our first recruits."

He set the com laser probing, and its red light glinted off folded limbs, fisted four-finger claws, sensor heads and three-section jointed bodies. One of these construction robots responded almost at once and began to unfold. The infective component within the signal began operating too, as this robot opened up a channel to its nearest neighbour, passing on Saul's recoding instructions, and it too began to unfold.

"Fuck," said Braddock—his frequent repetition of that word causing a flash of irritation inside Saul, instantly discarded.

The machine moved fast for something that would weigh in at half a tonne down on Earth, pulling itself neatly through the mesh of surrounding girders until it halted close by them. It possessed four grasping limbs extended, a pair each, from the rear two sections of its body, which it could swivel a full three-sixty degrees in order to position them. Two more limbs extended from the fore section, which both terminated in carousel tool heads. One was a multiweld kit capable of welding beams in place, spot welding and acetylene cutting. The other head bristled with a laser drill, diamond disc cutters and grinders, thread-tapping tools, a bolt winder and a riveter. The next robot to venture out lacked a welder, but in its place sported a spray head for depositing coatings piped from a varied array of tanks fixed on its back. More robots were now in motion till eight of them in all had positioned themselves nearby. Saul focused initially on the one with the sprayer.

"Once Smith figures what we're doing, he'll throw everything he's got at us," warned Braddock.

"But still not enough, I hope," Saul replied. "These things are built to withstand severe impacts from any materials they handle—like the end of a bubblemetal beam travelling at up to five metres a second. Station antipersonnel weapons won't be sufficient to damage them." He turned to look at Braddock for confirmation.

"Yeah, but that ain't all they've got."

"Agreed, but by the time Smith gets round to deploying something more effective, I intend to be down his throat." He did not add that, in order to do that, he would need to discover Smith's location.

The spraying robot clambered on to the walkway and, under Saul's instruction, moved along ahead of them, accelerating to the point where the walkway jagged left and reacquired walls before disappearing from sight.

"Where now?" asked Hannah.

"We stay out here much longer, we'll be caught," he explained. "It's time to move in now, but as we move further in, we'll start encountering the hardwired cam system and readerguns. Come on, let's go."

He led the way after the departing robot, while all around them came clattering and slithering as the other robots kept pace. Soon they reached a bulkhead door and a steep, rough-surfaced ramp which they descended to reach the next level. The robots followed one after another, folding their limbs so as to get through, then negotiating the ramp two abreast, and descending it neatly like a platoon of giant steel ants. After that, a short, filthy corridor led to yet another ramp, to another corridor, then some steps heading downwards, constructed for Earth gravity, which the robots handled better than the humans. Next they were entering a long, low-ceilinged and brightly lit room, into which natural sunlight was piped from the suncatchers positioned on the station outer rim. It housed several large cisterns containing water soup-thick with green algae.

Saul pointed up to the frameworks supporting the diffraction ends of the mirrored pipes leading from a suncatcher. "Do you see it?"

"What?" asked Hannah.

"The cam."

It was an old-fashioned design of security camera: a motorized socket made to take a disposable cam the size of a man's thumb. Both cam and socket were now covered with a rapidly hardening layer of orange safety paint. Linking himself through to the spraybot, as it now moved beyond this same room, he found that it had sprayed over twenty-three cams located here, and was now doing the same to the smaller pin cams stationed in the corridor beyond. He had initially been surprised to discover one huge gap in the security system here, for in an effort to cut down on triggering false alarms, and thus not waste resources, it did not bother to register the station robots. All that would happen now was that some program would note that the cams were out. It might even be the case that maintenance would be alerted before Smith was, but Saul did not hold out much hope for that.

The cams in the following corridor were not visible to the human eye, but the robot—its vision capable of focusing on beam faults just a few microns across—had detected them all with ease. As a result, safety paint ran in an unbroken line along the ceiling, and in a punctuated line along each side wall. But such ease of progress could not last, of course. Just as they approached the entrance to the next hydroponics hall, Saul saw, through the lead robot's eyes, that troops were now moving into position behind gulley tanks filled with distorted-looking potato plants and bulbous carrots sprouting from nutrient-laden sponges. He immediately instructed the spraybot to come to a halt, and to precisely locate every soldier waiting in ambush, relaying their positions back to its fellows.

"Hostiles ahead," he warned the other two.

"Security?" Braddock asked.

"Very definitely."

Braddock sighed, then reached down for one of the grenades clipped on his belt. Saul put a restraining hand out. "No need."

With a deeper link into the robots, he tampered with their safety protocols. Their systems had been keyed to recognize the human shape, so that they would not inadvertently injure anyone who got in their way while they were working. He now subverted that protocol and inserted new instructions where there would usually occur a 90 per cent drop in work rate or complete safety shutdown. The instructions were simple: grind here, drill there, cut this piece away, spraycoat that, weld this.

"Okay, step aside," he said. "Up against the wall."

Saul stepped back himself, and Hannah moved quickly up beside him. Braddock stood doubtfully staring at the robots, then hastily moved out of the way too, as they shifted smoothly into motion. They flowed towards the bulkhead door, which thumped up on its seals and swung open—already cued to allow through maintenance robots, like the sprayer robot that had gone through earlier. Saul gazed through their sensors, eight views opening up in the virtuality inside his mind. They were fast but then, while engaged in their usual jobs, they were as fast as any automated lathe or milling machine, or the kind of factory robots that assembled ground cars. Using simple location programs that he had no need to load, they followed the most direct routes to their targets, which had been efficiently prioritized.

Three of the robots sped up into the ceiling frames that supported diffractors, pipes and power ducts directly above the hydroponics gulleys; two went straight across the gulleys themselves, while the remaining three headed down the central aisle, turning into side aisles directly leading to their targets. Saul moved up closer to the door, to give them a better chance of maintaining laser link with him. Communication would become intermittent once they went out of line-of-sight, but that would still not upset their programming. Also, some of them would keep returning into view to update him, and he was running a program to smooth out the data flow. So there weren't really any noticeable interruptions.

"What the fuck is this?" he heard someone cry from inside the room beyond, before realizing that the robots lacked the facility of hearing, having been originally constructed to work only in vacuum.

One of the robots up in the ceiling continued reaching down, its claw closing around one soldier's neck and hauling him up. The man shrieked, raising an ionic taser and firing it, small lightnings erupting from its impact point. A diagnostic feed from the robot involved threw up multiple errors, but it still laser-drilled a precise one-centimetre hole directly through its captive's heart.

"Pull back!" someone else screamed.

Another taser fired, but to no effect.

"Guns!" someone shouted.

Gunfire from automatic weapons racketed about within the hydroponics room. A soldier stumbled away from the paint-sprayer, orange from head to foot and blinded, then another robot pinned him back against a wall, while it tried to weld a non-existent join running from his neck to his groin. The one with the cutting disc casually sliced off someone else's head, then turned to a smouldering corpse that had just been welded, and cut off its head too. The screams of agony were horrible, and usually quickly truncated. Within a minute they had ceased, as had the gunfire. Still, the robots continued with their allotted tasks until Saul instructed them to desist. Refinement was called for, and at the very thought he altered the programs, now specifying only one operation to be carried out per work task. No need for a robot to behead an electrocuted corpse.

"They're done," he decided, about to step through the door.

"Wait," said Braddock, "let me check."

He knew there was no need, but Saul allowed the soldier his professional pride, so he stepped aside and Braddock ducked in ahead of him. Gazing through the eyes of a single robot, Saul watched the man cautiously advance, then halt to stare up across at the robot still located in the ceiling. A human corpse still hung by the neck from its claw, and it hadn't moved since being hit by the taser. Diagnostics showed that the electric charge had corrupted its main processor, so it had been a mistake for the soldiers to switch over to automatic weapons, since they'd stood more of a chance using tasers. Braddock checked further, pausing to stare at a headless corpse resting in a bed of potato plants.

"Jesus fucking Christ," he gasped, obviously dumbfounded, his hushed tones still audible outside the hydroponics room, but admirably he went on to check every other corpse before shouting, "Clear!"

"It's going to be bad, isn't it?" said Hannah.

"Yes, it is." He watched her for a moment before continuing. "Alternatively, we could always just hand ourselves over to Smith—you know what the choices are now." It seemed necessary to emphasize the point, to keep her focused on the current reality of their situation.

"It's not the choices now I was thinking about." She chewed at one of her knuckles for a moment, still gazing towards the open door. Then, abruptly dropping her hand, she said, "Let's go," and led the way in.

It affected him more than he would have expected; the analytical part of his mind momentarily swamped by the emotional reaction. His views, through the robots, were clear—in fact provided much more clarity than through his own eyes—but besides hearing, they lacked one other sense. The robots did not possess a sense of smell and, on entering the hydroponics room the smell of shit assailed him, in the trousers of those who had died or from their ruptured intestines, accompanied by other warm butcher's-shop odours. Steam spread around the fresh corpses, their blood beaded the air.

He studied Hannah, trying to gauge her response. She stared at the dead, nodded to herself, before she went over to one man who had been neatly riveted through the forehead, picked up his weapon and then pulled the spare clips from his belt. Saul retrieved the gun from another corpse, and saw Braddock also collecting weapons and ammunition.

"Low-impact ammunition," Braddock observed. "It won't last."

"They won't know what happened here," Saul replied, then instructed the robots to move ahead of them to the next bulkhead door, the spraybot again leading the way. "Smith rightly assumed that the cams going out meant we were located here and he sent these men to seize us. They only went over to automatic weapons when they realized what was attacking them, so the tasers were for us."

"He wants us alive, then," said Hannah.

Saul nodded. "That won't last either, once he has some idea what I'm up to. The next ones will come equipped with ceramic rounds and probably something stronger."

Just then the whining in his head faded to leave a hollow emptiness. Obviously Smith had just decided to fix his communications problem, which meant he would be kept in constant contact with the next soldiers he sent against them.

"He knows something's wrong," Saul said. "The EM field is now out."

"Probably others further in heard the shooting."

That seemed likely.

Saul approached the next bulkhead door, transmitting instructions as he did so. He moved three of the robots to the rear, because knowing their location,

Smith might send troops that way, whilst the remaining four headed towards the door ahead. Saul also ensured that they would not include himself, Hannah and Braddock as targets in their work roster by tagging the design of their spacesuits. The spraybot went through, and viewing through its sensors he saw a woman wearing the uniform of an Inspectorate enforcer standing there holding a console, its optic cable plugged into a wall socket. At her feet crouched a single soldier armed with an assault rifle rather than a machine pistol, its stock up against his shoulder. He hesitated for just a second before opening fire, whilst the woman instantly detached her console, then turned and ran. Instructing it to now ignore the cams, Saul sent the spraybot in pursuit, just as the other robots followed it through the door. Diagnostic errors—that assault rifle being loaded with ceramic armour-piercers. Saul was only half aware of Braddock shoving him to one side and dragging Hannah along with them. Bullets zinged into the room they still occupied. Transmission from the robots ahead of them ceased as he crouched safely to one side, but when he moved back up to the door edge and leaned round it, laser com updated him instantly.

The spraybot hurdled the soldier, who tried to shoot it as it leapt over him. Before he could bring his weapon back down again, one of the following robots slammed into him at floor level and sank a grinding disc into his neck. His shriek curtailed with a spray of blood up one wall. Now the spraybot came down on the woman, just before she entered a vertical cageway running alongside a massive shaft which also contained the mechanical spindle and light-diffusion pipes leading to a single arcoplex cylinder. Saul instantly instructed the robot to just hold her, since it might now be worth his while gathering some information. However one of the other robots arrived and following its program perfectly, laser-drilled her heart. No matter; perhaps it was best they just move as fast as they could now. He summoned the sprayer back into the preceding corridor, and returned it to its task of blinding the cameras. That Smith now knew he controlled robots was almost instantly confirmed when all of their radio receivers activated at once, though whatever orders Smith had sent them could not bypass the ten-digit code.

"Come on," Saul said, "fast now."

He ducked through the door, no longer wanting Braddock to check ahead—they didn't have time. Leaving behind it the stink of paint, the spraybot disappeared round a far corner. Reaching the corridor beyond,

Saul shoved his machine pistol into his thigh pocket and took up the assault rifle. The three humans rounded the corner and entered the cageway. Just ten metres further out from them the cylinder spindle revolved slowly, surrounded by light pipes, and, peering down, he saw a massive mercury-lubricated bearing with numerous suncatchers set into its surface arranged to intercept the light from the ends of the stationary light pipes, as they passed under them, and transmit that harvest into the arcoplex cylinder itself. The robots worked their way down outside the cage, to reach floor levels whose construction had stalled. Yet again the stink of new-sprayed paint, but in this area he didn't think every cam could possibly be knocked out. Then came the familiar vicious sound of a readergun.

"Still low-impact," Braddock decided.

They wouldn't risk loading readerguns with armour-piercing rounds, not here.

Saul was now looking through the eyes of every one of his robots simultaneously. All were still functioning, though the diagnostic returns registered damage, and kept trying fruitlessly to instruct their recipients to return to the maintenance bays left behind them. The readergun was mounted on a column. Shedding splintered plastic all around it, one of the robots closed a claw around the gun's revolving turret, then laser-drilled inside it until something blew. Four more readerguns followed after that, then they reached an airlock out beyond the rim of the arcoplex cylinder. Whilst Hannah and Saul slid their visors across and ran spacesuit diagnostics, Braddock began operating the airlock's manual controls. Saul next allowed himself a low-level penetration of the computer architecture operating here, finding safety protocols and permissions for remote access to the airlock, and instantly shutting them down. That took him only a moment but, even in that brief time, he felt Smith starting to zero in on him. Then, almost inevitably, a jag of light flashed across his vision.

By now, all the robots were clustered around them, waiting.

"We'll send them all ahead," Saul instructed, his mouth feeling dry. No pain yet, and no thundering pulse in my head, but it would return, he felt sure.

For its first cycling, four robots crammed into the airlock like some weirdly compacted sculpture. It took ten minutes to get all of them through and meanwhile Saul's contact with them was completely cut off. However, if any soldiers awaited them on the other side of the airlock, the robots would continue to follow their pre-programmed instructions. The three humans stepped into the airlock next.

"Channel 37," said Saul, as the atmosphere drained out of the lock, slowly killing his words in the air. As icons flashed up in his visor, he approved them and then shut down exterior applications for inclusion, thus making their radio communications private, at least for a while. Shortly, they propelled themselves out into a tubeway still under construction, at present only a cage of girders curving round and then spearing downwards beside the massive revolving arcoplex cylinder.

"Mother of God!" Hannah exclaimed, her voice crackling with interference.

On its outer rim, the station had seemed huge enough, but here, within the wheel, its vastness delivered more impact. From behind, to their left, the inner surface of the wheel's rim curved almost imperceptibly inwards; while over that way, gazing through the inner structure of the station, they could just see an ore-transit tube foreshortened by perspective. Immediately to their right turned the great curved wall of the nearest cylinder world—the nearest arcoplex extending down to where it connected, at its further end, to the asteroid itself. However, the view of that was blocked by countless intervening tubeways or buildings suspended in the mesh of girders, like insect carcasses trapped in a spider's web. Ahead and above, where a latticework of girders divided the starlit sky into diamonds, Saul could just see the technical-control building jutting up from the asteroid itself. This entire massive station, he now understood, represented what the Committee had been bankrupting Earth in order to build. Thus there had to be more to it than simply providing a base of operations for the satellite laser network.

Now clear of the airlock, Saul once again linked back into the personal network with his robots, and only on doing so did he spot the flashing of weapons ahead. Next he registered a detonation, though silent in vacuum, as it erased one of the robots from his network, and with human vision he saw a couple of its steel limbs clinging to beams nearby. As they propelled themselves down towards this spot, and to where the tubeway acquired walls, Saul replayed recorded data and saw a spacesuited soldier lurking in the shadows with a carousel launcher—a big weapon equipped with a round magazine, as on a tommy-gun—but the man didn't succeed in getting off a second round. Saul was still refining the programs, so it wasn't a corrupted work order that made the next robot tear off the human assailant's head, but new programming.

Heavy machine-gun fire next, a ten-bore hastily clamped to a beam, armour-piercing rounds cutting out from the tubeway's mouth to punch their way through bubblemetal beams and sheet. The silence of this destruction created an illusion of disconnection, and safety, but the firing didn't last long. Three robots entered the tubeway, and after one of them had torn the gun crew apart, Saul paused it there and gave new instructions. It picked up the heavy machine gun in one of its clamp claws, swivelled back so as to walk upright on its hind legs, then advanced further like some nightmare ape made of steel.

"Pretty toy," said Braddock over com.

Saul thought the soldier referred to the upright robot, but in fact Braddock had retrieved the missile-launcher and begun examining it. Saul flicked a glance sideways to watch the headless corpse of its previous owner gyrating away from the walkway to impact on the outer surface of the arcoplex cylinder, then be flung on to a new trajectory.

They entered the tubeway with a few of Saul's little army of homicidal machines moving ahead of them, some inside and some outside the tubeway itself. Rails ran along the floor here, but they soon petered out, just a short section completed. Then walls, floor and ceiling withered away too, the tubeway once again becoming a cage that continued snaking through the open substructure of the inner station. Here large and stationary habitation and factory units hung suspended in the substructure, even more cageways and tubeways running between. His robots continued to spread out through this, seeking new jobs to perform. The one with the big gun opened fire as it advanced. Then, suddenly, new laser com feeds began to open up.

Whilst maintaining the communication between himself and the robots, Saul had left open the option to summon other robots into the same network, their com lasers probing all about them in search of new recruits. First another four, too distant to see clearly but from the feedback he ascertained that they were construction robots put to work on the lower bearing structure of the arcoplex cylinder. He summoned them into the fight, and even as they began moving they hijacked yet more robots near to them. Another five construction robots and a big hauler loaded with tonnes of building materials joined his army, then smaller robots, the size of cats and used to clean out one of the newly built habitation units. They swarmed towards the conflict, moving up on the flank of the attacking enforcers.

Braddock rapidly propelled himself along the incomplete tubeway, with Saul and Hannah following. The soldier turned abruptly to one side and fired his missile-launcher. In elegant silence, the blast ripped open a partially constructed wall fifty metres to their right, and a burning corpse fell out from behind it, the fire snuffed the moment the suit air feeding it ran out. They were right in the middle of it now, since the open structure all around them made it impossible to maintain a single front.

"Stay beside me," Saul instructed Hannah.

"How far to go?"

"Half a kilometre to Tech Central," he said, pointing ahead and upwards.

Directly ahead now, and visible below their destination, lay the rough surface of the asteroid. Saul, at last, restarted his modem and began carefully probing the data spaces all around him. Yes, Smith was there, but at first Saul didn't venture so deep that he couldn't pull out in an instant. However, he felt a sudden satisfaction as he mapped signal traffic on to his schematic of the station. Most of it issued from the region of Tech Central, which meant that Smith had to be either there or somewhere nearby.

"A shoddy application of tactics." Smith's observation came through to him, as if they were sitting together in the same room. "And certainly doomed to failure, Citizen Saul."

13

THEY NEVER SUFFER

Once the Committee had firmly tightened its grip on Earth, it distributed wealth only on the basis of its own survival. In the beginning, "zero-asset" citizens received just enough to keep them fed, clothed and housed, whilst "societal assets" could receive considerably more, calculated on the basis of their use to the Committee and how much more of a contribution could be derived from them by allowing them more. But the Committee itself sucked up the bulk of world wealth through building the infrastructure of utter control, and it maintained its upper executives at a level of luxury never before witnessed on Earth. However, as the population continues to grow and production does not, inevitably there will be a resource crash and ensuing Dark Age. Those at the bottom of the pile will starve and die in their billions, whilst those at the top will perhaps have to forgo their caviar and biscuits.

As robots located down on the surface of the asteroid began to respond to Saul's laser communications, he rather thought Smith was mistaken. However, even as he considered that, the number of robots he was hijacking ceased to increase, while other robots again were clearly on the move. Smith had evidently begun taking control of the remainder and was turning them against him. Saul received data on the first robot-on-robot clash less than a second later.

"I'll be on top of you very shortly," he replied to Smith. "That doesn't look like failure to me."

He began probing, feeling out the network—gritting his teeth at a familiar stab of pain in his head—and started recording large chunks of code to then run through the processors lodged inside his skull. This was slow progress, however, because though he realized a lot of the activity he was currently picking up would involve tactical information and attack orders, that stuff only gave him a vague lever for code-cracking.

"You've made a miscalculation based on badly collated data," Smith explained, arrogantly confident of his own abilities.

"You think so?" Saul asked, probing behind the Director's latest words to where they'd passed through the same coding as served the entire station's network. Just eight words and one contraction enabled him to crack 18 per cent of the overall coding of voice and text transmission, and also enabled him to recognize the image files of visual feeds, but he was getting nowhere with the hardware instructions to cams, readerguns, and other station security devices.

"It would appear you are now heading for Tech Central, expecting to seize control there. That could be considered amusing if it were not for the people's resources I must expend just to deal with you."

Smith's love of verbiage had now given Saul a further 47 per cent of all voice and text transmission, then, within a few seconds, he had all of it. He erased all recorded text and voice data from his mind so as to concentrate on the rest, his head immediately feeling less *congested*. At the same time he realized that, whilst he had partially penetrated Smith's comlife element, Smith had been probing him likewise in an attempt to crack the ten-digit code keeping the robots secure.

"You're *not* in Tech Central?" Saul enquired, pretending ignorance.

"That's not the kind of information one should volunteer to an opponent."

Saul supposed Smith must think him really stupid, assuming that Saul believed that, by taking physical control of Tech Central, he would thereby gain control of the station. He'd never thought that for an instant, of course. Having expanded himself just as Malden and Saul had, Smith could control the station from any location he chose, and therefore it was him Saul needed at gunpoint, or dead. He probed deeper still, trying to get a handle on visual feeds being routed from the same source as Smith's voice. And that's when Smith pounced.

Smith was into his mind, a search-engine link stabbing deep down into its processing spaces, like a barbed harpoon. Saul tried to cut it off, but the engine instantly began searching the software he used to control his modem, and his instructions queued up like print orders to an overloaded printer, whilst the pain between his eyes rapidly increased. This is how Smith did it, he realized; this is how he got Malden. He simply overloaded everything within his prey until its programs started to hang. Malden had probably failed because his first instinct, like most other people's, would have been to retreat, defend himself, try to get this intruder out of his head. Saul realized now his advantage over Malden, and maybe over Smith himself: he had more firmly accepted that his self did not reside only in this body of flesh and blood. Like a salmon leaping up through a waterfall, he battled his way up through the informational tsunami to get to Smith himself. Even as the pressure of data began to shove him back down, and lights began flashing across his organic vision, he copied the weapon Smith had used against him—that search engine possessing a huge requirement to find, without any clear definition of what it must find—and flung it straight back towards Smith.

"You fucker!" Smith exclaimed, losing his usual laborious manner of speech.

The thing thunked into the man's brain like a crossbow bolt into wood, and before Smith got a chance to clamp down, Saul saw for a moment through his opponent's eyes, and then through the cams in his immediate vicinity. Smith was making his way along a wide tubeway, four guards surrounding him, all of them suited up for vacuum. Despite his apparent assurance earlier, he was fleeing, and Saul realized that, by deploying the robots, he had caught the man out. He now precisely located Smith on the station schematic—in a tunnel over to his left and further down, leading away from Tech Central. And, as Smith struggled to drive out Saul's probe, he was forced to retract his own from Saul.

Now they were swirling around each other in the network, like immiscible fluids. Feeling the other man's panic, Saul realized he had a chance to win this. However, it could not be through direct mental confrontation like this, because the steady growth of pain in his head made an eventual loss of control inevitable.

Within a second, Saul punched into Tech Central, grabbing the readerguns, and from that point also spreading out virally to contest for control of additional guns and cams. Smith seemed weakest at Saul's point of penetration, as was the case in Tech Central itself, yet, even beyond a certain point where the sheer density of data began interfering with Saul's usurpation, Smith could not seem to hold on. He tried to retain control of the readerguns, but only managed to trip safety protocols designed to prevent the weapons being hijacked, thus crashing their systems and burning out critical hardware. Meanwhile even as he fought for control elsewhere, Saul was focusing through the cameras of Tech Central itself.

Smith had abandoned the staff working the consoles in the main control room, and they were now trying to make sense of what was happening. Outside that room itself, two Inspectorate guards had tipped a couple of steel desks onto their sides and were crouching behind them for protection. Saul gave instructions to the readergun in the ceiling immediately above them, and two short bursts of fire wrote them out of the equation. Then, despite Smith's interference, he managed to reprogram the same gun, as well as others in the vicinity, to respond only to his ten-digit code. Smith, unfortunately, was not in range of any gun Saul could fire. Time now to finish this, because Smith must not be allowed to escape.

"Braddock," Saul called, as he came to a halt and squatted behind a pallet of sheet metal.

The soldier leapt to one side as shots exploded across the walkway in front of him. He then turned and fired his stolen machine pistol over to the right, emptying it completely, then tossing it away. A weapon tumbled away down there, not because its owner had been hit, but because he was desperately trying to fight off the robot which was attempting to tap a twenty-millimetre thread through his back. Braddock retreated fast towards Saul and Hannah, his own machine pistol in his left hand and the missile-launcher in his right. He crouched low beside them.

"The both of you, head up into Tech Central." Saul focused on Braddock, meanwhile sending new instructions to two of his robots. "Those remaining there are not armed, and the readerguns there are now under my control."

"You've won? You've won already, haven't you?"

Saul shook his head, then quickly wished he hadn't when it felt as if something began snapping loose inside. He was trying to keep thousands of separate functions open to his conscious perception, striving to keep the pain under control. Smith's informational assaults on him were constant and it took all Saul's effort to retain control of the robots and readerguns he had already seized, his attempt to code them to respond only to himself becoming a continuing battle.

"I've got an advantage over him in the immediate area, simply because of the robots and readerguns I control," he explained. "But I don't know how long I can hold on to that."

One of the robots drew itself up into the cage of girders, causing a shudder of metalwork, whilst another passed below on its way towards the required destination. Saul meanwhile replaced the ammunition clip in his machine pistol with the ceramic ammunition clip from the assault rifle, then tossed the emptied weapon away.

"What are you doing?" Braddock asked.

"Smith isn't in Tech Central, so I'm going after him."

"Then I'll come with you."

"Go where I told you to go," Saul instructed, before he propelled himself over towards the squatting robot and caught hold of its bullet-scarred cowling. He then focused on Hannah. "Justice now, I think."

Hannah merely nodded, her expression unreadable behind her visor. Braddock's expression, however, was an open book—the man obviously angry and ready to protest. Saul slung one leg over the robot and jammed his fingers into a row of data ports inset in its upper surface. It leapt from the walkway, claws closing on beams in the latticework, then propelled itself onwards through the internal structure of the station wheel, like some magical lion in a VR fantasy.

The machine exhibited none of the jerkiness associated with robotics of previous ages; instead his metallic mount flowed smoothly towards its destination, keeping him seated safely by choosing a route to ensure he wouldn't be knocked from its back—or, rather, Saul was doing that himself, because his mind lay as much inside these machines as in the grey fat inside his skull. Through other eyes—or rather sensors—he saw Hannah and Braddock reach the airlock that led up into the entrance block of Tech Central. There they would be safe, at least for a little while.

Finally, his robot mount landed on top of the wide tubeway snaking down and away from Tech Central, and after he had stepped down it joined its fellow in cutting and levering up a section of the bubblemetal ceiling. *Faster*, he needed to move much *faster*. But even as he registered that thought, he saw from another viewpoint the missile speeding down towards them.

Saul hurled himself forward, every instinct now concentrating on personal physical survival. He shouldered the floor and rolled into the gap below the plate the two robots were levering up, then shoved himself downwards. Even as he was falling through he pulled the machine pistol from his thigh pocket, aimed it and fired. Two of Smith's guards flew backwards just as the missile detonated above, shaking the tubeway violently. As he hit the floor, he initiated the gecko function of his boots and propelled himself forward, firing again to send a third guard spinning and bouncing backwards in dreamy slow motion, vapour jets pinpointing the punctures in his spacesuit.

Behind Saul, an undamaged robot slipped through also, but as it tried to right itself, a robot under Smith's control hurtled along the tubeway leading from Tech Central and slammed into it, a collision silent in vacuum, yet noisy in interference over com as internal components shorted. Shots tracked along the nearby wall as the last guard tried to regain his balance and get a bead on Saul—but by then Saul was on him. He caught the barrel of the man's gun and pushed it aside, whilst pulling himself in closer. A heel-of-the-hand blow to the man's visor, then again and again, air leaks starting to create vapour trails all around it, his gun barrel hot, and vibrating in Saul's gloved hand, as it spewed a stream of bullets. The guard tried a hook punch, but Saul turned him towards the wall and chopped at the back of his neck—once, twice and then again to feel something break.

"Smith!" he bellowed, with com set to broadcast.

Smith had abandoned his guards and fled out of sight, somewhere ahead.

Glancing back, Saul saw the two robots still locked together, their movements growing sluggish as they died. The tools they used for their work were as effective against each other's bodies as on the metals they manipulated, and in very little time they had managed to nearly cut each other apart. He summoned more robots towards the tubeway, certain he would need them, then grabbed up a machine pistol and went loping after Smith.

In the network, Smith then went for him, closing the virtual gap between them. Through surrounding cams they could now see each other. Smith was down on one knee, armed with some sort of wide-barrelled assault rifle aimed back along the tubeway. Within Saul's mind, Smith delved into the organic interface, this interference firing off nerves in Saul's body. He staggered, his inner ear telling him everything was spinning, while those jagged flashing lights blinded his human eyes.

Saul fought back by going for a more specific effect, looking for a physical function already queued up, and forcing it. Smith's finger pulled tight on his trigger, so his weapon emptied itself on full automatic. Recovering as Smith's attack on him weakened, Saul saw armour-piercers punching through the wall just ahead of him with shreds of paint showering away like snow.

"Acceptable," Smith said, and copied his opponent's attack.

Saul's own trigger finger closed, low-impact slugs denting the floor by his boot, scattering fragments of blue plastic in every direction. Smith abandoned the assault rifle and drew a side arm, but access to that trigger response had become easy for both of them, and Smith nearly shot himself in the leg before managing to drop the weapon.

Round the corner now, and there he found Smith waiting, those ridiculously blue eyes glaring from behind his spacesuit visor. Saul was finding it difficult to walk by now, just as Smith was finding it difficult to turn and run. They were rooting deep into each other's hardware and software, feeding back instructions through the organic interfaces they both possessed. Robots, friend and foe, were closing in on the tubeway from all around, and Saul had no idea which side would get there first.

This had to be finished, soon.

Saul reached his opponent, closed a hand on his shoulder and spun him round again. Smith's fist came up towards Saul's throat, but he managed to turn enough for it to glance off the side of his helmet. But the knife in Smith's other hand lunged straight through the fabric of Saul's spacesuit and into his side. Agony surged through him as Smith tried to tilt the knife upwards through Saul's liver, to find his heart. No good: grip all wrong. Smith extracted the blade to try again, which gave Saul just the break he needed. All but blind now, he grabbed Smith's hand and turned the knife away, driving it back towards the man's throat, below the metal rim of his helmet. But instead it went lower, going in just above Smith's collarbone, and sent the other man staggering backwards. Saul now tried to seize sufficient mental control to make Smith pull the weapon out and stab again, but, with a spastic convulsion of his arm, Smith flung the knife away.

Now the entire tubeway shuddered under the clash of combat. Through multiple sensors Saul observed the robot-on-robot battle outside, and realized he had no way of knowing which side would win. If one of Smith's robots made its way inside this tubeway first, then Saul was dead—though the reverse applied too.

"You are a greater enemy of freedom than I considered," declared Smith ludicrously, one hand at his collarbone, where blood and suit sealant had begun welling underneath. He looked grey and sick and—to Saul's eyes—scared.

Saul didn't bother replying. Navigating only by cam view, he grabbed a nearby safety handle, propelled himself over to the knife and snatched it up, his shoulder jarring against the floor and causing something to twang painfully in his side. He then rolled through the air, bringing his feet down to adhere, pushed himself upright again and held the knife ready. However, this time Smith did not seem inclined towards hand-to-hand fighting. He resorted to a mental assault instead, but it bounced away as Saul now recognized it and closed down that route into his mind.

Smith suddenly turned and fled, propelling himself along the tubeway, perhaps knowing he would lose in any physical encounter, but not knowing that Saul could hardly see him. Saul tried to slow him by interfering with the operation of his limbs, but Smith had closed down that route too and, in retreat, presented a sheer and slippery surface that Saul could find no purchase on. Tracking him by cams, Saul stuck with him to the limit of his own domain.

Smith hauled himself to a halt before moving beyond the last of the cams that Saul controlled. Hand pressed to his knife wound, he gazed up at the nearest lens.

"We will conclude this matter later, Citizen," he managed to gasp.

Then he was gone.

***

Outside the tubeway itself the robot-on-robot battle continued, but the ones Smith controlled were now steadily retreating. This might look like a victory, but Saul knew otherwise. Smith might have pulled back, but mentally he seemed stronger. Though by using the element of surprise Saul had carved out a little realm for himself, Smith still controlled the rest of the station, its personnel, and the bulk of the robots. And now those jagged flashes of light were killing the last traces of Saul's human vision, his side hurt even more than his head, and he was beginning to cough up foamy blood. Without medical attention he could soon die here, he realized, but he needed to give himself a breathing space.

Taking a firm grip on the readerguns he did control, he began opening up on security personnel, but even now many of the troops were withdrawing into those grey areas where the readerguns were out of commission. Only those whose escape routes were blocked by the guns or robots that Saul controlled were still trapped.

As he lay there, blood bubbling in his lungs, Saul perceived a number of options. He could continue this local slaughter until no one remained standing against him, but with cold calculation he realized that he might need personnel on his side to finally win this place. That meant demonstrating some compassion, even if it wasn't genuinely there. He therefore shut down readerguns and put his robots on hold.

"Lay down your weapons," he broadcast to those trapped soldiers, through personal fones and spacesuit com systems.

Through a thousand cams, he watched security-force personnel still firing on the robots poised to fall upon them. Some had already destroyed readerguns that had turned on them, that had been blocking their retreat. Hundreds of messages slid into the network, seeking instructions from the commander, or from Smith and his immediate subordinates, but so far no replies seemed to be forthcoming.

"This section of the station is no longer under Smith's control," he informed them, his lips merely miming the words, but the com system turning them into something stronger than he himself could physically manage. "I am now in control of all local computer systems, robots and readerguns, so you will drop your weapons immediately and either leave the area extending between Arcoplex One and the Arboretum, and including Tech Central, or return to your quarters to await instructions." With that, he made the robots in the area jerk forward menacingly like war dogs pulling at their leashes, and set readerguns in motion momentarily, but did not allow them to fire.

A fit of coughing racked him suddenly, more blood emerging, his breath becoming noticeably shorter. Saul rested for a moment whilst watching the security forces scattered about the area. Listening to the exchange of orders, he finally managed to locate the military commander of all these troops. It was a guy called Langstrom, so he opened up com with him.

"Political Director Smith has abandoned you," he explained. "I now have absolute control of this section. The only choice you now have is whether you obey me and live, or disobey and die."

Momentarily transferring his attention to Tech Central, he saw Braddock herding all but three of the staff outside and sending them on their way. Hannah meanwhile held the remaining three at gunpoint, so perhaps it was Braddock's idea to keep a limited number of hostages. But they needed to be people Smith actually cared about, and Saul doubted that such people existed. He next explored Tech Central's schematic, in his mind, quickly finding what he required, then connected to a simple cleaner robot nearby and sent it over to Hannah's location. Finally he summoned one of the least damaged construction robots remaining just outside the tubeway.

"Who is this?" Langstrom responded, with seemingly admirable calm.

About twenty troops had retreated into another tubeway, where they had eliminated the nearest readergun. They were obviously on the point of heading for the next gun along, just as Saul started making his announcements. Langstrom was a wiry black man clad in the same style of vacuum combat suit as his soldiers, except with a silver diagonal bar across the front, and he now stood near an uncompleted section of tubeway, gazing out into the web of girders running between the latticework walls. Within view were soldiers who until then had been fighting desperately against robots that Saul controlled.

"My name is Alan Saul, but that of course means nothing to you."

"Precisely," Langstrom replied.

Just a mental nudge caused all the robots within view to once again advance slightly. Firing broke out again, until Langstrom issued orders into his helmet mike.

"If he really controls all the readerguns and robots, like he says he does," observed a huge bulky man standing just behind Langstrom, "we don't stand much chance of getting out of here."

"And if he's lying, and we surrender our weapons," said Langstrom, "you know damned well what Smith will do with us."

"Have you recently received any word from Smith?" Saul interjected.

Langstrom shook his head involuntarily, then said, "No word, as yet."

There was nothing to stop Smith from communicating with his troops isolated here, but it seemed he considered them even more dispensable than the robots he had withdrawn from the fighting earlier. Saul also wondered if Smith was now receiving medical treatment, just like he himself would need very soon.

"He wasn't lying about these readerguns here," said the bulky man, eyeing two corpses sprawled at the edge of the tubeway. "And he's not lying about the robots either."

Langstrom nodded. "What guarantees are you offering?"

"You know I need to offer you none," Saul replied.

The man again tried for some response from Smith, but got nothing. He then cursed and tossed down his machine pistol.

"Smart move," Saul remarked.

"You're watching?" Langstrom asked.

"As I told you, I have control in a limited area, but my control there is absolute."

"You'll let my men come in?" Gesturing up at the nearest cam, Langstrom pointed out the robots that hovered menacingly.

"So long as they don't try anything stupid, Langstrom," Saul agreed.

Langstrom nodded briefly and waved his men back. Speaking over com, he called them all in, and soon they began retreating.

"What is it you want?" was his parting question.

Right then, Saul wanted more than anything to not be leaking so much blood inside his suit.

"Not your concern right now," he replied.

As the commander moved off, Saul opened com with Tech Central. "Hannah," he began.

Braddock was now back inside, too, where he had ordered the three remaining captives to call up views of the surrounding area on their screens. Both he and she looked up simultaneously.

"A cleanbot has arrived just outside, and I want you to follow it."

"Where to?"

"There's a surgical area located one floor below you."

"I see," she said, suddenly looking worried.

Just then the construction robot arrived, dropping through the hole in the tubeway roof, and advanced towards him. He could only see it through the cams, as he programmed in its next location, retracing Smith's escape route along the tubeway, before giving it very careful instructions about how to pick Saul up. Even so, the world greyed for a moment as its claws closed around him, but it seemed that unconsciousness remained out of his reach.

Hannah felt overcome by a sudden atavistic fear at the sight of the construction robot crouching in the corridor with bloodstains on its cowling. When she saw Saul slumped in front of it with his back propped against the wall, she assumed it must have attacked him. Then she noticed the Caduceus symbol on the door he was resting beside, and logic triumphed. She stepped over the cleanbot that had guided her here, and rushed over to kneel before him.

"Smith...got away," Saul managed.

Those were definitely not the words she wanted to hear. She stared at the blood plating the outside of his spacesuit, dried out and turned oak-brown by vacuum. "Where are you wounded?"

"Side." He gestured with one blood-smeared glove.

Hannah peered at the mess of suit sealant that had boiled out of there. "Can you move?" A weak shake of the head. "I'm going to need Braddock," she decided.

After a pause Saul replied, "He's coming now."

Braddock arrived in double-quick time, armed and looking for a fight, but as soon as he saw Saul, his face turned white. Was that because without Saul their chances of survival became precisely nil?

"The prisoners?" Hannah enquired.

"I locked them in the toilet," Braddock told her.

"Okay, help me."

They carried Saul as carefully as possible through the door and into a surgery prep room.

"Get his suit off," Hannah instructed, as she herself frantically began checking the cold stores and equipment cupboards ranged along one wall. It was good that the level of gravity lay as close to zero as made no difference, otherwise Braddock's task would have been much more difficult. By the time she had found trauma dressings and a pair of scissors, Braddock had removed the spacesuit to expose the blood-soaked undersuit. Whilst he held Saul in place Hannah cut away the undersuit, and soon located the wound. She then affixed a trauma dressing, which quickly formed itself over the wound while infusing it with coagulants. After that they loaded Saul on to a special gurney which closed pads securely over his arms, legs and forehead, before rolling him through the clean lock leading into the operating theatre.

"What about Smith?" Braddock asked.

"He got away," she replied bluntly, trying to stamp down on her fears. She just had to be pragmatic; no use wondering when Inspectorate enforcers would come piling in here to drag them away, no use thinking about what lay in store if Smith managed to get to them.

"So we're fucked," replied Braddock, equally blunt.

She quickly stripped off her spacesuit and undersuit, hardly noticing Braddock's embarrassment as he turned away. She then propelled herself through into the surgeon's lock, quickly donning surgeon's whites and forgoing the decontamination process. Now in utterly familiar surroundings, she connected up a pressurized blood feed to her patient, before administering a general anaesthetic through it. While Saul was relaxing into unconsciousness, she began sifting through the tools she required, picking up a wound ring of the appropriate size.

"We need him awake again as quickly as possible," warned Braddock, from the other side of the isolation window, having obviously located the intercom. "If Smith discovers he's out of it, his people will be down on us in a second."

"No, really?" said Hannah, sarcastically.

She stripped away the dressing to expose the weeping hole in Saul's side, then folded up the wound ring and inserted it into the gash, before opening it out to leave a neat round hole into his body, out of which oozed black, jelly-like blood. Next she swung over the microsurgery unit and positioned its slow-worm head in the mouth of the wound. The head pushed its way in, tentatively exploring inside the patient's body, suction pipes slurping as they cleared out yet more congealing blood or leaking fluids, while sensors mapped out the internal damage to its screen, for her inspection.

The knife had penetrated his side, slicing straight through his liver and pancreas, and, just missing the splenic artery, had twisted upwards and into the lobe of one lung. The comprehensive damage ended only a couple of centimetres from his heart, but, even so, the lesser vena cava had been nicked. Starting with that vein, Hannah began repairing the damage, working the microsurgery head gradually back out, cauterizing and gluing on its way. Most of this repair work could be left to automatic programming now the damage was mapped into the machine's processor, but she did pause it a couple of times to inspect the situation more closely. This was all wrong, she soon realized. Some of the damage within Saul had already begun to heal up, and checking his bloodwork, she found it flooded with unassigned stem cells and other elements she just did not recognize. And she felt renewed awe of the man he had once been.

The work continued until the slow-worm head slipped obscenely out of the wound carrying the wound ring with it. Micro-manipulators then drew it closed, the astringent smell of wound glue arose, then a brief sound like that of a fingernail being run along the teeth of a comb as the surgical head stitched in a neat row of staples just to make doubly sure.

"I'm done now," said Hannah.

"That was quick," remarked Braddock.

"Left untended, a normal person would probably have died quickly," she explained flatly as she folded the microsurgery head back down into its sterilizer. "He was already beginning to heal up."

"Heal up?" Braddock echoed, puzzled.

"His predecessor's nano-viral fix."

"Nano-viral fix?" asked Braddock. "Predecessor?"

"It's a long story," she replied.

"Right," Braddock snarled, obviously annoyed. "So what happens now?"

"You think I know?" Hannah spat back.

She shifted the microsurgery unit away from the gurney, then headed over to the drug dispensary. There she tapped her requirements into a touch screen, and waited while it buzzed and hummed to itself. Shortly a drawer emerged, holding three loaded syringes: one containing a counter-agent for his anaesthetic, the second a mix of sugars, antishocks, viral and bacterial applications, the third a wide-spectrum stimulant package. She injected just the counter-agent and waited.

Saul lay utterly still for a short while, then suddenly jerked, his left hand rising to touch the wound in his side. He opened his eyes and licked his lips, then slowly sat upright, using his arms to lever himself up. Just as well, because straining his stomach muscles didn't seem like a great idea right then. For a moment Hannah assumed that the chilly distance of his expression was due to the drugs, then she realized that he was back inside the station's computer network.

"The pain…has gone," he slurred. "And I can see again."

See?

He reached up and probed his forehead, closed his eyes and for a moment fell utterly still. Then abruptly his eyes reopened.

"Unbelievable," he said, the slur vanishing from his tone.

"What is?" demanded Braddock from behind the glass, before peering suspiciously at the door behind him, cradling his machine pistol even closer.

"The Argus satellite system," Saul explained, shaking his head slowly. "There are seven thousand satellites in all, of which only ten per cent are functional. I've just managed to achieve a limited penetration, but that's enough to interpret how it's intended to run."

Saul carefully swung his legs off the gurney, then didn't appear strong enough to proceed any further, besides which, the pressure feed was still plugged into his arm.

"How, then?" Hannah asked, as she uncapped each in turn of the remaining two syringes.

"All queued up and ready for mass slaughter," he continued. "But in the typically fucked-up way of any operation run by government."

"How fucked up?" asked Braddock.

"The satellites can pick up ID implant signals and target individuals, but what criminal or revolutionary ever sticks to the same identity?"

"True enough."

"So they tried recognition systems." Saul glanced across at him. "The satellites all possess high-definition cameras capable of reading the writing on a cigarette packet from orbit. The images they obtain can then be run through complex recognition systems—the aim being to target selected individuals."

"Yeah, and so?

"A slight problem is that such recognition systems are keyed to a human's face, not to the top of his head."

"You're shitting me."

Hannah held her syringes ready. "So that means the Committee's dream of being able to identify and eliminate single insurgents from orbit is still very much a dream?"

"It is, but governments never let go of a bad idea."

Saul finally pushed himself away from the gurney, standing up for a moment, still wobbly. In Earth gravity, he would already have been flat on the floor. Hannah stepped forward to squeeze the larger syringe into the pressure feed plugged into his forearm. Then she swabbed his biceps before injecting the smaller syringe, containing stimulants. Saul watched this procedure with a kind of impatient detachment.

"So what're they using now?" Braddock asked.

"A rather less specific option called DAS."

As the stimulants began slowly kicking in, Saul straightened up and began to look marginally more alert. He gazed around the surgery, eyed the blood pooled on the gurney for a moment, then turned back to meet Hannah's gaze. He gave a nod of acknowledgement. "Thanks."

"Think nothing of it," she replied. "It wasn't exactly brain surgery."

He managed a grin, but it seemed an expression delivered by rote.

"Is that portable?" He was pointing at the pressure feed—a device positioned on the side of the gurney, into which square blood packs were plugged like ink refills.

Hannah detached the object from the gurney and held it up.

"We need to get into Tech Central itself." He reached out for the pressure feed, took it and tucked it under his arm.

Exiting the aseptic surgery was less of a problem than actually getting into it, though a little screen did flash up a warning about them taking contaminated clothing outside. After she had helped him pull on a pair of disposeralls, cutting through one sleeve so as to feed the pipes through, Hannah overrode this warning and they moved outside to join Braddock. Now that Saul was mobile she could see how the sugars and stimulants were kicking in faster and how he propelled himself purposefully towards the door. But on gecko boots, Braddock got there ahead of him, opened the door and helped Saul to make his way through.

This display of oversolicitousness annoyed Hannah. She understood how their lives now depended on Saul, but there seemed more underlying Braddock's behaviour than that. It seemed the soldier had found someone new to serve.

Once in the corridor outside, Braddock asked impatiently, "What the fuck is DAS?"

"Defined Area Suppression," Saul replied, flicking his gaze towards the robot that had carried him here. "The entire planet has been segmented into a grid whose smallest area measures about a kilometre square. Feed a square number of the grid into the system, and the satellites will burn anyone found inside it. Even now, data is being uploaded from the surface to define those places on Earth that are being sectored: five square kilometres here, seven there, and ten over there. In fact, sectoring has been worked on the basis of the grid already present in the computer system here—which means they've been planning to depopulate those sectors for some time."

Hannah absorbed this in silence and looked away. She wasn't sure why he felt the need to repeatedly drive home the murderousness of the Committee. Perhaps to justify the actions he himself intended to take?

Saul turned to Braddock. "Agricultural land is also covered, as are large areas of the sea, since government vessels broadcast their position on a particular frequency and won't be targeted. Someone has also been feeding in masses of data related to tenement and office blocks, houses, reservoirs, universities, schools, specific streets…basically any area or structure that can be comprehensively 'defined.'" He almost spat the last word. "I guess this ensures that the Inspectorate can more easily call in a strike." He paused, his gaze swinging back to Hannah. "They've gone one step up on the pain inducers. With this system up and running, the next riot would end quickly—and that *burning pain* would be real."

She could see his anger, which seemed to flare out of his red eyes. She might have felt that such *human* emotion should make him appear to be more human, but it seemed to expose something unhuman in him, instead. Noise behind, then, and she glanced over her shoulder to see the construction robot back up on its feet, turning round in the corridor and heading away.

"What happened with Smith?" she asked.

"I think he is definitely stronger than me, but I managed to catch him by surprise."

"But then he surprised you?"

"Yes." Saul pressed a hand against his side.

"Can you defeat him?"

"I don't know. I stuck his own knife back in him, and he ran."

"That's not the answer I was looking for."

"It's the only one I can give."

14

SCRAP MARS

A question that has often been raised is: "What interest does the Committee have in Mars?" To which the answer has to be that in the beginning it had no interest at all. The early Mars missions were part of a project jointly pursued by the Asian Coalition and Pan Europa; an affirmation of the ties that eventually led to the creation of the Committee itself. However, as the Committee increased in power, some of the delegates initiated a sequence of moves to scrap the Mars project—one such being arguably the reason why the first base, in Valles Marineris, failed. However, more far-sighted Committee members kept the whole project going because, utilizing data produced by assessment and focus groups, they came to the conclusion that the Mars missions could ultimately lead to a tightening of their control over Earth. The project's infrastructure would enable them to obtain crucial metals from the asteroid belt, which in turn could provide the basis for a space-based industry large enough to construct the Argus satellite network. Beyond this, they had little interest in the red planet, though one discussion point was mooted: if travelling to Mars became an easy option, it might become useful as a prison planet.

ANTARES BASE

"I see," said Ricard, "that you now have entered Hydroponics, which is one of the most critical areas on this base. Doubtless you have also murdered my two men stationed there. Be assured that by threatening our food supply, you cannot hold the people of this base to ransom."

"Speaking for the crowd again," observed Var.

They looted the two corpses but, disappointingly, this provided them with only two machine pistols and five clips of plastic ammunition. It seemed that even Ricard hadn't thought it wise to arm guards located inside Hydroponics with weapons and ammo capable of penetrating the geodesic dome.

"He'll be sending his men soon," Lopomac warned.

"He can't send all of them."

The public-address speaker system now emitted a feedback whine, and Ricard started speaking again, but this time without the echo in the background. Obviously he was now addressing them directly, rather than including the whole base.

"So, Var, what will you do now?" he began. "I have six highly trained Inspectorate personnel here with me, and I've provided them with antipersonnel grenades, and Kalashtek assault rifles, along with a crate of ceramic ammunition. I also have all the rest of the base personnel locked up in the Community Room, many of whom are friends and associates of yours."

Var noticed the com icon flashing down in one corner of her visor. Ricard wanted to talk to her privately, but what really was there to say?

"He's in Hex One, right now," observed Carol.

"He must have loaded up a crawler and taken it round," suggested Lopomac.

Var had perhaps underestimated Ricard, having expected him to stay hidden in the safety of Hex Three.

Ricard continued, "By my estimation, you yourselves must possess some weapons—mostly plastic ammunition and, I see from the base manifest, maybe one seismic charge. You have two choices now. One is that you rebalance the atmosphere in Hydroponics, then, once the bulkhead doors can be opened, you come at us through the adjoining wing—where my men will be waiting for you. Your only alternative is to exit via an airlock and try to gain access in some other way. However, the second shepherd is waiting outside for you, and it is now adjusted for shredding rather than capture mode. You might even get lucky with the one seismic charge you possess, but I doubt that, since our robot is now broadcasting local EM interference so that any radio detonation signal simply won't work."

"What the hell do we do?" Carol wondered. She sounded weary, and defeated.

"We don't have much time," admitted Var, at a loss.

"We can't take off the head now," said Lopomac, "but we can still deliver an ultimatum to him and Silberman, and to the remaining enforcers. They'll have heard Le Blanc's speech and will know the situation: they can't run this base by themselves. We demand that they surrender their weapons, and their authority, and that from now on we run this place separate from Earth, and on the basis of the needs of all here. No more political thought police—we can't survive like that."

"Yes, that's the most logical step," said Var, "but Ricard won't see it that way." Lopomac was just babbling, just hoping to see some clear way of dealing with this.

"You'll have to play the cards you've got," said Kaskan, who, Var noted, was now holding the seismic charge. "There'll be more weapons available in Hex Three."

"Got any suggestions on how we get there?" Lopomac asked.

Kaskan shrugged, then began walking right across the hex towards the airlock. "You cut the power and you threaten to kill them all, thus forcing Ricard and his men to go after you."

Var just then registered the words Kaskan had used: *You'll have to play the cards you've got.* He was talking like someone who wasn't included in their predicament.

"And kill everyone else remaining on the base?" asked Carol. "You know how fine the dividing line is between unconsciousness and death, once you start running out of air." She pointed to the two corpses lying on the floor.

"Var here has already demonstrated extreme ruthlessness," said Kaskan. "She'll surely be able to convince Ricard, then it'll be a straight fight."

Var suddenly understood what he was doing.

"No, Kaskan!"

But he had already opened the airlock and stepped inside.

"I loved Gisender," he called back to them. "You've no idea how much."

He closed the inner airlock door.

ARGUS STATION

The jagged lights were gone from his eyes, and his head no longer pounded, but that might be as much due to the drugs Hannah had fed him as anything else. Whatever, he must use every second he remained functional.

At that moment, Smith did not seem to be active, perhaps himself lying drugged in some surgical facility, and currently beyond Saul's ability to locate him. However, already the Committee was responding, and four space planes had been launched from Minsk. They had to be dealt with so, as carefully and as quietly as possible, Saul returned his attention to the systems in Tech Central that controlled the laser satellites. Very quickly he discovered that their security had already been breached. The set-up originally required at least five members of the Committee acting jointly to bring the system online, and then input the targets. But Smith had created a back door for himself so that he could take full control, which showed how in recent times he'd been working to his own advantage only. Checking status next, Saul discovered that only 10 per cent of the network was ready to use but, even so, that was nearly seven hundred satellites, each of them fusion-powered and firing a multi-megawatt laser capable of incinerating a single human being right down on the surface.

He could do a lot of damage, but only for so long as he retained control.

As Saul moved slowly down the corridor, catching at wall handles to propel himself along, even the adhesive quality of his sticky soles seemed too strong in his present weakened state. Nevertheless he concentrated beyond his own body, slowly infiltrating the satellite control system through the same back door that Smith had created. He studied the limitation to what he could achieve before alerting Smith to his intrusion—not a lot really: just run computer diagnostics and power-source tests. Using the latter test routine, he sent the requisite instructions to power up the seven hundred available satellites. Readings at once started climbing, as fusion reactors dumped their loads into advanced super-capacitor storage, and Saul knew that within a few minutes the satellites would start signalling their readiness to him—and, unfortunately, to Smith.

Saul couldn't use the satellite weapons to stop the space planes already heading up here. Two of them had gone into SCRAM, and there was no point in trying to laser them, since their carbon nanofibre hulls were designed to disperse point temperatures and comfortably withstand temperatures that would melt steel. But he could certainly prevent further planes launching.

"You okay with this?" Hannah asked him, as they reached the cageway at the very end of the corridor.

Saul looked up. Of course he was—after all, he weighed nothing here.

"I think I can manage," he said, reaching out to one of the struts.

Just then, something else came to his attention. Message traffic from Earth, and from the approaching space planes, was being responded to by people aboard the station itself. As he slowly propelled himself up towards Tech Central, he ran traces that discovered these replies were coming from partially isolated computers scattered throughout.

Smith.

In a structure called the Political Office, situated down between Arcoplexes One and Two, Smith—obviously yet to visit the infirmary—sat strapped in a seat with a blood-soaked dressing taped across his bare chest. Other Inspectorate staff were busy communicating from various small security offices, while Commander Langstrom was speaking from the security force's barracks. Right then, Saul couldn't break the code used for the actual transmissions but, whilst the transmissions were coded, Smith stupidly hadn't blocked Saul's access to station microphones and cameras, so it was still possible for him to listen to any audible exchange. This gave him pause for thought. It was surely such a basic requirement to ensure secure communications, yet it seemed his erstwhile interrogator had neglected to do so. Perhaps, while Smith had underestimated Saul, Saul had equally overestimated Smith?

Saul netted all the conversations at once, and processed the resulting audio data. Langstrom was giving a pretty good assessment of the situation on the station and received orders to back up the assault troops, once they arrived. Smith was meanwhile notifying someone on Earth that he intended to arrest and adjust Langstrom once this was all over, since, as Smith had noted before, Langstrom had been showing signs of incorrect thinking. Checking data relating to this Saul discovered that, as Political Director, Smith was also in overall charge of the adjustment cells located aboard the station. Saul hadn't so far picked up on the fact that they operated such facilities here.

"What about the robots?" Langstrom asked.

Saul understood the man's concerns, because just then he took a look into the barracks' hospital, where medics were still struggling to repair the damage resulting from hand-to-hydraulic-claw combat. It wasn't pretty, and the surgical facilities available weren't quite so good as those Saul had recently used. He now realized that he had occupied the kind of surgery reserved for the upper echelons, who were rated "more equal than others."

Apparently the answer to the robot problem was the PA50 TB, and further research identified the "Pulse Action 50 Tank Buster." This was an electromagnetic weapon developed to knock out the electronics of modern tanks, and like many such weapons had been sidelined when the Committee decided the only people left to fight would be armed merely with bricks and Molotov cocktails.

"Langstrom," Saul spoke directly to the man, through his fone, "here's an audio file you might like to listen to." He then sent him a nice clear recording of Smith's earlier conversation about future "adjustment"—then turned his attention elsewhere, as satellite after satellite reported readiness to fire.

"Trouble on the way," he informed Hannah and Braddock.

"What kind?" Braddock asked.

"Four space planes loaded with troops in vacuum combat gear." Saul finally brought himself to a halt at the top of the cageway, and stepped out into the short corridor beyond. "They're also bringing EM weapons capable of knocking out the robots. Should be quite a party."

"You seem rather unconcerned?" Hannah ventured.

"I *am* concerned," he replied, "but I'm also busy."

Now alerted by the readiness signal received from the satellites, Smith tilted his head for a moment, obviously rapidly processing data, then peered up at the camera Saul had pointing towards him. Feed from that particular cam blanked out, and, a moment later, Smith began closing the gap in his security. Saul immediately launched an attack on the Political Office, trying to infiltrate it, but Smith hit back and Saul found himself fighting a savage informational battle, striving to hold open his control channel to the satellites, while constantly rewriting code.

Only two of the ten per cent of functional satellites were positioned geostat in range of Minsk. Saul fought for control of them all, but focused primarily on retaining control of just those two, ready to sacrifice the others.

Saul was in a position to sector the critical areas of the spaceport and unleash the laser weapons, spreading burning corpses across the carbocrete. But that wouldn't stop the next two nearly fully loaded space planes from taking off, and he had no way of punching through their hulls to get to the troops inside. He deliberately sacrificed control of the anthropic targeting programs of the lasers to Smith, which left the man juggling with a huge mass of additional data, and meanwhile identified installations and support equipment down at Minsk, then began selecting specific targets, and planning the most effective firing pattern. Next he routed a firing order to all satellites, allowing Smith to take nearly half of them away from him, simply to ensure control of the critical two.

Using high-definition telephoto cams positioned all about the Argus Station, Saul focused on one of the satellites he'd ordered to fire. The cylindrical object measured ten metres long and five in diameter, four solar panels extending like wings fore and aft to complement its fusion-power source, while impellers were dotted about its surface. A hyox engine jutted out to the rear—used to first position the satellite where needed, but also to reposition it should demand from some other hemisphere require it. As it fired, the beam wasn't immediately visible, only flashing into view way down below, at the point where it punched through a thin layer of cirrus. The first strike hit the side of a fuel tanker parked right beside one of the loaded space planes, but only heated up metal and set it smoking. The second strike did the real damage. A spout of flame erupted from the side of the tanker, hosing across all the umbilicals and installations nearby, then shooting underneath the plane itself. Then the tanker blew, its front end blasted clear of the ground and the whole vehicle turning a complete cartwheel. The space plane juddered sideways, then crashed down on its belly as its landing gear collapsed.

This damage was done in less than a second, and Smith, still struggling to fortify his hold on the satellites Saul had now allowed him, hadn't even noticed.

But no tanker stood beside the second plane, and already the ground crews were retracting all the umbilicals, and preparing to withdraw all the loaders and passenger tunnels. Again and again, Saul hit the points where those tunnels connected to the plane, until he could see fire and molten metal erupt, then begin to spiral out from that point, crippling loaders and vaporizing chunks out of the caterpillar treads that the mobile access buildings moved about on. Then he got lucky, because one of the loaders on the ground, obviously hydrogen-powered, exploded and rolled underneath the plane. Even if they could manage to detach the passenger ramp and get the airlock closed, it would still take them a long time to clear the rest of the debris out of the way. Time for some insurance, just as Smith—probably informed of what was happening by his contacts below—now tried to seize control of the two active satellites.

Eight fuel-tanker trucks were drawn up in a neat line inside a heavily secured compound, with a ninth tanker parked alongside the big overground pumps that drew fuel up from an underground cistern. This one tanker was currently being filled, hoses trailing from it across the carbocrete. He didn't know if the other eight were waiting to be filled or already full, but it didn't matter. He hit the hose first, then concentrated his aim on the pumps, all to spectacular effect.

Burning liquid fuel flooded from the ruptured pipe, pursuing three personnel trying to escape across the carbocrete, but even when they reached the compound fence and tried to climb it, they weren't quick enough. The firestorm expanded from the compound in a steadily widening tide. Within, it flowed underneath the tanker parked beside the pumps, then spread across and underneath all the other tankers, so that in moments their tyres were burning. Next the pumps blew, hurling chunks of heavy machinery high into the air. The blast rolled the loading tanker straight into the neat row of its fellows, spewing a jet of flame from its filler port. At this point, a tanker in the middle of the row exploded, overturning the one next to it. Then the underground tank began itself to spew blazing fuel, erupting from where the pumps had stood like a mini-volcano. Saul saw fences sagging and collapsing, with a few burning remnants still clinging to them of those who had been trying to flee. It was so hot down there that the wire began melting. Another tanker blew, and yet another, a moment later, then his view was blotted out by the thick black smoke cloud rising from the firestorm.

Saul immediately turned his attention to securing his gains but, oddly, Smith merely retreated from him.

"Hopefully I've delayed any more launches out of Minsk for a while," Saul declared, "but there are four planes already on their way up here, and we need to find a way of dealing with them within the next hour."

The short corridor led directly into the lobby of Tech Central, where Saul could see the result of one of his earlier actions. Two guards sprawled motionless behind overturned metal desks, large portions of their heads spread across the floor and up the wall behind them.

"And how did you stop further launches?" Hannah enquired, her tone flat, her face pale.

"You'll see," he said.

"I want to see, too," said Braddock, glancing at Saul with something akin to admiration.

They entered Tech Central to the sound of hammering from within the adjacent toilet.

"Be quiet!" Braddock bellowed.

A couple of surprised exclamations issued from within, and the noise ceased. Saul peered through the two cams in there to see a man and two women clad in the cheap standard garments of technicians. Then he turned to study the rest of Tech Central as he began finessing his control of every system that originated from here, and still remained within his compass.

This room was just like the one he had seized control of in the cell complex at Inspectorate HQ London. It bore some resemblance to a flight-control room, with outward-slanting windows running around most of the exterior, but in this case overlooking the asteroid and the full extent of the station wheel radiating all about them. Below the windows lay a range of consoles and screens, which also ran around those walls lacking windows. Saul moved over to a work station with three much larger screens mounted above it. He pulled himself down into a swivel chair and rested his blood pressure-feed on the console. The console was laden with controls he didn't need because, by just using his mind, he now brought up a repeating series of views on the middle screen, including a close-up of the fire raging down on Earth, and a more distant shot of the whole spaceport.

"Minsk," he murmured.

"You used the lasers?" Braddock frowned. "I thought they had only anti-personnel capacity?"

"A rifle, too, is an antipersonnel weapon, but it's amazing what happens when you fire a tracer bullet into a petrol tank."

"Point taken," Braddock conceded.

"Now these." Saul gestured, as on all three screens he pulled up views, through the sat cams, of the space planes approaching.

"And you can't use the lasers against them," said Hannah, pulling up a swivel chair beside him, and sitting astride it with her forearms resting on the back.

"No, they wouldn't be able to penetrate."

"So you've no usable weapons out there now?"

"On the contrary," replied Saul, an idea taking shape in his mind, "I have a number of satellites at my disposal."

"But you said Smith—"

Saul held up his hand to silence her. "Please, I need to think."

It was all about trajectories. The less atmospheric pressure around the planes, as they continued rising, the more dependent they became upon steering jets rather than ailerons and wing-repositioning, and the less manoeuvrable they thus became. The two satellites were still within range and remained under his control, while his defence against Smith's perpetual probing attacks was steadily growing stronger and almost self-maintaining. He pulled up some nice close-shot pictures of each on two of the three screens and set the cameras to tracking them whilst maintaining a view of the approaching planes on the third screen. "What are you doing now?" Hannah asked.

"It's nice that they're bringing those planes up in such a tight formation," he noted.

She shot a look of puzzlement at Braddock, who brought his two fists together with a thwack, and then grinned. Then she nodded in understanding.

"Now I need to disarm Smith," continued Saul.

He opened fire from the other satellites under his control upon the ones that Smith controlled. Smith was quick to reply, and their incandescent battle must have been clearly visible from Earth, as lasers repeatedly targeted fellow satellites. But the whole thing was taking longer than Saul had expected, and on checking stored schematics he discovered that all these satellites were protected externally by a layer of ceramic tiles.

The contest centred at first on the two satellites located over Minsk, but then it spread. Three hundred satellites in all were disabled within the first six minutes—ten times the timespan involved if they had not been protected by those tiles—so that massive areas of the globe dropped out of coverage.

Smith's expected attempt at communication came through shortly after the first satellites went down, but Saul ignored it. The man probably hoped to dissuade Saul from such a mutually destructive battle. Only when those satellites that Saul wanted disabled were out of action did he cease his attacks, whereupon Smith's attacks ceased a fraction of a second later. Now, of course, Smith had nothing left within range of Argus—or of those two satellites down below.

Saul began calculating vectors in his head, loading engine-thrust calculations, and even then using the steering jets on the satellites to turn them, whilst simultaneously starting up their engines so as to set them on a rough vector he could correct later … four seconds later. The two satellites now shed their panels, folding and twisting away like discarded Christmas decorations.

They were now well on their way, but Saul maintained his mental link to the steering thrusters, so he could still make instant adjustments.

"Twenty-three minutes," he noted. "Long before then, either Smith will warn them or they'll figure out what's going on and start evasive manoeuvres."

Just then a scraping sound issued from the toilet, as someone tried to force the door open.

"Let them out, Braddock," he said, "then bring them over here."

Braddock nodded, without questioning the order, and headed over to the toilet door. A panel beside it contained a motion detector to open it automatically whenever anyone approached. That was until he had put a single shot through it, after the three prisoners were inside. Now he just landed a boot against the door and burst it open inwards. Someone yelled in pain and Saul glimpsed the man tumbling backwards holding his head.

"Out," Braddock ordered the three of them.

The two women pushed their way out first. Both had cropped blonde hair, probably because keeping long hair clean up here was nigh an impossibility, and they were of very similar appearance. They looked remarkably young to Saul, seeming little more than teenagers, but that merely meant they might have been using anti-ageing drugs. He checked personnel files stored in Tech Central itself and discovered that they were twins. Angela and Brigitta Saberhagen were very bright twins who had been born in Berlin twenty years ago, then turned into societal assets from the moment they started dismantling computers at the age of five. The man was bearded, balding and running to fat. Despite the clean technician's clothing, his hands were ingrained with dirt, and Saul found that somehow reassuring. His name was Girondel Chang, home city Nanking in China, but he certainly didn't look at all Chinese. Braddock ushered them over and mustered them in a line, but far enough away that he could still bring any one of them down if they decided to attack Saul.

"Do you have any survival gear in or near here?" Saul asked them, even though he already knew precisely what was available.

The twins merely looked at each other, and it was their bearded companion who replied, "Emergency survival suits in the lockers." He nodded towards a column of locker hatches that rose up one wall.

"Well, get yourselves suited up, then," Saul instructed, "and fetch two extra suits out for myself and Hannah—Braddock here is fine in his spacesuit." He paused for a second. "My name is Alan Saul." He had used their names deliberately, to humanize them, to help transform them from nameless terrorists into real people.

"We already know your name," said Brigitta, the twin who, from her record, he had known would speak first. She turned to study the screens, perhaps instantly understanding the need for survival suits.

Saul nodded to Braddock, and the soldier herded them towards the lockers, where they retrieved baggy survival suits that could easily be pulled on over their clothing. Here and there, wherever views were obtainable, he saw other station personnel already opening similar lockers and donning similar suits. They all clearly knew what was coming. However, there didn't seem to be enough suits to go around, and in some areas people were already fighting over them.

"What do you want of them?" Hannah whispered.

"I've got limited control of some sections of the station computer network, and I can also program some of the robots, but even if we manage to deal with Smith, I still cannot become omnipresent and omnipotent." He glanced at her. "If I gain full control here, I'll be needing people, so I may as well start recruiting them now." It was a lie, of course. If he gained full control here, he could easily keep the place running with just the robots. But what to do with the humans then? Slaughter them all?

"That's good to hear."

"I don't think there's any need for sarcasm, at this point, do you?"

"Actually, I think there's a very great need for it." She eyed him carefully.

"Keeping me grounded, Hannah?"

"I try, but perhaps it's already a bit late for that."

He smiled tightly, but let that go.

The three staff returned with Braddock, but had yet to pull up their hoods and seal their visors. Hannah got up and accepted the two suits Chang had draped over one arm. The barrel of Braddock's gun rested against the back of the man's neck while Hannah was so close. Saul gestured to three chairs over to his right—the ones he knew they had occupied previously.

"I want you three to oversee the safety of whatever station residents you can contact," he told them. "Direct them towards any survival and spacesuits still available. You can perhaps also send some of them to better-protected areas, or put them in EVA vehicles. You have about forty minutes for that. No need to bother about station security staff, as it seems they've quite enough vacuum gear available to them."

"If we do what you say, we'll end up in adjustment cells," protested Brigitta.

He shook his head. "You can, of course, refuse to help your fellows," he said. "In which case the adjustment you face will come from the barrel of Braddock's gun. Make up your minds."

After a short, almost embarrassed, pause, Chang announced, "Those in Arcoplex One will be in the most danger, since they're not trained personnel."

Saul eyed him steadily, and began frantically accessing station data. What he found there surprised him immensely. When Janus had originally gathered data regarding this station, the population was about a thousand; now it seemed to have climbed to four thousand. The numbers of the workforce, along with security and political monitoring personnel, had initially doubled, then a surge of a further two thousand had arrived. Most of these newcomers were located in Arcoplex One, and as he checked the relevant data the true situation began to emerge. The Committee, or some part of it, had already begun the process of relocating here. Delegates now occupied the arcoplex cylinder—including names he recognized—along with political staff, all their families, and others whose presence here he suspected was due simply to powerful people they knew. But all of these he would have to deal with later.

"Whatever," he said, expressionless. "Just try and keep *your* people safe."

He carefully turned his chair away from them as more chatter suddenly started becoming accessible to him. It seemed that the security hole Smith had recently closed had reopened in the barracks where Langstrom was located. This had to be some sort of trap, surely, involving deliberate misinformation.

"We have more serious challenges to respond to right now," said Smith. "We can discuss your rather minor problem once we have nullified the current power instability here within the station."

"Well, there we have a problem. I want to discuss this now," replied Langstrom.

Three other soldiers were with him and, checking records, Saul noted that they were all sergeants. They all wore the pale-blue uniforms of Inspectorate enforcers, but specially adapted for the near-weightless environment. No one here was clad like an Earth-bound enforcer as the net broadcasts had shown—those broadcasts were either seriously outdated or had simply been falsified. Checking further, Saul began to discern the true shape of the hierarchy here.

Smith and his Inspectorate execs were the arm of government in overall command of security, political oversight, and ensuring that everyone did what they were told and thought what they were ordered to think. However, someone in the Committee had realized that, where survival depended on science, the scientists and technicians must be allowed independence, therefore authority over technical issues within the station had been handed over to someone called Le Roque. This situation had not lasted too long, for apparently Le Roque now languished inside one of Smith's adjustment cells. Langstrom's soldiers, who reported to Smith and his execs, were military-wing Inspectorate enforcers, and the best—as far as the Committee was concerned—that "service" had to offer. Which probably meant that they were all utter shits.

"The space planes will arrive on-station in just half of one hour," Smith insisted.

Saul flicked his attention to the robots he controlled, already running self-diagnostics and stretching like cats. They needed to become a little bit more sneaky if they were to end up going against weapons that could fry their electronics, so he began programming them to that purpose. A suitable name for that program was "Ambush Predator." Except for just a few still gathered about Tech Central, he began dispersing them to the outer limits of the area he currently controlled.

"Fuck the fucking planes," was Langstrom's rejoinder. "You've been down on me from the start just because I wouldn't back you up on Le Roque."

"It is advisable to exercise some caution during discourse," Smith warned him mildly.

"Oh, right, I might get myself in trouble."

After a brief pause, Smith said, "It is unfortunate to note that you have disconnected your system from Political Office Oversight and lowered your security firewall. In circumstances such as the current ones, this must be considered an adjustment offence."

Saul was on it in a second, realizing that everything in the barracks now lay open to him. He began seizing control of readerguns and cameras, locking them into his own network, while locking out a sudden flanking attack from Smith—an information serpent looping round to try and shove its way through the same hole Saul was using. Next, Saul had control of the air, the power, even the medical machines. He could kill them all off in an instant, and meanwhile the realm he controlled had just grown significantly in volume, because now his reach extended over to the other side of Arcoplex One. If this was some sort of trap, Saul could not detect it.

"Yeah, right, so I might end up in an adjustment cell for that!" Langstrom responded. "Oh, too late, seems I'm already destined for one of your cells, because you don't like the way I think."

"So at this crucial time you betray our plans to enemies of the state?"

Langstrom smashed a hand down on the computer keyboard, cutting off further communication.

"That's pretty shitty," remarked one of his sergeants.

Langstrom nodded, his expression resolute, then turned on him, pulling a side arm. Without further ado, he raised it and shot the speaker straight through the face, spraying his brains over the door. The impact jerked him up off his gecko boots and sent him tumbling between the two men behind him. His corpse hit the door and bounced, before it began to drift away again. Globules of blood and brain and chunks of skull fell about the room like red-and-pink snow.

"Fuck, you could have warned me." The muscular soldier with coal-black skin flicked a fragment of skull off his shoulder, then raised a boot to field the corpse and press it down to the floor. Blood went on pumping from the head wound, winding out in a thick snake across the floor, its back rippling like red mercury.

"Right, sorry, Jack. Next time I'll say, 'Step aside because I'm just about to shoot Smith's weasel through the face.'" He holstered his side arm. "What about the others?"

"Two in the hospital and eighteen in the disciplinary cell."

"How many of the rest are in this with us?"

"Thirty-two."

"So that means we've got about a hundred and fifty who might be a problem?"

Jack shook his head. "A hundred and eleven, since our friend in Tech Central killed forty-eight."

"Do you two have reservations?"

"None at all," said Jack.

The other man, whose name Saul now ascertained, from reading the bar code on his uniform, was called Mustafa, said, "I've been waiting for something like this to happen all my life."

What was going on?

The one called Jack had mentioned "thirty-two," and a check showed Saul that thirty-two soldiers were gathered in Barracks One, while the rest were ensconced in the four other barracks. The first thing noticeable about the soldiers was that most, like Langstrom himself, were black men. He started scanning bar codes on their uniforms, and quickly realized that all these soldiers had been transferred from an Inspectorate assault group located in South Africa, specially trained for ground assault and hostage extraction. Though this hinted that they were proper soldiers rather than secret police, it did not necessarily raise them in his estimation.

"Alan Saul," enquired Langstrom, "are you listening?"

"Always," he replied, through their public address system.

"We're with you, then. Just tell us what you want."

"You'll excuse me if I reserve judgement on that." Saul paused for a second. "Though I perfectly understand your change of allegiance, I don't see why any of your men should want to stick with you, especially since assault troops are on the way."

"Then you obviously haven't spent most of your life shovelling Committee shit."

"Apparently not."

"Just tell us."

"Very well." Saul considered the situation, and decided he wasn't going to let Langstrom or his men get anywhere near Tech Central. "Since I disarmed you and sent you away, I see that you have all rearmed yourselves. I want you, Mustafa and Jack, and the thirty-two other men formerly of SA22 Assault Group, to now disarm and confine those other hundred and eleven soldiers with you."

The three men just stood staring at the source of his voice for a moment, till Jack was the first to snap out of it.

"Just bring 'em through one at a time," he said, gazing fixedly at Langstrom.

Langstrom shook his head. "No need. They'll follow orders now Smith's spies are out of the way."

"Smith's spies would be the eighteen held in the disciplinary cell?" Saul suggested. "And our friend down at your feet."

The gory detritus in the air, Saul noticed, was all heading towards the louvres of an air cleaner, which began to make a sound like an air-locked central heating system as it gobbled them down. Langstrom glanced down at the corpse, taking a step back from the spreading blood. He then glanced up at a nearby cam, as if hoping to catch a glimpse of Saul. "Yeah, they're not so hard to spot."

"Once you've disarmed the rest, SA22 should be ready to fight the troops it was formerly ordered to assist."

"We knew that would be necessary."

Saul studied Langstrom carefully. How was he to judge this man? Could all this be some elaborate scheme to get a killer close enough to Saul to end things quickly?

"It will only become necessary if their space planes manage to evade the satellites I'm dropping on them ... but be ready, all the same." He left it at that, returning his attention to the screens in front of him, and the vector calculations inside his head.

"The pilots have spotted the satellites," Braddock informed him.

The four space planes were now separating, their steering jets blasting, and contrails whipping away from their almost retracted wings. Saul adjusted the paths of his two satellites and after a minute, the planes reacted to that. Perfect, they were dropping lower while extending their wings, hoping for greater manoeuvrability within atmosphere. Saul made another course correction to the satellites, whereupon one pilot—obviously a lot smarter than his fellows—raised his plane's ailerons to aerobrake hard. All the steering jets pushing the plane down, it dropped out of formation just as the pilots of the other planes got wise, too, and tried to do the same thing.

Too late.

He had imaging from the two satellites displayed on the screen, imaging from other satellites, too, and from the station itself. A grandstand view. One of the satellites streaked in, striking a space plane trying to throw itself into a turn. The target became an explosion fifteen kilometres long, stabbing past a second plane, the blastwave setting the second plane into a spin that he hoped it couldn't correct. The next satellite hit the third plane, shearing off its rear half and leaving the rest to tumble through upper atmosphere, on and out of sight. Calculating its vector, he realized it would never actually hit the ground.

"It's recovering," Braddock noted, gazing at the spinning plane as it gradually stabilized.

The spinning craft finally managed to correct, then abruptly extended its wings and began arcing down.

"Heading back to Minsk," Saul noted. "Or maybe one of the emergency runways in Australia or Canada. Must have been damaged."

"It's out of it, then?"

"Yes, but we still have this problem." Saul called up an image of the plane that had dropped out of formation first. It was once again rising through the upper atmosphere. "But we have time," he continued. "It'll have to do a full orbit of Earth"—he ran some calculations based on the fuel the plane had available and its optimum approach speed—"which gives us twenty-two hours."

"Can you hit it with some more satellites?"

"No, they'll be watching out for that now." Saul turned his chair so as to face both Braddock and Hannah. "We'll have to kill them near or actually inside the station, if we're still alive by then."

15

DRIVE TO FUSION

When, back in 2035, the first commercial fusion reactor went online, scientists speculated that they were now just ten years away from using the same technology to build a fusion drive. It was to prove, however, a lot more difficult to develop than they supposed. Within ten years, the first prototype was assembled in orbit, then towed out from Earth for test firing. It worked for just six tenths of a second before sputtering out, yet it took the engineers a further five years to find out why. The problem was gravity. On Earth, the engine tolerances were correct, but once away from gravity the device distorted. In fact the engine was far too sensitive, since the slightest misalignment could shut it down. It took a further ten years to design and build a more robust machine, and only five years after its first successful test, the next massive fusion engine was being installed in the steadily growing hull of the first Traveller spacecraft.

Chang and the Saberhagen twins ensured that everyone they could communicate with was made as safe as possible. They found every available spacesuit or survival suit and assigned them, before ensconcing those people still without suits in the safer, inner areas of the living accommodation—the sections that could be sealed with bulkhead doors. But in total that amounted to less than eight hundred people, because the moment the three of them tried opening com with those outside the area Saul controlled, Smith shut the communication down. Just as he seemed to be shutting down so much else, for all construction and maintenance work aboard Argus had now ceased. Even the ore carriers were no longer running between the station itself and the smelter plants, which had started folding up and closing their huge mirrors.

"You've now lost your chief security force here," Saul observed, "and now only one of those space planes looks like having a chance of ever getting here."

Smith's image flicked into view on the middle screen, the communication link having been immediately accepted. "It has been a consideration of mine at what point you would resort to the infantile gloating of a terrorist. But I feel it necessary for you to understand that, whilst you consider yourself of great significance, to the state and to the people at large you are merely an irritating inconvenience."

"Your laser network isn't looking too healthy." The jibe was out of Saul's mouth before he could stop it.

Smith shook his head as if hearing the absurd logic of a child. "It is true that over eighty per cent of the seven hundred satellites are temporarily in need of maintenance, but we have over six thousand satellite lasers on the point of being activated."

"That's not going to happen."

"Not within your own limited lifespan, I would suggest," Smith replied, allowing himself a nasty smile.

"Only one space plane." Saul held up a finger.

"That plane contains over fifty highly trained military personnel, armed with state-of-the-art suppression hardware. The robots you have stolen from the state will not be sufficient to interfere with their mission, Saul. Not in the least." Smith paused, then shrugged. "It is my own opinion that the dispatching of four planeloads of troops was the hysterical overreaction of untrained personnel down below."

Saul leant back in his chair. "I wonder, Smith, how some of your masters might overreact if they were told that you've created a back door through which to seize control of the entire satellite network?"

"Your naivety is perhaps the result of a sheltered upbringing, or maybe the consequence of some mental debilitation suffered under adjustment."

"Perhaps you would like to elaborate?" Saul suggested calmly.

"My deserved political status as delegate for Argus Station was approved a year ago, during early-session Committee hearings. After the Committee is relocated here, it is inevitable that I will be voted in to replace Chairman Messina, almost at once. It is my experience that the Earth government is always practical about the realities—which is why it has survived so long."

"You threatened to fry them?" Saul suggested.

"Very practical of them to avoid such unpleasantness."

"I see," said Saul, feeling he now saw even more than Smith was admitting.

By reducing to just one the number of space planes about to dock with the Argus Station, Saul felt sure he had actually done Smith a favour. Did that mean that Smith hadn't fought as hard as he might have to prevent Saul destroying those other planes? It now struck him as highly likely that the force, ostensibly dispatched here to counter the threat Saul himself presented, would also have received instructions concerning Smith. That those troops had been dispatched so quickly indicated that they had been assembled and waiting long before Malden had launched his coup. They had been ready to seize the station back from Smith, and thus re-establish Chairman Messina's control here.

"Are those people over in Arcoplex One your hostages?" Saul asked abruptly.

Smith gave him that nasty smile again, and cut the communication link.

Saul continued staring at the blank screen, assessing and calculating, then began mentally probing towards the Political Office. But there he hit a wall, for Smith had pulled back and consolidated, so his grip over the Political Office and the rest of the station now seemed absolute. He was clearly playing a waiting game, perhaps hoping Saul would squander his robots against the forces aboard the approaching space plane, thus weakening two enemies simultaneously. Saul realized even more urgently that to succeed he needed to eliminate Smith before that plane arrived. The situation would have been hopeless had it not been for Langstrom's defection, which in itself still gave him grounds for suspicion.

Saul shook his head, wished he hadn't when he instantly felt dizzy and sick, then with a thought summoned up views of Braddock, who was now guiding Chang and the twins back down to Tech Central accommodation, located three floors below. As Braddock stepped back to let the three others file into the accommodation section, then closed the door on them, Saul addressed him through the intercom, while simultaneously engaging the locks.

"You should find yourself somewhere to rest, Braddock," he suggested. "Get some sleep."

Hannah, after recently removing Saul's blood pressure-feed, was already fast asleep in a wide comfortable hammock in Le Roque's former apartment adjoining Tech Central.

"Yeah, I'll go get some sleep," Braddock agreed, gecko boots slamming down heavily as he marched resolutely towards the cageway.

Meanwhile, the last of those whose loyalty to him Langstrom was uncertain of were being ushered into Barracks Two and Three. Sergeants Jack and Mustafa then shut the bulkhead doors and engaged the electric locks, finally securing a hundred or so potential problems.

"Okay, Langstrom," Saul said, "time for you to prove yourself further."

"How?" Langstrom sat in his office, gazing at station schematics on his screen.

"Smith's adjustment cell block is only a hundred metres away from your barracks, and it's situated close to the Political Office."

Both the adjustment cell block and the Political Office lay between Arcoplexes One and Two, and had been built well inside the lattice walls. The reason for this was obvious, since it gave them both room to expand. Langstrom called up images of both structures on his screen and began to study them intently, only glancing round as Mustafa and Jack rejoined him.

"I want you to hit the cell block first," instructed Saul. "Secure the place so that you won't have any of Smith's guards at your back, and then move on to the Political Office."

"What about the readerguns?" Mustafa enquired.

Via the multiple viewpoints provided by construction robots clinging to nearby station frameworks, Saul focused first on the barracks, suspended within inner station structure like a starfish caught in a net, then on the cell block that lay a little further away. Certainly, readerguns were in evidence, but it seemed that not one of them was functional.

"They're disabled in the cell block itself, and along your route to the Political Office," Saul informed them. "Smith and I both sacrificed readerguns to prevent them falling under each other's control. However, it seems likely they're still in operation within Smith's domain."

"Why not use the robots to attack?" Mustafa asked.

"I could, of course, but I'm offering second chances." That was not entirely true, because though he could use his robots, it struck him as unlikely they would prove sufficient to penetrate the Political Office. He needed soldiers, but before he could trust them he needed to assess them in action.

"We never even had a first chance," grumbled Mustafa. "Your robots gonna leave us alone?"

"My robots will leave you alone," Saul confirmed.

The three of them now headed off to Barracks One, where their men checked and loaded their weapons while Langstrom delivered the briefest of briefings Saul had ever heard: "Guys, we hit the cell block, let the prisoners go, and stick the guards in the cells."

"What if the guards resist?" asked a tall Nordic-blonde woman.

"I didn't say they had to go into the cells alive, did I?"

General laughter greeted this, so it indeed seemed no love was lost.

Within minutes they set off again, propelling themselves, by wall handles, down a long corridor leading from the barracks to a point where it expanded into a tubeway, then through a large airlock, then further along the tubeway for about five hundred metres, until they reached a point where any construction of walls and ceiling ended. From there they progressed along a wide walkway, now down on their feet using their gecko boots. As they proceeded, Langstrom issued brief comments over radio, which his sergeants translated into orders.

"Five in the admissions section, maybe six," observed Langstrom.

"Peach, your guys in. I want 'em disarmed and on the floor," ordered Mustafa. "Use zip-cuffs."

As they reached a crossroads in the walkway, Langstrom gestured right and then left. "We need to cover the other entrances."

Sergeant Jack raised a fist, held up three fingers, twice, then also gestured right and then left. "Three minutes," he added. "Let us know when you're in position."

Breaking into long loping strides, twelve troops went right and twelve went left. This confirmed for Saul that the men were organized in units of four, below the sergeants. Langstrom now slowed his pace, gazing up at three robots moving through the scaffolds above.

"They ain't moving the same," remarked Jack.

"Yeah, I know," Langstrom replied.

Saul was surprised but a brief analysis provided the reason: the programs that he'd put in place—almost completely displacing their previous programming—displayed his own particular coding quirks, and the robots moved more like living creatures now.

Soon the soldiers reached a point where new wall and ceiling construction extended out from the cell block.

"Top and bottom," said Langstrom. "The four blind wings."

Two fingers up from Jack, then a thumb stabbed up and down. Eight men detached their gecko boots from the floor, propelled themselves up on to the top surface of the tubeway and set off. A further eight men headed over one side of the walkway and began making their way across the scaffolding underneath. Saul again checked a schematic of the complex, and immediately saw what Langstrom meant. Four diverging corridors possessed only one conventional way in, and finished up against the exterior walls. However, temporary airlocks were positioned above and below each end to facilitate future installation of vertical shafts. Perhaps waiting for when further levels of cells needed to be added, which indicated the way Smith and his kind thought.

Soon they entered the tubeway into the complex, at which point he lost sight of them, since the staff inside had disconnected the cam system.

"There's about forty prisoners over there," Langstrom reported eventually. He paused for a moment. "Are you watching, Saul?"

"Certainly," Saul replied, though it had taken him a moment to realize he could. Via the barracks, he keyed into the feed transmitted from thirty-five pincams, each fitted at the temple of every soldier and connected to their fones. Langstrom was currently pointing to a doorway above which hung a big blue sign proclaiming: "Adjustment." Now another view: Peach turned out to be the big blonde and, noticing she had removed her suit helmet, Saul decided they must have already passed through an airlock in the tubeway. She and the other three of her unit were approaching Admissions, where four guards were crouching behind a makeshift barricade composed of tacked-together sheets of bubblemetal.

One propelled himself out as Peach and her men approached. "Good," he said peremptorily. "It's about damned time."

"Time for what?" Peach asked, still moving forward.

"About time we were relieved," he continued. "You had no problem getting through?"

She paused beside him, while her three fellows stepped on round the barricade. Almost negligently they swung their machine pistols sideways to cover the three crouching men there.

"Drop your weapons," said Peach.

"What the—?" The standing man's protest ended in a coughing gurgle as he tumbled back through the air in slow motion, clutching his throat. Her karate chop had been almost too fast for the eye to follow, so Saul replayed it in his mind out of analytical interest. The remaining three were frozen in disbelief, until one of Peach's men fired into the ceiling, and they discarded their weapons.

"I don't know why you're doing this," protested one of them. "We've done nothing wrong." Even then, they thought this was their own people arresting them—some mistake, perhaps.

Two of Peach's unit remained outside, gathering up weapons and securing plastic ties to wrists. The Admissions reception area contained an armourglass guard booth to one side, a long desk on the other, with storage cupboards lining the walls behind it. One man began getting up from his desk, while another behind him was already pulling a machine pistol from a rack. That's what killed him, for as he turned, Peach did not hesitate. A short burst of fire sent him slamming back into the weapons rack whilst the other man began shrieking, "Don't shoot! Don't shoot!" and stabbed his hands in the air, his eyes closed. Whilst the survivor was cuffed, Langstrom and the others moved on through, into the cell blocks.

Just then, Braddock rejoined Saul, so he selected some of the scenes he was currently observing in his head and put them up on the screens. Without comment Braddock strapped himself down in a chair, laid his weapon on his lap, and gazed at the changing images with fatigue-reddened eyes.

Saul enjoyed observing the steady military efficiency of it all. Anyone inside the complex made a wrong move, and they died on the spot. After Langstrom had finished, twenty-eight guards occupied the cells, though one cell containing five served as a temporary morgue. Langstrom released forty prisoners, some of whom were now detailed to help others over to the barracks infirmary.

"Could your men have taken them?" Saul turned to Braddock.

"Huh?" Braddock's head jerked up, betraying the fact that he'd dozed off. He shook himself awake in irritation, then said, "The idea was to avoid a fire fight."

"Get some sleep, Braddock," Saul urged him. "Go and join Hannah—I'm sure there's room on that hammock for the both of you."

"What about you?"

What about him? Yes, he felt utterly weary, but his mind had not slowed down at all. Gradually he was embracing more and more of the overall function of his area of the station: its cams, microphones, motion and heat sensors becoming his extended senses, and its readerguns his immune system. By the same analogy the robots had become his eyes and hands. It was as if, during the initial stages of his taking over this area, he had dissipated himself throughout the station network. To him the station had originally felt messy, bits and pieces not integrated as a whole, but now it felt like an extension of himself.

"I'll be fine, Braddock," he assured him.

Even as he spoke, he watched Langstrom moving out of the cell block, watched released prisoners heading for Accommodation Sixteen, and noted the space plane at last rising over Earth's horizon. He was simultaneously refining his robots' attack programs, and making layered plans about how to deal with the impending assault. It all depended on where the incoming troops penetrated the station.

"Okay, I'll sleep," agreed Braddock, wearily unstrapping himself from the chair and propelling himself off to join Hannah. Saul watched him go; watched how careful he was not to wake her as he lay down on the wide hammock beside her.

Now that he wasn't fighting for his life, Saul decided it was perhaps time to prepare for an option that until then had remained only in the back of his mind. He allowed his senses to range across the station, bypassing the Political Office and zeroing in on an area neither he nor Smith had so far paid much attention to, yet had been of great interest to Malden.

The wheel of Argus Station was interrupted—a quarter section missing from the rim—and below that break, attached to the asteroid itself, sat the Mars Traveller fusion engine. Through various cams in the locality, Saul now studied this behemoth further.

A section of the asteroid had been ground flat, then layered, three metres thick, with the foam composite on which the engine framework rested. This was just a secondary shock-absorber, since the first impact of the engine firing was sustained by the massive hydraulic shock absorbers positioned evenly about the framework, and secured to plates bolted directly onto the asteroid itself. From nearby housings, built into the lattice walls and girder structures, a great number of ducts, cables and pipes fed in just above this secondary layer and connected to the spherical fusion reactors used for start-up, and for maintaining the nozzle fields of the combustion chambers. Above the reactors stood pairs of large cylindrical fuel tanks containing, respectively, liquid deuterium and tritium talc. Above these again were the dome-shaped, pellet-aggregation plants, and above them the six fusion-combustion chambers rose in a rectangular cluster, each surrounded at its rear by fuser lasers and the deuterium-tritium injector guns. The whole massive structure stood half a kilometre tall, secured in place by a web of steel and a framework of I-beams, all of it fixed with integral pivot points so that the engine would be allowed to move against its shock absorbers.

When this thing was up and running, deuterium droplets sprayed into the aggregation plants, where they froze, and were next electrostatically coated with tritium dust. The resulting microspheres were then conveyed to the injectors, to be fired into each combustion chamber. Once a sphere reached the chamber's centre, it was briefly captured in a magnetic bottle, then targeted with the beams from high-intensity stacked gallium-arsenide lasers. With each ignition, the bottle expanded to form a tubular containment field, focusing the resulting blast out of the rear of the engine. The lasers fired, igniting fusion, then this process repeated itself a hundredth of a second later, and from then on kept repeating. The resulting plasma explosion from the engine provided thrust measurable in millions of tonnes.

Saul ran a diagnostic check through the Traveller engine, just to assess its present condition. As he had learned from Malden, it had still enough fuel to hurl the space station down against the surface of the Earth with catastrophic consequences, or even to throw it out of Earth's orbit altogether, and take it up to an appreciable portion of 1 per cent of light speed. He received some dodgy readings from two of the injectors in a combustion chamber, but that's why they installed the chambers in an array of six. If one started to go wrong it simply shut down, while the rest would keep on working. The only other problems seemed to be the cooling system, which was frozen solid, and how frangible some of the engine's components were at such a low temperature. This meant the engine could not be fired up at once, but would require several hours of warming up, during which process further faults might emerge.

Saul carefully considered the options opening up here, aware of being poised on the brink of some understanding that still eluded his grasp. When he finally transmitted the code that would start the engine-warming process, it seemed like he had made a decision impossible to recall. He waited then for some response from Smith but, after a minute passed with no reaction, he knew Smith could not have been paying attention to the engine. Saul finally let out a long slow breath, and withdrew.

Quiet now, alone at the centre of it all, Saul peered down at his hands, which were resting in his lap. He noticed a large bruise on the back of the right hand, and how thin they looked. Inset amidst numerous other controls on the console before him was a big keyboard, with virtuality half-glove indents on either side of it. He already knew this console from the inside, and directly manipulated the flows of information it controlled. Never again, in this place, would he have to physically press a button, shift a pointer, or open up frames in virtual displays. What use were his hands?

He raised them off his lap to inspect them more closely, and noticed how they started shaking. What was wrong with them? He knew his body was exhausted, and injured, but what was the problem here? He needed to find out, for whatever his present disconnection from his body, he couldn't manage to do without it. Right now, if his physical self died, he died too.

Deciding to take a risk, for it seemed Smith was still perfectly content to await the arrival of the assault force, he began closing down his connections to the station network—which seemed almost like deliberately blinding himself, blocking his ears, numbing his senses. By slow degrees that took many minutes, he reduced himself, returning to the primitive level of humanity. The process seemed like trying to cram something into a box too small for it, but eventually he was there in that box, and it wasn't comfortable at all.

His head ached horribly, both inside and out. His stomach felt tight, his mouth dry, and something seemed to be twisting internally below the iron knot of his knife wound. It took him a moment to recognize the quite simple signals his body was sending him: a full bladder and a thirst so intense that it felt like something solid stapling the back of his throat to his neck bones. He felt sick too, but he reckoned that must be what remained after the hunger pangs departed. Also his back, his legs and his buttocks ached, and if he had been in Earth gravity he would have assumed this discomfort resulted from remaining seated for so long, but it was the result of his body remaining utterly motionless. With a huge effort of will, he loosened the straps securing him to the chair, and propelled himself upwards. Dizziness overwhelmed him and, failing to press his adhesive soles to the floor, he rose to the ceiling. One hand raised against it propelled him back down sufficiently for him to grab the console edge and press his feet floorwards.

With a further effort of will, Saul took firm control of his body, ignoring discomfort and just moving. Shambling like a reanimated corpse, he headed over to the door leading to the toilets, again finding it an effort just to tear the adhesive soles of his survival suit from the floor. Once inside, he paused for a moment, unable to make up his mind what to do first. He chose the toilet, attaching the hose and urinating for so long that he felt he might shrivel up and drop to the floor. The pleasure of the relief was practically euphoric. Next he went to the sink—deep with an incurving rim to hold water in at practically nil gravity, and an extractor bowl above—turned on the tap, and then dipped his head to sip water that shifted gelatinously. Not enough. Mouth closed around acidic metal he allowed the pressure to shove the water down his throat. He only stopped when his thirst started to give way to a further twinge of nausea.

Standing upright again, he gazed at himself in the mirror. His eyes, but for the pupils, were still utterly red, which seemed odd because he felt sure that should have been fading by now. At least they were no longer a dark wine-red, but more an albino pink. The glued and stapled wounds traversing his skull were obviously healing effectively, with a fuzz of pale hair shoving up scabs of dry blood and wound glue, like new grass raising the leaves scattered on a lawn. He looked painfully thin, even the bristles on his face failing to hide how closely the skin clung to the cheekbones and how evident the skull beneath. Conclusion: he needed to take better care of this storage vessel containing part of his mind. He turned, headed to the door, and stepped out.

***

Hannah stood by the console, her gaze flicking from screen to screen. One showed the approaching space plane, while the other two kept cycling through a limited selection of views of Earth: Minsk spaceport, Brussels, London and another urban sprawl she did not recognize. She turned as she heard Saul exit the toilet, pleased to see him showing at least that sign of human frailty.

"I brought this for you." She pointed to a plastic tray resting on the console.

He moved over, trying but not quite succeeding in hiding his physical debility, sat down in the chair and strapped himself in. He lifted the transparent cover from the tray to find noodles mixed with cubes of vat meat, chopped-up local vegetables, grown in Hydroponics, pancake rolls and a dipping sauce, accompanied by a steaming double espresso.

"They live well here," he remarked.

"Le Roque's private stash," she replied. "He's got a fridge full of luxuries, which I bet came up in crates listed as essential supplies."

"You cynic, you."

"Who isn't these days?"

"Have you eaten?" he asked.

"Some…but I'll have some more later."

After being woken by Braddock stretching himself out next to her on the hammock, and then lying there for some while, still reluctant to move, Hannah had got up to investigate Le Roque's large fridge. Almost shocked by the bounty inside, she had stuffed herself with cold food until a sense of guilt compelled her to stop, assuaging her guilt by preparing the tray for Saul. She was now glad she had, since borderline malnutrition, initial surgery, followed by injury, then further surgery, had all combined to knock him down. But she rather thought it was the hardware in his skull that was sucking the physical bulk from him, almost fast enough to be visible. It seemed a fire now burned inside his head—one she herself had ignited.

"What's that?" She nodded towards the screen as the urban sprawl she did not recognize appeared once again.

"The Luberon Sprawl in southern France," he explained. "Rather disconcerting to find a disconnected part of my own mind calling up that image. It shows how I am as much inside the machine as the machine is in me."

He picked up a combined fork-and-spoon implement and shovelled some noodles into his mouth, making, it seemed to Hannah, a deliberate effort to chew slowly, swallow carefully, and then pause between mouthfuls. Both he and Hannah had been gradually starving since they had fled the underground bunker, so if he bolted such rich food he would probably throw it all up over the console. But then he wasn't unique in his hunger; billions were starving down on Earth, and many millions dying of hunger.

He glanced at the screens as he ate and his expression went blank, oddly disconnected. The image cycle disrupted, to be replaced by a randomized feed of views inside and outside the station.

"You were more human, just for a moment, but now you're back in the system."

Even when she had known Saul as a lover, he had always seemed one step away from being truly human, but not in a way that had seemed dysfunctional. He had been strangely unencumbered by the burdens of physical or mental weakness and the millstone of emotion, but now he was partly machine, these traits seemed to be sharply emphasized. This distanced her from him further and, beyond his intention of taking the satellite network out of Committee control, she did not even know his ultimate aims. Perhaps they involved delivering some payback for the billions suffering down below, but was that all he actually intended?

He glanced at her, then deliberately seemed to be fighting something, emotion returning to his face. He turned and gazed at the screens, a sadness, a regret, filling his expression.

"What are you thinking?" she asked, finally.

"About how it all went wrong," he said. "And also of how it was inevitable."

"Inevitable?" She sat up straighter.

"Yup, just human nature."

That was so dismissive of human nature, she felt the need to challenge it.

"I think it's a little more complicated than that."

"Really?"

She gazed at him intently, gathering her mental resources, remembering things she had considered over many years but never allowed herself to voice out loud. "Crises used by politicians as excuses to stifle freedom, kill democracy and grab yet more power. Terrorism, energy crises, financial meltdown, climate catastrophe…all, of course, global so those same politicians could extend their power *globally*. Everyone made obedient to the state in pursuit of the so-called greater good."

"And your point is?"

"Well," she was on a roll now, "all those crises strangely seemed to disappear once the state had gained a sufficient stranglehold on the populations it was supposed to serve. Bit of a joke, really, when fossil fuels genuinely started to run out and we hit the human population upslope. Real crises then, and what was the response? To expand the state into a behemoth even more wasteful than the people it governed."

He just sat there silently waiting for her conclusions.

"Less of such waste and they might have actually developed the appropriate technologies to handle the problem."

"Ah," he said, "you're an optimist."

"Perhaps." She shrugged, feeling uncomfortable with that label.

"We've got fusion power, remember, Hannah. What we actually needed was a technology that's been around for a couple of centuries. It's called birth control." He shook his head and gazed pensively at the screens. "The real problem is manswarm."

"The fault here is ideology," she said, feeling sudden doubt upon hearing him use such a dismissive label. The Committee was very definitely a bad thing, but humans were better than that—could *be* better than that.

"What?"

"You know, the forerunners of the Committee weren't interested in population control. They weren't interested in making things better, because people who are well off and comfortable wouldn't be likely to vote for the crappy ideologies they promulgated. Urban sprawls packed with ZAs were perfectly in tune with their interests."

She had never spoken to him like this before, even in past times when they had lain in bed together. But of course, even during such intimacy, talk of this kind would have been dangerous, their words recorded and reviewed on the following day by a political officer.

"But none of them prevented people using birth control—only religions tried to do that."

"They deliberately created underclasses and gave them a financial incentive to breed," she insisted.

"True," he said, "but in China, in the twentieth, they actively discouraged breeding, yet China still went into the twenty-first with a population of over a billion. Sorry, but that doesn't cut it, Hannah. In the end, you can't engineer a society to go against four billion years of evolutionary instinct."

His pessimism scared her. Okay for someone to be a pessimist when he was just among billions of other powerless human beings, but it certainly didn't seem such a good thing when that person might soon be able to seize control of technology capable of slaughtering millions, or even billions.

"There's no light in your world, is there?" she commented. "None at all."

Hannah didn't know how to take this conversation any further.

***

The water from the shower hit like needles, before it spattered and diffused in slow motion, filling the air all around him. Across the transparent shower door it ran as thick as jelly, before being sucked into holes in the three walls of the shower and even in the door, linked by vacuum pipes running through the glass. Without this constant suction, he imagined it would be quite easy to drown taking a shower in near-zero gravity. Even as it was, the moisture hanging heavy in the air made it difficult to breathe.

After washing the rest of him, he applied a soapy sponge carefully to his head, wiping away sodden scabs, a couple of wound staples and flakes of wound glue from his scalp. Flicking these off the sponge he watched them swirl about him until sucked away. Next he turned his attention to the knife wound below his ribs. In itself it was relatively small, but the pain lingered, and kept him mindful of the damage that had been done there. After that he just luxuriated till Le Roque's shower abruptly shut down. He was then blasted with hot air but, not prepared to wait for it to do its job, he pushed himself out of the booth and grabbed up a towel.

"I think these should fit." Hannah gestured to some items of clothing she'd draped over the double hammock. They consisted of an undersuit, cut off at knee and elbow, and a vacuum combat suit equipped with expansion seams enabling it to cover a range of sizes.

Saul pulled on the undersuit, then thrust his feet into the integral boots of the VC suit before releasing the fabric concertinaed at the knee in order to get the right leg length, then finally tightening the upper section around his torso. It was a useful hard-wearing garment fitted with armour pads and inlaid shock and penetration mesh, suitable for stopping any missile from a plastic bullet downwards.

And it certainly seemed likely that he would be needing such protection.

Once the space plane was only four hours out, he attempted putting some satellites on an intercept course, but those aboard were obviously checking satellite positions constantly, and the craft made a sufficient deviation before he could even apply any serious acceleration. Having expected this, he swivelled one satellite, its laser still functional, and fired on the plane, probing all the way along it to look for weaknesses. No result, however, and infrared imaging indicated the point heat dispersing almost immediately.

Next he selected a communications satellite positioned within a few kilometres of the plane's forward course, and shot at it with the laser until he hit something, like a high-density battery. The satellite flew apart, hurling fragments in the plane's path: chunks of metal, ceramic and plastic, that it couldn't hope to avoid. When the plane reached this debris half an hour later, Saul observed a series of impacts on its outer skin, but they neither slowed nor diverted the craft, and he had no idea how much damage they might have inflicted. All this while Smith did nothing to stop him, which seemed merely to confirm Saul's earlier speculation about the true mission of those aboard the approaching space plane.

Meanwhile, Langstrom had been moving his men in all around the Political Office, which was a pill-shaped building eight storeys high, both its top and bottom ends terminating against the exterior lattice walls running between two arcoplexes. Simultaneously processing numerous different viewpoints, Saul watched four of Langstrom's troops hurtle for cover as a continuous fusillade, at two thousand rounds a minute, shredded structural metal behind them. It seemed Smith had no intention of coming quietly.

Langstrom cursed long and hard, before opening communications with Saul. "We're going to have to cause a lot of damage here. He's got those fuckers posted at every entrance and, knowing him, probably all through the building."

"Just keep them covered for now," Saul advised.

Now feeling suitably clad, he picked up the suit helmet and a shoulder bag full of items that would soon be necessary, and headed for the door leading out of Le Roque's apartment. Hannah instantly fell into step behind him. Out in the Tech Central control room, Saul checked that Chang and the twins were now back at their consoles, ready to assess damage, or to move station staff to safer locations. Braddock turned towards him, eyeing his new clothing doubtfully.

Saul glanced up at a screen, confirming that the approaching space plane was now only two hours out. This business needed to be resolved before the plane got here—which meant Smith had to die.

"Hannah," he said, "I want you to keep watch here. Braddock, you're ready?"

"I am," the soldier replied.

"Then we go."

Braddock and Hannah exchanged an unreadable look, then he handed her one of his collection of machine pistols. She armed it and glanced over at the three seated at their consoles, who looked back at her with some trepidation. Perhaps they thought Saul had just issued their execution order.

"So you still intend going out to join this Langstrom," she stated.

"Certainly," he replied. "If I can get direct physical access to the Political Office, I can end this pretty quickly."

"This entire situation might have been manufactured just to lure you out there."

"Let's hope not," he said. In reality, without Langstrom they didn't stand a chance.

"You're sure?" she insisted.

"Sure enough." He turned towards the door.

He couldn't be totally sure, of course, but who could be totally sure about anything? Perhaps undergoing such a dramatic mental transformation could have impaired his judgement. Maybe he had missed some secret communication, some covert agreement between Langstrom and Smith, or between Langstrom and his officers, or perhaps they were following some plan put together long before he arrived here? He just could not know what was going on inside their heads—or, at least, beyond his enhanced ability to read the outward expression of their thoughts. Just as he had already told her: he wasn't omnipresent nor omnipotent. Yet.

Out in the lobby, they crossed the bloodstained floor. Braddock had been keeping himself busy by dragging the corpses into a storeroom off to one side. Later they would go the way of all corpses here: fed through the digesters that also processed all the sewage and other organic waste, the water drawn off and recycled, the residual compost spread below the twisted trees of the Arboretum. During the planning stages of this project, the idea had been that all materials imported up here must be recycled. Even the ash from the smelting plants was turned into a conglomerate building material. However, this hadn't been entirely successful and, like a body ridding itself of accumulated toxins, some materials ended up ejected into space within the first year. Later, as demand for foamed metals increased, and ore was even shipped up from Earth, more and more waste was thus ejected, creating meteorite streaks across Earth's skies.

"So you want me to take this role," said Braddock.

"Certainly," Saul replied. "I leave it all to your judgement." He eyed the soldier keenly. "I'll also be watching them through the readerguns and robots." Some of those robots were now armed with weapons that Langstrom's troops had earlier abandoned.

They headed for the main cageway running down through Tech Central, then after closing up their suit helmets, passed through an airlock into the same tubeway in which he had fought Smith earlier. They soon passed the two wrecked robots, and the sight of blood spatters decorating the walls, which started the hard lump of Saul's knife wound throbbing in painful recall.

Eventually the tubeway extended beyond its wall panels to give an unhindered view out into the open structure beside Arcoplex One. Saul glanced aside to confirm the presence of the robots he'd summoned, then picked up his pace, propelling himself forward in a gliding, almost skating stride calculated not to raise his feet too high off the floor. He could have instead just flung himself forward until he encountered something solid, but leaving himself no way to quickly change direction, should there be hostiles nearby, did not seem like a good idea.

The tubeway ended at a junction already completed, a flattened cylindrical chamber with track-switching gear set in the floor. The worm of a stationary train blocked the branch they wanted, but they entered a pullway running alongside it. After exiting at the other end, a few more minutes of travel brought them into unfinished tubeway again. Now the robots were moving along the lattice walls immediately above and below them, like wrought-iron apes. After a further ten minutes of such progress, human figures started becoming visible waiting beside the entrance into the cell complex.

Checking via numerous cameras, Saul identified Langstrom, Sergeants Mustafa and Jack, and the big blonde woman they called Peach. Braddock moved ahead, his machine pistol raised. Saul took his time, however, as he brought the robots in closer. When he finally drew near, one quadruped robot that seemed to have bits of both lobster and earth-mover in its ancestry landed on the beams of the tubeway cage above, whilst numerous other robots became plainly visible beyond it. The four humans looked up pensively, then turned their attention back to Saul. He studied their immediate reaction: the tightening of hands on the weapons slung in front of them, their shock quickly hidden, though Sergeant Jack also took an involuntary step backwards.

On receiving a radio query through his suit, Saul linked up coms.

"Alan Saul," began Langstrom, as Saul stepped up beside Braddock.

"The same," Saul replied.

"What do you want?" Langstrom asked.

"Is that a question general or specific?"

Langstrom shrugged.

"Generally, I want to be free of the Committee. Specifically, I want to get into the Political Office—and to a particular location." He unhooked his shoulder bag and passed it over to Braddock. "Braddock, your new commander here, will explain further where I want to go." He fixed Langstrom with a steady gaze, noticed a flash of rebellion quickly suppressed, then he turned and strolled away, to apparently gaze unconcernedly through the lattice gaps at the distant arc of Earth. But he was still watching carefully through numerous electronic eyes, including one set belonging to a robot armed with a ten-bore machine gun.

Braddock retrieved a laptop from the shoulder bag, placed it down on a girder, then peremptorily gestured Langstrom over. The man stared at Saul's back, then, perhaps realizing you don't argue with the chicken farmer about your position in the pecking order, he moved over to stand beside Braddock. After a brief hesitation, the other three followed him.

"Here," said Braddock, calling up a schematic of the Political Office and outlining one particular section in red.

"The transformer room," Langstrom noted. "But why there? You could cut their power from outside, but it'd make no difference. They've got hydrox generators in there, and enough fuel for at least twenty days."

"We don't intend to cut their power."

"What, then?"

"Did you question your previous commander like this?" Braddock enquired.

"Not a healthy option."

"What makes you think it's a healthy option now?"

Langstrom shrugged. "Stupid optimism?"

"Okay, here's the deal. We're all as good as dead now if the Committee regains control of the station." He surveyed the faces of those around him. "*All* of us."

"We get that," said Langstrom.

Braddock lowered his voice, with a slight nod in Saul's direction, and hissed, "He look human to you? Well, he ain't. He's all that's stands between us and the Committee, and we do it like he says." He shook his head. "He don't need us—he doesn't need anyone here on this station. We're just a convenience to him, for now. So let's talk about how we get him where he wants to go, shall we?"

Saul hadn't coached Braddock on how he should present this, but essentially the soldier's words were the truth. He now allowed his attention to stray away from them, ensuring his robots were all in position, checking to see if Smith was in any way responding. Nothing evident as yet. Saul tried to discover any holes in his own reasoning, but could find none. In the virtual world, Smith had lost the fight about Saul's point of penetration, but even if that didn't happen again this time, their battle for the Political Office should result in that safety protocol that had kicked in before, kicking in again and disabling the readerguns. This should give Langstrom the time to seize control of the place.

"Okay, we're done," said Langstrom abruptly.

Returning most of his attention to his present surroundings, Saul turned to see Braddock close the laptop and shove it back into the shoulder bag.

"Shall we go?" asked Langstrom.

Saul nodded. As Langstrom stepped through the skeleton of the tubeway and launched himself into the station structure, he followed, with Braddock close behind him. Progress then consisted of leaping from I-beam to I-beam, until they began to discern the lights of the Political Office amid the tangled gloom. Whilst they advanced, Langstrom continued issuing instructions, so that by the time they arrived on the lower lattice leading to the ground floor, still more of his men were ready, waiting. Saul had meanwhile summoned closer some of his robots, though he hoped not to need them. In terms of utterly ruthless calculation, they were more useful to him—and more trustworthy—than Langstrom or any of his men.

16

RECYCLING TALENT

For the first fifty years, fusion reactors had required highly specialized fuels like lithium pellets, tritium microspheres, Bellington glass or Islington lead. However, the scientists continued to work diligently, and eventually attained their next goal: a reactor using full-sphere laser compression to cause fusion in a wide range of materials. But even these reactors were limited to fusing solid materials, and the final goal of devising a water or gas reactor seemed permanently out of reach. However, finally, a scientist working under Committee political oversight made the breakthroughs that resulted in the water reactor. A simplistic explanation is that he merely froze the water, thus turning it into a solid, but it is still to be revealed how water is kept frozen while being introduced into a reactor core as hot as the sun. The same scientist went on to create the first gas fuser, able to fuse hydrogen down into iron. Though these were brilliant achievements, the identity of the scientist is known only to the Committee, and Subnet rumours claim that, after he showed signs of burnout, his political director considered him too dangerous to live, so his final resting place became a community digester.

ANTARES BASE

The airlock seemed to be taking for ever to cycle. Perhaps it was malfunctioning? No, the ready light now came on, so Var pulled down the handle and pushed open the door. She could grab Kaskan, pull him back inside. But, as she stepped outside, she realized she was already too late.

Ricard must have had the shepherd waiting right outside, and it was already retreating through a cloud of dust, hauling its prize up towards it. Kaskan wasn't even struggling, just hung inert in tentacles straining to wring him out like a wet dishrag.

"Build a monument…uh…something," he managed to say to her over com.

His voice sounded strained, and at that moment she noticed the horrible angle of his leg. So far it had not managed to penetrate his suit, but then his helmet fell away, with a great gout of vapour exploding outwards around his exposed skull.

At that point he chose to manually detonate the seismic charge.

Light flashed underneath the shepherd, and Kaskan was just gone. The blast wave picked up Var and slammed her back against the airlock. The robot's body rose vertically, its legs blown off out to each side. Something smacked into Var's chest and she peered down at a wormish segment of one of the shepherd's tentacles. She batted it away and looked back up again, but no sign of either the robot or Kaskan now remained. By detonating right underneath it, the charge could have propelled the robot's body for kilometres, while Kaskan himself would have instantly turned to slurry. Her back still against the door, Var slid down into a crouch, but then felt it moving, so stood up again and stepped away.

Lopomac came out first, then Carol, and for a moment they stood in silence staring at the wave of dust rolling away from them. Then Var broke into their thoughts.

"For that to mean something," she said, "we have to succeed now, so let's move."

She broke into a steady lope, making sure that the others were keeping with her. Ahead, the wave of dust broke over the walls of Hex Three, then continued beyond it, dimming further the already waning light of the setting sun. Kaskan's sacrifice, Var realized, had crystallized the hard determination within her: *Ricard was not going to win.* They were going to survive here without him and his enforcers, or they were not going to survive at all. If he did not respond in the way Kaskan had predicted, the power was going to stay turned off. Better they all died now than by whatever selection process Ricard had in mind, or by the gradual collapse of the base's systems later on. She knew that maybe she wasn't being fair to others, but, damn it, this must end—and soon.

The damage she had already caused to Hex Three soon became evident. They rounded the structure to reach the only remaining airlock—the one into the garage—which took them nearly a quarter of an hour to get through. She entered the garage first, with her machine pistol cocked just in case Ricard had left one of his men behind, but there was no one there.

"No action yet?" said Lopomac, stating the obvious as he stepped out behind her.

"Weapons," decided Var. "He won't have taken everything from the cache."

Kaskan had given them this. Ricard had rightly believed that they stood very little chance indeed of dealing with that shepherd outside Hydroponics. But he had not included in his calculations the fact that one of them might be prepared to die in order to destroy it.

The garage contained a single crawler, parked on the ramp accessing a passage leading down underneath the hex to the workshop in the adjoining wing. The doors leading into the workshop would be sealed, that being the first area Var had opened to the Martian atmosphere. Spare wheels and engine parts were stacked along one wall, while along another one a row of super-caps was being charged up. To her right a heavy door stood open and she headed over to peer inside. Ricard had been in a hurry, so had not bothered to lock up safely. Assault rifles rested in a rack, also machine pistols and side arms. Stepping inside, Var discarded her machine pistol, selected a rifle and filled her hip pouch with clips of ceramic ammunition. The grenade rack, unfortunately, stood empty.

"The reactor," prompted Var, after the other two had made their selections.

It resided in a room of its own at the centre of the hex, cut off from the Political Director's control room and the Executive's and enforcers' quarters by bulkhead doors now tightly closed. Four pillars supported the reactor's housing, a thick coin of bubblemetal, veined with pipes, from which ducts containing superconductive wiring diverged into the walls. A simple console and screen controlled the reactor itself, while most of the other equipment crowding this room was the tool set for taking the thing apart and performing vital maintenance on it.

Var dropped into a chair facing the console and screen, and started by calling up the menu. Then she glanced round and noticed Carol beginning to remove her helmet.

"Find some more air," she instructed. "We won't be staying in here."

Carol stared back at her, looking terrified, but she nodded obediently and left the reactor room.

Having used the reactor's simple menu a number of times before, while doing some work on the old injectors, she keyed through it quickly. This time she didn't want to shut the reactor down, just cut the power. In a moment she had a schematic of the entire base up on the screen and, using her finger, selected every section of it except Hex Three, hesitating for only a brief moment over Hydroponics. She did not want to give Ricard a place to retreat to, nor think for a moment that she did not mean what she would shortly be telling him. The lights brightened for a second, then settled again. There, it was done, and now the rest of the base lay in darkness. Var used her wrist console to open a channel via the still flashing icon in the bottom corner of her visor.

"Hello, Ricard," she began.

It took a moment for him to respond, and he sounded angry, of course. "Really smart, Var. I see they must have missed something during your psyche evaluation."

"I don't think they did," she replied. "They've always been aware that intelligence is not a trait normally found in obedient little drones—but that intelligence is needed in places like this. They just took a calculated risk. However, there was no risk with you, Ricard—they roll your kind off the production line every day."

"So rather than surrender yourself to the legitimately established authority here, you'd kill us all."

"Yes, because I know that you won't let me, Carol or Lopomac live. And I also know that under your stewardship, this base will fail within months, so better we all die now. You, Ricard, now have two choices. You can either do nothing, in which case you'll begin running out of air within a couple of days, and the heat will have bled out meanwhile so that everything in Hydroponics will be dead, or, if you've got the balls, you can come over here and try to get the power back on."

"You wouldn't do that," he said.

"Yeah, my psyche report didn't label me as the kind who would so readily kill Inspectorate staff. Just as Kaskan's psyche report didn't have him down as the kind who might sacrifice himself to take out a shepherd. I'm therefore guessing that those psyche reports aren't really so reliable."

"A hundred and fifty people here would suffocate—that'll be on your conscience."

"See you soon, Ricard," she said, cutting the connection and spinning her chair round to face Lopomac, and Carol, now back with an armful of spacesuit air bottles.

"We can't lose Hydroponics," said Carol.

"It won't come to that. He'll send his men over soon, and maybe he'll even come along himself."

"He might try to wait you out. He might realize you're bluffing?"

"Carol," said Var firmly, "I'm not bluffing. We go independent here or we all die. And I'm making the choice that if we are due to die, that will occur over the next few days rather than a few months down the line."

"I'm with Var on that," said Lopomac. "There are no half-measures we can take."

Var stood up. "I'm sure they'll blow out the windows and come in that way...though they might try bringing a crawler into the garage." It was what she would do. Yes, she could now destroy the garage's door mechanism to keep them out, but she didn't want them out. She wanted them inside, then dead. "Ricard will probably hold off, hoping we'll give in, but once the cold starts killing off Hydroponics, he'll have to act. So let's get ready for him. Let's use some of our brilliant technical know-how to prepare a reception."

She had doubts still, but couldn't show them. Ricard might hold off for too long—certainly he could take all remaining air stocks for himself and his men. He might even use this as a method of thinning out base personnel, that way managing to lay the blame on Var. But, no, he would act before the air supply ran too low, and he'd act before he lost Hydroponics. Surely he would.

ARGUS STATION

"Hit it," Langstrom instructed over com.

A series of explosions ensued, punctuated by the stuttering light of the ten-bore machine guns, all utterly silent in vacuum. Missiles flashed across above them, bullets and tracers sparked off beams, and fires bloomed as of a city under siege at night. In loping strides of three metres each, starlit vacuum visible below them through the lattice partition, they approached the base of the Political Office. Some distance ahead, Peach's unit reached the blank wall, against which two of her men stuck incendiary worms. Off to the right a ten-bore flashed, tracers streaking across above the lattice-work, before striking an armoured shield. Then from the point of impact a missile was fired back, hitting the original source of fire. The detonation flung chunks of debris out amid the surrounding substructure.

Peach's people stepped back as the incendiary worms burned, cutting a doorway, which was then opened by the blast of a centrally positioned charge. Atmosphere blasted out, carrying all sorts of unidentifiable detritus, then just as abruptly it shut off. Two of her unit went through, one of them shouldering a missile-launcher. Detonation inside, lighting the interior, the burr of a machine pistol over com. Peach and the other man followed next, and five more after them.

Langstrom listened to com for a moment, then turned to Braddock and Saul. "We're clear. We can go in now."

Saul nodded briefly, then held up a restraining hand: *just one moment.* Through his boots he felt its approach behind him, and through its robotic eyes he noted Langstrom's startled expression as the construction robot moved up beside him. It loomed over him like a guardian bear, but this particular bear had six limbs, and in one of its tool-wielding paws it clutched a heavy machine gun.

"Is that thing really necessary?" Braddock asked.

"It may be useful," Saul replied, not yet ready to rely on the soldiers' protection alone.

Langstrom led the way into a corridor filled with tendrils of smoke dissipating into vacuum. Blood smeared the floor, blackened by absence of air, yet there was no sign of any corpses. Off to the right lay further wreckage, and the remains of a machine gun embedded in a wall. They headed for a secondary airlock, and after Langstrom opened it, Saul sent his guardian through first. He watched through its eyes as the inner airlock door opened, admitting the robot to a corridor filled with smoke. He and Braddock stepped through next, and at once he picked up sound: suppressing fire from four soldiers racketing like power drills somewhere out of sight. With Langstrom following they proceeded left, then right, the sounds of gunfire almost continuous ahead of them. Saul glanced up at the wrecked dome of a readergun located in the ceiling, surprised that it seemed to have cost no lives.

Next, three corpses at the foot of a vertical cageway—Saul guessed they were Smith's people, though it was hard to be sure, and odd that the blood on their uniforms looked so dry. They launched their way up the cageway, their progress covered by three of Langstrom's troops, who began firing into any exposed sections of the Political Office. They continued on through, bullets zinging constantly off surrounding metal. Something thumped against Saul's thigh, but didn't penetrate. Smoke lay thick and heavy in the air as they departed the cageway, before entering another corridor where the smoke stank of burning meat. Someone started screaming, but he couldn't locate the source. Next, a blast ahead, doors disappearing, Langstrom's troops piling straight in amid gunfire. One of the men bounced out again, blood jetting from his open mouth.

Braddock caught Saul by the shoulder and pulled him down, as the fire fight continued. A minute later, the fighting ahead of them was over, though all about them the Political Office resounded with continuing gunfire and explosions.

"It's clear now," said Langstrom.

Braddock preceded Saul into the room beyond: a horizontal cylinder with two bulky transformers protruding from the right, one of them showering a steady stream of sparks and molten metal from its bullet-riddled armature. A man hung from one side of it, his hand melted in place and his body beginning to smoke. Langstrom's troops were down at the far end, in the corridor extending beyond, crouched behind a barricade consisting of a couple of metal tool cabinets against which they had set doors ripped from their mountings.

"Here." Saul pointed to a mass of fibre-optic and power-cable junction boxes, and consoles running along the wall facing the transformers, then launched across and steadied himself against the unit he required, planting his gecko boots back on the floor. Removing his helmet, he flipped up the unit lid to expose six teragate sockets, then held out a hand to one side. Braddock delved in the shoulder bag for a coil of optic cable, with teragate plugs at each end, and silently handed it over.

"We don't have long in here," Langstrom remarked, watching with curiosity as Saul pulled the plug of synthetic skin from his temple and plugged the cable into his skull, before jabbing the other end of the cable into one of the six sockets, randomly chosen.

Instant connection filled an empty space within his being. Smith was already waiting there, but the man's attack on him seemed utterly ineffectual as Saul speared his way into the isolated Political Office network. It felt like satiation of vast thirst as he sucked up data, modelling the entire Political Office inside his head, while noting the positions of everyone within it. In a sudden heady rush of power, he swatted Smith aside, felt him retreating, withdrawing—the man now outmatched.

Two major fire fights still continued, and he saw Peach and the remaining two members of her unit pinned down by machine-gun fire from some of Smith's people positioned on a gantry above them. Only twenty metres away from Saul, another four of Langstrom's troops, led by Mustafa, were caught up in a shoot-out with more of Smith's men, who were busy moving additional firepower into position, in the shape of another big machine gun. Elsewhere, Langstrom's units were intermittently engaging the ten-bore machine guns at the five main entrances, simply to keep them tied down. Whilst he delved into Smith's database, loading the ID implant codes of everyone currently under Smith's command, he individually seized control of the readerguns in two relevant areas, and powered them up. Should he give Smith's soldiers a chance to surrender? Should he hell, since just moments' delay could result in soldiers on *his* side dying. Within a minute Saul provided the readerguns with specific targets. And it took the readerguns a further ten seconds to complete.

Their dome turrets flashed like halogen lamps, turning then flashing again. The one positioned in the ceiling immediately above the men trying to creep up on Peach and her two comrades flashed brightly for a full three seconds. Five partially dismembered bodies were blown from the gantry, sailing in a cloud of shattered flesh and bone over above the three below. Another reader then took out those running the machine gun. Just two short bursts left one jammed underneath the great weapon, his form no longer recognizably human, whilst the other one cartwheeled away to one side leaving an arc of blood in the air. Similar scenes played out amongst those attacking Mustafa, and, even from where he stood, Saul heard the sound of the guns through human ears.

"Readerguns," observed Langstrom.

"Yes," Saul replied, turning to gaze at him, but feeling he had nothing more to add.

Smith he finally found in a room filled with yet more computers, screens and consoles than Tech Central itself, but the computers there were used solely to control the station's hardware and direct its staff. This array ran complex programs to monitor the behaviour of all working aboard Argus Station and thereby try to divine what was going on inside their heads, so that corrective instruction could be issued. Here lay the essential power base of the thought police.

Smith had pushed himself out of his chair and was floating backwards, hand up against his head as the hardware there transmitted his spoken orders. Already others were turning away from their consoles to look round at him. Having just learned that the readerguns were killing his people, he didn't look as alarmed as he should, but then no readerguns overlooked this particular room. Saul guessed that Smith must be aware of the 5 percent malfunction rate, and wanted to cut down the odds of some nasty accident happening that might involve himself.

Speaking through the intercom so as to broadcast his voice throughout the entire Political Office, Saul began, "This is Alan Saul speaking, and I now control the readerguns here. So put down your weapons and surrender yourselves. This is not a request."

Smith extended a hand to catch hold of a stable piece of hardware, then pulled himself floorwards and turned to gaze up at the nearest cam. Meanwhile, the gunfire inside the Political Office began stuttering to a halt. As soon as those operating machine guns by the entrances became aware that the nearby readerguns had targeted them, they too began shutting down their weapons and awaited further orders.

"Smith," he continued broadcasting, "issue the surrender order."

"Before I can do that, you must acquaint me with whatever guarantees you are laying on the table," Smith replied, stalling for time. Saul ensured his response was broadcast as well, and studied the defenders' reaction to it.

"I guarantee that any of your people who don't put down their weapons, and surrender instantly, will be dead within a very short time."

With a look of intense frustration on his face, Smith seemed momentarily at a loss for words. Saul had no doubt that this man was prepared to sacrifice any number of lives, just so long as they didn't include his own. However, already some of his fellows had abandoned their weapons and were moving away from them. Some of the machine-gun crews, too, were drifting out of the Political Office, while others still inside were trying to keep their hands up while propelling themselves clumsily towards Langstrom's men.

Smith knew that he had lost; it was now a matter of whether he was still prepared to allow pride and stubbornness to sway him. Saul did not like what he was reading in the man's expression, or in the pose of his body, or the way he closed a hand over the weapon holstered at his belt.

"Can't you just finish him?" Langstrom asked.

Saul focused on the question. "No readerguns installed in his control room."

"Typical."

Studying their immediate surroundings, Saul noted that with Smith's men surrendering in the near vicinity, certain routes now lay open. He reached up and detached the optic from his head. Access stuttered for just a second, then the Political Office was once again included within the framework of the whole station network.

"Braddock, Langstrom, let's go and have a chat with the Political Director."

The three of them set off.

"It will be interesting to evaluate how you managed this," sneered Smith. "But that will be after you have found the challenges of Argus Station too much for you. Do you honestly think that a few traitors and revolutionaries can withstand the concerted might of the Committee and the People? We command the resources of an entire world: hundreds of millions of military personnel, countless space planes and ICBMs. You must know that resistance is futile."

"Yet you neglect one obvious fact," replied Saul as he strode onwards. "They are all down on Earth, while I am up here. Give it up, Smith. Why waste yet more lives?"

"Surrender is not an option open to me, as it would represent a betrayal of trust. Government forces are currently on their way, therefore it is certain that any who betray the people by putting their own physical survival first can be sure ultimately of a visit to an adjustment cell."

Saul could have cut Smith off the moment he realized what he was about to say, but he wanted everyone here to understand how low was Smith's regard for their lives. Yet there seemed to be something more to his response than just that. Smith could not hope to hold out until the space plane arrived, so he must surely know that, after making such a statement, his own life would be forfeit. Besides, it seemed certain those aboard the approaching space plane would not have his best interests at heart.

They reached the door leading into the control room, which opened with surprising ease since Saul had expected it to be sealed. As they entered, Smith turned away from the screen he was watching and stepped out on to an open area of floor. At once Saul sensed something was wrong, and he instinctively groped for a view through the eyes of his guardian robot. But, of course, having received no further instructions, it still squatted in the transformer room; just a heap of inert metal.

"I suggest that you have been guilty of the same sort of arrogance, and lack of intelligence that resulted in your friend Malden's demise," Smith announced.

Saul began to turn. "Braddock—"

A shot rang out and Braddock spun past him, with a quarter of his head gone. Saul turned back just in time to notice the blunt object Smith clutched in one hand. Sheer agony ripped through him from head to foot, the impact tearing his boots from the floor. In that moment it felt as if he had been plunged directly into a furnace. Saul tried desperately to link up with his robots, with the readerguns, with anything, but the code had become just a scrambled mess of migraine lights flashing through his skull. He felt a hand close about his arm, shoving him to the floor, and a foot pressing down on his chest.

"Now that was costly," said Langstrom. "I could have taken him down long before now."

"His value to the people outweighs the level of casualties we have sustained," said Smith calmly. "And, for the benefit of the people, it was necessary that one of my status should be seen as able to render him harmless, thus reinforcing Committee command structures."

"Still, there are people out there lying dead who didn't need to be."

"I think not," Smith replied. "The moment you so much as pointed a weapon at him, one of his robots would have torn you limb from limb. Anyway, since when has the extinction of subordinates ever been a problem to you, Langstrom?"

"I was just saying," the soldier replied.

"Anyway, all those men against you were primarily loyal to Messina, so that's been to our advantage. The same with those space planes he destroyed."

Through a blur of vision, Saul stared up at Smith smiling down at him.

Then the man took his foot away and fired the disabler again, and Saul was once again in the furnace. He heard someone screaming, only realizing it was himself just before the world slipped away from him.

***

"The Political Office is back online," reported one of the twins—Hannah wasn't sure which of them it was.

"Yes, evidently," she replied, studying the screen as some of Langstrom's soldiers began making their way out of the office building. "Any sign of Saul?"

The other twin began flicking through cam views, till she picked up Saul currently propelling himself along a pullway beside a stationary train. She then tagged him with a surveillance program and shunted the image over to one of the three larger screens. Hannah reached out and manually operated the camera focus, trying for close-ups, but failing. Saul appeared uninjured, but that was all Hannah could discern. As the program tracked him back towards Tech Central, she wondered if Braddock was still safe. What had happened in there, and how many people had died? She'd witnessed the fire fight from the outside, and later recognized the vicious sound of readerguns over com. Did the interior of the Political Office now resemble an abattoir?

"So he now has full control," suggested Brigitta, her voice devoid of all emotion.

"So it would seem," Hannah replied.

She closed her eyes for a moment and tried to suppress the feeling of helpless terror. Looking again at the screens, she watched the space plane inexorably drawing closer, only a half-hour away now. She then returned her attention to Saul himself, and watched as he finally passed the two wrecked robots on his way in. He seemed stronger now, snapping himself forward by the wall handles with obvious impatience. Soon he headed through the Tech Central door and Hannah spun her chair round to face him.

"All done?" she asked.

Moving forward, Saul dipped his head and began undoing the catches of his suit helmet. Only then did Hannah understand the doubt that stirred inside her. She spun her chair round and began to reach for the machine pistol lying on the console. Shots thundered into the console, flinging the weapon out of reach. She shrank away just as a hand closed on her shoulder, tipping both herself and the chair over backwards, banging her head hard on the floor. The hand now closed about her neck and the hot barrel of a machine pistol was almost touching her face.

"Greetings, Hannah," said Smith.

Smith must have used the simple ruse of wearing Saul's vacuum combat suit to get himself here, but the ruse hadn't really been necessary. With Saul now captive or dead, only one option was available to keep herself out of Smith's hands, but she wasn't prepared to kill herself. Now, looking straight into his face, she knew he would be in no hurry to kill her either. She noted the red eyes, the broken blood vessels around them, and the veins standing out in his forehead. His breath smelled rank too—characteristic of someone maxed out on cocktails of painkillers, stimulants, ACE inhibitors and beta blockers. Though perhaps not yet as screwed up as Malden, he must know he could not carry on living like this.

"Commander Langstrom." Smith spoke into the vacuum suit's mike. "Now would be a suitable time for you to be present here." Then, after a pause, "I do not see any difficulties in that regard. All the robots are currently inactive, as Saul did not program them for completely independent action, or to engage in hostilities without direct orders from himself. Therefore, once I have divined the basis of his code, they will be mine once again. Now, please do not make me issue a reprimand, as I require your presence in here right now."

Smith stood upright, hauling Hannah to her feet by her neck, before transferring his grip to the front of her survival suit. He then swung his attention to Chang and the twins, who remained standing by their consoles.

"We had no choice," said Chang defensively.

"In no known situation are choices lacking," Smith replied. "We must therefore work diligently together to reveal how difficult your choices were."

Hannah could see the sudden terror appearing in their faces, for they knew the techniques Smith would use to discover whatever version of the truth suited him. Chang moved forward slightly, but Smith swung the machine pistol towards him. For a moment, Hannah thought Chang might charge him, but the big man desisted, holding his hands out to his sides. "What do you want of us?"

Smith hesitated, flicking his gaze to the three large screens, all of which now instantly changed images to show different views of the approaching space plane.

"My current preference is for you to seat yourselves again, and then refrain from further comment," he said.

Shooting worried looks at each other, they obeyed him. Maybe if they just kept their heads down, he would forget about them. Hannah did not think so, but understood their bunker mentality.

"What happened to Saul?" she abruptly asked.

Without even looking at her, Smith released his grip, swung his arm away, then struck her hard with the back of his hand. The blow felt like it dislocated her jaw, and the adhesive sole of one of her shoes ripped free of the floor. Lights flashing in her vision, she tumbled over backwards, her spine jarring against the floor. In an instant he was crouching over her, the machine pistol again in her face.

"Saul has suffered a misfortune, for him at least, in that he is still alive." He grinned nastily. "Presently he occupies an interrogation cell, and is enjoying recurrent inducement—just enough to keep him from regaining full mental coherence."

Hannah felt sick. The Inspectorate used that technique to break people: give the victim just enough time to regain consciousness and some awareness of his situation, before hitting him repeatedly with an inducer until the pain again knocked him out. At that moment Saul would be in hell.

"Didn't you already do enough to him?"

"It would appear that I did not and, though I feel more than his current mental retraining is required, I don't want to damage the hardware and software installed in his brain, do I?"

She knew at once what he meant: Smith wanted for himself to possess the more advanced hardware and biotech inside Saul's skull. It seemed pointless, life-threatening in fact, to try explaining to him how very different was Saul's organic interface from Smith's, and also how it could not now be removed.

"Okay," she said, giving a little nod. Pretend to knuckle under, pretend that to survive she'd do whatever he wanted. But why not? Before Saul had freed her, that was how she had always behaved.

Just then the doors opened, and in came Langstrom accompanied by three of his soldiers. Smith stepped back, hauling Hannah upright. He beckoned to one of the soldiers, a heavily built black man. "Restrain her."

"You want her in a cell?" the man asked.

"No, restrain her here within my sight."

The man picked up the chair she had been sitting in, gripped Hannah by the biceps, and towed both of them over to one side of the room. Quickly and efficiently, he slipped a plastic tie about her wrists, then used strong tape to bind her to the chair. Meanwhile, Smith and Langstrom were busy studying the images coming up on the screens.

"In twenty minutes they will be joining us here on Argus Station," Smith announced.

"You've told them that we've solved our little problem?"

"Yes, I have so informed them, but such information will not prevent them from docking." Responding to a limp hand gesture, one of the screens changed to show a massive airfield in some desolate desert location. Hannah squinted at the image, realizing, with a sudden lurch in her gut, that the thirty-odd shapes revealed were space planes, some of them in the process of launching.

"I thought they were meant to wait until after full commission of the Argus Network?" observed Langstrom.

"That was the original intention, but it seems that, now the predicted societal collapse has begun, things are accelerating." Smith shook his head slowly. "In all regions we must rely on extreme measures to quell insurrection, but throughout most of South America, North Africa and Southern Europe we are not preventing the collapse, and have therefore withdrawn resources back to our bases, in preparation for later intervention."

Hannah felt a surge of contempt. Smith had always spoken like this, in such a convoluted manner, and sometimes it was difficult to work out exactly what he meant. The Committee had completely lost control, so was using gas, live ammunition and robots programmed to kill in order to prevent itself being overrun by the starving mobs. In the three areas mentioned, its forces had withdrawn to their bases for the time being.

"And with the few remaining lasers that you and Saul didn't wreck, between you," said Langstrom, "there's no way of reversing that disintegration now." The soldier said it without emphasis, but the hint of criticism was there. Smith, however, did not seem to notice it.

"One must await the appropriate time," he replied, and pointed to the screen showing the launching space planes. "Messina is aboard one of those planes, which is already on its way here, perhaps to oversee any future interventions."

Langstrom gazed steadily at him. "Is he going to try and take the station away from you?"

"He may indeed wish for primacy."

"You've warned them over in Arcoplex One?"

"There is no necessary benefit in doing so. Alessandro Messina will not establish himself in control here by means of policy statements or Committee votes, therefore my pet delegates would not prove effective in such a situation."

As they both returned their attention to the screens, Hannah digested this reference to delegates. Didn't Saul say earlier that Smith had opened a back door into the laser network? It seemed he had been clawing for power, and control of the network had been one chip in the dangerous game he was playing. Meanwhile, he had used his bargaining position to get all those delegates prepared to back him transferred up here, only now things had drastically changed. Perhaps the Committee had hoped to retain control down on Earth with the seven hundred satellites previously available, using mass slaughter as a tool, when necessary. Now that so few laser weapons were immediately available, it seemed Messina and the rest of the Committee were ready to abandon the planet, for now. Whatever way it went, the power base was now up here on Argus, and that's where all the politicians wanted to be. And once they got up here, they would fight, as ever, to become top dog.

"Let us assemble a small reception committee," said Smith. "I believe you should ensure it consists primarily of those whose martial usefulness is in question. The rest of your men should be deployed around the core installations: here at Tech Central, the Political Office and the cell complex."

"More sacrifices, you mean?"

Smith tilted his chin towards the screen. "I am ignorant of the orders issued to those in the approaching space plane. Whoever meets them can direct them straight to the nearest rim-side accommodation and, if they agree to go there, that will give time for you to move out there from the core, and be ready to negate their interference." He turned his gaze fully on Langstrom.

"Once they dock on the rim they'll probably head straight in towards the core," suggested the soldier.

"A more likely and even preferable scenario, because we'll then know Alessandro's true intentions. Militarily it is preferable, too, since a great number of readerguns and robots lie conveniently between the rim and the core."

"They're going to be well equipped and there's no guarantee they'll use a dock at all," Langstrom observed.

"I have enabled access for your men to Kalashtek assault rifles, and ceramic ammunition capable of penetrating VC suits," said Smith, "and you may also wish to deploy carousel missile-launchers wherever feasible." When Langstrom still did not seem in any hurry to depart, he snapped, "Is there anything further?"

"Nothing at all, sir." Langstrom gestured for his men to follow him and, even as he departed, new staff were arriving and taking up positions at the consoles around the room.

"You three," Smith indicated Chang and the twins, "return to your accommodation for now. We will discuss that 'choice' you mentioned at a later juncture."

So much for keeping their heads down.

***

The nightmare was a repeat of one he'd experienced more times than he could count. He was strapped naked to a cold steel wall, while in front of him stood a bench scattered with the kind of tools to be found in any workshop: screwdrivers, pliers, wire cutters, a soldering iron and an angle grinder. In this nightmare, however, he could hear the words.

"The people," declared Smith, "need to know."

It wasn't Smith, however, who now stepped into view, but some interrogation-block technician—no, not even that; just some recorded mock-up of a human being. Saul could distinguish the man's enforcer uniform underneath his transparent plastic overalls, but no sign of his face, for he wore a hazmat filter mask and green-tinted goggles. Careful not to tear his surgical gloves, he picked up the angle grinder, removed the grinding disk and replaced it with one used for coarse sanding.

"In what manner precisely did you alter the functions of your body?" asked Smith, now also stepping into view. "We need to know why the viral nanite you created has killed all the subjects we've tested it on. And how does it function in combination with the anti-ageing drugs, and what alterations did you make to those drugs themselves?"

Saul stared at him, dressed in his immaculate white suit, looking so incongruous in this dark and filthy place. Everything Saul had done appeared absolutely clear in his mind: the way the viral nanite had been modelled on his own individual DNA, therefore was in many ways equivalent to the bespoke magic bullets already used by the medical profession; the way he altered the fix so that some parts of it worked more slowly, thus allowing the virus to finish its work before sealing it perfectly. The whole wonderful complexity of what he had achieved lay there opened up to the inspection of his inner eye. But he could not explain this to Smith: the man was just too stupid to understand, and Saul didn't possess the words to make it clear. Furthermore, at the core of him lay a rebellious stubbornness and a disinclination to communicate which just locked him into continuing silence.

The enforcer started the grinder rotating and brought it up close to Saul's chest.

"As a consequence of the antishock drugs we have injected into you, you will undoubtedly stay conscious for an appreciable period of time," Smith explained, in his usual laborious fashion. "Blood loss resulting from this treatment will not be sufficient to render you unconscious." He indicated a set of blood bags tubed into his victim's arm, which Saul hadn't noticed before.

The sanding disc came down against his chest, producing an unbelievable explosion of agony. Saul shrieked, and struggled against the restraints, blood and skin spraying all about him. He now wanted to tell Smith, wanted to tell him everything, but the words remained locked up inside him. And even in his agony he noticed that not one fleck of the bloody detritus had marred Smith's pristine white suit.

Saul retreated from this nightmare of pain, but just couldn't locate himself in time or space. His groping mind tried to incorporate a thousand cam views, tried to get a grip on the huge traffic of computer code surrounding him, yet found it frustratingly slippery to his mental grasp. He sensed robots stirring in recollection, from wherever they crouched amid the inner-station substructure like roosting birds, felt others blocking him out as they began to move under someone else's instruction. Such exploration was almost instinctive to him, yet at least it gave him his own location.

I am aboard the Argus space station.

An outside view suddenly of a space plane coming in to dock. He felt a sudden surge of panic at the sight, but had no idea why. He needed to take control, needed access, but it all now seemed far too confusing. First he needed to return to himself and locate himself precisely in space and time. He needed to rediscover his fleshly ego, and from that firmer basis regain memory and purpose. But which of these thousands of views came through his own human vision? The only way to find out was to disconnect from all obvious cam-signal traffic, which he did as rapidly as he could, and finally he opened his eyes.

A cell?

He felt as if he had been beaten from head to foot, and his skin scoured with acid. Because he was bound upright, naked and cruciform against a white-tiled wall, with manacles about his wrists and ankles and a steel band about his waist, he instantly thought he had returned to the world of nightmare. But reality possessed a much sharper edge, and a particular pain throbbing in his side reawakened memories of Smith's knife going in, and his surroundings smelt of shit, which he realized must be his own as soon as he saw the pain inducer projecting from a ceiling-suspended framework. Turning his head slightly, he noted an optic cable trailing from his temple to a box mounted on the wall, just above his shoulder. From this, yet more optics ran up the wall and across the ceiling, connecting into the hardware above the inducer. And then he remembered precisely how he had got here.

"The three...bodies," Saul had managed, after being dragged down here from the Political Office, and when the two soldiers secured him to the wall.

"Three bodies?" Smith had enquired with interest, standing with Saul's VC suit draped over one arm. "What three bodies?"

"On the way in...the blood on them was dry."

"Oh, yes." Smith had nodded. "I used some of the casualties from our previous encounter, just to set the scene. I also needed to let you kill a few yourself, just so you would feel confident enough of victory to come directly against me. Rather negligent of you to leave your robot behind, but that wouldn't have mattered anyway, since I had one of my officers standing by with a PA50 tank-buster, just in case."

"Why?" Saul had asked.

"Why what?"

"Why the charade, if you had suitable weapons...to hit my robots?"

"I only have the one, you see. Initially, I could have sent my soldiers directly against you, but that would have resulted in too many deaths, and I will be needing them now. It was better just to manipulate you, which of course was so easy. You even destroyed those three space planes for me, which of course I can now deny responsibility for." Smith had smiled.

Despite the pain in his head, Saul had retained enough analytical capacity to realize that Smith could have brought him down much earlier. It seemed that this whole charade had not been necessary, but merely to satisfy Smith's enjoyment of manipulation.

Saul had blinked, the ache in his head partially receding, and he had begun to probe the computer networks in his vicinity, first picking up on the cam view inside the cell itself, then venturing beyond it to see soldiers moving about in the corridors of the cell block. He had reached further, trying to get in contact with Hannah—but then Smith was there, blocking him, undermining him.

"I did consider shutting you completely out of the station network, but it seems that switching off your internal modem would require either destructive computer intervention or even surgery," Smith had said. "I then considered keeping you unconscious until we two found an opportunity to spend some quality time together, before I got Hannah to surgically extract all that hardware in your skull, but the problem is that while you're unconscious you are not suffering, and I so very much want you to *suffer*, Alan Saul."

Smith had stepped back and, with a surge of dread, Saul could clearly see the inducer in the ceiling. The man had continued, "Then I figured out the perfect solution: recurrent inducement. For any normal subject, periods of unconsciousness last between ten minutes and an hour, but I feel certain, in your case, the recovery period will be quicker. Let's see, shall we?"

The agony, as ever, had been unbelievable. He roasted, screaming, in invisible naked flame, his contorted body pounding against the wall behind him like it was being electrocuted. Blackness had overcome him...then, seemingly in no time at all, he had been back in the cell, and trying to remember who he was, where he was...

"That took only four minutes," Smith had said, checking his watch. "Remarkable." He had departed, slinging Saul's vacuum suit over his shoulder.

Then the agony once more, again and again, Smith's voice recurring too, after the first two times. How many times thereafter, Saul had lost count.

"Readings indicate that you are now fully conscious," declared that hated voice.

Saul licked desiccated lips, trying to think of the words to beg for relief, even though he knew he was merely hearing a recording.

"And once again it is time for instruction."

"No...please..."

A light appeared, up there in that hardware, blinking from red to green, and in the next instant every square millimetre of Saul's skin began to burn. He felt a moment of utter disbelief that such agony could be possible, as he glimpsed his arm, corded with veins, and could not understand how the skin wasn't melting. He screamed repeatedly and tried to tear his manacles from the wall till, after an eternity of just ten seconds, his mind escaped once more into comfortable darkness.

Saul crept into wakefulness like a wild animal approaching a suspicious bounty of food. He couldn't remember where he was or even when he was, but knew danger lurked close by. He therefore needed to move fast. With a feeling of déjà vu, his mind groped out and tried to incorporate a thousand cam views, tried to latch onto the huge surrounding traffic of computer code...

Not fast enough.

17

RETIREMENT WITHOUT PENSION

As the Committee steadily expanded in power, it grew far too large and complex, until in danger of ceasing to function in any meaningful manner. Sitting above the massive bureaucracy there were over three thousand delegates representing countries or regions across the Earth. Even minor matters, like the standardization of paperclips, became the subject of debates that raged for years, while vastly more important issues were consigned to a political wasteland. However, a winnowing process was already at work as some of the delegates clawed more power to themselves, and created factions or supporters, whilst others of their kind were consigned to a political void. Secret decisions began to get made as an ostensibly egalitarian regime shed any pretence of equality for all. This was the time of the efficiency experts, promoting the division of Earth into larger regions and thereby the dismissal of delegates who failed to secure their hold on power. And, as with all such regimes, the penalty of failure was inevitably severe. It has, ever since, been the case that very few delegates will go into quiet retirement. And the word "retirement," in Committee circles, has become a euphemism for something a great deal less pleasant.

"It is essential that you remain within the arcoplex," declared Smith. "You will be perfectly safe there and, at present, facilities external to the arcoplex are unable to guarantee your full protection."

The man peering from the screen frowned, and Hannah felt sure she recognized him from somewhere but could not place him just then. Meanwhile, the view over his right shoulder was distracting, for it showed a window through which the interior of Arcoplex One could be seen, which resembled a city distorted through a fish-eye lens.

"Why have you shut down rotation?" the man enquired. "Zero gravity is making a lot of people in here feel sick."

"It is a safety protocol, Delegate Shanklin, which negates the possibility of catastrophic failure of the cylinder motors, should they suffer munitions damage."

Shanklin was the Committee delegate for East India, and therefore controlled the Asian voting bloc, but other than that, Hannah knew little about him.

"Yet you didn't shut it down when either Malden or Saul penetrated the station?"

"The threat they presented to the structure of the Argus Station was negligible. Should those currently approaching us aboard the space plane be prepared to use force on Messina's behalf, they will be equipped to the highest level of Committee military requirements."

Shanklin stared at him for a long moment. "I'm hoping, Smith, that we haven't all made a big mistake with you."

"Considering that you have," Smith replied, "the time in which you might have corrected that mistake has already expired." Then he shut off the transmission.

"Your backers?" Hannah risked asking him.

"Committee delegates tend to get overly attracted to power and its trappings," he replied distractedly.

"How many are here?"

Without looking round he replied, "Fifty delegates in all, along with their staff and families. Over two thousand people." Coming from him it was a surprisingly direct response.

"So they got you here, didn't they?" ventured Hannah. "And now they're just a millstone round your neck."

He turned to give her an unreadable look. "They certainly would have been useful in re-establishing the rule of the people back on Earth, but a further one hundred and seventy delegates have made a provisional commitment to back me for the chairmanship."

To Smith, it seemed, "the people," "the state" and "the Committee" were all the same thing, but only if it meant he himself got to give the orders.

"Would have been?" she asked.

He shrugged. "Alessandro Messina's tyrannical arrogance is such that he would likely not let it come to a vote."

Hannah glanced out through the windows allowing a view across the wheel of the space station. From where she was seated, she could just about see the space plane dropping down behind the station's rim. Next she transferred her gaze back to the screens, one of which now showed the space plane moving in to dock, whilst another displayed the interior of that same dock.

"His failure is inevitable," Smith added, studying the screens.

The docking pillar, one of five sticking out from the rim, was pentagonal in section, each external face of it wide enough to encompass the largest type of space plane. As the plane settled against it, she could just about discern the docking clamps engaging underneath it. A belly lock in the plane could be opened to the inside of the docking pillar for loading and unloading cargo, whilst a separate passenger airlock would be engaged via an extending tube. She focused on the interior of the dock, wondering if Smith's reliance on such views showed how less able he was than Saul, who had no need for such extra aids.

The interior view showed four of Langstrom's troops making their way alongside the cargo train that serviced the dock, and then descending an internal face of the pillar itself. Ahead of them emerged one end of the passenger embarkation tube, a cylinder three metres high and two wide. As the soldiers approached, the two doors in its side opened to show three figures clad in VC suits, and upside-down. They instantly pushed themselves out, flipping over to come down upright on the floor, legs bending to absorb the shock so that their boots did not disengage. They then moved back-to-back, checking their surroundings.

To one side of the passenger tube, a pair of long double doors hinged up from the floor, opening directly into the belly of the plane. Out flew an object a couple of metres across, looking not unlike a balled-up mass of water pipes.

Smith hissed with anger, and immediately readerguns opened fire, sending the three men tumbling away, but seemingly uninjured. The balled-up thing opened, into a chaotic collection of robotic arms terminating in twin-barrelled guns which at once began firing, so it seemed rather like a flaming tumbleweed. Munitions debris spread out in a cloud as readerguns exploded all around the dock. Then, even as the onslaught diminished, the three figures in vacuum combat suits righted themselves and started firing too—at the four personnel who had come to greet them. Hannah found herself flinching as she watched bullets tearing into their bodies, jerking them about helplessly, spewing chunks of flesh and bone out in every direction.

"Low-impact ammunition in the readerguns," observed Hannah. "You should have thought of that."

Smith glared round at her and, by the look on his face, she half expected him to come over and hit her.

"They were dispensable," he replied coldly.

Did he mean the human troops who had just died or the readerguns themselves?

In the dock itself, more troops in VC gear piled out of the airlock, as the big robot settled quietly to the floor. One squad of about twenty troops moved swiftly to the base of the dock and through, down beside the train there, whilst others began removing equipment from the space plane's hold. Smith watched this activity for some minutes before speaking again.

"I am assuming that you were watching that, Langstrom?" he demanded.

Down in the righthand corner of the screen a frame opened up to show Langstrom. "I saw—and we're ready. We've got ten-bores and rocket-launchers deployed," the commander grimaced, "which we'll need seeing as they've got a spidergun with them." He glanced at something off-screen. "The first of them are not coming straight in but, as you predicted, they're heading for the upper spindle anchor. Maybe they'll pass through Arcoplex One to get down here."

"Most unlikely," Smith replied. "Though an arcoplex offers them cover, traversing it will be a slow process, for they would consider it necessary to use urban-warfare techniques. There are also few exits, all of which could provide ambush points."

"They'll blow it?" Langstrom suggested.

"This is not likely either, since Chairman Messina will want as little damage done to the station as possible." Smith raised a hand to the side of his head, an unconscious gesture as new information became available to him. The screen previously showing Delegate Shanklin now revealed the first squad of invading troops deployed in and about the massive machinery at the far end of Arcoplex One. Some were gathered about an airlock, which opened even as she watched. One of them made some adjustments to a package, then tossed it inside before the outer airlock door closed again.

THE DEPARTURE

"They are physically bypassing the airlock's electronics," explained Smith. "In those circumstances there is little I can do."

Now a fresh view: the interior of the arcoplex cylinder. It resembled a long street of buildings tilting inwards, with further buildings projecting from the sides and down from overhead, some of which were actually connected to the cylinder spindle. Sunlight flooded from the dispersal units positioned at intervals along the spindle jacket, bathing everything in a bright, almost Mediterranean light. Enough illumination, therefore, to see a troop of enforcers heading towards the airlock situated at the street's end, while civilians were heading in the opposite direction. Men, women and children were down on the street itself using gecko boots, while others higher up were propelling themselves from surface to available surface, or aboard a couple of aeros. Most of those fleeing the scene carried bundles and bags just like any refugee throughout history.

Then the airlock opened.

Hannah could not understand what the attackers hoped to achieve here if they were not using the arcoplex as a route to the station core. The inner door of the airlock just stood wide open now, and nothing much seemed to be happening there at first. But next some sort of detonation within the airlock blew out a cloud of vapour like smoke from the muzzle of a cannon. It dispersed as rapidly as milk in water and, almost at once, people started writhing in mid-air. Then one of the aeros slammed into the side of a building, and stuck there, its rear fan spitting out debris. Several enforcers rose from the floor, tearing at their clothing, while the others just began contorting where they were. Within just a few seconds all of them were motionless but for those on trajectories they'd set themselves upon as they died.

"Quick," observed Langstrom.

Smith replied, "In my opinion, they have just made use of the Novichok agent the Department of Warfare was developing. It was efficiency-tested during the Chicago riots and found to be very effective."

"Take some clearing up."

"That nerve agent has an active life of only about an hour," replied Smith dismissively, "so in itself should not be a problem for us. Though effecting sanitary measures to clear up the human detritus might not be so pleasant." He pondered this for a moment. "I will follow Saul's lead and reprogram construction robots to accomplish the chore. They can move a proportion of the deceased to cold sections of the station, to prevent any immediate overload of the digesters."

This exchange seemed so blandly conversational that Hannah felt a creeping horror. The two men were talking about the death of two thousand fellow citizens, yet Smith's biggest concern seemed to be organizing the funeral arrangements.

***

Somewhere down in that part of his mind where decisions were made even before coherent thoughts could express them, some dreg of pure reason alerted Saul to the impending agony, utterly certain, the moment the optic plugged into his skull registered his rise to full consciousness. In a state between unconsciousness and waking, Saul rejected wakefulness and yet, deep amid a morass of dreams and undesignated data, he managed to apply logic and found the ability to think. He discerned reality below that filter that led into the conscious world, and without any sense of self he managed to process it. His organic brain demanded that he return to that world above the surface, but what did it amount to? Just the fleshly vessel for part of his mind, a part that he'd so far found necessary only because within it lay his reason for physical existence. He remained detached from the now and, on one level, wondered how long it would take him to decide not to bother continuing with such an existence at all.

"It's monitoring him," said a vaguely familiar female voice.

"Just unplug it?" suggested a male voice. "Do something like you did with the cams?"

"Dangerous."

"Smith's busy out there."

The words murmured out of some abyss, and seemed almost irrelevant to him. All but the last four words made no real sense to him, but with those Saul felt a need to agree. For, in the current halfway house of his mind, his awareness of fighting out in the station seemed like a raw point inside his own skull. But to agree with the words he needed dangerous consciousness, and that was not an option.

"This is not a great idea," came a second female voice, very like the first.

Saul's semi-awareness strayed far enough to capture numerous views scattered throughout the Argus Station, and there he witnessed the battle in progress. Troops clad in vacuum combat suits had penetrated the station rim by the docks, and were quickly entrenching themselves there. He watched a great multi-limbed robot propelling itself about across one lattice wall, guns blazing from the end of each limb. The word "spidergun" arose at once out of his inner chaos.

Above the endcap of Arcoplex One, the underside of the station rim was criss-crossed with gunfire, missile streaks and explosions. Saul saw shattered bodies go tumbling through the dark amid fragments of metal, plastic, flesh, bone and globules of blood. His awareness straying further, he next saw a great fleet of space planes entering an orbital vector leading them towards the station.

"What are you doing?" asked the male voice nearby.

"He's in REM, and the unit's set to respond to his EEG. I just copied that." A pause. "Have you disconnected the restraint monitors yet, Angela?"

"They're now on manual release."

"Okay, here goes."

Saul felt a tugging sensation at his temple, which seemed to shift his entire perception. He did not consciously understand what had happened, but his knowledge of how the human brain functions made him aware that the state of consciousness was thoroughly overrated. He accepted its resurgence anyway, the chaotic fragmentation of mind slamming together, with an almost physical sensation, into a strong coherent whole. The spectre of agony assailed him, because his animal mind knew that his body must be a roasted ruin, but his whole mind denied it—did not allow it to affect his essential self. He opened his eyes, and again saw with utter clarity, absorbing hundreds of cam views and data flows, while processing them with a speed even he himself found frightening.

Surely this was some fragment of a dream remaining with him—how could he have integrated so much information so fast? The answer came at once, via a factual assessment of processing speeds alongside active and inactive memory capacity. But he should not be like this because, after suffering a real-time one hundred and forty-three minutes of agony, which subjectively seemed like a thousand years, his mind should have become a total wreck. Therefore something else must be happening inside his head, something beyond the melding of his mind with that of Janus. There must be something else, he realized, that Hannah hadn't told him. He would find out later. Other concerns came first.

On the other side of the cell, Angela Saberhagen squatted beside an open access panel, wires running from her palmtop, resting on the floor nearby, into the electronics revealed. Sweat beading his brow, Chang stood some way back, by the door, and looked ready to run. Brigitta stood right beside Saul himself. She had unplugged the optic from his temple and plugged it instead into a small optical drive, which she now released to hang by that optic cable.

"You're awake," she observed.

"I am," Saul agreed, his voice hoarse. He looked down at the manacles still pinning him to the wall. "You can release me now."

"Why should I?" she asked.

"Because that's what you came here to do."

She showed a flash of annoyance. "Don't you even want to know why?"

Saul dipped his head in acknowledgement. "Because Director Smith is never going to forgive you even the small amount of assistance I forced you to give me. He intends to stick all three of you in cells just like this, put you through hell, and probably end up killing you. You have surely realized by now that he only seeks excuses to satisfy his lust for inflicting pain, and that he is, in fact, insane."

"And are *you* sane?" asked Angela, now standing up.

Saul glanced at her. "By which definition of sanity?"

"Ours," was her simple reply.

"I have killed, and I will continue to kill," Saul replied. "But torture is not something I take pleasure in, nor is it something I would ever feel the need to use."

Brigitta reached up alongside his wrist, pressed a locking button, and the padded manacle sprang open. He swung his arm free of the wall, aware of the psychosomatic pain shooting all along it, but noticed only a slight reddening of the wrist, where it had fought against the manacle. He reached round to undo the other manacle, as Brigitta unclipped the metal band around his waist, before squatting to deal with the restraints about his ankles. Saul pushed himself away from the wall, feet light against the floor.

"Are you okay?" Chang asked.

Was he? All his two-year lifespan now lay open to his recollection but seemed distant, utterly shorn from the now by his time under induce-ment—by that subjective thousand years. To his recollection, he had sur-faced to awareness seventeen times, only to be driven under again by the same mind-destroying agony that had deleted the original Alan Saul from existence. This time, however, that same pain, operating in synergy with something new inside his skull, had driven deep into him an awareness that his physical body was not actually him, nor were the computer systems, nor the programs running within his fleshly skull, nor any implanted or external processors. He was all of these, yet none, for he was in a perpetual state of flux. He was not the sea but the waves riding upon it, and not even the same waves from one moment to the next. His definition of self seemed a hazy thing, but that knowledge of self was total. Smith had tempered him all too well in the fire.

"I have much to do," he replied, gazing down at his naked body, then at the shit spattered on the floor. "I'll be needing a VC suit."

"They have some here," said Brigitta, "but I don't think the guards will care for the idea of you taking one."

Saul's perception snapped towards the cameras positioned in the entrance foyer. Three heavily armed figures were watching the progress of the battle on two screens. Another screen nearby showed an image of Saul himself, still manacled to the wall—the twins had looped the image feed. Check-ing further, with a touch as light as gossamer, Saul felt Smith's presence extended throughout the station network, waiting ready at the readerguns that the attackers had ceased to advance on, reluctantly tasking robots to attack only to see them trashed by that spiderlike cousin of theirs.

Langstrom's forces clearly outnumbered the invaders, but since their pur-pose seemed only to establish a beachhead until the other space planes ar-rived, Langstrom wasn't making much headway so far. Looking elsewhere, Saul noted that Arcoplex One had become a mortuary, so he tentatively tried to penetrate stored image files. No reaction from Smith, since Saul chose to play those files at high speed within the memories of the cameras that had recorded them. In just a minute, he had assimilated an outline of what had been happening, surmising that if Alessandro Messina and the delegates he had brought with him now took over, the situation here would be no better than if Smith remained in power.

"It seems Messina is on his way here with about two hundred of his core delegates," Saul observed.

"Their arrival here won't relax their grip on things down below," Brigitta replied. "Not in the slightest."

He gazed at her. "At some point they will completely lose control of Earth, and billions down there will die."

Brigitta looked a little sick upon hearing this.

"They will later re-establish their authority, once they get the rest of the laser satellites up here running," he continued. "But I will try to ensure that those who manage to survive have a chance to establish something new, rather than fall back under the rule of the Committee. I am therefore glad that Messina is coming here." He reached back to the wall so as to propel himself off it, towards the door.

"We can get you out the same way we came in," suggested Chang, as Saul caught hold of his shoulder, then pushed on towards the door.

"That will not be necessary."

Smith was so very busy now, and by actually interfering with programming he found it surprisingly simple to create another video loop apparently recording from within the cell block. The cameras in the lobby would thus report no change at all. The readergun positioned there was one Smith had lost control of earlier, its software scrambled and the safety protocol thereby shutting it down, and therefore of no use to Saul. However, as he mapped, within his mind, every object in the lobby, every dimension, calculating probable reactions and their precise timings, he decided he did not need it anyway.

The three of them followed him out into the corridor.

"You can't go that way," hissed Chang.

Saul glanced back at him. "No need to be concerned."

The way through into the lobby stood open, the security doors retracted into their recesses. The three guards were still concentrating on their screens. Their minds, despite their time on this station, were still locked into that perception instilled in them by living on the surface of a world. Saul launched himself up to the ceiling, towed himself through the top of the doorway and propelled himself up to the ceiling of the lobby, then glided across it. He was nearly above them, and descending, when the bearded guard standing behind the other two noticed movement, precisely as predicted.

The bearded guard began to turn, reaching down for his side arm. Saul gave him time to draw the weapon before he dropped behind the man and locked his legs around his body. Left hand on top of his skull, the other gripping his chin: a single twist and wrench. Hand now moving down to the gun, redirecting the weapon as his own finger slipped in over the man's trigger finger. The first shot punched its way into the skull of the seated woman, the weapon's recoil flinging it free of the bearded guard's hand. Saul used his grip on the guard whose neck he had broken to propel himself towards the one remaining, the edge of his hand slamming into the seated man's nose as he turned, his hand then withdrawn, and the heel of it sweeping up in a perfect arc to deliver a jaw-shattering impact. The second man was unconscious as Saul drew the woman's side arm and shot him through the forehead.

It took less than four seconds, and by the time Brigitta Saberhagen dared peer nervously into the lobby, Saul had already donned an undersuit and was pulling a VC suit out of an open locker. Drops of blood and bits of brain still tumbled through the air, as she stared at him, lost for words.

"Hide somewhere safe," he urged her. "Somewhere in the outer levels might be the best choice." He paused in thought for a moment. "Be sure to wear survival gear, and try to find some way of immobilizing yourselves."

"What are you intending to do?"

"Something rather more than I originally came here to do. I am going to free Earth of the Argus Network, and incidentally free it of the Committee, too. Now you go."

Brigitta ducked back out of sight.

With his VC suit fully secured, Saul collected various weapons, gratified to find a couple of short Kalashtek assault carbines. He slung them on his back, along with a large pack of ceramic ammunition, then belted a side arm round his waist, after discovering it could fire the same bullets. He also broke open a computer supplies cupboard to find some neatly packaged optic cables, which he slipped into a pouch on his belt, before heading out towards the cell-block airlock, switching himself over to the VC suit's air supply as he went. Exiting the half-completed tubeway, he watched the fireworks display far ahead of him, noting all the troop positions within the lattice walls. He knew precisely what he was going to do, but the time for that was not yet right. He needed Messina, along with whatever forces the man had brought up into orbit, landed on the station itself, and preferably embroiled in battle further in than the outer rim.

Then he would kill them.

***

Despite his initial confidence, it seemed Smith was not so sure of himself now. His forehead was beaded with sweat and he kept gobbling painkillers and stimulants like sweets. From a recent fraught dialogue between him and Langstrom, Hannah gathered that the assault force had unexpectedly fortified its position around the dock and, despite Langstrom sending troops against them, stubbornly refused to be drawn into an all-out conflict. And now it seemed that an entire fleet of the space planes was on its way up, obviously bringing in reinforcements as well as Messina and his inner circle of trustworthy delegates.

"You're going to lose," said Hannah.

Smith seemed not to have heard her, his concentration perhaps focused elsewhere in the station, then he jerked upright as if some subsidiary part of his mind had only just brought her words to his attention. He turned to stare at her, his expression somewhat puzzled.

"The blame for current circumstances lies with Alan Saul," he announced. "Alessandro Messina will soon realize why I have so few readerguns at my disposal."

Hannah tried to make sense of that statement, but just couldn't fathom it. It was almost as if Smith expected Messina to forgive him for him proving unable to kill Messina's troops. Always, on hearing Smith speak, she had been conscious of there being something about his convoluted verbal structures, his strange emphasis on certain words and inappropriate emotional reactions, that combined to hint at some sort of malfunction inside his head. However, now it seemed utterly plain to her: Smith had completely lost his mind. Hannah did not get a chance to take this conversation any further because, almost as if that mention of his name had summoned him, Alessandro Messina himself appeared on one of the screens. Smith turned back to it, nodding to himself, as if Messina's appearance somehow confirmed his most recent statement.

"Good morning, citizen," said Messina, "or whatever part of the day it is where you are."

There was something odd about Messina's appearance now, on this high-definition screen, that Hannah had never noticed before in his regular broadcasts to the people. At first glance, he looked like a thirty-year-old, with those clear eyes, clear skin and black curly hair, but closer inspection revealed a shiny, almost plastic, texture to his skin, teeth that were altogether too perfect, and a nose and ears that seemed strangely out of proportion to the rest of his face. That skin tone she assumed must be the result of some early anti-ageing treatment he had undergone. The teeth were clearly ceramic implants, and the ears and nose were so big because those earlier treatments did not halt the continued growth of nose and ear gristle which was found in the very old. Messina, after all, had been alive for nearly a hundred and ten years.

"By current Argus time, it is just after midday," Smith volunteered.

"Ah...well, the sun was just rising as we departed Earth, so for me it's still mid-morning. How are you Smith, no ill effects from those cerebral implants, I trust?"

"I am perfectly functional, Chairman Messina," Smith replied. "All the same, despite the superior mental functions I now enjoy, I am puzzled as to why your troops arriving here felt it necessary to murder at least fifty Committee delegates before seizing part of this station. I therefore wonder if the rest of the Committee is aware of this action."

"Most of the remainder of the Committee now accompanies me, aboard these planes. I want to keep them close so as to ensure their...safety. Oh, perhaps you have not yet heard about the latest tragic event? During the recent insurrection, some terrorists managed to release nerve gas inside a hall in which about one hundred and seventy delegates were assembled for an off-the-record meeting."

Smith stared at the screen for a long moment, before repeating numbly, "One hundred and seventy."

"Yes," Messina continued with relish, "and for the duration of this emergency the remaining delegates have voted me a position worthy of my ancestry. They have made me dictator for life."

"Yet that still does not explain why your troops have embarked upon such a hostile penetration of this station," Smith insisted.

"The Argus Station, as far as we are aware, is under the control of someone evidently hostile to the Committee. How else to explain the laser attack upon Minsk, the subsequent destruction of two space planes, and then the systematic disabling of most of the working portion of the Argus satellite network?"

"One Alan Saul, a person of whom you have knowledge, temporarily took control of a section of this station. He now languishes in a cell, under inducement," said Smith, "so now I take it I can expect the hostilities up here to cease?"

"It will be necessary for me to assess the situation personally," replied Messina, putting on a sad expression. Then a thought seemed to perk him up. "However, I do look forward to renewing your acquaintance, Smith. I look forward to that very much."

Messina's image blinked out, to be replaced by Langstrom's.

"What is the current number of planes approaching?" Smith asked him.

"Twenty-eight," Langstrom replied.

"And in your estimation, how many troops?"

"Messina knows exactly how many are based here, and therefore the resistance he may expect to face," said Langstrom. "He'll be bringing up no less than two hundred troops, but with that number of planes, he could be bringing as many as a thousand."

"Then it is my requirement that you mount your defence on that basis."

"We've got no defence that'll work."

"When you have your plans ready, submit them to me at once."

"Sir, we don't stand a chance."

"You should also prepare a hard copy to keep on file, whilst transmitting a data copy down to Central in Brussels. It is best not to be incautious in such matters."

Langstrom gazed at him in silence for a long moment, before he said, "Whatever," and shut off the connection.

Hannah felt no pity whatsoever for Smith. He had tried to seize power for himself and was about to be stomped on by Messina; however, she could see utterly no hope for herself or Saul, either. If neither of them got killed during the impending battle, she herself would end her days in perpetual slavery, whilst Saul would finish up in one of the station's digesters. She bowed her head, wanting to weep in despair but determined not to.

"There will be a degree of damage done to the station," remarked Smith abruptly, "but nothing major. Again, the problem will be to find somewhere suitable to store the resultant human detritus. It is a great shame that inducers and tasers will not be effective over the ranges involved, else I would instruct Langstrom to use them and thus there would be less of a mess."

Hannah looked up to focus for a moment on the spittle foaming at the corner of Smith's mouth, then she bowed her head again.

About twenty metres out from Saul, a three-man crew was manoeuvring a heavy machine gun into place, its barrel protruding from a curved metal shield. He paused for a moment to study them, and, even though one of them shot him a glance, they then ignored his presence and continued busily securing the gun to an I-beam. They were preparing for the imminent arrival of Messina's forces, and, naturally, any soldiers seeing his VC suit would assume he was one of them.

Saul moved on, but abandoned the walkway before it became enclosed again at the point where it entered Langstrom's barracks. One shove of his hand sent him dropping steadily down towards the asteroid's surface, and on the way he tried to pick up more information on the present situation; tried to infiltrate further the station network without alerting Smith. Again it seemed so very easy.

Perhaps Smith did not notice him because he was currently focused on the invading troops entrenched above, or upon working out what Messina intended. But Saul doubted that, because this new ease of penetration seemed more likely to be due to the way he was now using his mind. Having utterly subjugated his own organic component, he had assumed a semblance to the station's computers, till in fact he was just software running within them, and less of a presence, even to himself. Whereas before he had just about been able to match Smith's abilities, his adversary only withdrawing deliberately so as to lure Saul deeper into a trap, it now felt as if he had taken a decisive step beyond the man. However, this advantage did not place ultimate power neatly in his hands. Even if he could now manage to seize control of the station network, that would not be enough to give him victory over Smith and his troops, or over Messina and his men. Too many readerguns weren't operating, and against hundreds of troops the robots available here could not win. And, as ever, in this present disconnected state, he did not know how long he would actually care about winning, or even living.

Certainly, Messina was approaching the station with enough troops to ensure capturing it, therefore, despite the hatred he felt in his organic mind towards Smith, Messina's troops were the greater danger to him. And this he must now prepare for.

The surface of the asteroid came up at him fast, and he hit it bending his legs just sufficiently to absorb the shock, so that he didn't bounce off and away again. Exactly locating his current position, he headed off in bounding strides for the base structure of Arcoplex One. As he circumvented this, he continued to thrust his mind further inside the station network.

Smith had managed to crack the code Saul had used to secure his small army of robots, but only for a short while before it underwent one of its hidden transforms, and so had not managed to take all of them away from him. Saul found the remaining robots scattered about the lattice walls lying between him and the rim, but most were concentrated around Tech Central, which now loomed up to his left, cast into silhouette by the sun. From their slumber he woke up five construction robots, which he summoned to him along with those smaller members of the robot ecology that Smith had ignored, perhaps because they were of little use against the power of Messina's troops. Remiss of him, for Saul now linked into them, found twenty belonging to a specific subspecies of maintenance robot, and gave them instructions little different from the kind they would normally receive. He then dispatched them throughout the station to repair disabled readerguns and make them accessible only to him. However, he knew that those readerguns, and the construction robots now heading towards them, would not be enough to bring him victory.

Ahead of him lay a mining complex, out of which an ore transit tube rose, like a massive redwood, towards the station's rim and the smelting-plant dock located there. A huge robot equipped with twin digging wheels sat there frozen, having been shut down in the process of hacking chunks of ore from the ground and transferring them into the fat carrier comprising much of its body. A giant drilling rig on gecko-treaded tracks stood at rest only thirty metres beyond it, its extended robotic arms clamped around an anchor pillar that speared up into the station's inner structure above his head. It held a new section of pillar destined to fill the gap where a large mass of ore had been removed below. Of course, as they mined out the asteroid, they built the station inwards as well as outwards. All around Saul could see where massive I-beams had been extended downwards and re-anchored, even cases where a few, which had once abutted the asteroid surface some metres apart, now intersected each other and had been joined into one. After kilotonnes of ore had been mined from it to turn into bubblemetals, the asteroid was now substantially smaller than when first brought here from the asteroid belt.

Circumventing the complex put both it and Arcoplex One behind him, and now only the Arboretum cylinder lay ahead, bright in the sunlight peeking round Tech Central over to his left. As he rounded the base structure of the Arboretum, his suit grew uncomfortably warm in open sunlight. Here, no more cylinders lay ahead, just lattice walls rising above him to the station rim. However, these diamond-pattern partitions now terminated up against a solid wall rising sheer from the asteroid surface ahead, marking the near edge of the single break in the rim wheel. A series of ribs braced this great wall, on which monitoring stations and work habitats clung like shellfish to a sea cliff. This barrier hadn't been here when he had researched the vicinity down on Earth, but it appeared on the station schematic inside his skull. He realized that it had been built to protect the girders of the inner station from the heat generated by the Traveller engine that lay beyond.

Saul approached and entered a tunnel cut through five metres of foam insulation at the base of the wall, finally coming against a thick bulkhead door with a single armour-glass window incorporated. He brushed aside asteroidal dust and peered through, studying the massive Mars Traveller VI engine standing beyond it, looking like a steel church dedicated to some ultimate god of fire.

A god he now intended to awaken.

18

DEMOCRACY IN ACTION

At one time, the Committee Chairman was elected to office by the delegates, and occupied that position for no more than five years. Originally it was a position no one could be elected to more than once, but then Alessandro Messina's predecessor, Chairman El Afraine, used a manufactured terrorist crisis to defer the election of a new Chairman. Unfortunately for him, his most likely successor, Messina, already had more allies in the Inspectorate than he did, and manipulated that "crisis." The terrorists themselves—a small group of Subnet seditionists who had been monitored by the Inspectorate for years, but left alone precisely because El Afraine wanted to use them for his own ends—suddenly managed to obtain weapons and Hyex explosive, as well as El Afraine's itinerary and information regarding the gaps in his security. After El Afraine's scramjet detonated over the Adriatic, Messina swept to power in less than a day. When his own five years drew to a close, the sudden unfortunate demise of any suitable successors kept him in power for another term. Henceforth, nervous candidates were overcome by a great reluctance to put themselves forward, otherwise he lured out the bolder ones by hinting at possible retirement, though not in the usual sense of Committee "retirement." After the first ten years, the five-year rule was quietly dropped and thus Messina occupied the position of Committee Chairman, on Earth, for forty-three years, before deciding to relocate his power base to Argus Station.

ANTARES BASE

A control room was no longer a necessity when even the most complicated of systems could be operated from a simple console, even just a portable one. That Ricard had insisted on a full control room and the executives to staff it demonstrated the usual Inspectorate mindset: that being in charge required inferior ranks to obey you, a precise territory to piss-mark and dominate. And the more important you were, the bigger the office and the larger the staff you had to have, even if neither was strictly necessary.

Finding a wall console rarely used, in a room turned into a store, Var accessed a wide range of the base's systems. Plenty of the information she could not review, since only Ricard knew the codes, but she still found enough for her purposes. Lopomac and Carol had knocked out the internal cam system throughout the base, but they hadn't disrupted the external ones, or even the feed originating from the satellites orbiting Mars. After checking those external cams first, she keyed into the satellite feed. Ricard had locked down all communications to and from Earth, and she didn't have the time to break his codes, but she was still able to pick up image data from satellites orbiting Earth which was being relayed to those immediately above. This she did to confirm that the Mars Travellers really had been decommissioned, and soon discovered that they had. The only evidence she could find of their existence was the nose section of Traveller VIII out in the orbital complex in which the Travellers had been built, but where it was being dismantled. Frustratingly, the shielding around Messina's private building project prevented her obtaining image data of the *Alexander*, but while looking she found something else—something odd.

"We're done," said Lopomac.

Var glanced up to see him and Carol enter the room, and beckoned them over. She pointed at the image on her screen. "What do you make of this?"

"You're getting feed from Earth?" said Carol.

"Satellite cams—that's all."

"What do we make of what?" asked Lopomac, clearly puzzled.

The screen revealed one hemisphere of Earth, with satellites glinting above it. Using her ball control, Var moved the pointer up alongside one of the satellites, pausing it on a lengthy vapour trail.

"I see," said Lopomac. "Maybe they've been repositioning them?"

"Maybe, but there are plenty more vapour trails, and what looks like wreckage of some kind." Var paused, called up a menu and selected a long list of cam numbers, then scrolled down through it and selected again. "Then there's this."

Argus Station was distantly visible, and rising towards it were more space planes than Var had known existed.

"Something big, I guess," said Lopomac. "Maybe we'll be able to find out about it later, if we're still alive."

Var frowned, clicked back to exterior cam views of the base itself and was abruptly returned to reality when at random she selected one focused on the area just outside the main garage doors. Though this was night-time the cams possessed light amplification so that everything remained clearly visible. Spotting Gisender's pathetic dried-out corpse, Var swallowed drily and rapidly checked other views. Still no sign of further action from Ricard, and there was work to be done. She reached out and slid over a laptop she had found earlier, checked its Bluetooth link with the console, and ensured she could call up all the cam views that could help her.

"Have you fixed the garage doors?" she asked tightly.

"I've rigged up the supercaps there for full discharge through the garage airlock," he replied.

"How are you delivering it?"

"If they bring a crawler in, they have to open the outer garage doors and close them behind, then pressurize the airlock before opening the inner doors. I've just linked up a power line through the gate valve to the door mechanism and to the inner doors themselves." Lopomac stepped over to the console and linked into the internal cam system. "As you asked, I put the inside of Hex Three back on camera too. I cut the optics running into Hex One and triple-encoded radio, so Ricard can't access it, and, as you said, he probably won't even realize the cams are working." He clicked through a list, calling up a view inside the crawler airlock. "When that gate valve opens, it feeds power straight into the electronic control of the doors' hydraulics, burning them out and seizing up the doors. Their only option then is to open them manually. The moment one of them touches a door, he'll get a full discharge straight down through his body and into the floor."

"Rubber soles," said Var. "Insulated suits."

"About as much defence against this as against a lightning strike. Even less in fact. The doors and frames are bubblemetal but contained in bonded regolith, therefore insulated from the metal floor. This means I can run the full discharge of five in-series crawler supercapacitors to them. What's left of whoever touches them we'll have to scrub off the walls."

Five in-series supercapacitors: enough to power five crawlers over distances amounting to nearly a thousand kilometres each.

"How many discharges?"

"One at full power, the next one at half—exponentially downwards. I don't suppose any of them will volunteer to touch a door to check if it's still live, after the first of them has done so. The only way they might get by this is if they use something, some lump of metal, to make a connection between the doors and the floor to discharge the capacitors. Even then, it's likely the locking mechanisms will have become fused."

"You also located that mountaineering equipment I mentioned?"

"I did, though I've yet to see what use it will be to us."

"You will." Var turned away from him. "Carol?"

"Nothing so dramatic," she said. "If they blow out all the windows, as you suggest, it'll equalize pressure so that all bulkhead doors linking the outer sections of Hex Three can be opened, whilst anyone still in the internal compartments and corridors will be trapped."

"It's what I would do," agreed Var. "If they blow out all the windows they can hunt us down in the outer sections, but if we're in one of the inner sections after that, we'd be trapped and no longer a problem."

Carol nodded, then reached into her hip pouch for a long, pressurized bottle. It took Var a moment to recognize it but, when she did, she felt a stirring of macabre amusement. "Contact adhesive," she said.

Carol nodded. "A Martian mix based on Terran hyperglues. Whilst exposed to Martian air, it remains in gel form, but the moment it is sealed against atmosphere, for example when sandwiched between metal and a gloved hand, it takes only about two seconds to set. I've smeared some on the exterior frames of any unbroken windows, also on the window frames and bulkhead door handles of the sections you've already opened to atmosphere."

"What about the door handles inside the pressurized sections, like here or in the garage?" Lopomac asked.

"In Earth atmosphere the glue oxidizes in about three minutes," Carol replied. "I could maybe fix that once we see them coming, but only then."

Var considered that. Once Ricard and the rest made a move, assuming they used a crawler, they could get themselves here within ten minutes. Only ten minutes for Carol to spray glue on every bulkhead door handle within reach, then get safely back to the reactor room.

"Too much of a risk." She shook her head. "You'd be very exposed and there's a chance they could either kill you or cut you off from us before you got back to the reactor room." She called up a schematic of Hex Three on the computer screen. "Including Ricard himself, there'll be seven of them," she decided. "He won't know for certain where we are inside the hex, so he'll keep one or two men outside to snipe at us if we try to escape. They'll blow each remaining window in turn, searching each room after its window has been blown. Almost certainly they'll throw in grenades before entering, and probably spray the interiors with gunfire too."

"But they can't come through the garage windows, because there aren't any," observed Carol.

"Precisely," Var glanced at her. "Which is why I wanted Lopomac here to set up a booby trap."

"But even if we do manage to kill some of them in the airlock, the rest will still enter through the bulkhead doors. They'll know we're either in the garage or in one of the closed-off inner sections...as we will be."

Var nodded. "Certainly. They'll blow bulkhead doors leading into the garage, and then secure it just as they have all the other outer rooms of the hex, before they move on to open each of the inner sections and search them."

"We'll be trapped in the reactor room, so what's our angle?" asked Lopomac.

"The roof," said Var.

ARGUS STATION

It was now evident that the warming process was well under way. When he reached his hand to rest it against the door, Saul could feel the vibration of machinery through his fingers, and through the window saw plumes of vapour jetting here and there from the engine itself. Probing the computer network in the immediate vicinity, he checked to see how close the engine was to firing temperature, then inspected the diagnostic data. Despite a couple of minor faults, the engine was now ready and, with just a thought, he could start it running. However, even though the process of shutting it down was a lengthy one, Smith could initiate that with a thought too.

Saul moved back out into the open, then skirted the wall, studying in his mind a schematic of all the hardware nearby as he progressed. Finally reaching a certain point, he looked up, and noted a mass of optic cables that emerged from the wall above, then ran along a beam continuing out of sight somewhere behind him. He leapt up towards it, caught hold and pulled himself over, coming down astride the cables just at the point where they exited the wall.

Here the sheer mass of cables was further distended by a great number of connector plugs all gathered together. Slowly and methodically he checked the codes etched into the side of each plug, till on the eighth one found the optic connection he sought. This plug, however, could not simply be pulled apart, being tightly secured by a ring of screws. Saul pulled it away from the others, drew his pistol and fired a shot. The cable was whipped out of his hand, the shattered plug parting, while the frayed optic cables provided a display of green and yellow laser light. Retrieving the plug, he could now pull it apart. That ensured that the hardwire connection was removed and, when the Traveller VI engine fired up, the EM interference produced would make it impossible to issue radio instructions able to shut it down. Saul propelled himself back to the floor. Time now to stack the dice even further.

Saul waited at the entrance to the tunnel leading through the wall insulation, gazing back at the Arboretum cylinder. How much force could the structural beams here withstand? They were much more widely spaced than would be required for a building on Earth, but would soon be subjected to levels of stress halfway approaching the same. Since he had set the engine to fire up at its maximum, the initial thrust would be in the region of half a gravity. He paused for a moment to make some complex calculations and discovered that, though the massive shaft spindles of the Arboretum and the arcoplexes would take a huge amount of the resulting strain, there would be substantial damage caused to the intervening areas. That was unavoidable, however. As he finished making calculations which confirmed that any internal buildings still under construction—like the Political Office and the cell block—might tear loose from their mountings, he finally sensed that his five construction robots were approaching, and turned to face them.

With animal grace they headed down the face of the asteroid, coming from Tech Central, and he began firming up his connection with them and further preparing them for action. Soon they were gathered around him, his pack of eager steel wolves. Instructing them to follow, he turned and entered the short tunnel that took him to the edge of the engine enclosure. Bracing his feet against the ground, he hauled up a simple mechanical latch and pushed open the door. The engine loomed above him, and when he gazed up past it he could see the stars. Now he propelled himself upwards, catching hold of occasional protrusions from the inner ceramic-tiled wall to keep himself close to it, and avoid flying out into open vacuum. In another moment he ascended past the open throats of the fusion chambers, and then understood why the insulated wall had been built. Remembering the specs of the Traveller VI engine, he knew that the fusion torch would lance out way beyond the station, its length nearly two kilometres, and producing sufficient heat to melt anything nearby. He glanced down to see his robots following him up the wall, their limbs never out of contact with its sheer expanse of tiles.

Finally, near the station rim, he caught hold of the protruding end of a beam end and halted his climb, then pulled himself over to stand upright on the rim itself, which curved away from him like a long hill on some massive highway. Looking up he could see the smelting plant, whose dock lay just beyond the point where the Arboretum cylinder terminated. The plant resembled an ugly spined iron fish now that its mirrors were furled. That was something else he would have to deal with because, once the station started moving, the smelting plants would swing round on their cables and come crashing down with catastrophic force. However, returning those things to their docks would certainly alert Smith to his presence.

His five robots escorting him, Saul picked up his pace, knowing he must cover nearly six kilometres to reach his destination. Entering one of the half-constructed levels enabled him to speed up since, with a ceiling above him, he could propel himself forward confidently without any danger of floating out into space. Emerging into the open again, he paused a moment in wonder, because the arc of Earth itself was now visible. Moving on, he quickly rounded the structures located directly above the Arboretum, and then came in sight of the massive pit of the smelting-plant dock, which he circumvented too. The pillars of the space-plane dock loomed into sight ahead, as if he was trudging the highway towards the tower blocks of a city centre. However, the illusion was dispelled by a single space plane moored to the nearest pillar, like a dragonfly larva clinging to a reed.

One of the Argus Station's massive steering thrusters jutted up between him and his destination. It was a thing the size and shape of a railway carriage, but tilted at forty-five degrees on a turntable fifty metres wide. When he had first studied this station from Earth, these things had resided at the ends of twenty-metre-tall structures constructed of reinforced girders, which projected outwards from the station rim. Now, by contrast, this particular thruster lay only a few metres from the surface, the rim itself having been extended out nearly far enough to encompass it. As he gazed at this object, Saul detected movement and swung his attention back to Earth, where the swarm of space planes was rising into view.

He quickly headed into the hard shadow of the thruster, and almost at once found the maintenance hatch he was looking for. Though he needed primarily to get to the docks, approaching them across the rim itself would have been foolish, since the troops entrenched there would be on the lookout for a flanking move by Langstrom's men, and would be sure to spot him. Besides, even though most of the laser satellites nearby were disabled, Smith still controlled a few usable laser satellites within range, and might spot him too.

The maintenance hatch was not designed to be opened by human hands, but a simple instruction called one of the robots over, which inserted an outsize Allen key to disengage the locking mechanism. A slight puff of vapour blew out as the hatch hinged open, but that probably wasn't station atmosphere but the result of fuel spillage. Summoning his five robots to follow him, Saul dropped inside and found himself in a narrow space alongside the huge stepper motor used for driving the turntable mechanism, powering a great cog above him which engaged with a massive toothed ring.

Skirting around this motor he found a tunnel leading to the distant space dock. Built to accommodate robots, it was also lined with fuel pipes from the silos there. As the last robot closed the hatch behind it, the lights went out, but he had two of the robots light up their fault-inspection lasers, and damp coherence, to illuminate his surroundings in lurid red. Ten minutes of propelling himself along the tunnel brought him to a point where many of the pipes diverged upwards to connect with the various silos located along the base of the docks above. However, other pipes ran ten metres further in, before curving upwards into the nearest docking pillar, there to connect to the pumps used to fuel space planes engaged in orbital duties.

Climbing up alongside these pipes brought him to an inspection point for human technicians. Here secondary pipes branched off to connect to the fuel pumps positioned immediately behind the hydraulic systems that extended concertinaed fuel hoses out to any plane currently docked. Saul opened the adjacent manual airlock and entered, summoning just one of his robots in with him. Once the lock had cycled, he opened the inner door and stepped into a maintenance area containing a spare pump, a variety of pipe and hydraulic fittings, along with some of the heavy-duty machinery required to install them. Here seemed as good a place as any to set things in motion as he meanwhile guided the remaining robots through the same airlock.

Saul delved deep into the station network, making no attempt now to conceal his presence. Seeking first to crack their control codes, he probed Smith's remaining readerguns and robots. Smith reacted immediately, the shadowy presence of his mind thrashing like a hooked bloodworm before he started shoring up his defences. This was just what was needed for, whilst keeping the pressure on him, Saul slipped past Smith and into long-dormant portions of the station network, to gain access to a process only rarely called for up here.

On occasion a smelting plant required major maintenance that could not be conducted out there in space, and therefore it was winched back into its dock, furling its solar panels and burrowing into the station skin like the head of a tubeworm. He now set this process in motion for both plants, and watched as the folded panels withdrew into their soot-stained bodies. Under his feet he felt the station's heavy thrumming as giant cable drums began to revolve, winding in kilometres of cable thicker in diameter than his thigh. It took a moment for Smith to realize what was going on, but instead of trying to stop this process he focused his attention on the cell block, and after a moment he spoke.

"Saul," was all he said, his voice ghosting across the network.

"You should have killed me," Saul replied.

"You had not ceased to be of use to me." Now, probing began into the informational architecture that Saul was fortifying. "I am now puzzled as to why you feel the need to retract the smelting plants."

"I'm ensuring Messina has no place to land but on the space-plane docks themselves."

"Ah, so you recognize the dangers in Messina's assumption of ultimate power, and are therefore prepared to ally yourself with me to ensure his defeat?"

Saul paused in the midst of checking the readings on the air sampler strapped about his wrist, but it took him just a second to realize that Smith had finally gone over the edge. No sane man could ever expect to make an ally out of someone he had subjected to inducement. Saul shook his head in disbelief and returned his attention to the sampler. The air was pure CO_2, thin, and rapidly getting thinner, so he could not remove his VC helmet. This was not surprising because, as he understood it, airlocks like the one just behind him had been designed for some future era when the entire docks themselves could be pressurized—but now they remained airless.

"I fully understand that at present Messina is a greater danger to me than you are," Saul replied carefully. "I also understand that, should he try to get his troops into Argus like Malden did, you probably still control enough long-range satellite lasers to burn them off the station's surface."

From the cam systems under Smith's control, an image feed opened directly across into Tech Central itself. Saul quickly noticed that all the available seats were occupied, while Smith himself stood in front of the three major screens. Off to one side he could see Hannah bound to a chair, and clearly Smith must be routeing his voice through the intercom, because now she was looking up with interest.

"And what other approaches might you suggest?" Smith asked. "I would be interested to discover your unique perspective on the matter."

A cracked and desperate mind would be easier to manipulate, Saul surmised, but it was also likely to spin out of control and head off in unpredictable directions.

"I still control some resources," he replied, "but you'll understand why I'm not keen to reveal what they are, or how I intend to use them. For the moment, however, I will cease any attempt to take readerguns or robots away from you." Saul halted his mental assault on these devices. "I would rather they were used against Messina than we render them useless by fighting over control of them." He paused, wondering how best to conclude this. "I'll do what I can against Messina—but then I'm coming after you, Smith."

Stepping away from the screens, Smith moved over to stand next to Hannah, pressing a hand down onto her shoulder. "Once I have fully re-established my position here, I certainly look forward to that encounter."

Perfect. Smith had not looked beyond Saul's explanation about the smelting plants, but his threat regarding Hannah was clear. Saul studied the scene further and assessed her position. When the steering thrusters turned the station round, the effect there would be negligible, but once the Traveller engine fired up, over half a gravity would surge through Tech Central horizontally. Her chances of surviving that, strapped in a chair as she was, he rated at about 70 per cent. He could do nothing about the uncertain 30 per cent, for if her head slammed into the consoles just to her right, she'd probably end up with a broken neck. Nevertheless, in her present position, he doubted she would resent him taking that chance.

"Later, then," concluded Saul. "The first of Messina's planes will be docking here within twenty minutes, and I'm sure you have plenty to do."

The image feed cut off, though, unlike before, it now remained unblocked so Saul could seek it out whenever he wished. Instead he checked out other areas of the station, noting how Langstrom's troops were scattered in squads of four throughout the lower section of the inner core, but far enough above the asteroid so that it was not right up against their backs and therefore blocking a retreat. Most of these four-man units controlled hefty machine guns and missile-launchers, though Langstrom himself had taken the controls of a weapon Saul now identified as Smith's one EM tankbuster. Between them and the outer rim, robots were constantly on the move, laying antipersonnel mines activated by wires strung nearly invisibly between the structural beams.

Arcoplex One had also been secured. Inside it, Smith controlled a good number of functioning readerguns, and a team of soldiers was busy loading them with ceramic ammunition. But that wasn't a route Messina's troops were likely to be taking—why enter an obvious killing ground? No, they would come straight down on Langstrom's troops through intervening girderwork of the station, possibly using shields and deploying more spiderguns. They would certainly face heavy losses, but Saul doubted that would much concern Messina, as in the end sheer numbers would prevail. A greater worry to Messina would be the serious losses Saul was intending to inflict.

Saul crossed to the large sliding door separating the maintenance store from the dock's interior, his robots following sneakily as if they sensed his need of increased caution. He probed for some access to the nearby cameras, but found that, though the system remained live, little image data was available from within this particular dock. Messina's first arriving troops had obviously destroyed the cameras, just as he knew they had disabled the readerguns here too. However, one camera continued to function, and on switching it up to its 270-degrees setting revealed enough of the dock to show that no guards had been posted actually inside.

Unshouldering one of his carbines, Saul moved over to the door control. He pressed it once and watched the door judder as it slid aside, aware how it would have made a considerable racket if the dock had been pressurized. The moment it opened wide enough, he pulled himself through and, with another of those slightly disorientating changes of perspective, brought his feet down on the dock floor on the other side. In a squatting position he checked his surroundings. To his left stood a cargo train, while from the floor directly ahead rose the personnel access tube leading to the space plane, and just beyond it the cargo-access doors stood wide open. He turned to study the far wall, noting the tunnel cutting through it for the train, and numerous open corridors leading into the station rim.

He rose and headed rapidly over to the access tube, detailing one of his robots to the cargo hold, one to follow him, and dispersing the remaining three about the dock. Within seconds he was gazing through the sensors of the first robot, to confirm that the cargo hold now contained only a few crates of munitions. Descending through the tube to the plane's airlock, he paused to study its controls, and found nothing more difficult than an electronic lock. He stepped inside the airlock and waited till the red lights turned to green before he removed his helmet, then opened the inner door on to a muttering of voices. Before he stepped further, he summoned the robot into the airlock behind him, instructing it to wait there—an unpleasant surprise for anyone who tried entering the plane after him.

The forward seats had been detached from the floor to leave a clear area, where three soldiers clad in VC suits had jury-rigged a console and a pair of screens providing views across the station rim outside the space plane. The one seated at the console glanced round with mild interest until, feet braced against the floor, Saul fired off three short bursts of ceramic rounds. The bullets punched through the seated man's body, blowing away chunks of armour, along with flesh and bone as they fragmented. The two men standing nearby were slammed against the bulkhead separating this area from the cockpit. Even as they died, Saul launched himself towards the cockpit door, swooped through it high and fast, covering the four seats it contained and then the area immediately behind them. Another man began rising from his inspection of an open box, his mouth hanging open in shock. He dropped the beaker of coffee he held and raised both his hands, as Saul circled him to ensure that any rounds he fired had less chance of puncturing the plane's outer skin.

"How did you—?" the man began.

Now in position, Saul switched to single shots and put one into the man's forehead. As the man bounced off the bulkhead, the jet of blood from his head beading the air, Saul bent over the console to inspect a view of one of the smelting plants sinking into its dock with gargantuan ponderousness. He then returned to the passenger compartment to find one of the two displays was still working, then manipulated a ball control to call up the widest view of the fleet's arrival.

By now both smelting plants had entered their docks and were locking down. Ten space planes were already docking, and others coming in. Saul studied them all closely and, predictably, found his main target by its obvious display of arrogance. This was a much more recent design of vessel, bulging all along its length with armaments. That it carried the Chairman on board was evident from the "United Earth" logo inscribed on its side with high-temperature metallic paints. Whilst he focused on this single vessel, he registered the sound of docking clamps and airlock tubes engaging, even as the ball control vibrated under his fingers.

Gazing through the sensors of his dispersed robots, he watched cargo doors opening from the five interior faces of this pillar, and VC-clad troops swarming out, shifting heavy weapons from the holds, along with a number of large discs, each a couple of metres across, with small cylinders attached around the rim. One of the cargo holds also discharged other multi-limbed robots, before, in squads of twenty, the troops began to head for the pillar's exits, where doubtless their earlier comrades now awaited them. Estimating by the number of men exiting the five space planes here, Saul reckoned on upwards of four hundred troops, and possibly five of those spiderguns—more than enough to flatten Langstrom's force. No doubt the attack they were about to make had already been carefully planned to rule out delays, but still the plane Saul had identified as Messina's kept its distance. He wanted it to dock, *needed* it to dock.

Saul took out one of the optic cables he'd found earlier and plugged one end of it into the socket in his skull, the other into a dataport in the console. The coded network being used by the attackers was simplicity itself to encompass, and there were no codes to crack since the console was included in that network. It was previously for such access that he had come here, since for his plan to work he needed to get some accurate timings on how things were likely to proceed, and above all needed access to those multi-limbed robots. Within a second, he was listening in on the com traffic and learning how Messina's force intended to attack.

Messina, or some general of his, hadn't yet considered the obvious move of using EM blocking. All about control, really: though such blocking would reduce Smith's power, it would also cause all radio communications with both troops and robots to crash, and Messina was probably frightened of becoming blind and powerless to influence the course of the battle. Saul filed that thought away for future reference: the powerful did not sacrifice control, even when it became an actual hindrance.

The big guns would remain in place above, targeting similar guns and troop concentrations below. The discs were armour-glass, laminated with shock-dispersal fibre; the cylinders spaced around their rims were "bottle motors." Units of four men each behind these shields would descend on Langstrom's forces to engage. The big armoured spiders would then descend just behind them. Judging by this arrangement, Messina clearly valued those machines over the lives of his men, certainly realizing that booby-traps would have been laid.

Locating com channels that shunted computer code only, Saul allowed himself a smile, then routed the feeds into his mind, and learned that his estimate had been spot on. There were five spiderguns here—and, moments later, they fell under his control. However, he did not immediately block the orders they were already receiving, and though tempted to turn them on the crowds of troops moving around them, he did not. Only five of them might not prove enough against four hundred professional soldiers, some of whom sported tank-busters, so that number first needed pruning.

Saul paused just then, knowing that within the last minute he had all but won. Keeping a minimum link to the spiderguns, he prepared to initiate the program he had already loaded into them—the one that would include them in the same network as his construction robots, and thus exclude directions from anyone else. Searching the station network, he soon uncovered the ignition sequence for activating the huge steering thrusters located around the station's rim. Constantly kept online in order to make minor corrections to the Argus Station's position, which was often changed through the shifting of large amounts of internal materials, the thrusters required no warming up.

Smith did not try to stop him and, having other things on his mind, he probably didn't even notice Saul exploring this option. Checking image feeds from cameras nearer to the asteroid itself, Saul observed that the massing of Messina's forces was more clearly evident from down below. Troops kept swarming out onto the inner surface of the ring like refugees from a disturbed ant's nest. Saul watched them for a moment, then, dragging the console after him, he retreated to one of this space plane's remaining seats, where he sat down and strapped himself in. Ten space planes were still hovering out there, but on checking their positions, Saul calculated that, if they remained roughly where they were, they would soon be facing serious problems. It was all becoming rather neat really.

Ah, Messina...

The big United Earth plane was now shifting away from the crowd and coming in to dock. He watched it manoeuvre carefully and surmised that Messina wanted to be in at the kill.

Good.

Other planes began following it in, and Saul guessed they contained Committee delegates and their entourages. After watching till Messina's plane was firmly docked, he could wait no longer.

It's started.

Bottle motors spurted plumes of vapour, and Messina's troops began heading in towards the centre of the Argus Station, even as the docking clamps locked down on the Chairman's plane. With a thought, Saul relayed an instruction to fire up the two equatorial hyox steering thrusters, while simultaneously instructing the spiderguns to grab at and fold themselves around the nearest structural beams. Light glaring from the space plane's cockpit confirmed that one thruster out there had now definitely fired, and a second later the ponderous revolving of the space station pressed him gently down to his seat. Whatever his intentions, this provided the additional benefit of kicking in the safety protocols to lock in place all the docking clamps. But to absolutely ensure there would be no escape for Messina, Saul transmitted further instructions to two of his construction robots, and sent them off to weld those clamps shut.

From the screen, he now observed one plane—just about to dock—suddenly find its docking pillar receding from it. The plane docking on the other side was not so lucky. The pilot began firing off thrusters, turning his vessel in the hope of sliding it safely past the pillar rapidly heading up towards it, but to no avail. The pillar caught the side of the plane full on and, in silent slow motion, it folded in on itself and split. Atmosphere blasted out of it, spewing a fountain of detritus that included two people who obviously hadn't been properly strapped in. Wriggling about in speeded-up motion, desperately trying to snatch hold of vacuum, they left vapour trails behind them as their lungs emptied, even as their internal fluids began boiling and blood vessels ruptured. Those still inside the plane would have died little differently.

Within the station, both attackers and defenders were now in total disarray. The neat formation of attackers had slewed in one direction, crashing into beams or into each other, whilst nearer to the asteroid many of Langstrom's men had been jolted from their designated positions. Then the thrusters cut out, leaving the station still spinning ponderously. Saul had some leeway now, since he could make adjustments later, so he waited until the station had turned far enough to align a particular portion of it with the remaining eight space planes that had not yet docked.

Now.

Saul sent one more instruction; the one that had been sitting in his mind like a precious jewel hidden in his pocket.

And the giant Mars Traveller engine cleared its throat, and breathed fire for the first time in decades.

19

YOU ARE A RESOURCE

Robots steadily displaced human beings working in industries across the world, until the only ones left were robotics engineers and programmers. But Committee delegates did not like to see so much power residing in so few hands, unless of course they happened to be their own. As a result the same engineers and programmers became some of the most heavily scrutinized and politically supervised people on Earth. A similar displacement of human labour was also taking place within the Inspectorate military, seeing that the likes of a single spidergun could deliver the firepower of a whole platoon. However, the danger there was not from having some small number of individuals in a position to bring industry to a halt—a problem the Inspectorate military could easily deal with—but the risk of them being able to bring about the swift obliteration of their masters. This was a possibility the Committee delegates could not allow, so they carefully balanced the number of war robots against the number of human soldiers, and then ensured that the engineers were kept separate from the programmers, and that both were kept separate from the machines they created. That separation often involved confinement in a secure cell, so long as they were still considered useful.

Someone grabbed hold of her chair and began turning it slowly. Hannah looked about her in confusion, then realized that the whole station must be revolving as, through the windows, she saw Earth itself begin sliding round.

Smith staggered briefly before dragging himself back to the console.

"Good, that's good," he said, gazing at the chaos now revealed on one screen, amidst conflicting forces. "Very good, Saul."

What the hell was Saul up to?

Smith summoned up another image that showed a space plane nearly torn in half, and slowly falling away from the dock it had just crashed into. Hannah could see a couple of people out there in vacuum clad in smart business suits, vapour misting from their mouths.

"Did you do that…sir?" Langstrom enquired, his face suddenly appearing in a new window opening at the bottom of the screen.

"No," replied Smith, "that was Alan Saul who, due to inadequate cell-block security, has escaped. However, he has managed nevertheless to destroy a space plane filled with treacherous delegates, and I see that he has also disrupted the main attack by Messina's troops."

"Yeah, great, but he's managed to 'disrupt' our defences at the same time."

Smith did not seem to be listening. By now he had summoned up another image on a different screen, this one showing space planes still hovering out in vacuum. "I think I know his—"

A great flash of light, and the screen went blank for a moment, yet the light still blazed in through the windows behind Hannah, feeling hot against the back of her neck. The screen image reappeared as autocontrast tried to make the image clear. Some of the space planes were now missing, while others seemed to be tumbling away beyond the perimeter of the Traveller engine's fusion blast, though it was difficult to tell because they were rapidly disintegrating. Another of them tried to escape, till a detonation starting in its engine travelled up inside the craft to peel it open like a banana. Even as Hannah realized what was happening, the thrust of the massive engine made itself felt.

Half a gravity of thrust cut horizontally through Tech Central, and her chair shot backwards to crash into a console. Glancing aside, she saw the nearest technician actually pinned against the window above his console. Others were thrown from their seats, chairs and people all falling in the same direction, though Smith managed to stay put, clinging to his console like a drowning man grabbing a piece of floating timber. All of Tech Central seemed to tilt right over onto its edge, so that what had once been the floor now rose vertically like a wall.

With a surge of horror, Hannah realized what Saul was doing. Having recognized the hopelessness of their position, he must now be following through on Malden's plan. The space station would burn on its way down, and Tech Central would be scoured off the asteroid by re-entry fire. She gazed back up towards the main screens, just as Smith lost his grip and tumbled back across the control room, crashing down somewhere over to her right. The first screen just showed the glare of fusion flame, the image feed breaking up into squares as the camera sourcing it began to fail. The middle screen had blanked completely, whilst the remaining screen still focused on Messina's invading forces.

In the time it took Hannah to realize that the half-gravity currently jamming her up against one side of Tech Central would be affecting all the troops outside too, the first of them went flying past outside. She turned her head to track his progress, as he began leaving a vapour trail, before disappearing in light too bright to gaze at directly. He must have been one of Langstrom's men, for they were closest.

Returning her attention to the screens, she watched the fate of Messina's forces. Many of them kept slamming into beams between the lattice walls, others bounced out into space, away from the station. There must have been screaming, and if Hannah had been tuned in to a radio channel she might have heard it. Then came the rumbling of multiple impacts all around.

"Oh my God!" someone cried, as a soldier from outside slammed into a forward window, his split glove issuing vapour as he slid across it, smearing blood, then dropped out of sight.

It was raining soldiers. Men and women who had been preparing for an attack in practically zero gravity now found that what had once been a long gap they needed to propel themselves across had turned instead into a drop of two kilometres. Trying to grab hold of vacuum, yet more figures hurtled past Tech Central, many of them jetting air from torn VC suits. Equipment rained past, too: heavy guns, circular shields, packs of ammunition. It lasted for just a minute, but by the time it ended, most of the attackers and many of the defenders had simply vanished, burning up inside that bright light that lay behind.

"You have achieved your aims," said Smith, out loud. He stood upright, parallel with what was once the floor, his feet on a window and his gaze now fixed on the same screens Hannah had been watching.

He continued, "It would perhaps be wise for you now to shut down the Traveller engine which, it appears, I cannot gain access to."

"I have not entirely achieved my aims," Saul replied through the intercom.

"At its present vector," said Smith, "Argus Station might eventually crash into the Moon, but if you shut down the engine now, we should be able to reinsert ourselves into orbital position just by using the steering thrusters."

"In actual fact I can no more shut the engine down than can you. It will follow its firing program," said Saul. "You're also wrong on two other points:

first the station will not crash into the Moon, but in twenty-four hours it will slingshot round it, putting it on an optimum course for Mars; and, second, I have no intention of letting you or Chairman Messina get anywhere near Earth ever again."

Hannah felt some relief that Saul wasn't intent on crashing the station into Earth, but otherwise, had their situation improved? Though many invading troops had been incinerated out there, some would have survived, and would still be armed—and against them, there was only him.

***

Saul unplugged the optic from his temple. The interference caused by the EM output of the fusion engine reached even as far as the space dock, but he overcame it easily by running programs to clean up the data and by double-layering the code he sent. After ensuring that their programming was capable of handling the half-gravity, he summoned three of the spiderguns, whilst dispatching the other two down towards Tech Central. Viewing through their sensors, he observed survivors clinging to the intersecting beams within the station ring, but now there were only a few of them. Messina's force had for the most part been approaching the station core sheltering behind those discs, so had necessarily distanced themselves from the structural beams, and that had killed them. A larger proportion of Langstrom's force had survived, having built armoured hides about junctures of beams. Saul estimated he had killed about three hundred and fifty of Messina's force in all, which left about fifty; and about seventy of Langstrom's, leaving only thirty to forty. That was a massive slaughter, but he felt as much concern for them as they would have felt for him. He even considered instructing the robots to kill the rest of them, but relented.

First he successfully penetrated Langstrom's military com, which involved working through some tangled coding, then—already in the com network Messina's troops were using—he broadcast a message to both sides.

"Those of you that can hear me," he said, "should be aware that I am now in control of the spiderguns. You will first abandon all your weapons, then, as acceleration cuts, as it will do in three minutes, Messina's remaining troops must withdraw towards the station ring, whilst Smith's force will head back to their barracks. Failure to obey these instructions means I will be forced to use the spiderguns. That is all for now."

He immediately picked up on numerous minor communications: soldiers trying to find their commanders, others pleading for medics, many others complaining that they were in no state to go anywhere. Then arrived com traffic from Messina's space plane, as some general instructed the troops to "maintain their positions" and "retain their weapons." At which point Saul decided it was time to butt in.

"So you are actually instructing all your men to commit suicide," he said, making sure that his words—and any replies—would be heard by all the troops outside.

"Who is this?" demanded the general.

"I think I have been here before," snapped Saul, "and I've no patience with it any more. Here is the position: Argus Station is presently set on a course away from Earth, and while it is under acceleration, all your space planes will remain locked down. I have destroyed the majority of your force and I now control your spiderguns. If your troops do not withdraw immediately as instructed, I will send the robots to kill them all. After that, I'm coming for you personally. I can detect that some of the nerve gas is still available, and a little bit of that released inside your plane should conclude this matter."

"This is Alessandro Messina speaking." The Chairman's voice was instantly recognizable from so many broadcasts back on Earth. "And you, I take it, are Alan Saul?"

"I certainly am," said Saul, rather distractedly.

The two robots Saul had sent off to Tech Central still had half a kilometre to go. When some of Langstrom's men opened fire on them, their reply was brief and wholly destructive: five human beings converted into flying chunks of flesh interspersed with shreds of VC suits, all raining down on the asteroid beneath. This fusillade had also turned their gun to unrecognizable scrap, but now Smith was moving hundreds of station robots in between the pair of spiderguns and their destination.

"We have much to discuss," continued Messina. "I can understand your anger towards Director Smith, since it seems he has subjected you to the most—"

"Yes, do let's have a discussion," Saul interrupted him. "Relay my order to your troops, or I come over and kill you. Meanwhile you remain aboard your plane. End of discussion."

Saul cut the link and left them to it.

He now reviewed the progress of the construction robots he'd previously sent into Dock Two. They'd already secured Messina's plane and three others, and were proceeding towards the last one on that docking pillar. He checked on timings and saw everything running to plan: less than two minutes left till shutdown, and by then the construction robots would have finished their job. His three spiderguns were in position within the same dock, so he sent them instructions to kill anyone who tried to step out of the space planes. All neatly tied off there, time now to deal with Smith.

There was only one life that Saul felt ready to save, and unfortunately it now seemed Smith had realized that. Once again intercepting the image feed from Tech Central, Saul discovered that Smith had untied Hannah from the chair and forced her, at gunpoint, out into the corridor behind. They were now both standing on what might once have been considered the wall, as Smith held out to her a lightweight survival suit—which she accepted with reluctance and began to put on.

So, once the acceleration cut and movement about the station again became easier, Smith obviously intended to take her somewhere outside Tech Central. Saul paused to think, after ordering the two spiderguns to hold still where they were. If he allowed them to continue towards Smith's robots, the battle around Tech Central would be in progress just as Hannah left it, which risked her getting hit by a stray round. The robots controlled by Smith also came to a stop once they had positioned themselves. Even if Saul tried to seize control of them, it would take up time he did not now have.

There had to be a neater, and more satisfying solution—and his adversary gave it to him:

"Retain your weapons and retreat to the Political Office once acceleration cuts," was Smith's brief instruction to his men. Saul could have made threats, but this scenario was perfect: lots of troops heading for what he assumed would be Smith's destination.

Malden's original target had been the EM shield, and once that was down he had tried penetrating the station network. But Smith had been waiting for him within the same network, and had promptly killed him. Smith had also used the shield to cut out Saul, but then shut it down once it became a tactical disadvantage. At no stage after that point had he tried to shut Saul out of the network in the same way, instead leading Saul into a trap. Saul now understood Smith's reluctance to start up the shield: when linked into the station network he was powerful, he could see so much, control so much, but cut off by the shield from all that, he reverted to just a normal human being. Saul now probed the network till he found the virtual controls for operating the shield, and its "on" button.

The minutes ticked by as Saul watched Smith laboriously herding Hannah as far as the airlock accessing the tubeway leading out of the lower levels of Tech Central. Then the fusion drive cut out, the harsh brightness of it fading, till the station dropped back into shadow and practically zero gravity. Saul now breathed easier, his seat straps loosening. He unclipped them and pushed himself away, donning his suit helmet as he headed for the airlock, while instructing the robot posted there to open it ahead of him. In a moment he was through, the schematic of the station fully clear in his mind. Smith was definitely heading for the Political Office, which he had a greater chance of fortifying, for it was still staffed and had heavy machine guns still in place. Time now to engage the EM shield.

Nothing stood in the way of him accessing those virtual controls. Smith had not even thought to defend them, perhaps not comprehending why anyone with the capability of reaching them would want to turn the shield on, and thus sacrifice access to the station network. As he turned the device on, an explosion of static began fragmenting neat structures in his mind. He at once felt blind and powerless—almost like a normal human again. But Smith would be feeling the same, and almost certainly would head straight for the Political Office control room, for access to the shield's manual controls there.

Quickest route?

Saul propelled himself across the dock, shouldering into the side of the monorail train to halt himself, then propelling himself down through the rim to the airlock through which Messina's troops had delivered their package to Arcoplex One. Though Smith had directly controlled the readerguns in here, with the EM shield operating he could no longer access them. There was some risk that they might fire on him automatically, though Saul doubted Smith had taken the time to program them. Manually opening the outer airlock door, he glanced down at the remains of the backpack, with its ruptured chrome cylinders still protruding. He closed the door behind him and after the airlock had pressurized, opened the one ahead, stepping into a massive cylindrical mausoleum. Buildings were lensed around him; a chunk of city rolled into a tube at ground level. The corpse of a woman clad in a long silky dress revolved through the smoky air directly ahead. To his right, fire belched from various windows, and fragments of metal went shoaling about like small fish. There were surprisingly few other corpses in sight.

Saul launched himself towards the central spindle, which seemed the quickest way to the other end. Using the handholds, he propelled himself feet-first towards the base of the cylinder, his speed gauged precisely such that he wouldn't break any bones as he reached it. As his destination came in sight, he realized why so few corpses had been visible where he had entered the cylinder, for the same acceleration that killed Messina's troops had propelled all their victims in the same direction. The base cap of the arcoplex now resembled a medieval depiction of some level of hell. A mass of corpses lay tangled together, limbs jutting out at odd angles and sodden with blood. In zero gravity, Saul had to literally dig his way through them to reach the further airlock. As he exited into vacuum, their blood rapidly freeze-dried on his VC suit, flaking away like black leaves.

***

Had he been a normal person Smith might have been terrified, but as far as Hannah could see, he seemed to be showing only an intellectual curiosity in the sequence of events. It seemed he had stepped off the far side of weird some time ago.

"That was an excellent tactic, well thought out and precisely applied," he had remarked, his voice crackling through the button speakers set into the fabric of Hannah's survival suit. "I might have used it myself, but the Traveller engine has always resided outside of my calculation structure."

Meaning he hadn't thought of it.

Once the half-gravity of acceleration had cut out, Hannah had tried throwing herself away from him, but his hand had closed instantly on her shoulder as he jammed the automatic into her side. Now he kept her close, digging the gun in deeper every time she tried to slow down. So what, she wondered, was the situation now?

Saul had killed most of both the attacking and defending forces. It seemed he also had control of the spiderguns out there but, judging by the robot host gathered between her and these weapons, he did not have full control of the station. It looked like a stand-off to her, and one that none of them could survive. If Smith and Saul continued fighting for control here, much of the equipment would get wrecked, and as they drew further and further away from Earth, they would increasingly need that equipment to survive. But did Saul even care about that? He'd successfully cut the head off Earth's government, taken away one of its biggest technological toys; he'd struck a blow, had his vengeance, and now Messina and his corrupt crew would have no chance of taking up the reins of power again. Saul had then chosen to fling the Argus Station out into space, rather than down towards Earth, so perhaps he was not entirely suicidal, but what would he do now?

Corpses were draped over nearby beams, others had broken free and were floating about between the lattice walls, as now the Political Office loomed ahead. *Where are you Saul? What are you doing now?* Part of the answer reached her almost at once, as Smith lurched abruptly to a halt, his gun hand rising up alongside his head. Hannah tried to pull away again, but his other hand still tightly gripped her shoulder. She could see him saying something but, over com, nothing but static. Roughly, he shoved her forward again, their pace now even faster. Nearby, the robots hovered inert, whilst moving through the station structure ahead she could see soldiers entering the Political Office.

After another half a kilometre, she and Smith entered an enclosed tubeway, passed a machine gun tipped over on its side, and finally came to a double-door airlock. When these doors did not open on their approach, she realized what that burst of static meant. The EM shield was turned back on, preventing Smith from delivering mental instructions, but it also meant Saul was out of that realm too. Both were now as blind and powerless as anyone else in this place.

Smith shoved her up to the doors, tapped a code into the console immediately beside them, then pushed her inside as soon as the doors opened. He gripped her shoulder as the airlock cycled, then after dragging her through finally released his hold on her. Stepping back, he gestured at her suit, then flicked his hand to one side, obviously wanting her to remove it. She considered pretending to misunderstand him, but this garment did not offer her the same protection as a VC suit, so there seemed little point. She laboriously stripped her way out of it, as other people began to appear—most of them looking like the kind of desk jockeys that ran the Committee's bureaucracy, though they included a few of Langstrom's soldiers, whose battered appearance suggested they had just come in from outside.

Smith removed his helmet. "You," he pointed at one of the soldiers, "clear the lower three floors, but bring up whatever weapons you can find there."

"Sir?" the soldier glanced dubiously at the anxious-looking staff standing all around them.

Smith nodded. "Organize teams to guard all the entrances. See that no one gets in unless you can confirm their identity. Am I understood?"

"Yes, sir."

Smith waved the man aside, then caught hold of Hannah's shoulder and hauled her along after him.

"Saul's turned the EM shield on," she remarked. "That means you're blind."

"I can turn it off directly from my control room," he replied.

"If you two keep fighting, there won't be anything left here," she said.

"Once I have dealt with Saul, though unfortunately at a distance, I should be able to gain mental access to the steering thrusters and the Traveller engine." He glanced at her, and continued, "He is aiming to set on course towards Mars. I, however, will bring us back. I can then dispose of Messina—probably dump him into one of the station's digesters. You see," he gave a strange twisted smile, "Saul has made my victory complete."

"But you'll have to deal with Saul first."

He turned suddenly and slammed her back against the wall, his face thrust forward till it was almost touching hers. "Even with the shield turned off, he controls only a few robots and some unimportant systems inside this station." He stepped back, gesturing to his chest with the weapon. "I will take them all away from him, and then hunt him down with his own machines. He simply does not possess the moral strength to defeat me."

Moral strength?

He pulled her from the wall and pushed her ahead. They entered a cageway rising to another floor, made their way along another corridor, then through double sliding doors into a large control centre. It looked more like a slaughterhouse.

Two corpses lay on the floor, a third drifted through the air whilst another lay draped over a console. Bullet holes riddled the equipment and a stratum of smoke hovered in the air just above head height. The place stank of burnt plastic and something was sizzling behind one of the screens.

"What?" exclaimed Smith, looking round, his grip slackening momentarily.

Seizing her chance, Hannah threw herself sideways, turning to hit the wall hard with her back, the breath knocked out of her. She scrabbled to get away from Smith, even as he swung towards her. Across the room, Saul rose from behind a console, a carbine up and braced against his shoulder. Two shots slammed into Smith's chest, hurling him back into the closed doors. He bounced away, brought his feet back down onto the floor, struggling to raise his weapon. Saul rounded the console and headed over, caught Smith's hand and shook the weapon from it, sending it tumbling away through the air.

"The shield will shut down in a moment," explained Saul. "I estimate it will then take me only half an hour to crack all your codes. Then this station…" Saul paused contemplatively. "No, this *spaceship*, will be mine."

Smith started to say something, but only blood issued from his mouth. Hannah pushed herself upright, keeping well back. She now just felt exhausted.

"There's nothing more I need to say to you, really," Saul finished.

He raised his carbine to Smith's forehead and pulled the trigger. Smith was slammed back again, the rear of his skull exploding outwards, hints of metal glinting inside. He hit one of the double doors again and bounced away, slowly tilting forward like some kind of ancient monolith. Hannah just stared at the blood beading the air, at a piece of scalp gyrating away from him, then, abruptly and violently, she threw up.

"This feels somehow disappointing," remarked Saul, still staring at Smith.

"The EM shield?" Hannah finally managed.

"With the EM field up, he could not get into my head and I could not get into his," said Saul. "But most important he was blind, and that's what enabled me to sneak in here."

Both dried and fresh blood covered his VC suit, she noticed, the fresh blood looking the same colour as his eyes. A fuzz of white hair now covered his scalp, concealing most of the scars, but to Hannah as he turned to face her, he just didn't look human.

"How did you get in here, then?" she managed.

"I just walked in along with some of Langstrom's men," Saul shrugged. "I knew Smith would come here directly to shut down the EM shield."

"What now?"

He raised his head slightly as if listening to something. "That's the shield down again. Now I'm running code crackers on everything he controlled." A humourless smile. "Since I'm no longer fighting him or need to perpetually look to my defences, I can use station computing…there, I have the reader-guns. The robots next."

"But again, what now?"

He looked momentarily pensive. "Presently I have this station set on a spiral course outwards from Earth. At the end of that course, it will swing itself around the Moon. By then, all necessary decisions will have been made."

"Decisions?"

"Yes, Hannah, decisions."

***

Saul revelled in the new feeling of freedom and safety as he cracked the last of Smith's codes, whereupon the last of the functioning readerguns and station robots came under his control. Human feeling like this he now allowed himself to indulge in, since it seemed to give him a reason to continue existing—after all, what was the use of victory if it could not be enjoyed? However, despite this sudden extension of his power, and with areas he had previously been almost blind to now opening up to him, he remained merely a fragile human being in a space station filled with those who, given the chance, would kill him.

"So that's it. He's gone." Hannah turned to gaze back at Smith, rather than query Saul's comment about "decisions."

Saul reached out and grabbed the front of Smith's VC suit, kicked the dead man's feet away from him to detach his soles from the floor, and lifted him higher.

"He won't get much deader than this," he observed, then shoved Smith away to send him drifting across the room.

What now? Hannah had asked. When Saul had fired up the Mars Traveller engine, his decision to fling the Argus Station away from Earth had been founded on the notion that his human self would want to survive. Now, by allowing human emotions to emerge, his reason for going to Mars was obvious: his sister was there. But wouldn't the moral choice now be to first neutralize Messina and the remaining delegates, then return to Earth to do whatever possible to mitigate the impending horror there? Quite simply, he did not know the answer, for he could do little to avert the catastrophe, and he wondered if he really wanted to set himself up as some kind of arbiter over it. The human race had walked blindly into this disaster, so it was theirs to deal with, wasn't it?

"I can see more of the station now," he informed Hannah, as the doors swept open ahead of him. "It possesses enough fusion plants and enough raw materials and equipment to continue functioning for a century or more without any need of the sun."

"What about food?" asked Hannah, following him out into the corridor beyond.

"The Arboretum and zero-gravity hydroponics can provide enough food for all those presently on board, and because they sent nearly the entire library from Gene Bank up here, along with tonnes of frozen samples, there's enough biodiversity available to iron out any instabilities occurring in the ecology." He shot her a glance. "Arcoplex Two is full of state-of-the-art technology, including the necessary biotech to turn any of those samples into something living. We could resurrect whole species here that Earth hasn't seen for centuries, or even millennia."

"But we're not going back to Earth."

Saul paused as he mentally riffled through the inventory of the equipment, laboratories and technologies contained in Arcoplex Two. There he discerned a laboratory and surgery even more advanced than the one Hannah had been using down on Earth, along with hundreds of copies of the hardware that had ended up inside both Malden's and Smith's skulls. No doubt this had all been laid on for Messina and his core delegates, so they could elevate themselves to a state of post-humanity. But, as Saul well knew, such equipment could provide a two-way street; what could expand the mind could also be used to scrub it, to totally erase it. He felt that thought for future reference; a viable alternative to death. And, when the time seemed right, he would let Hannah know that this alternative existed.

"If we went back to Earth, what could I do?" he asked.

"You could…save people."

"Yes, I could, but how exactly would I do that?" He gazed at her steadily. "Whilst in orbit, the tools I would have at my disposal to interact with Earth would consist of the satellite laser network and my ability to penetrate the computer systems down there. I cannot make more food available. I cannot build more power stations or more efficiently channel water supplies. In the end all I could do to ensure that some lived would be to choose which others should die."

"But isn't that what you want to do?"

He felt a wholly human flash of anger at that. "The only power I ever wanted was that of deciding my own destiny, which was something I could never hope for while the Committee still controlled Earth. I know that total individual freedom is about as real as the tooth fairy, but I still wanted more than I was being allowed. The power I've never sought is that of deciding the destinies of billions of others. I absolutely don't want such utter power over life and death."

But even as he said them, those last words rang hollow in his mouth, and he could see by Hannah's expression that she could hear the echoes. In pursuing vengeance while dressing it up as "power over his own destiny," he had already changed the entire course of history. The lives of a population of just over two thousand people now aboard this station were currently in his hands and, by removing both the Committee and the big stick that was the Argus satellite network from Earth, he had changed the fate of the billions remaining down on the planet.

"The Committee came to power largely through the complacency of Earth's population," he said. "Should I really be interested in them, Hannah? Should I be interested in the manswarm?"

He had influenced events on a massive scale, and in his hands lay the power to influence them further. He had obtained freedom of choice but, seemingly, no freedom from responsibility. Power was not something that would simply go away, and the decisions he now made, though unlikely to prevent the death of billions, could still change a very great deal.

"What would *you* do?" he asked.

"Whatever I could," she replied.

So easy for her to say that. He decided then that there was one decision he would delegate to her, to see how, given power, she handled it. Then he would finally decide on his own course of action. There was time, more than enough time, even though the station was steadily drawing away from Earth. In the end, Earth would still lie within his grasp even from Mars, for even from there he could still penetrate Govnet and thereby so much else. But what about here in the station, inside his own domain?

An idea hard to rid his mind of was that if he set the readerguns to killing, over half of those aboard the station would be dead within the next ten minutes. Turning the rest of the robots, including the five spiderguns, on the survivors would result in a space station full of corpses within six hours. He could then use the robots to clear up the mess and, needing to look to his own survival only, he could gradually reprogram the robots to replace any essential personnel. A plant for producing more robots existed in Arcoplex Two, so making replacements or increasing the robot population would not be a problem either. Then he could be alone and utterly free of contemptible humanity. Only Hannah's presence, and some remaining dregs of compassion, enabled him to resist this temptation.

"Stay behind me," he said, and perhaps meant more than just those words.

Peering through the cam network, he saw Langstrom limping down a corridor, with Sergeant Mustafa, the Nordic woman Peach and three other soldiers accompanying him. Obviously they had survived the acceleration. Just a thought and the readergun positioned in the ceiling of the intersection ahead would finish them off. Instead Saul spoke, his voice transmitted through the Political Office public address system, and then, because it seemed easier, throughout the station.

"Okay, everybody, listen very closely. Security Director Smith is dead and I, Alan Saul, am now in complete control of Argus Station, which is, as you may have noticed, no longer orbiting Earth. I now repeat my instructions to all the troops still aboard this station. Those who were engaged in attacking will withdraw to the outer ring; those defending will return to station barracks. Furthermore, all technical control staff will return to Tech Central to organize and assign essential maintenance and repair tasks. And, for the present, all construction work will remain on hold."

He watched Langstrom and the others come to a halt, and then gaze up at the readergun just ahead of them. Saul proceeded to limit the transmission of his voice to the Political Office only. "And you, Langstrom, and those with you, will place your weapons on the floor." Just to drive this point home, Saul made the readergun swing towards them and begin rotating its three barrels.

Langstrom was the first to react. He drew his side arm, held it up in plain view, then ducked to place it on the floor in front of him. In that same moment it occurred to Saul that there would be an excess of weaponry scattered all about the station, which perhaps would not be healthy for him and Hannah. He would have to do something about that, soon.

Langstrom's companions followed suit, till shortly a stack of side arms, machine pistols and assault rifles lay on the floor. Saul began to walk again, beckoning Hannah after him. They rounded the corner just as Langstrom and crew were turning to head off again. They swung back and just eyed Saul carefully. As he advanced, he studied them too, through his own eyes and through the sensors of the readerguns behind him and also behind them, their electronic triggers at the ready, and a program already loaded that would have them responding to the detection of any overlooked firearm.

Saul came to a halt ten paces away from them.

"Smith's back there?" Langstrom enquired, jerking his chin towards the dead man's one-time control centre.

"He is."

"What do you intend doing with us now?"

Saul gazed at him steadily. "You live or die at my whim. At present it is my whim that you live."

"No change, then," the commander replied. "We lived or died at Smith's whim."

"And yet you obeyed him and deliberately led me into a trap. Also you killed Braddock."

"I'd seen what happened to those who ever disobeyed him."

"There then is the difference between myself and Smith."

"Oh, yeah?"

"Yes—I wouldn't torture you for disobedience, I'd just kill you. Now," Saul paused in apparent thought, "most of your companions here can return to barracks, but for you," Saul pointed at Peach, "and you," he indicated Langstrom, "I have another task."

When Langstrom just stood motionless, Saul added, "Now."

Langstrom waved a hand and all but Peach retreated, glancing behind them as they went. Despite Saul's claim otherwise, they probably thought he meant to kill Langstrom—and the commander himself probably thought so too. Saul felt he could perfectly justify that to himself, as vengeance for Braddock, but, no, he actually had something else in mind.

"So what's this task?" Langstrom asked.

"I want you to go and collect Smith's body. Then I want you to take it to the nearest digester, which is at the bottom level of the Political Office. You'll have to strip him of his clothing before he goes in, as a VC suit won't digest." Now he turned to Peach, and pointed to the combat recorder extending alongside her temple from her fone. "You will film your commander here while he carries out my orders. I want clear images of Smith's face, and unbroken footage of him being taken to the digester and fed into it. Then, after you have both returned to barracks, I want that same image file made available to every console aboard this station. Is that clear?"

Langstrom nodded numbly, as Peach reached up and adjusted her combat recorder. Saul glanced at Hannah, who had been watching expressionlessly, then he nodded towards the corridor ahead. They set off, stepping round the pile of guns, then past Peach and Langstrom as the two moved aside. Saul did not bother to watch them further. If they tried to attack him, they would be dead in an instant, and he didn't want to show he was nervous that they might try. Soon they were out of sight, and by now Saul could see the exit airlock from the Political Office up ahead.

"Why?" Hannah asked.

"They need to be certain Caesar is dead," Saul replied, "before they can feel safe in obeying his replacement."

"I'm betting you have assembled enough image data of your own already."

"True enough, but the sooner I start issuing orders accompanied by implicit threats, the sooner it will be that I can issue orders without any need for threats at all."

Hannah nodded. "Yes, you need to firmly establish your rule here, which must extend beyond just the power to kill at whim."

"Because if I don't do so quickly," Saul continued, "there's going to be a lot more killing." Then after a pause he added, "And then I might just get bored with the whole idea of keeping *anyone* alive."

As they approached the airlock—presently closing behind a large troop of soldiers—he studied her reaction.

She shrugged. "I can see how it would become a trial to you."

As he suspected, his last words had come to her as no surprise at all. She fully expected him to stop playing games, and resort instead to the much easier option of mass slaughter. He had already decided not to follow that easier route and, of course, the avoid-killing-people test was about to get much harder now that he intended paying a visit to Chairman Alessandro Messina and the remaining delegates of the Committee—people whose own experience of mass slaughter made him look like an amateur.

But, no, that would be Hannah's test. It would be *her* choice.

20

I'M KILLING YOU FOR YOUR FREEDOM!

Freedom as an absolute does not exist since there are always constraints: genetic predetermination, surrounding environment, the society in which you live and, in the end, everything. Freedom is always a matter of degree: you cannot wish for the freedom to flap your arms and fly so long as gravity exists, nor can you wish for the freedom to breathe water. You are of course free to try both, but the results of such endeavours are not within your power. This is the big problem with freedom when it is taken up by some political ideology, for those who rely on the term are often trying to adjust the parameters of reality, and they simply cannot. And, when the revolutionary cries that he is fighting for "freedom," be sure to go running away from him just as fast as you can, for you can be damned certain he's fighting for the freedom to tell you what to do.

ANTARES BASE

Var gazed at the telescopic ladder now extended to the ceiling of the reactor room, its base clamped to one of the pillars supporting the reactor itself. Perched at the top of it, Lopomac was using a piton gun to drive the spikes into the bonded regolith of the ceiling, immediately around the big, recessed, double-door hatch situated up there. Because of its position, dividing internal air off from the atmosphere of Mars itself, this particular hatch's sensors did not extend to locking it down if they detected changes in the air mix, though it was locked down by the pressure differential. Its purpose had been to provide an opening through which to lower reactor components by crane. Var calculated that Ricard would know nothing about that.

"When they blow the door leading into here, they won't burst in spraying gunfire or tossing grenades," she said. "I'm guessing Ricard will send them in with plastic ammo only."

"That's a comfort," muttered Carol flatly.

She had just spooled out the control box, on its cable, from a multiple hoist: a device that could accommodate both forklift and crane attachments. Pressing one button made the device extend its wheels down, thus lifting its body from the floor, and by further manipulation of the controls, Carol sent it over towards the closed bulkhead door. She then brought the forklift tines right up against metal, forcing the door back on its seal, then lowered the machine back down to the floor, scraping glittering scratches on the door. Next to be sent over was a mobile tool chest, followed by chunks of reactor shielding to jam between the hoist and the door itself.

Var knew that Ricard's men would eventually get through. They would first use the least force possible to breach the door's seal, in the hope that, once pressures were equalized, they could just open it manually. Probably ceramic bullets would be fired at an angle through the bubblemetal, to reduce the chances of them hitting the reactor. They wouldn't want to risk major damage here but, on finding the door firmly jammed, they would have to use something more substantial—probably a grenade. This would hopefully take them the extra vital minutes that Var needed.

"They're coming," she warned, now watching on her laptop screen as a crawler headed over from Hex One and entered the pool of light cast by the exterior lights of Hex Three.

Carol looked round, her face white.

"You done there yet?" Var called up to Lopomac as a haze of releasing fluid drifted down from where he had positioned himself, hanging directly underneath the hatch on a rope strung between two pitons.

"It *should* open," he declared, now dropping a coil of rope attached to one of the array of pitons he had driven into the bonded regolith surrounding the hatch. "The motors are receiving power and the hydraulics don't seem jammed."

"Okay Carol," said Var, waving her towards the rope.

Carol headed over, pulling on her suit helmet, already wearing her harness and electric climbing motor. Var pulled on her own harness then donned her helmet, Bluetoothing the laptop to her visor display before closing it and putting it into her hip pouch. Carol ascended to the hatch along with Lopomac, who had moved to another section of rope, and positioned herself just below the seam of the double-door hatch. Var walked across, undid the clamps holding the ladder in place, released its telescopic lock and collapsed it. She carried it over to jam it against the bulkhead door too, so that an enforcer spotting a telescopic ladder in here would assume its purpose was to add to the obstacles preventing him and his fellows getting in. Returning to the rope, she attached her own climbing motor, engaged the friction wheels and set the motor running. In a moment she was up beside Lopomac, on the opposite side of the hatch from Carol, and also just below the seam.

"Remember," Var urged, "stay low. The dust baffles up there around the edge, as well as the external lights, should keep us concealed from any snipers Ricard leaves outside."

"If he does leave any snipers outside," said Lopomac.

"He's doing that right now," replied Var, a flick at her wrist control flinging up an exterior cam image in the lower half of her visor. One enforcer had already exited the crawler and positioned himself behind a boulder, his scoped rifle resting on a small tripod on the boulder itself. On the other side of the hex, the crawler had now stopped to discharge another sniper. This man set off at a steady lope, then abruptly dropped into a hollow in the ground, before setting up his rifle too. After a moment he rose from a crouch and gestured to the crawler, which set off again, this time turning in towards the hex. The imperious gesture was enough to make Var realize something.

"In fact," she added, "Ricard is one of those two snipers."

"Makes sense," said Lopomac. "He wouldn't want to put himself at risk in here. I'll bet the other sniper is Silberman."

The crawler drew over beside Hex Three at the point where Var had blown the windows, there discharging another three enforcers behind the water tanks. Whilst one covered the two nearest windows, the third ran over to the intervening wall, where Var now lost sight of him from the roof cams. Switching to an internal view, she saw a hand briefly appear in one window, then some object bounce inside. The view whited out and from where she hung above the reactor Var heard two hollow booms.

"Grenades," she said, "just as predicted."

"Damn," Carol exclaimed. Var glanced at her questioningly, and she explained, "The glue, it's photo- and thermoactive too."

"So a grenade flash will make it set hard," said Lopomac. "That's great."

"Score one for Ricard," said Var. "But it's not like your glue is something he's deliberately and cleverly neutralizing." She did not mention her thoughts about lucky generals, instead focusing on the crawler as it rounded the hex and turned in towards the garage. Again it went out of sight of the roof cams, but Var now switched to the cam positioned in the airlock.

"The crawler's entering the garage airlock," she said.

Lines of vapour cut across her view into the airlock itself as the outer doors ponderously drew open, and the crawler rolled inside. The doors behind it closed and sealed, and she could tell that the gate valve had now opened to pressurize the lock as, over a long five minutes, the same vapour dispersed. How long would it take them to realize that the inner doors weren't opening?

Ah, now.

The small airlock of the crawler itself opened and an enforcer clambered out. As he paused to stare up at the cam, the resolution was good enough for Var to recognize his face. His name, she remembered, was Liam... something. He walked over to the door and peered at the electronic panel beside it, then moved directly in front of the door, unclipping a grenade from his belt and thumbing off the safety cap. He reached over for the manual lever, and arc light blossomed between hand and lever even before they connected. The cam view fizzed for a second, then cleared. The man's body was bent over, and smoking. There came a bright flash, whereupon the cam view blinked out. Var heard the whoomph of the grenade going off, followed by a massive rumbling blast. Multiple explosions, she realized, as she braced one hand against the rim of the hatch and switched to a view inside the garage. The whole hex was shuddering, and flakes of stone were falling from the ceiling.

"Score two, and three to us," she announced.

The garage was depressurizing. The inner and outer doors were gone, the crawler airlock empty. Switching to an exterior view, she saw the same vehicle's wreck lying some distance away from the hex. It struck her as highly unlikely that its remaining occupant was still alive or, even if he was, would be capable of causing harm.

"What do you mean?" Lopomac asked.

"Your supercapacitor output detonated all the grenades the enforcer was carrying—took out him, the crawler, and presumably the driver."

"Good," said Lopomac, but he did not look at all happy. He looked sick.

As she now coldly calculated the odds, Var guessed that some people found it much harder than others to turn killer. Another hollow boom reverberated, dropping another shower of regolith flakes from the ceiling, but this time it was followed by the sound of rushing wind. This meant the other three enforcers had blown out a window and were moving closer.

ARGUS STATION

Clad in a VC suit obtained from a store by the exit from the Political Office behind them, Hannah looked up and noticed that many of the station robots had been assigned new tasks. One resembling a truck, with legs instead of wheels, braced itself between beams while construction robots loaded it with all the corpses that had not gone flying outside the station. Robotic iron starfish, moving like gibbons, were busy collecting stray weapons, and had already fully loaded a smaller version of the truck robot, and it was moving off. Glancing left, she observed yet more robot activity where the lattice walls connected to the asteroid, but then more of the dead would be impacted there.

A couple of spiderguns not included in all this activity were now approaching. As one of them dropped into the unfinished tubeway lying ahead of her and Saul, while the other took up position behind them, Hannah seized the chance to study one of these machines more closely.

Though possessing the eight limbs of its namesake, the closest living thing she could equate it to was a vaguely remembered image of a sea spider—a creature seemingly without body or head, because its eight limbs simply conjoined where normally a body should have been. All the components normally found in a robot—like power supply, processors and sensors—were distributed along its limbs. This gave them a misshapen look and, to add to its oddity, the machine's joints were universal, so the limbs could hinge in any direction. It propelled itself along with just a light flick at its surroundings, the weapons terminating its limbs constantly zeroing in on any objects of suspicion. But this was lethal cutting-edge technology, and its oddity stirred no feeling of humour.

The machine she was studying seemed to be leading the way towards the lower end of Arcoplex One, where a great mass of partially finished buildings constructed against the face of the asteroid housed a massive mercury bearing and the drive mechanisms at this end of the cylinder world. They entered via a monorail tubeway, exiting it again at a small station located beside the arcoplex bearing itself, then heading upwards to reach the central spindle, aiming for the airlocks in the cylinder's endcap.

"Do we have to go this way?" Hannah asked.

"It's the quickest route," he replied, then paused and turned to stare back the way they had come.

"What is it?" she asked.

He glanced at her. "Readerguns. Warning shots. Four of Langstrom's soldiers were reluctant to abandon their weapons...Well, they've abandoned them now."

"What about Messina's men?"

"His remaining soldiers have withdrawn to the outer ring but have refused to obey Messina's orders to seize Dock Two."

"Refused?"

"Yes, their commander sent three soldiers to take a look. Seeing three spiderguns were guarding the dock, they reported the mission 'militarily unfeasible.'"

"Brave of them to defy Messina?"

"Being killed by a spidergun is more certain than any threats of Messina's at present."

"Those things are that effective?"

"They can deploy all eight of their guns at once, each with a rate of fire of a thousand rounds a minute, at four thousand metres per second. The rounds themselves are depleted uranium beads." Saul held up one hand, finger and thumb just a few millimetres apart. "They deliver the same kinetic energy as an eight-millimetre readergun round, but over a smaller area, and each robot carries about two thousand rounds in each of its leg magazines. So, yes, even discounting the other missiles they can deploy, they're that effective."

"Messina won't give up easily."

"Yes, I hope so."

Feeling suddenly uncomfortable with the direction of this conversation, Hannah now glanced up at the arcoplex soaring above them. "How do people get in and out when it's rotating?" she asked, deliberately changing the subject.

Saul pointed in over the structure housing the drive mechanism towards the dark throats of several access tubes leading towards the cylinder's spindle. "There's a tube elevator that goes in through the spindle itself, then curves down to the cylinder floor." He pointed downwards. "You enter it upside-down, in relation to the asteroid, then experience an apparent increase in gravity until you step out in the arcoplex. You'll soon see."

They went through the airlock and, waiting for the two spiderguns to follow them, all Hannah could see was a nightmare scene of corpses lying entangled all about her.

Even though many of the victims were guilty of killing citizens back on Earth, others were merely wives, husbands and children. Saul was right: human life, it seemed, had been cheapened by its sheer quantity.

"Come on." Once the spiderguns had joined them, Saul propelled himself up the inner face of the endcap, and Hannah quickly followed, gliding over the corpses until she could snag a handhold projecting from the spindle, sitting beside a sunlight transmission panel that even then was growing dull. The spindle itself was over ten metres in diameter, with frequent handholds marking a course along it.

"There." Saul pointed to a tubeway exiting the spindle some twenty metres ahead, which curved down towards a building situated on the inner surface of the cylinder. "Engineering for environments like those found inside this station presents some interesting challenges."

Did he not even notice all the dead?

At intervals along the spindle they were obliged to circumvent buildings that actually attached to it, extending outwards like spokes. Peering through their windows, she spotted further corpses drifting like slow marionettes. Two thousand people wiped out here just because some of them weren't voting for Messina.

The journey soon over, they exited at the other end of Arcoplex One, headed past the main train station, and entered a tubeway leading into one of the docking pillars. A train blocked most of the tube straight ahead, but pullways were provided on either side to allow access for station personnel. They passed along one of these to enter the centre of Dock Two, where Saul proceeded down the rear wall towards one of the five docking faces. Glancing back, Hannah noticed a spidergun crouching on the millipede body of the train, while another waited on the floor they were descending to, and a third was poised three floors further round, on the other side of the docking pillar.

"What are you going to do about Messina…and the rest?" she asked.

"Messina deserves to die," he replied. "As do most of those aboard these space planes."

"But it's noticeable how you're not saying whether you're planning to kill them."

As they reached the floor he turned towards her, while issuing some unheard instruction that dispatched the two attendant spiderguns to other docking faces. After a moment he replied, "No, I'm not. I'm going to wait for your decision on that, so long as it does not include them returning to Earth."

He then turned and headed towards the nearest airlock column, to one side of which already squatted a spidergun. There Saul came to a halt and folded his arms.

"Chairman Messina," he announced, "you, and everyone aboard with you, will now exit your plane, and I want you to order those onboard all the other planes here to do likewise." He tilted his head, as if listening, then continued, "I've already told you the alternative."

Hannah felt her stomach churn. It was now her decision? Why was he making it hers? Then she understood the reason. It had been so easy for her to offer criticism whenever she suspected him of being tempted by the ease of quick and bloody solutions, and now she was paying the penalty. She could refuse to make any decision at all, of course, but that would dump the whole matter back in his lap, and whatever he did then would essentially be the result of her indecision. In either case, there would be no way of escaping guilt.

After some minutes, the sliding door of the docking pillar revolved sideways, and four figures clad in light spacesuits stepped out. None of these was Messina, though Hannah recognized one woman from broadcast sessions of the Committee. After a moment the name came to her: Delegate Margot Le Blanc of the French region. With her was an older man who might be her husband, and a younger one likely to be her son. The heavily built one with ophidian eyes, and subdermal armouring evident in his face, had to be Le Blanc's Inspectorate bodyguard.

"Move over there." Saul gestured to a space at the edge of the dock floor, where the spidergun unfolded with fast and eerie silence in the vacuum, three of its weapon-bearing limbs pointed at these four.

Delegate Le Blanc was clearly saying something, but it wasn't audible over com. Either Saul had not seen fit to include Hannah in the communication, or he himself just wasn't bothering to listen. She suspected the latter. The spidergun took a few paces forward and, after staring at the machine for a moment, Le Blanc bowed her head and with the three others trailing her walked over to the spot indicated. More people began to emerge, including other familiar faces, along with children looking pathetic and vulnerable in the smallest size of spacesuit available, concertinaed at the joints yet still hanging loose and baggy. The sight of them at once coloured Hannah's decision as to their fate: she could not allow Saul to kill them all—not now.

"Messina will come out last," she predicted.

"He's wriggling like a hooked fish," remarked Saul. "He's communicating with people back on Earth, with the rest of his soldiers here and with those still on the other planes, trying to find some way of getting a handle on this situation. It seems he just can't admit to himself that he no longer possesses any power."

Hannah detected movement at the periphery of her vision and glanced across at the next docking face, which tilted up at an angle from this one. People were now departing from planes there and, as she looked straight above, she could see others were emerging on all the other docking faces too. Doubtless Saul was still issuing instructions even while he spoke to her for, escorted by spiderguns, they started heading round to the docking face she stood on.

"There's nothing he can do?" Hannah asked.

"He still thinks so—a notion of which I am about to disabuse him." Saul paused for a moment, then continued, "If everyone could listen very carefully. Since Chairman Messina has seen fit to issue orders for security personnel to take a shot at me whenever they get the chance, be aware that, before entering this dock, I programmed the spiderguns to react to any weapons fire in one way only. They will kill all of you. Since their sensors range into the infrared, the spill from your suits will be sufficient for them to target every one of you—there will be no place you can hide."

"You're taking a big risk by just being here," said Hannah.

"Not really," Saul replied. "Messina's troops destroyed the cams in Dock One, but not here. If someone even raises a weapon, they'll get no chance to use it."

Hannah again surveyed the crowds now moving round towards them, then focused on those arriving through the nearest airlock. If Saul was confident he could detect an attempt to kill him from so many different sources, it meant he was functioning at a level way beyond that of most computers. She had always known such ability was possible for him, but hadn't quite registered the fact until now.

"You're really confident of that?"

"Confidence is not the issue, but speed of image processing, assignment of risk levels and reaction times are. The only chance of someone actually firing a weapon in my direction is if twenty-eight people were to attempt it simultaneously within the same four-second time frame." He glanced at her. "You yourself installed the hardware in my head, you know what I can do."

Hannah shrugged. "On an intellectual level, yes." She nodded towards the airlock. "Here's Messina."

Still watching her, Saul grinned. "Did you think I needed telling?"

He turned to the airlock from which Messina had just emerged, with four large and heavily augmented bodyguards gathered round him. The Chairman wore a vacuum combat suit, doubtless state-of-the-art, but perhaps still wanted to put some flesh between himself and potential bullets. However, rather than go and lose himself in the growing crowd gathered at the dock edge, he walked directly towards Saul, and came to a halt only five metres away, his bodyguards lining up behind him.

"Your decision," said Saul quietly.

Hannah assumed he had addressed the Chairman, but when Messina showed no reaction she realized the words had been for her ears only. She was tired and now wanted to just be somewhere safe, so she could sleep, but the implication of those two words had her chest tightening and her heartbeat thundering in her ears. Panic attack—she'd been here before. Perhaps this meant that somewhere inside she was feeling safe, sufficiently out of danger for her false friend to return. She tried to breathe calmly, to get it all under control: in through her nose and out through her mouth. Saul turned to look at her and waited. Messina was speaking, she could see. Saul probably listened to his words and discounted them. Messina's control of his own destiny had ceased some while ago.

"My decision," she managed, the thundering in her ears retreating but the tightness in her chest increasing. "I am going to defer my decision."

"That you cannot do."

"Yes, I can." She shrugged, trying to get angry enough to drive away the feeling of losing control. "It is my decision that, until I come to some final decision, all of these people will be confined to Arcoplex One."

Saul nodded, with a hint of a smile. "Yes, appropriate." He then turned back to Messina, snapping, "Shut up." Hannah heard Messina's last words tailing off, as Saul now included her and probably everyone else in the communication. "Here's what is going to happen." He glanced from those already huddled at the edge of this dock to those still filing across from other docking faces. "You will all head towards the back of this pillar, and proceed through to the endcap of Arcoplex One, where you'll enter through the airlock there. I see there are one hundred and ninety-three of you, so I leave it to yourselves to organize who enters first and who enters last, on the basis of air supply, since each cycling of the lock will take a minimum of two minutes and it will only hold four of you at a time."

"You can't put us in there," protested Messina.

"Why not?" Saul glanced at the man absently. "Because of the two thousand corpses inside?" When Messina had no answer to that, Saul continued, "You will of course need to work fast to feed them all into the five digesters inside the arcoplex. You'll need to strip them of their clothing and remove any metal augmentations that might jam the digesters. Since each digester can only process one corpse per hour, that means, with all of them operating, the whole process should take about seventeen days. By then it's going to get rather unpleasant in there, I suspect."

"So it amuses you to exact such a petty vengeance." Messina's every word was laden with contempt.

"No," said Saul, "it would suit me better to feed you, and every delegate here, feet first into a digester while still alive. And that might yet become an option. For now, I am going to leave two of my spiderguns here to ensure you follow my instructions. Please don't try anything foolish, since that would only result in a horrible mess any survivors would have to clear up." He finally turned to Hannah. "Let's go."

As she followed him, two spiderguns overtook them and headed off at high speed. Glancing back, she found just one of their fellows keeping pace behind—the two Saul had left still amidst the crowd back there.

"Where are they going?" she asked.

"To confront Messina's troops," he explained. "It's time for them to acknowledge the new regime here."

***

When Saul delivered his terse instruction to the commander of Messina's troops, whilst the two spiderguns he had sent ahead strode amidst them, he felt almost disappointed by their immediate submission. But, then, fifteen of the fifty or so survivors were stretcher cases, whilst another twenty were walking wounded. They quickly abandoned their weapons and began heading for a tubeway into the station, from where they would go to join Langstrom's men in the barracks, and its hospital.

Saul felt a void within him as, with one of the spiderguns still dogging his and Hannah's footsteps, he approached the airlock into Arcoplex One. He had not been sucked into Malden's revolution, he had finally got himself up to Argus Station and here defeated Smith, and as a bonus he had decapitated Earth's government. He had won, yet still that emptiness remained.

Depression? No, he checked the balance of his neurochemicals and they were fine. He checked his own blood: his blood sugar was low because he needed to eat, and various toxins were present, but this could not be the cause of his present malaise, for it was purely intellectual. He dismissed it, suppressed it, then focused his attention on the odd fact that he *could* now so easily check the state of his own body.

"There is something you didn't tell me, isn't there, Hannah?" he said, glancing at her.

"What do you mean?" she asked, looking slightly panic-stricken.

"Something about the organic interface?"

"I..."

"Let me put it this way: just a moment ago I wondered, because of the way I feel, if I was chemically depressed. Then I checked, which rather tells me that I am now hooking in to my autonomous nervous system."

"The interface," said Hannah, as they waited for the spidergun to proceed through the airlock ahead of them, "it's not a static organism."

As the airlock cycled, Saul glanced back at the other two spiderguns herding the captives towards the same endcap. Then, with negligent ease, he cracked the coding of transmissions passing between the captives. Messina was busy firing off orders and demands for assessments to all about him, though the replies came mainly from a couple of delegates who had risen high in the Inspectorate hierarchy before joining the Committee. The Chairman was demanding an escape—with a few inevitable losses, surely they could reach a different docking pillar and board another space plane? He was currently being informed that, even with only one spidergun watching them, such an attempt would be suicidal.

"Smith was stronger than me, to begin with, then weaker," Saul said, mentally instructing the airlock to open ahead of them now that the spidergun was through. "My integration process with Janus is still far from complete, but even so, that should not result in me being able to connect this way to my autonomous nervous system."

"The interface is growing."

He nodded as he entered the airlock ahead of her, and whilst they stood inside, waiting for it to pressurize, he mulled over the implications. Only when they were back inside the arcoplex did he speak again.

"Malden's was static," he said.

"Yes…"

"Mine, however, is growing a neural matrix throughout my brain." He paused. "What is the organism based upon?"

"Your own DNA," she replied.

He turned and stared at her. "So no rejection problems."

She nodded. "It uses your own neural stem cells and grows its matrix from them. After just one day, the connectivity between your organic brain and the hardware in your skull was about the same as Malden's. Now it should be about twice that."

"When does it stop growing?"

"Only when it matches up to the demand you place on the hardware. If you make further demands of it, the matrix will grow further to accommodate that."

It struck him as more than likely that such bioware was not on general release. If it had been, then Smith would have acquired it.

"It's a prototype, then," he stated.

As they propelled themselves up towards the arcoplex spindle, then back along it towards the asteroid-side endcap, Saul quickly tracked down a number of key individuals inside the station. Robert Le Roque, the Technical

Controller of the station, remained in a cell and seemed unhurt, and by checking records Saul discovered that he had not been subjected to inducement. Commander Langstrom was currently in the crowded barracks hospital, his knee undergoing a scan. This hospital itself was presently overrun by casualties.

"Langstrom," Saul addressed him through the hospital intercom, "I want you to collect Le Roque from the cell block and both of you to be in Tech Central within ten minutes."

A similar summons soon had other necessary staff heading up from their cabins to the control room. Chang and the twins he could locate nowhere, until he replayed recorded data that tracked their progress from the cell block back to Tech Central. They had ensconced themselves in an unassigned cabin, after looping the cam feed to perpetually indicate the same cabin as empty. To their joint surprise, he summoned them too.

Even as he and Hannah arrived at the far endcap, Saul registered a cycling of the airlock they had just departed, and glanced back to see the first of the captives already entering the arcoplex. As the pair exited through the second airlock, he considered an old story that might have informed Hannah's decision about Messina and the rest: how German civilians had been forced to bury the concentration-camp dead. He felt that her first decision was just, and he would go with what she decided next just so long as it did not endanger the Argus Station or themselves. Once the airlock had closed, he instituted another protocol.

"The airlocks at this end of the cylinder are sealed now," he explained, as they descended to the surface of the asteroid. "But perhaps I'll place guards here too."

Stirring up eddies of dust, their gecko boots did not function as well on asteroidal rock strewn with flakes of stone, so they proceeded slowly and with care. Lifting his gaze from his feet, Saul glanced over to his left, where a construction robot was busy scooping up the last of the corpses here. Next he viewed their destination: a steel chamber in the outer rim where the corpses were all neatly stacked, the same way round, so that one wall seemed to consist entirely of boot soles. He could have ordered the robots to hurl them out into space but, now that he had cut all supply lines from Earth, even corpses had become a potential resource.

Reaching an airlock in the base of Tech Central, which lay above the lattice walls, offered a clear view out into space. Saul caught Hannah's shoulder and turned her so that she could look straight across the station wheel, as far as the outer ring where the docks were positioned. These were now effectively the nose of the enormous spacecraft this place had become. He then gestured off to the right of the docks, where the Moon loomed large in the blackness.

"Three more turns around the Earth and we'll be ready for a low-fuel course change around the Moon," Saul explained. "I'll then fire up the Traveller engine once more to boost us on the correct course."

They finally entered Tech Central, shedding their helmets whilst waiting for the spidergun to follow them through the lock.

"I was about to remark that we're free of the Committee now," he said. "But, of course, *you're* not free of it, because you still have that decision to make." Hannah's expression was pained as he continued. "That decision aside, what will you do now there's no political officers to instruct you?"

A look of panic flitted across her face—perhaps signifying another of her attacks, or the reaction of someone who, having lived a life without choices, was now being confronted with them.

"Arcoplex Two contains state-of-the-art research and surgical facilities, in fact even more than you had down on Earth," he noted. "Whilst you decide precisely what you want to do, perhaps you can occupy yourself there?"

"More than I had down on Earth?" Hannah echoed numbly.

He nodded, glad that the option was now firmly implanted in her mind.

"And if I want to return to Earth?" she managed.

"That option stays open. A space plane would need half a full fuel load just to counter our present velocity, and one could be fuelled and made ready before we reach the Moon." He paused contemplatively. "But I wonder if you'd really want to return to Earth aboard a plane that would need to be crewed by Inspectorate military?"

"No," she replied firmly. "So this station definitely isn't going back."

"It isn't." He shook his head. "Mars, I feel, is just going to be a stopping point on a very long journey. You need to decide how you'll fit in here, now. That means more decisions and choices for you—they come with the territory known as freedom."

"Will anyone really be free aboard this station?"

"Freedom is not an absolute."

21

ALL THE LOVELY PEOPLE...

A belief was once prevalent in "modern" societies that the killer of humans, the murderer, is an aberration. At least this was what the rulers wished their subjects to believe, though, as they ordered their soldiers to war, they knew that the veneer called "civilization" was as thin as whatever ideology they themselves espoused. The truth is that an aversion to killing anyone outside of immediate family is a product of societal indoctrination (and then only in that slightly more than half the population who are not sociopaths), whilst within immediate family it is merely the product of that contradiction in terms called "genetic altruism." It is in fact a harsh reality that he who believes killers are an aberration is also he who has the boot planted firmly on his neck; whilst amongst those who rule the aberration is the one who is not a sociopath, and therefore reluctant to kill.

ANTARES BASE

Some cams had survived the grenades, but when she saw the extent of the wreckage through them, she almost wished they hadn't. All that valuable equipment destroyed: computers, hardware, infrastructure, and items like the crawler lying wrecked out there—all of it vital to their future survival here on Mars. Through the cams she'd also seen an enforcer crawl out of that same crawler, issuing vapour trails from his breached suit. She watched as he managed about three metres away from the wreck, before he started suffocating and desperately clawing at the ground.

Using what cover he could, one of the three enforcers risked loping out to his fallen comrade, and gently turning him over on to his back. What he then saw through the man's visor told him all he needed to know, and he scurried back to join his fellows as they entered the garage through the open crawler lock. It was crucial that they enter the garage, for Var now needed it open to the Martian atmosphere for all of her plan to work. She had expected them to go in through one of the adjacent bulkhead doors, but of course there was no need now.

Once inside the garage, they didn't resort to grenades, because here there were so few opportunities for an ambush. Soon they were out again and moving round close to the wall, towards the next window. From her perch up beside the roof hatch, Var felt another blast as they destroyed the window, then through a roof cam she observed a further plume of wasted air. More explosions as the enforcers secured that section too, then appeared outside again, edging up to the last exterior window.

"Okay," she said, "they're now going into the final bit."

"I'm not sure I can do this," Carol protested abruptly.

Var peered across at her, but could think of nothing useful to say.

Minutes ticked away as the enforcers searched this last section, then one of the snipers waiting outside the base stood up and loped in. Obviously, now that the enforcers had searched all the outer sections, Ricard thought it safe to send in Silberman as his deputy, though apparently it still wasn't safe enough for Ricard himself. From inside the hex, a fuzzy cam view showed the three enforcers on the move. Var tried tracking them for a moment, then gave up and switched to a workable view of the corridor leading straight towards the reactor room below her. About a minute later the first of the enforcers stepped into sight, with the other two close behind. At the door they hesitated, and turned as Silberman joined them, waving a hand to complement whatever instructions he was giving them over com.

"This is it," said Var. "They're right outside." Her stomach felt tight as a rock. "Carol, I want you to crawl over to the edge—up there." She pointed to that side of the hex beyond which Ricard had positioned himself. "Silberman is now with our three enforcers, but Ricard himself is still outside. He's got a scoped rifle on a tripod, so has every chance of killing you if you show yourself, so don't take a shot at him unless he actually stands up and starts heading in."

That put Carol safely out of the way, since if she was not sure she could *do this*, she might be a liability in the coming fire fight.

"Okay." Carol's jerky nod of agreement set her swaying on her rope.

Firing erupted: the chatter of an assault rifle accompanied by the sounds of ricochets inside the reactor room. Var glanced down and saw five bullet holes stitched across the door. Air began screaming through them, and the corridor outside began fogging up, those in there lost from view.

"Lopomac?"

He was peering up at the electronic control panel alongside the roof hatch.

"Not yet," he said.

The shrieking continued, slowly reducing in intensity, until it became like the wailing of wind over a desolate landscape. In the corridor the fog began to clear, and Var could now see the enforcers poised by the bulkhead door. They had laid their assault rifles on the floor and were now holding machine pistols. Plastic ammo, just as predicted. Var momentarily wondered if those assessing her in her childhood had chosen right about her education. Perhaps they should have trained her for the Inspectorate military instead. She felt some gratification in having got it right every time, yet her thinking all just seemed like the logical working of a machine, so there was no joy in it.

"Now," said Lopomac.

He keyed something into the control panel, waited a moment, then tried again. Outside, at that instant, one of the enforcers was handing his grenades over to Silberman. Var did not understand the reason until the same enforcer picked up one of the assault rifles, removed its ammunition clip and ejected the shell from the breech, then stepped over to the bulkhead door and balanced the tip of the barrel against the floor. Letting it go, he leapt back so the weapon toppled against the door. They'd obviously assumed this door might be electrified too.

"Fuckit," growled Lopomac. "Fuckit!"

"What is it?" she asked.

"Pump's fucked."

He started working a handle back and forth till the hatch doors began to bulge downwards and, with a clonk, the seam opened. He tried the panel again, and this time was rewarded with the familiar hum of a hydraulic pump in action. Slowly the doors continued hingeing downwards.

Immediately outside the bulkhead door below, the same enforcer tentatively stepped forward and tried the manual handle. The handle crunched over but, with the weight of the forklift pressing against it, the door would not lift from its seals, and therefore could not swing aside on its upper pivot. The enforcer drove his boot against it, but the door moved not at all.

Var turned her attention elsewhere—time to move.

She reached up around the rim of the hatch and, aided by the low Martian gravity, easily hauled herself up on to the roof. Carol pulled herself up almost simultaneously, with Lopomac immediately behind her. After they unclipped their climbing motors, Lopomac reattached the piton gun to the length of rope he had hung from and flicked over a switch on one side of it. This transmitted a low current to the pitons, operating micromotors inside them so as to withdraw their barbs. After a couple of tugs, he hauled up the ensuing tangle of rope and pitons. Meanwhile Var rechecked her visor screen, seeing all but one of the enforcers retreating along the corridor. The remaining one placed a grenade beside the lower rim of the door, then retreated too.

"Hurry!" she urged.

Already at the external console, Lopomac first keyed in the instruction to close the hatch doors, then grabbed the external manual pump handle and started to work that too. Slowly they began to close up—just as the grenade detonated below, causing the roof to jerk up underneath them. Smoke instantly filled the corridor, so it took a moment for Var to check if the grenade had been successful. Fortunately it had not, and though the door itself was bent inwards at the bottom, there was not enough room for anyone to slip through.

"That's got it," said Lopomac, as the hatch finally sealed shut.

"You go on," said Var, gesturing Carol over to the dust cowling along the edge of the roof. She herself began crawling on her belly towards another section of roof.

"I'll deal with the hatch," she said to Lopomac. "You put a piton in and give us a line."

The hatch above the reactor room was not the only access to the roof. A small vertical airlock sat directly over the garage, built in its previous incarnation when it had simply been a major storeroom. The hatch had allowed personnel access to the roof in order to make repairs to cams, lights and radio dishes, but it hadn't been used in years, and even the ladder descending from it had been removed. On reaching it, Var thumbed its console whilst Lopomac drove in another piton. The console screen instantly warned her of a pressure differential, but she ran a reboot and it corrected the error to show no differential at all. Finding the manual lever stiff and the seal stuck, she cautiously got up on her knees to provide herself with more leverage, and heaved. The outer hatch eventually came up with a thin tearing sound, strips of torn seal hanging from it. She dropped down inside, and clinging to the upper section of ladder that had been left inside the airlock, she released the lever of the lower hatch, then paused to check image feed.

Another grenade detonated by the bulkhead door leading into the reactor room. The blast sent the forklift skittering over to one side, and the door tumbling into the room beyond, where it slammed against one side of the reactor itself. Var winced—she'd have to check for damage—but at least Silberman and the others were still where she wanted them.

"Any movement from Ricard?" she asked.

"Nothing," said Carol. "He's keeping his head down."

"Lopomac, where's that line?"

"Coming." He dropped a coil of rope over the edge, then peered down towards her. She attached her climbing motor, then kicked down on the hatch, once, twice, until it fell open, then as fast as she could she lowered herself into the garage underneath. After a moment, Lopomac joined her.

"They're in the reactor room," she explained, unshouldering her assault rifle and knocking off the safety. The enforcer who seemed always to get the shit jobs had been sent in first, the other two rapidly following.

"Come on," said Var.

She quickly opened a bulkhead door, leading into the next outer section, then in towards the reactor room beyond. Lopomac unshouldered his assault rifle and held it ready. By now Silberman himself was entering the reactor room. Of course, he would be puzzled: how had they sealed the door like that and yet apparently disappeared? As she reached the junction from which the corridor led up to the reactor room door, she waved Lopomac ahead. "When I give the word."

He still looked a bit sick, but nodded and moved over to the opposite side of the corridor entrance, resting his back against the wall, with his assault rifle braced before him.

"The reactor?" he queried.

"Not in line of sight," she replied.

That was true enough, but a stray round might still hit it. She just had to hope the imminent fire fight damaged nothing vital, but it was a risk they had to take. Also backing against the wall with her rifle ready, she once more studied her visor screen.

Silberman sat himself at the control console to work through the menu. After a second, she realized he must be turning the power back on to the rest of base. This accomplished, he stood, gestured to the other three and headed back towards the door. What would he now be thinking? He must realize that there were few places they could be hiding in the outer section, yet would assume they hadn't been stupid enough to seal themselves inside one of the less vital inner sections.

"Ricard's on the move," announced Carol.

Var briefly switched to an exterior cam view. Ricard was now in a crouch, his rifle up against his shoulder as he swung it about to check the screen view through its telescopic sight. This told her all she needed. Silberman had just informed Ricard of the situation, and now Ricard was worried; he thought they must be somewhere outside the hex.

"Kill him, if you can," she instructed, flicking back to the previous view inside the hex.

Waving Mr Shit Job ahead, Silberman stepped out of the reactor room, the other two enforcers emerging behind him. Let them get halfway down the corridor…

They were a few paces away from the room when Silberman abruptly halted and gestured behind him. One of the enforcers turned, and started to head back. Silberman had clearly decided to leave a guard.

"Lopomac," she said, "now!"

As one, they swung round, facing along the corridor, rifles up against their shoulders. Lopomac went down on one knee, but Var remained standing. She opened up on full automatic, whilst Lopomac fired in short bursts. The lead enforcer was slammed back into Silberman, but the spray of blood and escaping vapour showed that his body had not been sufficient protection, for the bullets had gone straight through him and struck Silberman too. One of the enforcers behind spun against the wall, smearing bits of himself across it, steaming like raw meat dropped onto a hot stove. The last enforcer managed to stumble a few paces towards the reactor room, before shots stitched across his back and he went down.

Var took her finger off the trigger. "We got them," she said, for Carol's benefit.

"I missed Ricard," said Carol. "He's back down in his hollow."

"Keep your head down," said Var as she advanced.

None of the four scattered on the floor showed any signs of life. Simple as that: extinguished in just over ten seconds of gunfire. Var called up a menu on her visor screen, and keyed into a com icon that was presently dormant. It started flashing, down in the bottom right corner of her visor as the rest of the menu faded. Then it blinked out, and her helmet speakers beeped to let her know the new channel had been opened from the other end.

"You're alone now, Ricard," she said.

After a moment, he asked, "What do you mean, alone?"

"I mean Silberman and the last of your enforcers are dead."

"Then you've won."

Var turned and began heading back the way she had come, leaving Lopomac standing behind her, seemingly horrified by what they had just done. He wouldn't be strong enough, she realized, he wouldn't be able to carry this through to its inevitable and necessary conclusion.

"Surrender yourself now, Ricard, and you get to live until the base personnel decide what to do with you," she said. "If you don't surrender, then that's fine. You can stay out there until your air runs out."

Into an outer section now, blast damage evident all up the walls beside her, the broken window ahead where the enforcers had entered.

"Someone was shooting at me from the roof," he protested.

"Carol?"

"I hear you."

"You can come down now."

"Okay, on my way," the woman replied, relief obvious in her voice.

"I need some sort of guarantee," insisted Ricard, but his decision was already made. She could hear it in his voice—he was all out of choices.

"I give you my word that no one here will try to kill you, Ricard. I need you alive, and telling the people here what instructions you received from Earth. I need them to know."

She could now see him through the window, as he stood up, holding his rifle above his head.

"Put the weapon on the ground," she said.

By the tilt of his head, he was still gazing up at the roof, expecting shots from there. With care he lowered his rifle and did as instructed, then began walking in towards the hex. Var moved towards the window, detaching the mostly used-up clip from her rifle and slotting a new one into place. She vaulted the sill, boots thumping on to the dusty ground. His head jerked back down, seeing her now. She walked out towards him, closing the gap until they stood just five metres apart.

"The base personnel will understand," he ventured anxiously.

"Yes," she replied, "they certainly will."

She pulled the trigger and watched him dance for a moment, then tumble backwards through a cloud of dust. The base personnel would certainly understand that this man wasn't worth the precious air it took to keep him breathing.

ARGUS STATION

Twenty people waited in the control room. These included Langstrom, Peach and Mustafa, escorting a thin man with cropped grey hair standing hunched over in his prison overalls. There were also thirteen frightened-looking staff Saul had summoned, all of them clad in the same sort of technician's garb worn by Chang and the twins, who were also present. Saul glanced at Hannah and nodded to the console they had used earlier. Understanding at once, she moved over to it, then turned and stood with her arms folded. Saul moved past this small crowd to gaze out across Argus Station, leaving them hovering and unsure about what they should do. He didn't need to look round to know that the spidergun now loomed in the doorway. Even without the multiple views he could summon the sudden terrified stillness would have told him enough.

"You are Robert Le Roque," he began, still without turning.

"I am," the thin ex-prisoner agreed, straightening up and stepping away from Langstrom to move to the fore.

"Formerly technical director of this entire station?" Saul now turned to focus on the man.

"Until Political Director Smith decided otherwise." Le Roque smiled nastily and glanced towards Langstrom. "But Director Smith is currently being processed into fertilizer for the Arboretum, so he has turned out to be unexpectedly useful in the end."

"Yes, the station digesters are going to be busy for some time yet."

Le Roque folded his arms, as if feeling cold, and continued, "So what are your intentions now, and what do you want with me?"

Saul studied the man a moment longer. Certainly, to have reached the rank of Technical Director of this station, Le Roque must have had some less than savoury aspects to his past. But, having studied the extensive data filed in the Political Office, Saul knew political manoeuvring was not the main reason for this man's promotion. Le Roque was highly intelligent and capable; in fact if he had been less so, he would have ended up in a cell long ago, for he had been far too much of a free thinker

"I want you to resume the position you held here previously," said Saul. "I want you, and your staff here"—he gestured to the others present—"to prepare everyone aboard Argus Station for the moment when, in twenty-three hours' time, it swings about the Moon and I again fire up the Traveller engine to put us on a course for Mars."

Shock registered on the man's face, amid gasps from others in the room. Le Roque, however, recovered quickly. "And if I'm not willing?"

Saul shrugged. "I'll find someone else, then. But you and everyone here must understand," he surveyed the group before him, "that there's no going back. So food, water and air cannot be wasted on those who will not work for the survival of all aboard."

The expressions of shock were still there, but in some faces he could see the kind of cowed acceptance that resulted from a lifetime of being ground down by the Committee. There would be, he knew, some here—and throughout the rest of the station—who had loved ones down on Earth who they had expected to return to, and he had now taken that option away from them. Part of him wanted to offer them some solution but, having set himself firmly on this course, he simply could not afford to expend valuable resources such as those space planes out on the docking pillars. Also, he could not afford to show the slightest sign of weakness. What would they be returning to anyway? Even a brief inspection of the data flooding Govnet rendered the expected results. If they thought they would just disembark from those planes and return to normal lives down there, they were sadly mistaken. Perhaps he should now acquaint them with some of the facts.

"You realize, I hope," he said, "that even if you made it down safely to one of the space-plane runways on Earth, your first port of call would be an adjustment cell—where you would be interrogated until every last detail of what has happened here was extracted from you. After that there would be no release either—whatever authority remains down there would not want you blabbing your story to anyone else. Already the Committee "press officers" are at work, and Govnet is flooded with news of a successful test run of the Argus network, and the successful repositioning of the Argus Station."

He let that sink in for a moment, before turning back to Le Roque.

"What about…after?" The man's voice caught in his throat. "After we're safely on course for Mars? What will you want of me then?"

"I'll want you to get everyone onboard the station back to work, all previous maintenance schedules adhered to, the self-sustaining programmes recommenced and the researchers in Arcoplex Two back on the job. I also want the entire station secured for space flight, strengthening made wherever required, the tubeways fully completed, and work started on a full enclosure of the inner station."

"We will need the smelting plants back online," observed Le Roque.

Saul nodded towards the Moon now beginning to recede behind the Argus Station. "After we swing round the Moon, the smelters can once again be extended. They will continue to function with the existing arrays of mirrors for seven months, though with declining efficiency, and we can extend that period by manufacturing more mirrors."

"Mars?" said Le Roque.

"Yes."

Le Roque grimaced towards the others before refocusing on Saul. He ran a hand down his yellow overalls. "I would like to change out of these before I get to work."

"Of course." Saul gestured towards the door of the man's former apartment. "I want you to move your personal effects later to Smith's quarters in the Political Office, which I notice are more capacious than your apartment here. After that you can convert the control centre located there into a secondary version of this one." Saul stabbed a finger down at the floor. "I'm sure you'll find a better use for the rest of the Political Office—I note manufacturing space has been tight while valuable resources were squandered there, and also on the cell block."

Le Roque nodded briefly, and departed.

Saul turned to Chang and the twins. "Anything you want," he said. "Within obvious limits."

Brigitta glanced at her sister. "We want to transfer to Robotics." She paused as if not quite sure how far to push it. "Will you be running this place like Smith did?"

"No," Saul replied firmly, before turning to Langstrom. "As the new head of security here, you will now find that the list of punishable offences has been substantially reduced, so reading it won't take you long. All of the sections headed "Political Subversion" have been deleted, and you will be receiving no instructions from the Political Office. That's because it has ceased to exist, and you answer to me alone."

The legal system here had been merely a straight upload from Earth: unless something was actually approved, it was considered illegal—Roman law—but with the extra twist that all "offenders" were deemed guilty until proved innocent. Judgement and sentencing was delivered by an Inspectorate Executive, who would also have investigated the alleged "crime" they sat judgement upon. The catalogue of such crimes, their parameters nicely vague and open to Inspectorate interpretation, had been huge, but it took Saul less than a minute to hack it down by nearly 90 per cent. It was now not a crime, for example, to suggest that your food ration tasted "funny"—an offence that had merited being "interviewed" for five hours by an Inspectorate Exec, assisted by two enforcers and a pain inducer.

Langstrom looked thoroughly surprised as Saul continued, "Your men will only carry ionic tasers and nightsticks, and your main duty will be to ensure civilian order. However, I have some other chores for you to complete before then. First you must ensure that everyone is released from the cell block, and that all Smith's toys there are decommissioned."

One of those in the cell block was the food critic. His subversive criticism of the Committee had resulted in a two-day period of adjustment after his "interview." With the right treatment he might be able to recommence his job in Atmosphere Management in a month or so, when he regained control of his bowels and stopped dribbling.

"Very well," began Langstrom. "I've never really agreed—"

"I'm not interested in your opinion, Langstrom. I will judge you later by your actions." Langstrom kept silent as Saul continued, "Your next task will be to round up the entire executive staff of the Political Office, plus certain other unpleasant individuals who work under them—I've already forwarded a list to your computer."

It hadn't been difficult to draw up this list. The Executive contained few redeemable souls at the top, and those in the lower ranks who seemed destined for promotion all demonstrated the kind of inherent nastiness and lack of empathy required for future exalted positions. Saul quickly tired of studying the records of these people, and it had been simplicity itself to create a search engine fit for the exercise.

"You'll then take them all to Arcoplex One," he finished, "where they will join Chairman Messina and his surviving delegates."

At that, many in the room exclaimed in surprise, and he turned towards them.

"Yes," he said, "Chairman Messina and fifty of his core delegates are currently detained in Arcoplex One until Hannah here decides their fate. They are sharing their accommodation with the two thousand corpses resulting from the nerve gas Messina's troops employed as they boarded the station." Saul paused, seeking the right tone. "That way our political elite can quickly acquaint themselves with digester technology."

One of the staff let out a bark of laughter, then abruptly looked frightened. Others, too, showed shocked amusement, before dipping their heads to hide their expressions.

"Laughter is not an offence," Saul declared mildly. He turned back to Langstrom. "Any questions?"

"None I can think of right now."

"You and your men must adhere to the laws of this station too," Saul warned. "Since you'll be in a position of trust, any infringements will call for a harsher punishment than is dealt out to ordinary civilians."

"Understood." Langstrom would do as instructed—he had risen in the ranks rather than ended up in a digester. Saul gestured towards the door, and Langstrom set off.

"Does that answer your question?" Saul asked Brigitta.

"Some," she replied. "But how much freedom are we going to be allowed?"

"How do you measure it?" Saul asked.

"The Arboretum?" Angela asked.

Brigitta picked up on that. "We were never allowed in there."

"Unless there are contamination problems I don't see why that should continue." Saul paused for a moment. "Everyone here will have the freedom to go where they want within this station. You will all have the freedom to do whatever you want so long as the work is done and whatever else you do does not endanger others or this station."

"I hope you're telling the truth," said Brigitta.

"I am."

"Better living conditions would be nice. Better food too."

"You three can take apartments in the Political Office." He paused, checking the assignment of living accommodation and beginning to make alterations.

"I have just reassigned you to Inspectorate Executive quarters. Once building recommences in Arcoplex Two, and the living accommodation is completed there, you'll be reassigned to apartments near the robot assembly plant and the research laboratory." Saul waited a moment for a response, and when none came, he turned to Chang. "And you?"

"I'll stay here," Chang replied, nodding towards the nearby consoles. "But one of those PO apartments would be nice."

"It's done," said Saul, then turned to the others and gestured to the consoles lining the back of the control room. "Okay, grab your chairs and take your positions." He beckoned to Le Roque, now returned clad in a padded overall. "Get them ready."

As Chang, the twins and the thirteen remaining moved quickly to their various consoles, Le Roque headed over beside Hannah and gazed for a moment at the bullet-damaged console, then stepped away to select another one. They began powering up, and Saul watched them for a moment. Meanwhile he called up separate views on the three wall screens: the middle screen displaying a distant view of Earth, and those on either side relaying orbital views transmitted from the laser satellites.

"You seem to have everything well under control," Hannah commented as he approached her.

Saul went on studying the screens. "I see no purpose in wasting resources on regimenting every detail of people's lives, nor on trying to control how they think."

"There'll be problems later."

As Saul accessed the control systems for the entire array of laser satellites spaced around the Earth, he acknowledged to himself that, yes, there would be problems. But the niggling, annoying problems of administration, of *government*, would perhaps be the least of them. For a start, it was by no means certain that the station could be made utterly self-sufficient, or that they could ultimately survive out here.

"The people here are used to being told what to do, and when they begin to realize that I am not instructing them all the time, that's when the problems will start. It's also going to be difficult for those currently redundant," he said. "I'll need to decide what to do with all those bureaucrats who've spent most of their working lives driving a desk and enforcing misery on others."

"Do the digesters often need cleaning?"

"Generally not, though those in Arcoplex One might develop faults." He glanced at her. "Have you made a decision yet?"

Hannah winced.

And well she might. A glimpse into Arcoplex One revealed that the digesters had yet to be put to use. Chairman Messina, accompanied by forty-one delegates and a further twenty bodyguards, had pushed his way to the head of the queue and entered first. They had then occupied a conference hall and were currently debating the agenda, having thus far merely drawn up a list of important subjects to be considered—such as the assignment of living quarters, a resources survey, their negotiating position and who would chair the escape-assessment working group. No one had yet got round to mentioning the corpses, of which only a few had been found so far, the majority occupying private quarters or piled up at the far end of the arcoplex. The situation seemed beyond satire, and Saul wondered how long it would take before this "hard-headed organizational approach to extreme circumstances" completely fell apart.

"Most of them are guilty of murder," Hannah suggested.

"Every single Committee delegate has been responsible, to some extent, for mass murder. They're also ultimately responsible for every other atrocity the Inspectorate has committed."

She turned to look at him. "Nuremberg?"

"We don't have the resources."

"I have to think more about this."

She bowed her head and Saul thought she looked ashamed. He decided then that he would burden her with no further decisions of life and death. He caught hold of her shoulder and directed her across the control room, towards the door through into Le Roque's former quarters. As they walked, he summoned the spidergun in behind him.

"You must sleep on it," he said, as she went through the door ahead of him, then he turned to see Le Roque eyeing him curiously. "We're not to be disturbed," Saul declared, before closing the door behind them. He watched through the spidergun's sensors, whilst Hannah moved over to the hammock and pulled herself down on to it, its fabric adhesion clinging to her suit. By the time the multi-limbed robot had squatted down outside the door, and raised two of its weapon-bearing limbs warningly, Hannah was already fast asleep.

Saul soon joined her, but some time still passed before he descended to a level of humanity where sleep again became possible for him.

22

YOUR VOTE COUNTS

Democracy is a luxury enjoyed by simple low-population societies, though wealth can maintain it for longer than its natural span. However, societies grow in population and complexity, the technological apparatus of control improves, individual freedoms impinge upon others until they demand "action" from government that is generally eager to comply and accrue more power to itself, and democracy gradually sickens and dies. This is what happened on Earth, but out in space democracy dies a different death. On ancient Earth all the necessities of life were free to every potential user: air, food and water, the materials from which to build a shelter or craft the tools of survival. As we built more complex societies, more and more items on this list fell under the control of others, and ceding such control is the way we forge our own chains. Out in space, every single item on such a list has to be either transported there or produced there at great cost, under the control of small specialist groups, or the regime which put the project up in vacuum. Also in space, where decisions about survival must often be made quickly, there is rarely time for full debate, for a vote. In space, meritocracy is the nearest to democracy you can hope to get, and neither of them are rugged survivors.

A long grassy slope curved ever downwards away from her, and as she ran it grew steadily steeper. Eventually she would fall, but she knew all she required in order to fly was an effort of will. Shortly the slope disappeared from beneath her…but at that moment she knew she could only fly in her dreams, and so she fell. When dream slid into reality, the sensation of falling did not leave her even as she opened her eyes.

"How long was I asleep?" she asked.

Saul was naked, towelling himself down vigorously after using the shower. Hannah could not help but notice how he showed no sign of sensitivity when rubbing the area where he had been stabbed, which meant the wound must have continued healing at the same speed she had witnessed while she had been operating on him. She sat up, licking her tongue round a dry mouth. She felt grotty and was momentarily tempted to lie back and go to sleep again, but instead her guts tightened and a familiar feeling of panic arose. She closed her eyes and tried to calm herself.

"You okay?" Saul asked.

"Panic attack," she explained, and saying it out loud seemed to help her get a handle on it and suppress it. And even as the weight of the *decision* he expected from her descended again, she managed to stave it off. It was time to do something about those people in Arcoplex One. They weren't entitled to cause her such grief.

"They're not all guilty," she remarked.

He didn't even ask who she referred to, his mind operating so fast. "Define guilt."

"I believe it is no more than can be attributed to many others on this station." She stood and took off her VC suit and underclothes, then headed for the shower. "Messina is as guilty as hell, as are his core delegates and whatever staff implemented their decisions. But there must be members of staff, bodyguards, wives, husbands and children who are no more guilty than anyone else you'll find out there." She pointed to the door leading to the control centre, before propelling herself into the shower booth.

The spray was good and hot, as she washed away the grime, clouding the water with soap till she seemed to be floating in a pool of milk. As she came out of the shower, she found Saul standing motionless, his gaze distant.

"Forty-one delegates, plus Messina himself, have been involved in the decisions about sectoring, and the euthanizing of dissidents. All of those have blood on their hands, as do most of their staff and some of their family members. Most of the Executive present here are killers, too. However," he now focused his gaze on her, "how exactly do we measure guilt? They are all of them the product of a society where the only route to power and wealth was a career in government, and it was impossible to rise high anywhere in this regime without getting blood on your hands. Bucking the trend in any way would be suicidal, and altruism a fast route to poverty—and quite possibly to readjustment in an Inspectorate cell."

"Then the buck stops with Messina and his forty-one delegates," decided Hannah. "And anyone else who has directly ordered or committed an act of murder."

Saul blinked. "That means thirty-eight more, then, according to their records."

A tightness returned to Hannah's stomach, but this time it wasn't panic but a strange species of excitement—and awe. While just standing there, he must be processing hundreds of personnel files, running searches, decoding govspeak and assessing every one of all those people currently confined in Arcoplex One.

"The others must be allowed to leave the arcoplex," she declared.

"What do I do with them?" he shot back.

"Assign them quarters and find them work to do throughout the station. Give them a chance to redeem themselves."

Saul gave a doubtful sneer. "Generally, their skills aren't of the kind the station requires. These people are bureaucrats now deprived of their natural environment of endless micromanagement and interference."

"Then they must be retrained on the basis of whatever other skills they possess."

"Very well." Saul headed for the door. "But you still haven't told me what you want done with the remaining seventy-nine."

He wanted her to tell him that they must die but, even though she knew they did not deserve to live, she could not bring herself to make that pronouncement. In her eyes it wasn't right. No one should be forced to make such a harsh decision.

"They will remain in Arcoplex One," she pronounced, with as much firmness as she could muster. "Their task will be to feed the corpses into the digesters."

"And then?"

"Surely there is a way they can be dealt with?"

"Yes, I am sure there is a way," he said, staring at her while something hardened in his expression. "Let's go."

"Food first," said Hannah quickly.

He paused. "Yes…of course."

Hannah suddenly wanted to rage at the unfairness of it all, but instead she merely turned away. She found a fresh elasticated undersuit in one of the wall-length cupboards, then picked up her discarded one and just stood staring at it helplessly. Saul turned away from the fridge and pointed to a little door set in the same wall. Hannah pulled on the handle, hinged out a hopper, and tossed the soiled undersuit inside.

"Where does it go?" she asked, prepared to talk about anything but the previous subject.

"Ultrasound and gas cleaner," he replied succinctly. "All clothing worn here is made of material suitable for that kind of cleaning."

"One more job the bureaucrats can't do," she muttered as she pulled on her VC suit. Meanwhile he placed the two ceramic trays into a microwave cooker, and shortly she joined him to eat bean stew, followed by some sort of treacle pudding. A drinks machine provided frothy coffee and chilled bottles of flavoured water. It all seemed so very domestic, though the coffee had to be sipped through a spout, and the emptied trays went into the ultrasound cleaner, along with their dirty clothes.

"Now," said Saul, leading the way out after they had finished.

***

A different shift of staff occupied the control room now, though Le Roque remained in charge. Meanwhile, a crew of technicians was gradually replacing the plastic office chairs with the kind of acceleration chairs found aboard space planes.

"Good thinking," observed Saul, as Le Roque wearily turned to face them.

"We could take more out of the planes, but I wasn't sure if that's what you'd want."

"The chairs from the one space plane you've selected should cover your present needs."

After a momentary look of surprise at this, Le Roque said, "I don't suppose I'll be needing to make a further report to you then?"

It was something they would all have to get used to. Saul might stand amongst them like a normal human being, yet his mind could range throughout the Argus Station with the omniscience of a demigod.

"I can detect what you've done so far," concurred Saul. "All personnel are now aware of the direction of thrust, and where to position themselves, though they're not yet aware of the duration of thrust, which will be two hours at one-half gravity. You've prepared the hospitals, I see, and are presently getting everything loose tied down or securely placed on gecko matting. You should have everything ready within the next thirteen hours. Any additional problems I should know about?"

"The Arboretum, and hydroponics there and also in the outer ring," Le Roque replied.

Saul paused for a moment, tilting his head, then said, "The Arboretum topsoil is layered with a mesh into which most of the trees are rooted. That was done so they would not break free of the soil should it be necessary to use the emergency brakes on the cylinder. The mesh should be enough, and the hydroponics there should be fine too. Those troughs situated in the outer ring need to be drained into their cisterns. Do this precisely half an hour before acceleration and, whilst under acceleration, you should set the misters to operate constantly. That treatment should be sufficient to keep the plants alive."

"But some will get thrown free?"

Saul shook his head. "No, I'm going to use only a gradual increase in thrust. Inside the cylinder there will simply be an increasing fluctuation in apparent gravity, from half a gee to one and a half gees. There'll inevitably be damage to some plants—an approximate fifteen per cent loss—but we can live with that. Anything else?"

"That about covers it for now, Dir—" Le Roque paused, looking uncomfortable.

"I do not like the title 'Director,'" said Saul, sharply. "It's got too many unpleasant associations." Another reflective pause. "Call me by my name but, if you're not comfortable with that, then refer to me as the Owner—because I own this station now."

Le Roque merely nodded, then watched while Saul led Hannah towards the exit, the spidergun falling in behind them and now moving with a spooky fluidity it had not possessed earlier.

"Where now?" Hannah asked.

"Arcoplex One—I want this resolved before we round the Moon."

Once out of the control room, she queried, "The Owner?"

"For all our lives, everything we've laid hands on has been considered the property of the state. Even our own bodies were considered thus. But no more." He turned towards her, his face a mask pinned by weirdly pink eyes.

"Decisions, power, responsibility, Hannah. I am now the most powerful here and therefore the most free, yet inevitably, I am also the least free because I bear the most responsibility."

"That still doesn't explain it."

She caught a glimpse of irritation in his expression.

"I am now in charge and, whether I want it or not, I have the power of life and death over all those here with me, because I physically and mentally *own* this station, which is the only thing keeping them alive. In fact this entire station now feels to me just like an extension of my own body. It's something I will not give up, which is something they all need to be reminded of, and the title I've chosen does exactly that. I won't call myself Director, Delegate, Chairman, Governor or King. From now on I'm the Owner—that is enough."

Arrogance or truth? Perhaps both. Hannah just did not know for sure. Maybe his choice of title incorporated a degree of calculation that went beyond what he could easily express to her. She wondered if the irritation he had just shown was due to her tardy comprehension, though more likely it was because she still refused to sentence seventy-nine people to death.

They collected their helmets at the airlock and were soon back outside in the main station. Here Hannah could see crews busily engaged, welding arcs faring blue light across the lattice walls, work lights glaring white and casting black angular shadows, one-man EVA units moving ponderously here and there amidst the rapid insectile precision of countless robots.

"This is not going to be a democracy," Saul reminded her over com.

"That's a political system that probably can't work satisfactorily out in space," Hannah admitted. "It has to be a Captain and his crew." Then she couldn't help adding, "Or the Owner and the owned."

Saul merely snorted.

As they reached the base of Arcoplex One, two more spiderguns approached them down the length of the cylinder, like dogs eager to greet their masters, joining them just as Saul and Hannah propelled themselves up towards the endcap. The spiderguns proceeded first through the airlock, but on the other side Hannah saw no one they needed guarding against. She reached up to detach her helmet, but Saul caught her arm.

"The levels of putrescence in the air here have risen substantially," he advised. "Better remove it when we are a little further in."

Only then did Hannah notice the flies gathered around the blood-crusted mouth of a nearby corpse.

"Are all Messina's people confined in here now?" she asked, as they moved away from the mounded bodies and along a concave street.

"They're all here," he confirmed. "Messina and his delegates broke off for a recess after two hours of *exhausting* debate, and they have now secured themselves suitable apartments after ordering their staff to clear them of the previous occupants. Some of the staff even started using a digester to dispose of the corpses, but were ordered to desist until the Committee came to a decision on the matter."

"Are they total idiots?"

"No, just mentally hardwired, still adhering to the old hierarchy—whilst Messina himself can't accept that he now rules nothing."

It seemed they were now far enough away from the endcap, because Saul removed his VC helmet and hung it from a hook on his belt. As Hannah removed her own, she detected some of the stink. Perhaps those already here for a while hadn't noticed the smell increasing. But they would definitely notice once the corpses began crawling with maggots.

Ahead, now, Hannah could see people on the move, all of them heading for a large building extending right up to the central spindle of the cylinder. Many of them kept looking back towards her and Saul, while trying to propel themselves along faster. She glanced at Saul questioningly.

"I ordered them all to their conference chamber. The place has room to contain all of them, and is equipped with large screens."

"And what images will you display on them?"

"Enough, let's hope, to burn out some of that hardwiring."

***

Govnet opened up like a whore eager to get her business over with, and virally dispatching copies of the programs he was running aboard the station proved easier still. He particularly needed to shift round vast blocks of data, but not necessarily in his own mind, so he just hijacked a range of computer systems down on Earth and let them do the work instead. All this meant was that it would all take just a little longer to kick off. Essentially he was doing, on a vaster scale, what he had already done aboard the station at large, and this time no other comlife stood in his way. Leaving processes running, he now focused a small proportion of his attention elsewhere.

"Langstrom," he said, uttering the name merely in his mind, as he saw the new Security Director suiting up along with forty of his men.

Langstrom looked up. "I hear you."

"I want you positioned at the base of Arcoplex One. Some people will be coming out soon, and I want them escorted to their assigned quarters both inside the ring and in the worker units situated within the lattice walls. I've already sent the details to your palmtop."

"Chairman Messina?" Langstrom prompted.

"Is not your concern."

Saul refocused his attention on the activity within Arcoplex One.

Delegates arriving in the conference chamber were obviously annoyed to see so many others present and started gesturing back to the walls any who had the temerity to gather about the tiers of horseshoe tables and chairs. No sign of Messina there—he was still in his apartment questioning two of his bodyguards about where the other two had gone. The missing pair were already in the chamber, one clutching the hand of his young daughter whilst the other leant back against the wall, arms folded and his expression sour. Saul had already checked on an earlier discussion between them, whose content was little different from so many he had already heard. Messina was fucked, they had agreed, and now the time had come for them to look after themselves. Out of curiosity, Saul reviewed the data on these two men. The one called Ghort, leaning against the wall, had not actually killed anyone, so under Hannah's terms was salvageable. Unfortunately the one with the daughter had eagerly dispensed Messina's personal justice in the past, and even kept image files of the proceedings.

Finally Saul and Hannah themselves reached the entrance to the building containing the conference chamber. There he paused, gazing along the length of the arcoplex. It seemed not all had answered his summons. Two were in fact hiding nearby, in a room where they had first smashed all the cams. A recorded video showed them entering the place, while the station net had registered the toilet being used only a minute ago.

"If you do not both go to the conference chamber straight away, I will have to send a spidergun after you," he announced loudly, via the intercom inside their refuge. Hannah turned to him in puzzlement, then swung her gaze to follow his. After a minute a door opened and a couple of people propelled themselves out. They abandoned their hide at a reluctant pace, but speeded up once they registered the spiderguns.

"There, that's all of them," declared Saul, folding his arms.

"We were—" began Delegate Margot Le Blanc, as she approached him with her bodyguard.

Saul waved her inside. "I don't care what you were. And that's something you'll all have to learn very quickly."

"Very well." Delegate Le Blanc swept on past, her dignity somewhat diminished by her lack of experience in using gecko boots.

After a moment, Saul dispatched one of the spiderguns after her, while simultaneously watching through cams as Messina finally quit his apartment and entered the conference chamber. The Chairman took the prime seat at the horseshoe tables, and only when properly seated with his two remaining bodyguards behind him did he gesture imperiously and the delegates took their seats. As Le Blanc hurried in and sat down, Messina eyed her calculatingly. He seemed just about to say something, but then the spidergun entered. Some delegates leapt from their seats and began backing off, while an uproar arose among the surrounding crowd as they retreated further against the walls.

Saul grinned. "Let's go."

Entering the lobby, they climbed a spiral stair two floors up, then took a short corridor to the double doors leading into the chamber. These had meanwhile swung closed, muffling the uproar inside. This entire building, Saul had discovered, had been planned as the Committee base inside the station. The three tiers of horseshoe tables within the chamber had seating for no more than a hundred and fifty, so it seemed to have been intended for Messina and his core delegates only. Whether the remaining delegates were due to have been assassinated, or just abandoned on Earth, he did not know. He stepped up to the doors, with Hannah at his side and the second spidergun close behind.

"What do you want me to do?" she asked.

"You've not made your decision," he replied, pausing, "and I now realize you may be incapable of making one."

"But it's not my decision," she said. "You've already decided that Messina and the rest must die, and you just want me to confirm that."

"No, I want you to perceive the correct course." He turned to her, wishing he could force her into seeing what was so plain to him. "Tell me, if we were back on Earth, with unlimited resources, what would you do with them there?"

"Try them, then send them to prison for life," she replied. "They're guilty of too much wrongdoing to ever be released, and if they were released they would only scrabble for power again. They would never be genuinely useful."

"So a trial would be irrelevant because you already know they are guilty. It would just paint a gloss of justice over a course of action that is already just."

"Some might be innocent..."

"No, not among the seventy-nine."

Hannah shrugged, looked away.

He continued, "This Argus Station is not Earth, and its resources are severely limited. Keeping this lot alive, whilst they contribute nothing, would definitely mean others here dying. So what is the right decision?"

With her face still averted, she replied, "They should die." She then turned to him, her expression registering shock at her own words. Doubtless she was now telling herself that she was equally as bad as those she had judged. He tried not to feel contempt for her weakness.

"I am glad to hear you say that at last. Now consider this point: It has been within your power to sentence those people to death, but it is also within your power to allow them to live—and within your power alone. When the time is right, I am going to ask you whether I can offer them the choice."

She was clearly confused, for she hadn't yet seen that other option, but eventually she would.

He continued, "As for what I want you to do now, just go wherever you feel comfortable."

"I'd feel more comfortable not being here."

He glanced at her. "Which was exactly the position of many decision makers within the Committee who had dissidents killed or drew up the plans for sectoring."

Hannah showed further discomfort at that statement, but stayed by his side as he pushed open the double doors and strode through, heading straight out into the middle of the chamber. Behind him, he had one of the robots remain on guard at the door, whilst the second climbed the wall and scuttled across the ceiling, positioning itself up above like some macabre chandelier. The uproar quickly waned, for they were frightened, but from Saul's presence they now knew they weren't facing instant extinction.

For a moment he scanned the faces all around him. Seated as many were, they obviously felt themselves to be in a superior position, but no matter. In a bit of theatre, he waved his hand, and the six massive screens ranged high on the walls all around the room flickered on. The views he chose for three of the screens were the same as those displayed previously in Tech Central: one of Earth from the station, another of Earth from cams on the Argus satellites, and finally a view of some of the satellites themselves.

Messina cleared his throat. "What can we do for you, citizen?"

Most of those present were wearing fones, but some were not. Saul nodded towards a fourth screen, routeing through to it a list of the names of everyone in the chamber, excluding the seventy-nine. "There are one hundred and fifteen of you here who are, from the available evidence, not directly responsible for the murder of citizens you governed. You will see your names are on this list and, as soon as I have finished here, you may depart forthwith to quarters assigned to you."

"Doubtless my name is not there," said Messina.

Saul turned to face him. "No, it is not."

"So you intend to kill me and everyone else not on your precious list," Messina suggested, with lazy contempt.

"That decision is not mine, and has yet to be made." Saul eyed him steadily. "Some seem to find it more difficult to pass a death sentence than you do, Alessandro Messina."

"Perhaps that's because they are not properly elected representatives of the people," the Chairman replied. "These last few years have needed some hard decisions about the very survival of the human race." He sat up straighter and stabbed a finger towards Saul. "It seems to me that you yourself are demonstrating that you do not have the strength of character to make such decisions. You treat us with spite, whilst running away from Earth and all that must be done there."

"Yes, I may be fleeing Earth," Saul replied, "but I have nevertheless made some decisions." Again he waved a hand towards the screens. "Twenty-three of your satellite lasers are still functional, and they can each fire a shot every two seconds. They could keep that rate of fire up for five days, until depleting their fusion reactors of fuel."

Messina glanced at the delegate sitting beside him, a woman with her hands poised over an open laptop, and with some very sophisticated fones seemingly welded against her head. Saul knew her to be officially the delegate for New Zealand and the Antarctic Region, but that was an empty title since she was primarily Messina's personal statistical analyst.

"Yes," Messina continued, having just received some figures from her. "Enough to kill five million people."

"Not nearly enough," said Saul. A rumble of whispered conversation broke out, and hissed like a wave over shingle. Saul noted Hannah staring at him, appalled, but he kept his eyes on Messina as he added, "However, I have some extra proposals."

"Oh, yes?" The Chairman sat forward. Obviously the word "proposals" gave him the odd idea that he still retained some influence over events.

Saul changed the screen views, adding two more on the blank screens.

"Even though this station may be moving away from Earth, I still have access to Govnet," he informed Messina.

One screen now showed an aerial shot of a mass of buildings protected by high fences, and it was possible to see the readergun towers surrounding the place, and the hundreds of aero gunships lined up, row upon row, across an enclosed landing field. On the other four screens views appeared briefly only to be replaced by new ones. Some of these Saul snatched from ground-level cams operating in bright sunlight: they showed armed enforcers departing a gunship, armoured groundcars, a cell complex, warehouses, government bureaucrats hurrying busily to some new assignment, yet more enforcers overseeing prisoners clad in yellow boiler suits as they rolled drums out of a warehouse; several Inspectorate execs up on a roof, peering at something in the distance through image amplifiers, with the familiar shape of a spidergun squatting behind them.

"One of you here will recognize this place," Saul remarked.

"Inspectorate HQ Brazilia East," stated a swarthy individual who was seated five seats over to Messina's right.

"Of course you recognize it, Delegate De Sousa. It cost eight hundred billion, approximately ninety-three per cent of one year's budget, to build it, and brought forward by ten years the expected famine in South America, at a further cost, thus far, of over a hundred and eighty million human lives."

"Hard choices," replied De Sousa. "They were going to die anyway."

"Yes, quite. Billions are due to die anyway, and many of you here have been busy running the selection process." Saul paused. "Just prior to your departure, De Sousa, food riots broke out in central Salvador, but now no one goes hungry there since, on your way up here, you ordered your people to drop nerve gas. Under your orders, too, they're presently struggling to sector the North Salvador sprawl, but power outages keep taking the readerguns offline and therefore ZAs keep escaping."

"And what would *your* solution be?" Messina asked.

"You're about to find out."

Saul was already beyond the confines of the chamber, mentally, delicately tuning programs that controlled massive data flows. It was as if he was manipulating screen icons that governed the rotation of tornadoes or the rolling force of tsunamis.

***

Hannah felt like a child that had been summoned to her political officer to receive a lecture. With only herself and Saul and the spiderguns here, she still felt wrong-footed, in an inferior position, for surrounding her were some of the recently most powerful people on Earth. She wanted to fold up inside herself and disappear.

"Is all this drama strictly necessary?" Messina demanded. "Are you really using the hard decisions we were forced to make to justify killing us?"

He still sounded so superior, so in control.

"No, I need no justification for that."

Even as Saul said this, Hannah felt something akin to embarrassment. Why was he revealing all this? Certainly it could not be for the benefit of those here. It seemed more like grandstanding, showing off. Or was he demonstrating all this to himself, simply to justify the actions he was about to take? Could it even be extra data for her to integrate, so she could offer all those present that mysterious *choice* he had mentioned?

"Then there's HQ Athens." New pictures appeared on the screens instantly. "The Greeks, being such a contentious people, started rioting early. The enforcers don't have so much to do there now: merely deploying spiderguns to hunt down the remaining dissidents hiding among the olive groves." Here came a scene of ragged refugees running from a dilapidated stone building.

Sound now, too: Hannah was sure she could hear the sea over the pistoning of hydraulics and the drone of an aero's fans. Then came the crackle of high-speed machine-gun fire. Shots tracked across the fugitives and they all went down in a cloud of dust. As the viewpoint started to advance, she realized that the scene was actually being viewed through the eyes of a spidergun.

"I could go on and on," Saul continued. "But for every minute I stand here talking, your Inspectorate forces are exterminating, at their present average rate, one hundred and twenty thousand civilians across the entire globe."

Hannah turned to him abruptly. "You could stop it. You could stop the spiderguns," she pleaded. "You could ground the aeros, shut down the readerguns, shut down the shepherds. You could trash their computer systems."

As he turned towards her, she could see a bloody tear at the corner of his eye. "I could do all those things, but the infrastructure would still be there. Inspectorate enforcers would still be there, with their guns and their nerve gas. Some will then realize how it was done, and from where, and they'll take those readerguns, spiderguns, shepherds and aeros off Govnet, they'll shut down satellite com dishes, and switch over to different frequencies. It may take them days but eventually they'll cut me out of the circuit—a task all the easier as radio delays make my task ever more difficult. So, should I follow your suggestions?"

"You'll do precisely what you think best."

He returned his attention to the screens. "Yes, I think you may be right."

"And what is that?" Messina interjected.

"ID codes," he said. "And then infrastructure."

He pointed at the screens and everyone turned to watch, seeing the spidergun's point of view swinging round. A grounded aero slid into frame, Inspectorate enforcers fanning out from it. Shock registered in their expressions as the spidergun suddenly advanced towards them. One of them shouted something in Greek, Hannah did not know what. Machine guns sighed and picked them off the ground, tumbling them backwards in the dust.

"Fifteen million spiderguns, eight million shepherds and their numerous brethren," he recounted. "Now for the readerguns." He glanced again at Hannah. "As with the spiders, I loaded a complex virus which does one simple thing. It's now loading to their kill lists the ID codes of all local Inspectorate enforcers, execs, Committee officials and political officers."

"You cannot do this!" Messina roared. He stood up; some of the delegates stood as well.

Hannah only caught it at the last moment, as a spidergun here shifted. De Sousa, perhaps considering himself under as great a threat as Messina, raised something from his lap. The sound made by the robot weapon just seemed to ape that of the machines featuring on one of the screens, but the red streaks that issued from two of its limbs were painfully bright. Strapped into his seat, De Sousa juddered, fragments showering out of his back and all over the bodyguard behind him. The gun the delegate had held went flying upwards through the air. Screaming and shouting filled the chamber, and those of the crowd furthest from the exit swarmed towards it. But those nearest to it came face to face with the spidergun posted there and started pushing backwards, with the outcome a milling crush. More firing, and a bodyguard went spinning away with half his head gone, a female delegate vibrating in her seat, something like a make-up compact spilling out of her hand. Hannah found herself crouching, but couldn't remember dropping into that position.

"The spiderguns will only kill those of you stupid enough to draw weapons," Saul announced, his voice much amplified. "Just keep still!"

It took some minutes before the shouting stopped, before someone suffering hysterics was slapped into silence, and by the end of it the whole balance of the room had changed. Some of the delegates abandoned their chairs and joined the main crowd. Others sat alone, their staff and flunkeys having withdrawn. No longer a single entity, the crowd had now separated into protective huddles. Messina himself was leaning forward, his hands laid flat on the table before him. For the first time, he actually looked frightened. Hannah stood upright, edged closer to the real power in the room: Saul, standing there, still as a statue.

"A salutary reminder," he said, "that I can and will do this."

A number in the tens of thousands was now displayed at the bottom of a screen showing shepherds marching through some urban sprawl, and it began to rapidly increase. The views depicted changed constantly: a street somewhere with gunfire crackling across armoured cars, dead enforcers strewn all around; an aero gunship dropping out of the sky; blocks of offices now, Brussels perhaps, where corpses were strewn across the carbocrete and sheets of paper snowed from the sky. And during the time it took Hannah to fully register each scene, the number below had leapt into the hundreds of thousands.

"The aeros," Hannah managed, her throat dry.

A woman in the crowd was moaning loudly, pressing her hands over her face. Perhaps she was De Sousa's wife, or had some emotional tie to one of the others who had just died. Perhaps she recognized something from one of the screens, or simply did not like seeing her world being torn apart.

"If they're already airborne, I'm currently shutting down their engines. If they're on the ground I'm just feeding the same ID data to their antipersonnel guns," Saul explained.

Hannah wanted to beg him to stop, but was he actually wrong to commit such slaughter? Knowing that so many down on Earth would inevitably die, she could not think of any who deserved to die more. Also something ugly deep down inside her—some obscene voyeur—seemed to be taking righteous pleasure in this carnage.

Another scene appeared. Hannah recognized Maunsell Airport, just as a scramjet slammed down and disintegrated, spewing fire and debris over the edge and into the sea.

"Two thousand and forty scramjets are presently either airborne or in the process of landing or taking off. Their passengers will not be surviving the journey." His words fell like lead blocks amid a growing stillness.

Just then, a scramjet on one of the screens, crashing into a sprawl, buildings toppling.

"It's unfortunate," said Saul, "but there will inevitably be innocent casualties too."

"Isn't this…enough?" Hannah asked.

Saul indicated the figure flickering at the bottom of the screen. It took a moment for her to realize that the set of digits was now in the millions.

"No, I haven't finished yet. Even now, power is being cut to readerguns, spiderguns are being hit with EM weapons, and aeros are being taken off Govnet and switched over to manual control. I have already taken a large bite out of the Committee apparatus, but there's a larger bite I can still take."

Again the first views Hannah had seen, showing the satellite network arrayed about the Earth.

"Twenty-three lasers," he declared. "They are firing now, their target sectors primarily government installations. Five million is an overestimate, unless I reposition the lasers or become less selective in choosing sectors." He eyed her again. "Though only twenty-three lasers are currently operating, all seven thousand satellite drives are in perfect working order."

"What do you intend?" Hannah asked, and glanced at Messina, who was now focused on Saul like a rabbit mesmerized by a fox.

"The satellites are made of bubblemetal and each weighs upwards of five tonnes. They were even given ceramic shielding to armour them in the event of extraplanetary war—another one of those hugely wasteful Committee inefficiencies that no one thought to review later." He fixed his gaze on Messina for a moment. "As we know, the Committee has freed us from the likelihood of warfare."

Messina just licked his lips.

Saul swung his gaze around the chamber. "As such," he said, "the satellites can in most cases survive atmospheric re-entry. If we use the old-style nuclear weapons measurement of TNT yield, I calculate that the impact energy of each will be in the region of ten kilotonnes."

"Impact where?" some brave soul asked.

"I am still making the ballistics and re-entry calculations—which means I'm having to do some processing outside my head and in the Political Office mainframe. I should then be able to bring each satellite down within one square kilometre of its target area."

"Where?" Hannah repeated, when the previous questioner did not persist.

The overall view of Earth, seen on one screen, suddenly bloomed with seven thousand stars as all of the satellite drives fired up. Two of the screens now showed previous views, Inspectorate HQs Brazilia East and Athens, whilst a third and fourth showed other Inspectorate headquarters. The remaining screen still showed that same list of names.

"Where do you think?" He gestured to the screens. "There are just over eleven thousand world regional Inspectorate HQs, but I think I can take care of the main ones." He nodded to himself. "The first impacts will occur in the Asian Bloc, in about one hour and forty minutes." He raised a hand and immediately the spidergun at the door moved forward, leaving space behind and on either side of it. "Now, all those I have listed will exit this chamber and head towards the asteroid-side endcap. Those not on that list will remain here—and should they attempt to leave, they will die."

The main crowd made straight for the exit, almost falling over each other to get out, thronging down either side of the spidergun on their way. Even as Hannah watched, the machine swung one limb sideways and the weapon at the end of it spat red fire, just once. A woman was slammed back against the wall, the top of her head missing. Hannah did not get a chance to recognize the delegate, as her corpse was shoved to one side by the crowd.

"No warnings," Saul added.

Within minutes, only the designated murderers were left in the chamber—along with four corpses.

"Now, Hannah," said Saul. "I want to know if I can offer those who remain here the choice."

She stared up at the screens, and particularly at the one showing an Inspectorate HQ so very similar to her former prison: where she had done her research, where she had operated on people's minds and inserted ever more sophisticated hardware and bioware. In a place just like that she herself had invented the things that had made Saul what he now was. But in a similar place Smith had used similar hardware to erase the mind of the Saul she had once known and loved. Smith had used pain, because that was his personal preference and because the hardware in Saul's head had not been so sophisticated then. But now, using the new organic interfaces stored in Arcoplex Two, pain would no longer be necessary. It should be perfectly possible to rub out a human mind with the ease of wiping a computer file.

"Yes, you can offer them the choice," she replied.

ANTARES BASE

They had only two viable crawlers left. Var watched as the flat trailer towed behind one of them was loaded with the corpses from Hex Three, alongside Miska's, which had been recovered first.

"No reactor damage," reported Lopomac, over com. "But plenty of other stuff here is totally screwed."

"Is the hex recoverable?" Var enquired, now sitting in a chair back in her own quarters.

"We've got three replacement windows, and the rest can be sealed with regolith blocks. Martinez's crew is fetching all the materials now. Those aren't the possible problem, however."

"Possible problem?"

"Structural damage from the grenades. Martinez is in there right now, using ultrasound scan to check for it."

"Tell him to hand that job over to someone else," Var replied. "I want to see him and all the other chiefs of staff over in the Community Room in ten minutes. You and Carol, too."

"Still keeping the same chain of command?" Lopomac asked.

"We have to. Democracy and freedom are only available to societies that can afford the dithering and time wasting." She hated stating such a truth, because it sounded like it came right out of the Committee manual, but that didn't make it less valid.

Upon her return to Hex One, weariness had bludgeoned Var. With Lopomac and Carol, she then stepped into the Community Room to inform about a hundred and fifty personnel that the Inspectorate no longer had power over the base, and henceforth the technical staff would control it completely. There had been few questions to begin with; there never were many, since discussing orders or policy statements had never been allowed. Then Martinez had spoken up to ask some of the most relevant ones and, emboldened by his example, others then began to ask questions too. Silence fell again when Var informed them that the enforcers, execs and Ricard himself were all dead.

"Return to your duties, or to your beds if that's where you were," she urged them, "as I'm now going to my own. In the morning I want all the chiefs of staff assembled here at nine, when I'll tell you exactly what's happened—and what is going to happen."

Back in her own quarters, Var turned on her laptop and again took a look at image feeds from the satellites surrounding Earth. What she found there was utterly confusing at first but, on checking back through recorded footage from over the previous ten hours, the images began to make sense. It suddenly felt as if someone had grabbed hold of her intestines and twisted them, and the relevance of this to their own situation could not be denied. Since she had first studied the images from Earth, the situation had changed substantially, indeed catastrophically. She extracted the same footage for use later, at that morning meeting, then fell at once into a deep sleep.

***

Waking at six, Var showered and got some breakfast. Whilst she consumed scrambled eggs, she remembered Gisender telling her to never close her teeth here whilst eating, because the Martian grit made its way into every-thing.

After working with her laptop for nearly three hours, she had broken into and studied carefully a substantial portion of the Inspectorate database. She now had everything she needed and must use it to try and get things in order here. She finally closed the laptop and turned her gaze to the object lying on her bed. Undecided about wearing anything so blatant, she picked up the belt and its holstered side arm, studied it for a long moment, then abandoned it. She could not rule by force here, nor did she want to.

Next she turned to inspect herself in the wall mirror. Her spiky cropped hair gave her a boyish appearance, belied by a face subtly touched with make-up to make her look even harder, tougher, more capable. Var picked up her laptop, tucked it under her arm, and headed for the door.

Besides Lopomac and Carol, six chiefs of staff waited in the Community Room, along with a few of their subordinates. One was Martinez, a swarthy lump of a man who ran building and buildings maintenance, and particularly atmosphere security. Lopomac himself dealt with most of the other infra-structure, including water and power supply, air control and the recycling system, with Carol and formerly Miska acting as his lieutenants. Here also was Gunther, now assuming Kaskan's job as chief of Hydroponics and Ag-riculture. The three remaining were Chief Medical Officer Da Vinci, Rhone from Mars Science, which covered geology, meteorology and survey; and Leo from the Store, whose duties were to keep the base manifest and ensure the repair and maintenance of all equipment deployed on the base. They were now gathered around a single table, some sitting and some still standing. As Var entered, those seated stood up too, which seemed a good sign.

She headed to one end of the table, placing the laptop in front of her as she sat. The way to play this, she decided, was to approach it as business as usual—but without the political intervention from Earth. Following her lead, the others quickly took their seats.

"I assume you've all had a chance to see Le Blanc's broadcast?" she began. Nods all around and grim expressions. "Some of you will have learned more but, for the benefit of all, I'll go through it from the beginning. I'll meanwhile transmit the evidence to your personal computers." She paused to link her own laptop to the main screen on the wall, projecting an image of the first shepherd carrying Gisender's body.

"We all had our suspicions, mostly unvoiced, when Ricard cut Earth-com," she continued. "However, some of us—myself, Lopomac, Carol, Miska, Kaskan and Gisender—managed to free ourselves from surveillance long enough to discuss the matter and decide what to do about it. We arranged it so that one of us could go out and collect optic cable from the old Marineris radio station, meanwhile downloading from there the latest communications from Earth. It was Gisender who went, but what we didn't realize was that Ricard had access to the security cams in that station too. He saw what Gisender had found out, and had her murdered before she could return."

"How?" asked Gunther.

"One of the enforcers shot up her crawler from Shankil's Butte," Var replied, then went on covering the next events in cold detail: her removing of her ID implant so that she could go out and find out what had happened to Gisender; Le Blanc's broadcast, and then her own exchange with Ricard; all the stuff about the Travellers going into the Argus bubblemetal plants, and final rescue in fifteen to twenty years. By the lack of any interruption, she realized they had heard much of this already.

"So he intended cutting down on our population here, to make it easier to support those who remained?" suggested Da Vinci.

"Yes."

"How and who?"

"Not you," she replied. "I have the figures at hand now from the Inspectorate database. The plan was to gather one hundred and eight of the staff—those designated non-essential—here in Hex One, whilst moving the rest to Hex Three for an "Assessment Meeting," then to evacuate the air totally from Hex One. Ricard reckoned this would leave just enough people to keep the base running, but that wasn't the ultimate plan as far as Earth was concerned."

"They wanted us all to die," said Lopomac. "They planned for us to die as quietly and quickly as possible, using up as few resources and causing as little damage as possible, so as to leave this place intact for later reoccupation."

"You have proof of this?" asked Martinez.

Var shook her head. "No direct proof, but the most basic study of resource usage, which I have transmitted to your computers, allows us a lifespan here of five years, maybe a little longer. All living here now are essential, and without them, things would break down a lot quicker. Reduce the personnel and you don't stretch resources over a longer period, you just kill the base faster." After this introduction she went on to tell them the rest: how she herself had killed Inspectorate personnel; how Kaskan had killed the two in Hydroponics, and about his subsequent sacrifice. She noted some angry looks as she detailed the cutting of power to lure Ricard out, but, of course, as a result they had all been left sitting in the cold and dark waiting to die. She then bluntly informed them how she had killed Ricard, sensed their approval, realized that some were now looking at her with something approaching awe, or even fear. Finally she called up video footage recorded from around Earth.

"Whilst the three of us were preparing for Ricard's attack," she continued, "we found evidence of some sort of disturbance going on around Earth. Since then, it seems the action there has escalated. Here is recorded footage from over twenty hours ago."

"Mother of God!" Carol exclaimed.

"What the hell is this?" Martinez demanded.

Before answering, Var scanned the shocked faces around the table, let them take it in, begin to absorb the implications. "The Argus satellite network," she eventually explained, just as another ground-based explosion flared down on the night side of Earth. "When I recorded this, about half of the network was already gone. Someone's been dropping the satellites onto Earth. Something major is happening there."

"War?" Lopomac queried. "I did wonder —"

"Who with?" Gunther interrupted. "There's revolutionary groups down there, we know, but none of them has the resources to achieve something like this."

A spear of light cut across the night side, terminating in yet another blast.

"Civil war," declared Lopomac. "It's the only possible answer."

Var nodded, for that seemed to make sense. "A schism must have developed within the Committee. They're fighting each other."

Such huge events laid out there for them to witness, yet they had only one crucial point of relevance to what must now happen here on Mars.

"There's something else too," she said. "I'm not really sure what to make of it."

She flicked to another recorded view showing an object at extreme range but drawing rapidly closer.

"Argus Station," said Lopomac.

"It's on the move," said Var. "Someone must have fired up the Traveller engine on the surface of the asteroid."

"They're going to drop that thing on Earth?" said Carol, her voice hushed.

Var glanced across at her. "It doesn't seem so. Last time I checked, it was on a spiral orbit moving outwards from Earth. In fact that path should have intersected with the Moon's orbit some hours ago."

"They crashed it on the Moon?" gasped Carol. "I don't know," said Var, vexed that she hadn't checked the same feeds again this morning. But how important were they? Her co-workers had just seen enough that was of relevance to them, because it showed the truth of their own situation. Of course, she understood the concern of those here who still had family back on Earth. Her own brother might still be alive somewhere back there. There was just a chance that he hadn't ended up in an adjustment cell for, if anyone truly fitted the description her political officer had once applied to herself—*too dangerous to live, too valuable to kill*—it was her brilliant sibling, Alan Saul.

"But, in light of all this," she said acidly, "it seems likely that the rebuilding of Mars Travellers has been postponed way beyond the prediction of fifteen to twenty years. There might not be further missions heading out this way for centuries, millennia…or ever." She paused for a moment, realizing that none of them knew about Chairman Messina's private project, none of them knew about the *Alexander*—that massive spacecraft under construction out beyond the orbit of the Moon. It had been kept very secret, and the construction station it sat within was EM-shielded and invisible from Earth. Whatever, with the events occurring on Earth the project had almost certainly been shelved, if not destroyed.

"How can you be sure?" asked Gunther.

"Last night I ran a rough analysis on those same images," she replied, "and what you are seeing is not random. Someone is dropping those laser satellites directly onto Inspectorate HQs all around Earth. When I last looked, all seven thousand satellites were on the move. I'm guessing it's finished now. Someone just annihilated most of the Committee power base on Earth."

"I can confirm that," said Rhone, of Mars Science, a man so pale that, without the Martian rouge ground into his skin, he would have had an albino complexion. "We've also been picking up some Govnet chatter, though most of Govnet now seems to be down. It goes beyond what we're actually seeing. Some kind of computer attack has turned readerguns and military robots against the Inspectorate all across Earth, and even dropped government scramjets and aeros out of the sky. Prior to this, it's also worth noting, the satellite lasers fired on Minsk and then on each other. There was also a big launch of space planes from a hidden spaceport in central Australia towards the Argus Station. A lot of them didn't make it, as they got fried by the Traveller VI engine."

Var stared at him. Here was someone who had been accessing data she hadn't even noticed. Best to keep a close eye on him. Then she felt a sudden irritation with herself. That was unfair; that was Inspectorate thinking.

"Any speculations?" she asked.

"We've picked up nothing on Alessandro Messina or the Committee delegates—probably now hiding in a bunker somewhere." He paused, looking thoughtful. "I don't know who or what did this, but it seems likely to me that it's based aboard the Argus Station."

It was Martinez who got down to the practicalities. "But where does that leave us now?" he asked.

Rhone was about to add something else, but he desisted, just dipping his head. She watched him for a moment, then turned her attention to Martinez.

"It leaves us completely and utterly on our own." Var scanned the faces all around her. "We now have to make this place work, all of us."

"And how's *that* going to be?" Martinez asked, studying her intently.

"We repair the damage," she said. "We locate resources, finish building the Arboretum, graft damned hard and very cleverly to make sure we can continue surviving here. We have to make this place self-sufficient or it's our tomb."

Rhone raised his head. "I don't think that's the question Martinez was asking. I think he wants to know who's in charge now."

"I suggest I retain my present position," said Var. "The command structure the Committee established here had its faults, but most of those are now lying on a flatbed trailer outside. Remember, I was chosen for the position of technical director here. You all know my qualifications in all branches of science, and that I am the best synthesist you have." She paused for a moment, focusing her attention on Rhone. "Does anyone else have suggestions?"

"I agree," said Rhone. "You are the best one for the position, and have ably demonstrated the ruthlessness the position may require."

"I agree, too," said Martinez.

"I certainly don't want the job," said Da Vinci.

They all agreed in turn, without reservation, some of them evidently anxious to avoid what they assumed might be a poisoned chalice.

"Perhaps we should agree to reassess the situation in a year's time," Var suggested, knowing that by then it would be clear enough whether they might survive longer than the predicted five years.

"An interesting choice of timespan," said Rhone, obviously hiding something.

"So that's it," said Martinez. "Now we get to work."

"Not entirely," said Rhone. "Though we must now focus primarily on our survival here, there's another rather worrying fact we'll need to confront just after the one-year period you've mentioned."

What was he getting at now? Did he intend to suggest some kind of inquiry at the end of her rule, some sort of investigation and maybe a trial?

"Go on," she said, waiting for the knife in her back.

"Those images you showed us are rather old, Var." Rhone pointed upwards. "A few hours ago, Argus Station did a low-fuel course change around the Moon, and unless its vector changes or it makes use of its engine again, it looks likely to be sitting right above us here in one year and three months' time." He smiled at her. "Whoever or whatever just trashed Earth is now coming here."

ACKNOWLEDGEMENTS

Thanks, as always, to the people who helped bring this book to your shelves; to the Kindle, iPad or any other new-fangled electrical device that this science fiction author really ought to know more about, but is trying hard to ignore—mainly because he has less chance of spotting someone reading one of his books on a train, beach or elsewhere. Damn it, I can't sign a Kindle, nor can I sneak into a bookshop and move it to a more prominent position on the shelves!

The people at Macmillan are Julie Crisp, Chloe Healey, Amy Lines, Catherine Richards, Ali Blackburn, Eli Dryden, Neil Lang, James Long and others whose names have fallen through the sieve that is my mind. Further thanks to Peter Lavery of the legendary scary pencil and Jon Sullivan who might not even use a pencil but has certainly produced some scary monsters for the covers. And, as always, thanks Caroline, for keeping me grounded in the real world and in my fictional ones.

ABOUT THE AUTHOR

Neal Asher lives sometimes in England, sometimes in Crete and mostly at a keyboard. He climbed the writing ladder up through the small presses, publishing short stories, novellas and collections over many years, until finally having his first major book, *Gridlinked*, published in 2000 by Macmillan, who have since published sixteen of his books and whose schedule is now two years behind him. These books have been translated into 12 languages and some have appeared in America from Tor. 2013 marks a return to his other US publisher, Night Shade Books, who produced *Prador Moon* and *Shadow of the Scorpion* and will be bringing out his Owner trilogy—*The Departure, Zero Point & Jupiter War*, respectively in February, May & September.

For more information check out: http://freespace.virgin.net/n.asher/ & http://theskinner.blogspot.com/